NIMBULAN WHISPERED A SPELL IN THE MOST ANCIENT LANGUAGE OF CORONNAN. . . .

The water in the bowl clouded. Dark mists boiled up from the bottom where the agate lay touching the base of the poison-filled cup. He blinked away the ominous portent symbolized by the clouds, willing the mist to part and reveal the image of the one who had poured poison into the wine and sent it unbidden to the king.

Lightning crackled across the surface of the water. The clouds roiled and grew as black as the void between the planes of existence. More lightning flashed before his eyes. He dared not blink away the brightness lest he lose whatever brief glimpse might be granted. Streamers of color coiled and tangled in a giant knot in the air above the water.

The assembled men in the Great Hall gasped with awe.

Another blinding flash of light, bearing all colors of the spectrum, cleared the surface of the water.

Nimbulan peered eagerly for sight of the one he sought.

A face rose up from the depths of the bowl. The beloved face of Myrilandel. Her eyes searched right and left with an anxiety that filled Nimbulan's gut with fear. Behind her, desert-colored buildings rose in a tall circle, trapping her within their midst.

NO! Myri couldn't be responsible for this assassination attempt. . . .

Be sure to read these magnificent
DAW Fantasy Novels by
IRENE RADFORD

The Dragon Nimbus:
THE GLASS DRAGON (Book1)
THE PERFECT PRINCESS (Book 2)
THE LONELIEST MAGICIAN (Book 3)

The Dragon Nimbus History:
THE DRAGON'S TOUCHSTONE (Book 1)
THE LAST BATTLEMAGE (Book 2)

THE LAST
BATTLEMAGE
The Dragon Nimbus History #2
IRENE RADFORD

DAW BOOKS, INC.
DONALD A. WOLLHEIM, FOUNDER
375 Hudson Street, New York, NY 10014

ELIZABETH R. WOLLHEIM
SHEILA E. GILBERT
PUBLISHERS

First Printing, January 1998
1   2   3   4   5   6   7   8   9

DAW TRADEMARK REGISTERED
U.S. PAT. OFF. AND FOREIGN COUNTRIES
—MARCA REGISTRADA
HECHO EN U.S.A.

PRINTED IN THE U.S.A.

For Karen, the logical one.
For Linda, the flamboyant one.
For TJ, the action one.
Thanks. I couldn't write without you.

And to the patient staff of Applebees,
thank you for putting up with the cri-
tique group from outer space, who
never order anything but half-price
snacks, and monopolize too much room
for hours on end. At least we tip well.

CASTLE
KREJ
THE CLEARING
GREAT BAY

DELTA ISLANDS
HANASSA
PROVINCE OF SARIA
CORONNAN
BALTHAZAAN

BARIA
RIVER CORONNAN
ROSSEMEYER
BATTLEFIELD

SAMBOL

KARDIA HODOS

CHAPTER 1

"Another moon before your babe is ready," Karry announced to Myrilandel, holding her hands expertly on the younger woman's swelling abdomen.

"I've midwifed enough babies, you'd think I'd know how my own baby progressed," Myri replied to her friend. She rubbed the lower portion of her enormous belly where the baby kicked vigorously. While she looked at her ungainly bulk, she checked the magical cord that bound her to her husband, no matter how far away he was from her.

A pulse beat against her fingertips. Nimbulan's life force remained steady and true. She had never been able to delve deeper into the meaning of the unique phenomenon.

Amaranth, her familiar, mewed at her feet. He rubbed his black cat head against her hand as if adding his caresses to the unborn child. He kept his falcon wings carefully hidden beneath protective folds of skin and fur. No sense advertising that he was a rare and magical flywacket.

She'd never been separated from Amaranth, not since they'd been born twin purple-tipped dragons twenty years ago. Dragon lore demanded that only one purple-tip could be alive at any time. Either Amaranth or Myrilandel had to take another form or die. Myrilandel had chosen a human body. Amaranth had transformed into his flywacket form to remain near her throughout her life. She had seen him grow into his true dragon form only once.

Myri scratched his ears. "Sorry, there's no room for you in my lap, Amaranth. Not that I have any lap left."

"Mbrrrt," Amaranth purred loudly, in rhythm with Myri's stroking of her belly.

"At the first sign of labor, you send that boy you adopted to me. I'll come and help," Karry ordered, just as she ordered everyone in the small fishing village.

"I'm ready for this baby now," Myri laughed. "I want my magic talents back, so I can help in the village again. I need to repay you for all your kindness to me. I've never had a home like this before," Myri whispered. If only Nimbulan would return from the capital city, her family would be complete. She had many friends in the village now, but they weren't family.

"What do them dragons of yours tell you about the babe?" Karry asked, setting her simple home to rights.

"Shayla only tells me it's a girl." Myri smiled every time she thought of her dragon family.

Her only family, other than the two children she had adopted. And Amaranth.

She refused to dwell on depressing thoughts about her human brother, King Quinnault de Draconis, who had exiled her, reluctantly, for her rogue magic talent. A talent that had decreased as her pregnancy increased. Her husband, Nimbulan, had remained in the capital serving her brother as adviser and Senior Magician. She might have been born a dragon, but in this body she couldn't gather dragon magic—no female could. Without the ability to work in concert with other magicians through dragon magic, she had to accept exile along with every other solitary magician.

Nimbulan would return to her soon. He'd promised.

(Danger!) a dragon voice screamed into Myri's mind. *(Danger to you and the younglings!)*

Raised voices and pounding feet filled the village square.

Amaranth leaped to the doorway, back arched, fur standing up. The tips of his wings poked free of their protective skin folds in his agitation.

"Raiders!" Powwell, her adopted son, shouted.

Kalen, Powwell's half sister, dashed inside. "Myri, come, the storage sheds are burning. We have to flee, now! They are coming closer." She tugged anxiously at Myri's arm.

"Who?" Myri barely had time to ask as Kalen pulled and Karry pushed her outside.

In the open space around the Equinox Pylon, dozens

of villagers rushed madly from hut to hut. Smoke filled the air with an aura of menace.

"This way," Powwell half-dragged, half-carried Myri's bulky body toward the path leading up into the hills and their magically protected clearing. Amaranth kept close by her side, refusing to fly until she was safe.

(Not that way!) Shayla announced into Myri's head. (Evil men await you near your clearing.)

The carpenter's hut at the edge of the village exploded in flames. Three people, faces blackened with smoke, ran out the door, coughing. They beat uselessly at the bright green fire with blankets and cloaks.

The greedy flames ate at the dry timbers and thatch. The entire Autumn had been unusually dry and bright. Very little rain had soaked into the homes to protect them from the flaming arrows that sped through the air. A fisherman's home, near the cliff path to the beach, caught fire with the next barrage of arrows.

Powwell tried a magic spell to douse the fire. The flames shot higher, feeding off his magical energy as well as the thatch.

Smoke filled Myri's lungs. She nearly doubled over from coughing. Moisture streamed from her eyes. Cold Autumnal air chilled her skin.

A tiny cramp in her belly sent panic and new energy shooting through her veins. The baby wasn't ready to be born yet.

Amaranth circled her ankles, mewing anxiously. She almost tripped over him. Her senses distorted. She needed a moment to grab a hold on up and down, right and left, safety and danger.

Black-clad men appeared at the edge of the village. A dozen or more. They carried torches, swords, and bows with full quivers on their backs. Something seemed familiar about them—brightly colored vests and kerchiefs covered in silver embroidery—Rovers!

"Into the forest. They can't find us in the trees!" Karry yelled.

(To the trees. I will guide you to safety,) the dragon said. Amaranth agreed.

Instantly, Myri's vision spun upward. From the perspective of a dragon flying overhead, she saw the villagers running aimlessly in all directions. Some of the humans ran afoul of the black-clad men who approached from the North with fire and sword. Others disappeared amid the towering trees that spread up the hills to the South of the village.

She forced control over her double perspective. She'd done this with Amaranth many times. Part of her consciousness had to remain anchored to her body so she could flee from the danger.

Myri's empathic senses roared into life after many moons of dormancy. She stopped her running steps to absorb the full impact of her talent. The essence of every life around her slammed into her consciousness. She needed time to sort through them, to know who was friendly, who intended harm, who needed help, who could help.

Suddenly she knew that the lives who hid among the towering trees awaited the villagers with clubs and knives.

"We've got to hide." Powwell slipped his adolescent arm about her waist, guiding her. She sensed his magical armor dissolving as fast as he erected it. What magician led these raiders? She didn't think the Rover chieftain powerful enough to interfere with Powwell's magic.

"No, it's a trap! There are more Rovers in the forest." Myri reeled, not knowing where to turn.

Shayla circled the gathering of humans, screeching her distress. She spurted flame at the edges of the milling villagers, then withdrew it. She endangered the innocent along with the raiders.

"Yiheee!" a black-clad man screeched, running toward Myri with club raised.

"I need her alive," another voice shouted. "Catch the witchwoman and her familiar *alive.*" A voice she recognized. She should have known he was behind the raid the moment she recognized the attackers as Rovers.

"No," she moaned. "Not him."

Amaranth screeched and launched into the air. He extended his talons to rake Piedro, the man with a club. He threw his hands over his face, ducking beneath the flywacket's assault.

Amaranth raked the man's scalp and circled back for a new assault. Piedro came up swinging his club, blood from his scalp dripping into his eyes. He caught Amaranth on the tip of his wing.

"No!" Myri tried to rush to her familiar. Powwell dragged her back into the mass of villagers fleeing into the forest.

The flywacket faltered. Out of nowhere, a fishing net flew through the air, trapping him. He fell heavily to the ground, thrashing and hissing. He bit the knotted ropes that covered him.

He stretched and paled. His black fur shed light. His wings grew larger, forming wicked hooks on the tips and elbows. The net parted at one knot, then a second.

"Transform, Amaranth. Transform into a dragon," Myri cried with relief. She needed to stay and make sure he was safe. Powwell pulled her away, toward the trees.

An old woman flung herself over Amaranth's struggling body. She enfolded the enraged flywacket in a thick canvas sack, cutting off his access to sunlight. Without light, he couldn't transform into his dragon body. He had only cat claws and teeth to fight the net and the sack.

The cramp in Myri's belly intensified. She panted, trying desperately to regain control over her body and the people running and screaming around her. The line of trees loomed closer. Sanctuary. She knew how to hide in trees. But she couldn't climb anymore. The bulk of the baby kept her bound to the land.

A dark man stepped out from the concealment of a fallen tree. Myri tried to run from him. Kalen and Powwell dragged her in a different direction.

Help us, Shayla!

(If I flame those who threaten you, many innocents will be killed. You must flee and hide. Flee into the trees.)

The dragons' Covenant with the king and the magicians forbade dragons harming any human, for any reason. If Shayla broke that Covenant, even to aid her daughter Myrilandel, many dangers to every dragon would follow. She had only dragon dreams as weapons against murdering humans.

Shayla broadcast the vision of a blazing desert into their midst: Wave after wave of rolling, red sand hills met the raiders. Sun burned through their clothing, parched their throats, and drained their bodies of sweat.

Myri saw what they saw, but with a curious transparency. None of the illusions of heat and arid air touched her. But her empathic talent forced her to share their emotions and pain.

Desperately she clasped the silver cord attached to her heart with both hands, trying to communicate with her husband. It had never worked over this great a distance before. Maybe danger would fuel her pleas.

Nothing. She looked around for another avenue of escape from the raiders and from her own empathic link to them.

One man stood free of the illusion. He grinned at Myri and stalked toward her, swinging his club and whistling a jaunty tune—the same tune he'd whistled as he thrust a knife into Nimbulan's gut last Spring. Televarn. The Rover chieftain who oozed lies and tricks with every word he spoke, every magical spell he wove.

Shayla added the image of a blessed oasis with a creek to her illusion. The people stumbled into a real creek, pressing their faces into the refreshing water. Shayla pushed the image of a shallow pool, no more than half a finger-length in depth.

The true creek ran nearly as deep as half a man. The dragon increased the sun's temperature in the vision, urging the evil men and women to press their faces deeper, deeper into the water. Relentlessly she pressed the dragon dream into their minds.

Air evaporated from Myri's lungs in empathy with the men and women around her. Fleeing villagers as well as the dark-haired, dark-clad raiders staggered in the imagined desert heat. Only Televarn remained upright. He continued his approach toward Myri.

She tried to run. A new cramp stopped her. Powwell and Kalen weren't there to help her. They, too, rushed toward the creek to drink.

Shayla! Myrilandel shouted. *Stop the dream. They die. They will all die.*

(And so they should. They dared harm you. They must die, by their own foolishness.)

If they die, then I will share their deaths. I am linked to them by my talent. I feel what they feel.

(You will be free of them in a moment. You need not share their fate.)

Televarn, their leader, is immune to your visions, as am I. He continues his pursuit of us. The children can't flee with me because of the dragon dream.

The vision evaporated.

A harsh blow to the back of Myri's head shot pain down her spine. Black spots crowded her vision. She stumbled. Powwell recovered enough to catch her. Kalen dragged her forward.

(Not that way. Evil men await you there!)

"Yes, this way, it's safe. I know it's safe," Kalen insisted.

Myri tried focusing on the trees around her and the path Kalen followed. Two of everything swam before her.

Two Televarns grabbed her harshly by the neck. She flailed against him. He tightened his grip, threatening to choke the life from her.

Other men bound Kalen and Powwell with stout ropes. Powwell kicked at his captor. Piedro punched him in the jaw, smiling vilely. Kalen screamed and thrashed. Abruptly she ceased, staring ahead with blank eyes.

Myri lurched forward, trying to get to her daughter.

"One more move, and I slash your belly open. I have no use for another man's child, Myrilandel," Televarn hissed in her ear.

She stilled her struggles.

"That's better, *cherbein*. I always knew you loved me best. As soon as you are rid of Nimbulan's brat, you will be my mate again. For all time."

The trees seemed to double. The colors shifted and swirled into a mighty vortex. Had Shayla superimposed another form of vision on her eyes? What did it all mean?

"I can't have you remembering the way to your new home, *cherbein*." Televarn laughed as he pounded something into Myri's temple.

The silver cord connecting her heart to Nimbulan's dissolved. Just as blackness enveloped her, she heard Shayla bugle her distress to every mind that could hear.

(The Covenant is broken!)

No, Shayla. Don't break the Covenant, she sobbed. *Don't desert us when we need you most.*

CHAPTER 2

Intense magical power swirled around Powwell in ever tightening eddies. Pain assaulted his joints. A great roaring filled his mind.

His talent cried out for the opportunity to tap the surging power and use it. Almost instinctively he drew the power into himself as if gathering dragon magic. The special place behind his heart where he stored magic couldn't hold the energy. It coursed along his nerve endings and erupted from his fingers and toes and the ends of his hair to rejoin the force that generated it.

Then abruptly the sensation of being caught in an airless vortex ceased. Powwell's ears continued to ring in the sudden silence. His body ached as if he'd been dragged through the surf of the little cove by the village.

An enticing melody hummed within his mind. He knew a compulsion to turn around and reenter the vortex.

Intense fear of the unknown kept Powwell rigid, with his back to the alluring song.

Inside his tunic pocket, Thorny, his hedgehog familiar, gibbered in fear. The little animal's bristling spines pricked Powwell's chest through his layers of winter clothing.

With Thorny's help, Powwell oriented himself to the planet. He located the South Pole of Kardia Hodos. With that position firmly anchored into his consciousness, he knew up and down, right and left, night and day. Only then did he became aware of moving his body.

Pain throbbed behind his eyes. He tried to raise his hands to press his fingers against his eyelids.

Something held his arms at his sides, at the same time pulling his hands forward. He twisted a little and winced as scratchy rope bit into his chest where it pinned his arms at his sides. More rope bound his hands in front of him. A dark-skinned man dragged him forward by his wrist bonds. His skin chafed and burned beneath the constant pressure on the ropes.

Powwell risked opening his eyes a little and stumbled over rubble on a rough path. Black and gray surrounded him.

He was *underground.* The entire weight of Kardia Hodos seemed to press upon his head and chest, robbing him of air.

No. Only his imagination and fear made him breathe so shallowly, fighting for every scrap of air.

A new noise rushed toward him like surf over the dragon teeth rock formation in the cove. *Yeek, kush, kush. Yeek, kush, kush.* The sound grew with every step forward. It echoed and multiplied until it overshadowed the sound of Powwell's heart throbbing in his head.

The air heated until it rasped against Powwell's throat. He longed for a drink of water—even the sulfurous stuff in the hot spring near the clearing.

Despair washed over his emotions like a living entity, compounding the heat. He began to sweat.

He wanted to roll himself into a ball, just like Thorny did, and ignore the world until all this strangeness went away and he was safely back in Myrilandel's clearing.

He thought of cool green trees, shaded saber ferns, and clear mountain streams. The heat intensified.

"Move, move, move. We haven't much time!" Televarn whispered hoarsely. He prodded the man dragging Powwell with a stick—as if herding cattle.

Memory returned abruptly to Powwell. Televarn had raided the village with fire and sword. The Rover chieftain had kidnapped the pregnant witchwoman and her flywacket. He'd also snared Powwell and Kalen. Why?

At least their captor was Televarn and not Moncriith the Bloodmage. With Televarn, they had a chance to live and maybe escape. Moncriith didn't want any magicians or politicians left alive except himself.

Powwell hoped the Rovers hadn't brutally murdered anyone in the village. Moncriith would have burned them all in his obsession to burn Myri at the stake and thus rid the world of demons.

Quickly, Powwell checked the line of marching bodies

in front of him. An older Rover woman, clad in black highlighted by red and purple, pulled on Myri's bonds, somewhat more gently than the Rover man dragged Powwell.

Ahead of them, a younger Rover woman, also in black but wearing a fire-green vest and blood-red trim on her skirt, yanked at Kalen until the little girl fell flat on her face.

Powwell almost cried out in protest of the rough treatment.

Kalen appeared nearly unconscious as the Rover dragged her to her feet. Myri moved in the same disjointed daze.

Televarn ignored Powwell, as if he expected his captive to be unaware as well. The Rover wanted them dazed and obedient for a reason. Just before the massive field of magic had engulfed him, Powwell remember Televarn saying something about not knowing the way to their new home.

Powwell kept his eyes half-closed. He could still see, but Televarn couldn't tell that he was awake. He needed time to gather information and plan.

A dour-faced older Rover yanked on Powwell's bonds. He stumbled forward on nearly numb legs. Two half running steps later, full sensation returned abruptly to his body. His legs felt like tree sap in the grinding heat. His head pounded more fiercely than before.

"I said 'move,' *s'murghit*. We have to get to the surface before Yaassima finds us," Televarn hissed through his teeth. Impatiently he moved beyond Powwell. He strode ahead of the dozen Rovers to the first man in line who carried a heavy sack over his shoulder.

Amaranth was in that sack. Powwell remembered how fiercely the flywacket had fought imprisonment within the dark canvas. From the wriggling within the sack, Powwell guessed that Amaranth still fought for freedom. But his talons and teeth didn't seem to penetrate the heavy canvas.

"Follow me, Piedro. I don't want you getting lost down here and betraying the entire plan," Televarn said.

Piedro—the man who carried Amaranth—flashed the Rover chieftain an evil sneer, but he yielded the lead.

His scalp wounds from Amaranth's claws had clotted messily in his sleek hair.

The black-and-gray landscape resolved into a long tunnel broken by small caverns. Powwell didn't know of any cave system near the village and the clearing, other than Shayla's lair. The big female dragon would never allow Televarn to hold them hostage in the lair.

Powwell tested the strength of his bonds with a small magic probe. The ropes remained firmly knotted, sealed with a magic he couldn't understand. They didn't move against his sweat-slick skin. If he could break a single strand of rope, he could wriggle free and take care of Myri and Kalen. He'd promised Nimbulan he'd protect them. He'd never broken a promise before!

Who would help Myri when the baby decided to enter the world? He had to get her back home before then. Nimbulan depended upon him to protect the family while the Senior Magician was detained in the capital.

"Quickly. They'll change shifts in the pit in a moment. We have to cross the big cavern in just a few heartbeats," Televarn directed his people.

Powwell took a longer than normal step so that his hands were closer to his chest without changing the pressure on the lead rope. *Thorny,* he probed the hedgehog with his mind. He knew better than to touch his familiar without warning. Thorny hunched and rolled in response to the mental caress. Then he relaxed his spines and wiggled his nose. He relayed a series of scent impressions to Powwell. This place was strange beyond new. The hedgehog had never smelled anything like this before. No plants. Few insects. A lot of fear. And too much noise. *Yeek kush kush. Yeek kush kush.*

Thorny, can you talk to Kalen's familiar? Have the beast wake her up a little. He couldn't see Kalen's pet on her shoulder; perhaps it was hiding beneath her skirts.

Thorny hunched again and remained firmly locked in a defensive ball. He wanted water and quiet. So did Powwell.

A flicker of white moved at the edge of Powwell's vision. Lumbird bumps raised on his arms and back. He risked turning his head to see what threat he and Thorny both sensed.

Nothing. Just more black and gray stretching in all

directions. He almost gave in to the feeling of hopelessness. For Myri and Kalen, he had to fight the emotions that pressed against him from the outside. He had to appear bewitched for a little while longer.

The tunnel walls narrowed again and lowered. Powwell resisted the urge to duck beneath the heavy ceiling. Myri didn't duck in her unconscious movement. Televarn didn't either and he was only a finger's length taller than the witchwoman. To maintain the illusion of sleepwalking, Powwell couldn't cower away from the rocks that seemed ready to drop and crush him.

They passed through a large cavern. The path seemed clearer, well-trodden. He breathed a little easier, less aware of the tons of dirt and rock above him.

Televarn pointed toward another narrow tunnel. Piedro stepped confidently into the darkness with the now quiet Amaranth still in the sack upon his back. The older Rover woman yanked Myri's rope and followed. So did Kalen's leader. Powwell gulped uneasily.

"They'll wake up soon." Televarn inspected Kalen. The girl swayed as she walked. Her head bobbed. "We have to be aboveground before they come to. We can't have them suspect the dragongate exists." He prodded the lead Rover harshly in the back.

Dragongate? What was that? The alluring, unknown song lingered in his memory. He needed to go back to it, to join with the intense forces that threatened to tear him apart—at the same time the vortex hinted at joining with the great secrets of the universe. Secrets beyond comprehension to mere mortals.

Powwell risked a tiny turn of his head to search the cave system for something unusual. Only gray rock walls shadowed with black met his gaze. Where was the light that produced shadows? He didn't see any torches, nor did the light flicker like a natural flame. A steady glow seemed to come from the ceiling. But darkness followed them, engulfing the light soon after they passed by.

Where are we? He tried touching Kalen's mind. Their rapport was strong; she should respond to the lightest probe. She remained blank and unresponsive. Then he tried to bring his TrueSight to the front of his awareness—a harder task. His head throbbed and he lost focus. No magic responded to his quest. He reached deeper into his being in search of stored dragon magic.

Nothing. He was empty. He'd used it all trying to get Myri safely into the forest. There must be a ley line nearby. He could tap the energy embedded in the Kardia to fuel his magic. The clearing was full of ley lines and so was the village.

Nothing. Wherever they were, the land and the air were devoid of energy to fuel his talent.

He must have been unconscious for longer than he thought. But his inner awareness of the planet and the passage of time insisted that he'd only lost his senses for a few heartbeats. Thorny agreed with him. The tiny hedgehog gibbered of dark magic and holes in time.

Televarn urged them up the steep incline, increasing his pace with each step. Everyone breathed faster and more shallowly. Sweat poured down Powwell's face and back. If only he had a drink of water, he could think straight.

A gate of crossed iron bars blocked their path. Televarn touched the lock with a strange metal wand. It unlatched silently. Where did he get the magic to do that? Rovers supposedly had strange powers, but they had to have fuel like any other magician whether it be dragons, ley lines, or blood. Could Televarn tap the heavy emotions that pressed against Powwell?

Televarn pushed the gate open. The hinges didn't protest. It was well maintained by someone.

At last they emerged into broader tunnels that looked as if men had attempted to smooth the walls with tools Even without magic, Powwell knew that other lives drifted close by, possibly in adjacent tunnels. The air became sweeter and more plentiful. Each breath came easier. They neared the surface.

With the release of the tremendous weight on his senses, Powwell began to hope. He sought landmarks and avenues of escape within the limited range of his half-closed eyes. He stretched his hearing, praying for some hint of where Televarn had brought them.

He saw a flamboyant tapestry draped across another tunnel opening. Some private apartment?

If only he had some magic to reach out with. He

needed to know how extensive this cave system was and
how many people inhabited it.

They paused by a very large tapestry. It would more
than cover all the walls of Myri's little hut. Red, blood
red, dominated the scenes depicted here. Executions and
terrible tortures filled the weaving. Beheadings, hangings, dozen of arrows piercing a naked man. Racks and
hot pokers, victims writhing in agony. Powwell almost
had the impression he was watching the horrible events
unfold before his eyes.

Then they moved on. Televarn thrust aside the next
tapestry. It was as large as the previous one. Powwell
stared at the amazing pictures of naked men and women
coupling in bizarre and obscene combinations.

He closed his eyes in disgust. Where were they that
misery and perversion dominated the walls?

Embarrassed heat wanted to flood his face all the way
to his ears. He fought for calm, breathing evenly, looking
elsewhere. Desperately, he hoped his flushed face could
be attributed to the unnatural heat of the lower caverns.

Televarn peered behind the tapestry, seemingly unaware of the obscenities he held in his hand. Odd yellow
light poured out from a vast open space beyond the
woven wall covering.

Sunlight? No. Too yellow, like the glow in the lower
caverns that brightened and dimmed in response to the
passage of people. Powwell couldn't see any hint of the
normal green firelight. Thorny wouldn't be able to help
him figure it out. The hedgehog's eyesight was terrible.

Televarn beckoned his troop to enter the room beyond. He pressed his finger to his lips, signaling silence.
All of them moved cautiously on the balls of their feet.

They entered a large room with a dais running the
length of one wall. In front of the dais rested a rectangu-
lar stone of dressed granite. It stood about as high as a
tall man's waist. Powwell had the impression of an altar,
except . . . except a sturdy metal spike was jammed into
the rock of each of the four corners. Manacles dangled
from each of the stakes.

An altar all right.

But the benevolent Stargods had never been wor-
shiped here. This had to be a temple to Simurgh, the
ancient demon who demanded blood sacrifice. Powwell

had seen descriptions of similar underground temples during the moons he studied at the School for Magicians.

That hideous religion had been outlawed in all of the Three Kingdoms almost a thousand years ago. The temples to Simurgh had been destroyed and filled with rubble. But not here. Where were they?

"What pretty prizes have you brought me this time, Televarn?" an oily feminine voice asked from the center of the dais. No one had been there a moment ago.

A tall woman with white-blonde hair and almost colorless skin, similar to Myri's, stood at the exact center of the raised stage. Another tapestry, this one of a remarkably lifelike, rippling waterfall hung behind her. Not a thread on the wall covering fluttered to indicate recent movement. The woman wore a simple gown of glittering sapphire blue. Diamonds glinted in her nearly colorless hair, picking up the yellow of the uncanny light and the blue of her gown. She seemed to sparkle all over, sort of like a dragon standing in direct sunlight.

Powwell couldn't tell how old or young she was because of the odd light. She flicked her very long, talon-like fingers in an elegant gesture. The hideous altar groaned and slowly descended into the floor until it became another paving stone. With another gesture the woman sent the stakes into hiding as well.

No wonder the Stargods hadn't been able to find and destroy this altar!

"Yaassima!" Televarn opened his eyes wide in feigned innocence. "I did not expect you to be in residence today."

She smiled with a slight twist of one corner of her mouth.

Powwell didn't like the menace that remained in her eyes.

"Tell me about your prizes. I see you have found a relative of mine." The woman glided forward to the edge of the dais. A dozen black-clad guards appeared on the platform behind her. Each man wore at least three weapons. Four of them carried strange metal wands that appeared to be hollow.

The same kind of wands Televarn had used to open the gate.

"Bring the woman closer," Yaassima ordered.

"My petty hostages are not worthy of the attention of the Kaalipha of Hanassa." Televarn eased toward the doorway on the opposite side of the room. He dragged Myri's rope behind him. She had no choice but to follow.

Her eyes flickered slightly. Her hands moved instinctively to rub at her belly. She must be nearly awake.

Powwell sensed movement in the stretched skin that protected the baby. He hoped the unborn child merely kicked and this was not a portent of early labor. The baby wasn't due for another moon.

So far, Kalen had made no sign that her mind stirred beneath whatever spell Televarn had placed upon her.

"Nonsense, Televarn. Obviously you have found another descendant of dragons, one I did not know about. Who are you, child?" Yaassima seemed to float down the two steps to the main floor. Her sparkling gown hid all traces of her feet. She stopped directly in front of Myri. The guards followed her.

Powwell watched as awareness returned to Myri's eyes. She darted glances all around her, opening and closing her mouth in silent protest. Her shoulders hunched and she bent her spine as if protecting her belly—or withstanding a pain.

"She's just a simple witchwoman from the hills," Televarn replied.

"Is the child yours, Televarn?" Yaassima placed her hand familiarly on Myri's bulging belly.

Myri hunched gain. Her hands fluttered and clutched again. She groaned slightly.

Danger screamed from the last remnant of Powwell's magical senses. He struggled within his bonds. He had to get Myri home. Now. Before the baby came. Nimbulan needed him to take care of Myri and the baby.

No one paid any attention to him. All eyes seemed glued to the Kaalipha.

"No, the child is not his. I would never allow him to father a child of mine," Myri spat. "Release us immediately. I will have retribution from him for this outrage." She gritted her teeth and held back yet another groan.

"Such defiance. A worthy descendant of dragons!" Yaassima stepped back. A true smile spread across her pale features and her eyes opened wide in delight. "If

Televarn has no claim on the child, then where is its father?"

"My husband had business in Coronnan City. Televarn waited until we were alone and then kidnapped us."

"The husband of a witchwoman with business in the city? Magician Nimbulan is the only man that could be. And you must be Myrilandel—the witchwoman who saved the naive king of Coronnan. He's your long-lost brother, I believe. You saved him from death, and then he exiled you. And your husband allowed it. Not only allowed it, but he stayed in the city to serve the Peacemaker rather than follow his pregnant wife into exile. What a delicious scandal. Name your reward, Televarn. You have brought me a rare prize indeed."

"The Kaalipha is too generous." Televarn dipped his head in a gesture that resembled humility. But Powwell saw him bite back a protest.

"Then I give you the commission to assassinate King Quinnault, Myrilandel's worthless brother. I need control over Coronnan, and he stands in my way. There is a reward of one thousand gold pieces for confirmation of his death. And if his pet magician Nimbulan is caught in the backlash, I will add an additional five hundred gold pieces in Myrilandel's name. She will be free of the blackguard."

"Never!" Myri cried in protest. "I will never countenance . . . uuuugh," she ended on a groan of pain. Her hands pressed against her belly once more.

"Oh, and take these hideous children with you, Televarn." The Kaalipha ignored Myri's outburst. "I have no need of them." She flicked her wrist again, and a small knife appeared in her hand. Myri's bonds seemed to dissolve at the touch of the blade.

"You can't kill my husband!" Myri screamed. "I'll kill you myself, Televarn, before I let you harm my husband." She lunged for the Rover. Before she had gone two steps, she doubled over in pain. Her hands clenched at the sides of her belly.

Powwell lurched forward, needing to cradle her, protect her. The Rover who managed his ropes held him firmly in place.

"Now see what you have done, Televarn. She has gone into labor prematurely. You'd better hope the baby lives. I have never found another person who looks as much like a dragon as me. Therefore, we are related by spirit if not blood. Go now and complete your commission." Yaassima reached to cradle Myri in her arms. She beckoned to the older woman who had led Myri through the tunnels. "You there, Erda, you are a midwife. You will stay and see to her. Ease her pain with drugs— whatever will keep her quiet. Nastfa," she waved at the guard in the center of the phalanx, "carry Myrilandel to my private suite. Gently."

"Powwell, Kalen," Myri called weakly. "You must warn Nimbulan and my brother, the king. Kalen can talk to dragons, have her tell Shayla. You have to warn them."

Televarn yanked harshly on Powwell's rope. He resisted, trying desperately to guide his steps toward Myrilandel. Televarn smiled, squinting his eyes with malice. This time he yanked so hard on Kalen's rope that she fell to her knees. She cried out in pain as the paving stones tore patches of skin from her knees.

"You'll warn no one, Powwell," Televarn said through clenched teeth. He whipped out a knife and held it to Kalen's throat. "So much as a weak cry in the night, and I shall kill the girl and make you watch while I slit her throat. I have uses for you now, but they are not so strong I must keep you alive if you defy me. Murder is quite legal here in Hanassa, the City of Outlaws."

CHAPTER 3

"**D**on't touch that wine, Your Grace! It's poisoned." Nimbulan rushed into the Great Hall of King Quinnault's keep. He was breathless, and his heart raced from his run across the bridge from School Isle. The sense of danger intensified the closer he came to the king. Lumbird bumps stood up all along his arms and his hair stood on end at his nape.

Silence descended upon the busy hall. Servants stopped their endless routines in mid-step. Courtiers and petitioners halted their babbling in mid-sentence. Two architects stared at him as they poised over their intricate drawings. Ink dripped from their pens. Even King Quinnault's pack of hunting dogs ceased their constant yapping and quarreling.

"What do you mean, Nimbulan?" Quinnault, King of Coronnan by the grace of the dragons, sat back in his demi-throne at the high table. He left the golden goblet where the understeward had placed it moments ago. The servant still stood beside the king, jaw flapping, carrying tray clutched to his chest as if a talisman.

"It's poisoned, Your Grace. I saw your death and that cup in a vision through my glass." Nimbulan waved the gold-framed piece of precious clear glass. He'd been looking for a clue to his missing wife's whereabouts when the premonition of danger intruded.

Three weeks had passed since Shayla had announced to one and all that the Covenant with dragons was broken. No dragon had been seen in Coronnan since. The amount of dragon magic available to the magicians diminished each day.

Soon they would have to resort to illegal solitary magic to perform everyday tasks of communication.

Nimbulan guessed that the dragons' withdrawal coin-

cided with the disappearance of his wife, Myrilandel, and
the severing of the magical cord that bound him to her.

Nearly two weeks had passed since he had returned
to the capital after discovering her absence from the
clearing. The villagers had been extremely reluctant to
tell him anything about her disappearance. They were
too busy rebuilding after a disastrous fire.

Not a day had passed since that Nimbulan hadn't
searched for her. Fruitlessly. Every spell went awry. He
couldn't sleep. His concentration wavered at the most
inopportune times. He had to find Myrilandel soon.

Quinnault and the magicians wanted Myri found, too.
They needed to restore the Covenant with the dragons.
But Quinnault had ordered Nimbulan to remain in the
capital, while they monitored an attack fleet from Rossemeyer gathering in the mouth of the Great Bay. The
quest to find Myrilandel should go to a younger man.
No one doubted that she must be found and the Covenant with the dragons restored.

"Who wishes me dead, Nimbulan?" Quinnault pushed
his heavy chair farther away from the table and the
tainted goblet.

"I didn't do it, Your Grace," the understeward protested. "I only carried the cup here from the cellar. I
didn't . . ." He looked pleadingly toward his king.

"Who prepared the cup?" Nimbulan approached the
high table from the front, below the dais, never moving
his eyes away from the suspicious goblet. Moisture con-
densed on the outside of the cold metal. Quinnault's
favorite red wine was always served at room temperature, not chilled.

Nimbulan didn't have much time. If the poison came
from magic, it would dissipate quickly, leaving no trace
of the assassin or clue to the nature of the spell.

"Did you ask for wine, Your Grace?" Nimbulan
raised his left hand, palm extended toward the goblet,
fingers slightly curved. The sense of danger stabbed his
palm. Reflexively he jerked his hand away from the cup.

"No. But when it arrived, I welcomed it, not realizing
I was thirsty until then," Quinnault said as he slowly
rose from his chair. His eyes remained fixed upon the
cup.

"The new girl in the scullery told me to take it to you,

Your Grace," the understeward said. "I don't question things like that, sir. The steward could have asked her to take the prepared cup to me. The order could have come from any number of people. I didn't do it, Your Grace!"

"A new servant?" Nimbulan raised his eyes to the understeward. The man's aura radiated layers of blue truth shot with the nearly white energy of fear. At least he could still sense auras. If he'd had to throw a truth spell over the young man, who knew what his magic would do.

"There are always new servants, Magician Nimbulan," the understeward explained. "They start in the scullery, and if they last, they move up to more respectable chores. I've been with His Grace five years. I would never think of harming him."

"You might not think of it, but a rogue magician could plant the idea in your head and you'd never know it. Describe the girl." Nimbulan moved his raised hand in a circle, wrapping the dangerous cup in a web of magical containment. When he saw the noon sunlight sparkle against the magic, he relaxed a little. He'd managed at least this simple spell. Time would not touch the poison and humans could not touch the cup.

"Short." The understeward held his hand up to his chin, indicating the maid's height. "A delectable little mole just to the right of her mouth. Dark hair and eyes. Beautiful eyes . . ." He drifted off in contemplation of the new scullery maid.

"How dark? Olive skin tones or fairer—more pink?" Nimbulan transferred his gaze from the cup to the understeward in alarm. *A mole to the right of the mouth.* No. Televarn wouldn't dare send Maia to do his dirty work.

Nimbulan hadn't thought much about Maia since he'd met Myrilandel. He wanted to remember his brief affair with the Rover girl as a time of spontaneous joy. But his mind told him the entire sordid mess had been manipulated by Televarn, the head of Maia's clan.

A wrongness grated against his mind. Televarn was a power-hungry, manipulative bastard, but he had courage. If he wanted to kill someone, he'd do the deed himself; as he had tried to murder Nimbulan with a knife.

"Rover-dark hair, I think. Her skin was so smooth and clear, except for that delectable mole. . . ." The understeward fell back into his reverie.

"Guard, dunk his head in a steed trough, a very cold one," Nimbulan ordered the men who hovered close by, hands on short swords. "He's been bewitched, and I think I know by whom. Bring me the biggest bowl you can find—crockery not silver, filled with fresh creek water. Remember, a free-running creek, not a confined well." A Rover spell to catch a Rover assassin.

Fortunately, Rover magic required multiple magicians. Nimbulan wouldn't have to depend upon his increasingly erratic magic for accurate results.

He searched the pockets of his everyday working trews and tunic. The wand he sought eluded him. *S'murghit,* he'd have to levitate the wand from his private chamber. He pictured within his mind the necessary tool with the faceted crystal suspended from the end by a reinforced spiderweb, right where he'd seen it last, on his desk. He'd locked the door to his chamber with a mundane key to keep the apprentices on housekeeping duty from disturbing his research. No need for magic on the seal.

From this distance he couldn't guarantee the levitation or the unlocking of his door.

"What do you need, Nimbulan? I can send someone to fetch it," King Quinnault offered.

A guard appeared with a bread bowl, large enough to hold several pounds of rising dough. Beside him stood a second man with a pitcher of water, still dripping from having been dunked into the creek or river.

Nimbulan patted his pockets one more time in search of the wand he wanted. He fished a small rock out of his pocket instead.

"I've found what I need, Your Grace." Not a faceted crystal that had been made perfect by men, but a naturally beautiful stone polished by water and sand. Like the free water and the crockery bowl, this natural stone was a tool a Rover could use.

Carefully he set the bowl on the floor in the middle of the Great Hall. The rushes had been scraped clear of the stone flooring and the assembly of people and dogs hugged the wall, giving Nimbulan space to work. Sunlight streamed through the high windows, illuminating the bowl in a glowing warmth. Three hastily summoned magicians, including his senior journeyman, Rollett, knelt beside Nimbulan, linked to him in trance and by touch. They encircled the bowl.

Gently Nimbulan adjusted his magic to match the compounded energy his assistants gave him. They'd keep the spell aligned and focused, even if he couldn't.

Where in Simurgh's hell had Myri gotten to? What had happened to the silver cord that connected their hearts?

He filled the bowl with the fresh water. Then, together, he and the magicians levitated the poisonous cup into the bowl until it rested snugly upright, surrounded almost to the rim by fresh creek water.

Only then, did Nimbulan dissolve the web of magic wrapped around the cup. It fell apart much more easily than it had gone together.

"The clay that formed the bowl is the Kardia." He raised his voice as if chanting.

"Sunlight is Fire," Rollett picked up the chant.

"The source of our question rests in Water," Lyman added.

"The magic we add comes from Air," Gilby, the fourth magician continued.

"We stand at North, South, East, and West. The four elements combined with the four cardinal directions form the *Gaia*. All is one. One is all," Nimbulan finished. Subtly he shifted his body so that he stood at the South of the spell—the direction of the nearest magnetic pole. The forces of the pole should keep his magic under control even if his mind strayed.

Myri had to be safe, wherever she was. The dragons would have done more than announce that the Covenant was broken if anything had happened to his wife.

His wife. She should be at his side, not exiled, not missing.

Nimbulan forced his mind back to the problem of poison and Rovers, looking deep into the mystery of sunlight sparkling against the clear water. He dropped the agate into the bowl close to the golden cup. Ripples moved outward from the stone, spreading the sunlight up and out.

He whispered a spell in the most ancient language of all Coronnan. The words of the dead language fell clumsily from his tongue.

The water clouded, dark mists boiled up from the bottom where the agate lay touching the base of the cup. He blinked away the ominous portent symbolized by the clouds, willing the mist to part and reveal the image of the one who had poured poison into the wine and sent it unbidden to the king.

Lightning crackled across the surface of the water. The clouds roiled and grew as black as the void between the planes of existence. More lighting flashed before his eyes. He dared not blink away the brightness lest he lose whatever brief glimpse might be granted. Streamers of color coiled and tangled in a giant knot in the air above the water.

The assembled men in the Great Hall gasped with awe.

Another blinding flash of light, bearing all colors of the spectrum, cleared the surface of the water.

Nimbulan peered eagerly for sight of the one he sought.

A face rose up from the depths of the bowl. The beloved face of Myrilandel. Her white-blonde hair streamed out behind her, unbound and uncovered. Her long face with its straight nose and high cheekbones reflected the generations of aristocratic breeding overlaid with a feminine softness. Her eyes searched right and left with an anxiety that filled Nimbulan's gut with fear. Behind her, desert-colored buildings rose in a tall circle, trapping her within their midst.

NO! Myri couldn't be responsible for this assassination attempt. He wouldn't believe it.

CHAPTER 4

Nimbulan placed his gold-framed glass between his eyes and the water, moving it back and forth for better focus. He had to see the truth. Myri could not poison Quinnault. She valued family too highly, and the king was her only blood kin.

He had to believe that his lack of concentration had brought him the image he had sought in a previous spell rather than truth in this one.

The image faded until only Myri's pale eyes remained, pleading with him for . . . A scratch in the bottom of the bowl jumped into view, magnified many times its size by the glass.

Nimbulan stood up from his crouched position. His knees didn't want to unfold. They creaked and groaned for every one of his fifty years.

Myri had made him feel like a teenager again. Her youth and beauty sparked his vitality as well as his intellect. Every day without her weighed heavily on his soul and his heart. And now he didn't even have the magical silver cord that had bound them together.

He'd allowed that bond to suffice for too long. And now he couldn't find her at all.

"I saw the face of a Rover woman," Lyman, the eldest of all the Commune of Magicians, said. "Very pretty in a dark, exotic way. A man could get lost in those deep, dark eyes . . ." His voice trailed off, very much like the understeward's had. Then, abruptly, he roused himself with a visible shake. "She had a mole to the right of her mouth—positioned perfectly to entice a man to kiss her. I watched as she poured a very cold liquid into the cup and whispered words over it. I could not hear the words, but I recognized the lilting pattern of them. She spoke in an old language. A language that is almost forgotten within the Three Kingdoms. As she said the words, the liquid in the cup foamed and nearly boiled over the rim, yet I knew it to be a cold boil. Unnaturally cold."

"I saw her, too!" Gilby and Rollett agreed. As senior journeymen magicians, they often worked in concert with Nimbulan and Lyman. Nimbulan trusted them. Rollett's quick eye for detail was unfailing. Gilby was particularly adept at delving into symbolism for patterns that reflected truth.

"The image faded very quickly. As quickly as the poison in the cup." Lyman looked at the clear water in the bowl as if he could pull more images from it.

"Maia. The woman is Maia," Nimbulan said. But Maia had never had an original thought. None of her clan did. Every thought, every action was manipulated by Televarn. Nimbulan had experienced Televarn's direct mind control during the season he lived with the clan.

I heard a baby cry in the background of the vision, Nimbulan, Lyman said directly into Nimbulan's mind. *I knew instantly that the baby had pink skin and auburn hair. The same color hair as yours.*

"Maia has a baby? My baby?" Nimbulan whispered, praying that only Lyman heard his conjecture. The emotional blow almost sent Nimbulan staggering. A child of his own loins? Magicians rarely sired children. He'd given up hope of ever having a child of his own. He had to find Maia and claim his baby. He had to find Myri, his beloved wife.

How? When? Which first?

"You know the Rovers, Nimbulan." Lyman cocked his head as if listening to something in the distance. But he didn't take his eyes off of Nimbulan. "Did you see who you sought in the vision? Can you find these people again?" Mischief danced behind the old man's eyes. His words had more than one meaning. Possibly many more than two.

What was Lyman up to? Had he seen Maia or Myri in the vision? "Maia may have been the instrument of the delivery of the poison. But Televarn directed the assassination attempt, as he directs all within his sphere." *I will not have him in charge of my child's welfare. I must find them. Now.*

Where was Maia? Was she truly involved in the assassination plot against the king?

Where was the child? Why hadn't Maia told him she carried his baby? She could have sought him out after he left the Rover clan, or sent him a message. She must know that he had survived Televarn's knife.

Think, s'murghit. He had to think clearly. Relying on information given him by others grated against his nerves. but all he could think about was Myri trapped within a bowl of red sandstone walls.

"A search across the void would tell us for certain who tainted the cup, and where they hide," Quinnault offered. He'd had some training as a magician and priest before becoming lord of his clan and then king. While he knew magic theory well, he had very little talent and knew nothing of dragon magic. Though the dragons had partially awakened the king's telepathic powers, he shared them with none but the dragons.

"No, Your Grace, we can no longer access the void. By law, we cannot use rogue methods even to serve our king," Lyman replied. The old man clutched Nimbulan's arm, offering him unspoken support and confidence; taking charge until Nimbulan sorted his thoughts and could speak without blurting out his true vision.

Myri couldn't be involved. Quinnault was her birth brother though they'd been separated when Myri was two. Somehow, Maia was involved. Maia, the mother of his child. Myri, the love of his life.

His thoughts refused to settle on one idea.

Later. We will discuss your vision later. Trust me to know that Televarn and his Rovers are your enemy in this and other matters, Lyman said into Nimbulan's mind.

Nimbulan forced his circling thoughts into some kind of order. Rovers had been banned from Coronnan, along with all magicians who could not or would not gather dragon magic. Myri had been among those forced to leave. Myri and her two adopted children, Kalen and Powwell. Why hadn't he seen the children in the vision? Only Myri. Only the one he truly sought with his heart as well as his mind.

Suddenly Nimbulan's mind brightened. Myri was a healer; she would never harm anyone, especially not Quinnault. The king had been brother to the little girl

Myrilandel. When the girl-child nearly died, Amethyst,
the purple-tipped dragon had taken over the weakened
body and healed it. The two personalities had fought for
dominance and compromised on forgetfulness until Myri
had grown into the knowledge of both her heritages. She
would never harm her only living blood relative.

*I must go in search of Myrilandel. She is in terrible
danger. I sensed it in the vision, now I know for sure,* he
whispered to Lyman telepathically—the only way he
could be certain no one else overheard. Rollett was capable of eavesdropping, but he wouldn't. The boy respected privacy too much. Gilby found telepathy difficult
and relied on his other talents.

I must add Maia to this quest, Nimbulan decided. He
had to find her before Televarn tainted the baby's
upbringing.

"The Rovers are a race not known for their forgiveness, or short memories," Quinnault mused. "Guard
Captain, send all available men to search for the assassin. Any Rover found within two days' walk of the capital must be arrested and brought here for investigation,"
he said to the officer who paced anxiously behind his
chair.

The guard practically ran out of the hall, gathering
armed men as he went.

Nimbulan nodded his approval then turned his
thoughts back to the problem at hand. He had last lain
with Maia the night before Televarn tried to kill him
with a knife between his ribs. That had been in early
Spring, nearly three seasons ago. The babe would be
newborn about now.

"You can't go in search of your destiny yet, Nimbulan," Lyman whispered, drawing Nimbulan aside as if to
consult on the assassination issue "Soon, though. Wait
until we can make arrangements in private. King Quinnault has ordered you to remain in the capital rather
than search for Myrilandel. He won't take kindly to your
leaving on this quest either. He needs you to counter
whatever ploy the attack fleet from Rossemeyer plans."

They stared at each other in a moment of complete
understanding. They barely heard the commotion at the
entrance to the Great Hall.

"Your Grace, you can't be considering this draft of

the treaty. The conditions are preposterous!" Lord Hanic burst into the room, oblivious to the tension surrounding the bowl of water and the cup of wine still sitting on the floor.

"Lord Hanic to see you, Your Grace," a servant squeaked from the doorway somewhat belatedly. He straightened his stiff tunic in the new green-and-gold livery of the royal house. A stylized dragon was embroidered over his heart.

"Calm down," King Quinnault soothed, not at all flustered by the lack of protocol. He hadn't been king long enough to expect the elaborate courtesy that plagued other kingdoms. "All of those 'preposterous' clauses are negotiable. However, we should at least pretend to consider them so that Ambassador Jhorge-Rosse can tell his king that he presented them. We might also lull him into the belief that we are incredibly stupid because we do consider them. His natural feeling of superiority might make him stumble into a mistake in our favor." Quinnault ambled back to the demithrone at the table, ready to return to business as usual.

"Your Grace," Nimbulan interrupted. "You don't need me further. Allow me and my assistants to clear away this mess and join the search for the assassin." If he stayed, Quinnault would drag him into yet another endless discussion about the blasted treaty.

"Stay, Nimbulan. The weather has been clear for two days. The Rossemeyerian fleet could attack at any moment. We need to plan our defenses. Now." Quinnault glared at his magician with an expression that tolerated no defiance. A new expression for the king, learned within the last year.

"His Lordship, General Jhorge-Rosse, Ambassador from the Serene Kingdom of Rossemeyer," the harried servant at the door announced.

Quinnault turned his attention from Nimbulan to the tall desert dweller who swept into the room in his all-concealing black robes. An elaborate black turban added more height to his imposing figure.

Rossemeyer's primary export consisted of mercenaries. Mercenaries, not assassins. No desert warrior would stoop to the dishonor of magical poison when a knife duel worked as well or better. Every member of the government in Rossemeyer had to have earned leadership on the field of battle before entering the battle of politics. The "Rosse" suffix added to the ambassador's name was the highest honorific allowed his people. Only members of the royal family made the name a prefix.

Nimbulan motioned to the two journeymen to dispose of the bowl and cup on their way back to the school. He dispatched Lyman to organize the search for Televarn.

Was Rossemeyer's desert sand as red and black as Nimbulan had seen in the vision?

Rovers were known to seek refuge in the desert wastes of Rossemeyer.

Concentrate! he ordered himself. *Find out what you can and then leave quickly. Leave and follow your heart. Myrilandel.*

"Your Grace." Jhorge-Rosse dipped his head and perhaps one knee in a brief gesture of respect to the king. He glanced sideways at Nimbulan and ignored Lord Hanic.

Nimbulan wondered briefly if his mud-stained leather working clothes, dyed a common blue, earned him respect or dismissal in the ambassador's eyes. He didn't allow himself to dwell on it. He had to find Myri and Maia.

"Your Grace, I have read your proposals and find them nothing less than insulting," Jhorge-Rosse continued. "Are you aware that our fleet is assembled in the Great Bay ready to descend upon you if I do not report progress in these negotiations *daily?*" The ambassador's callused hand rested near his hip, where a sword or dagger might be concealed beneath his robe.

"You remind me of that *daily,* General Jhorge-Rosse. What precisely do you find so insulting in our proposal for a resumption of trade? We are making concessions in buying large quantities of beta'arack, a noxious alcoholic brew that we don't need and your only export, in exchange for food which you cannot grow." Quinnault leaned back in his chair, chin lifted, eyes cold and calculating.

"You and your magicians want my people to starve. Your tariffs are absurd." Jhorge-Rosse's upper lip lifted in a snarl.

Nimbulan edged closer to his king, fully aware of how dangerous a man Jhorge-Rosse could be.

"You have fertile valleys rotting from the neglect of three generations of civil war while my people starve, and yet you demand added export tariffs before selling us the food you would otherwise throw away!" Jhorge-Rosse's hand remained on the hilt of the concealed weapon.

"Tariffs and taxes are a natural means of earning income for the crown so that I may pay my troops to defend my borders, or hire your mercenaries from Rossemeyer if necessary." Quinnault narrowed his eyes. He made a point of placing both of his hands flat on the table. Jhorge-Rosse would earn no honor in murdering an unarmed man.

Nimbulan's magical armor snapped into place around his own body. He consciously extended it to wrap around his king, praying it wouldn't dissolve at his first stray thought. Quinnault was the one man who could hold together a government, demanding and getting the cooperation of all twelve lords of Coronnan. If Jhorge-Rosse killed or seriously wounded King Quinnault, the chaos and civil war that had plagued Coronnan for three generations would erupt once more. The bachelor king had no child to inherit the Coraurlia and the Covenant with the dragons.

The Covenant was broken. Shayla had proclaimed it. Because Myri was missing. He had to go after his wife, now.

He wrenched his attention back to his king and the volatile ambassador.

Jhorge-Rosse sniffed in Nimbulan's direction. He wrinkled his nose as if the magician, or his magic, smelled bad. "You are a coward who hides behind magicians. I refuse to deal with a man who cannot defend himself. Prepare for invasion! We will have unrestricted access to your rich farmlands." The ambassador stalked out of the room, robes flapping indignantly.

"Be prepared for your ships to run aground in the mud, General Ambassador Jhorge-Rosse!" Quinnault said. He exhaled sharply as if he'd been holding his breath.

Lord Hanic collapsed into the chair beside Quinnault.

"Am I mistaken, or did that man just create an excuse to invade?"

Quinnault nodded in silent agreement. "I'm surprised he waited so long. We've been trading insults for weeks. He could have invaded two days ago, as soon as the last storm settled."

"Now what?" Hanic raised troubled eyes to Nimbulan.

"The tide turns as we speak." Nimbulan sensed the subtle shift in the position of the moon in relation to the poles. "By sunset we will have a flood tide pushed by a storm still two days off the coast. The full moon will also raise the tide. The Rossemeyer fleet might very well negotiate the mudflats without mishap. That is why he chose today for his ultimatum."

"That is not an option, Master Magician." Quinnault leveled his gaze on Nimbulan. "We have six hours to block that armada. Three half-built warships and a scattering of fishing vessels won't stop them."

CHAPTER 5

Myri concentrated on Amaranth. Her mind blended with her flywacket familiar's as he flew to freedom with her message to Nimbulan.

She had only a few moments of privacy to send Amaranth on this desperate mission.

Warn him of the danger. Stay and protect him! She urged the flywacket above the bowl of the volcanic crater that formed the city of Hanassa. Deep within the Southern Mountains, this haven for outlaws, rogue magicians, and mercenary soldiers was lost to casual searchers. Only Amaranth could fly over the protections and lead rescuers back to Myri and the children. *After* he warned Nimbulan of the plot against him. If only she wasn't too late. She'd lost so much time and consciousness from the drugs Erda gave her—still gave her—and the concussion she had suffered during Televarn's kidnap.

(Who will guard you and the babe? I don't want to leave,) Amaranth replied even as he flew higher.

North. Fly North until you find my husband. Her shoulders hunched and her arms spread slightly as if she could catch the wind and fly with Amaranth.

She could sprout wings and fly with him to freedom— ending forever Kaalipha Yaassima's enslavement of her.

What if she couldn't transform back into her human body once she took dragon form? Her tiny baby, barely three weeks old, depended upon her for life and nurturing. Powwell and Kalen were also captive. She couldn't leave them behind in this city of cutthroats and thieves. She didn't dare escape—yet.

For the moment she and her children lived. She could extend her thoughts and cares beyond the immediate circle of her daily routine.

She had to warn Nimbulan of Televarn's treachery before Yaassima returned to the suite and prevented Amaranth's escape. Myri hated the decadent opulence of the rooms she shared with Yaassima. She might have rich food, lovely clothing, and comfortable furnishings, but it was a prison nonetheless. Nor did the two separate bedrooms with a large common room between offer the privacy and solitude Myri craved. Someone, a guard or a maid always hovered nearby.

She hadn't been allowed outside the suite since that horrible day Televarn had kidnapped her and brought her to Hanassa. The baby had been born the day she arrived.

How long had Televarn kept her mind blank while they traveled here? How long had her husband suffered, not knowing her fate?

If only the silver cord of magic still connected her heart to his, she would know if he lived.

Myri turned her attention outward again. She established contact with Amaranth's mind. A sense of free soaring overtook her. A cold wind blasted Amaranth's face and lifted his wings. Freedom!

Through her familiar's eyes she saw the wide curve of the Great Bay, the mudflats on the western shores, and the braided delta of islands that made up the growing capital city.

Almost there. *Quickly, Amaranth. Yaassima comes.*

Her breath shortened in anticipation. Within a few heartbeats she would see the beloved face of her husband. "Nimbulan," she whispered. "How I miss you, husband. What made you stay away so long?"

Deep within her mind, she heard Amaranth cry out. He'd spotted the palace where King Quinnault lived. New construction gave the ancient keep an untidy look. She didn't dwell on the changes that had occurred in the last three seasons. The island next to the palace was her destination; the island where a vast pool of magical ley lines slept, hidden beneath compacted mud and silt. She honed in on the quiescent power in the pool.

She directed Amaranth's vision in an anxious search for the man who had given her love and trust and a child when no other could.

Together, she and her familiar picked out the window

of the room in the ancient monastery, now the School for Magicians, where Nimbulan slept. She had shared the room with him for a few precious days before her exile from Coronnan. Her baby had been conceived there. Conceived in love.

And now the baby's father didn't even know she existed. Myri had never told him, waiting for him to come to her so that she could relay the joyous news to his face. She had waited impatiently for him to come, always hoping that tomorrow . . . Neither she nor Powwell nor Kalen had perfected the summons spell. The road between the capital and her clearing was still too dangerous to trust a messenger to get through.

Pain stabbed her neck and chest, hot and fierce. Amaranth had been stabbed! He faltered from the wound. Myri's inner vision darkened as the pain swelled to encompass her entire being. Amaranth's agony pulled her mind deeper into his pain. Each heartbeat spread the burning acid through his veins.

Poison. Magic poison pierced them. His pain became hers. A deep wound beneath his left wing, perilously close to his heart made him falter and lose altitude.

Myri clutched the baby to her breast. The warmth of the tiny body anchored her to the reality of her physical existence. The familiar pressure of milk swelling in her breasts kept her from following Amaranth deeper and deeper into paralysis.

Voices in the corridor warned of Yaassima's approach. Abruptly the pain ceased. Myri's vision swirled and brightened.

"Amaranth!" she screamed with her mind. Her voice remained a whisper. "Where are you?" Frantically she searched for some contact with her familiar. The door squeaked open. Myri couldn't allow Yaassima to break her precious contact with Amaranth.

Amaranth, fight the wound. Fight the magic. You have to live, Amaranth. You have to warn Nimbulan, Myri screamed again with her mind. The pain returned. Not the hot stabbing wound Amaranth suffered, but a dull aching loneliness that threatened to squeeze the life from her.

Don't die, Amaranth. Oh, please, don't die.

*   *   *

"We have no fleet of warships, Your Grace." Nimbulan said. "But we have an army of wily fishermen who work the mudflats every day of their lives." Nimbulan retrieved his gold-framed glass from inside his tunic. He walked to the nearest candle on the high table.

"The tariff on trade was merely an excuse to trigger an invasion," Quinnault said as he cleared the table of current projects with one sweep of his arm. "The warriors of Rossemeyer thrive on war, not food." The king summoned a map with a snap of his fingers. Two servants dashed to obey his order.

"My magicians, your fisherman, and every able-bodied person we can gather will have a long hard day ahead of them, but we have a chance, Your Grace." Nimbulan breathed deeply, seeking calm. He had a battle to organize, when he'd thought his days as a Battlemage were over.

He had to stay and fight when he'd rather leave on his quest to rescue his wife.

When his thoughts fell into order, he continued the breathing exercise—in three counts, hold, out three counts, triggering a light trance for the summons spell. No time to return to the school for magical tools and a treatise on naval warfare. He'd have one of the apprentices bring them from his private study. He couldn't levitate them through the locked door. Stuuvart, his steward, had a key.

Nimbulan finished his summons, then marched into the courtyard and the stairs to the top of the palace walls and the roof of the keep. He didn't bother to pocket his glass. He'd need it often in the coming hours. His head spun with ideas and plans, as it had in the old days when he prepared for battle nearly every week of the campaign season.

"Merawk!" The sharp cry of a large bird screeched through the glass, piercing Nimbulan's ears and mind.

"Mewrare."

"That sounds like Amaranth." Nimbulan ran up the stairwell. As soon as he opened the trapdoor to the watchtower he looked to the partially cloudy sky for signs of the half-cat, half-falcon he'd last seen in Myri's arms.

"Perhaps your wife's flywacket responded to your

seeking vision, coming to you with word of Myrilandel."
Lyman poked his head through the opening right beside
him. Nimbulan scanned the bowl of the heavens rather
than question how the old man had appeared so
suddenly.

They both searched through a long moment of silence.
Only a few fluffy white clouds broke the unending blue
sky. Cold and crisp now. Beyond the horizon, a fierce
Winter storm gathered energy. The tide raced ahead of
the storm, swelling the bay so that even the deepest-
keeled ship could sail into Coronnan City.

At last, Nimbulan spotted Amaranth's silhouette, far
out over the Great Bay, black against a white cloud.
Wings stretched wide, Amaranth could have been any
large black bird outlined against the sky.

"Merawk," the flywacket cried. He banked and circled lower.

Nimbulan triggered his FarSight with a tendril of
stored dragon magic. There wasn't much of it left. He
had to conserve it.

The flywacket's cat-face came into focus within his
glass. Amaranth searched back and forth as he flapped
his falcon's wings, seeking the air currents to keep him
aloft. His black fur seemed to absorb light, robbing the
clouds of their share of sparkling sunshine.

"Here, Amaranth. Come to me." Nimbulan held out
his arm as an inviting perch.

"Merew," Amaranth acknowledged the command. He
stretched out his legs in preparation for landing.

"He'll tear your arm to shreds with those talons."
Lyman draped his cloak around Nimbulan's outstretched arm.

"No, he won't. He's very gentle when he lands," Nimbulan protested. But he didn't remove the cloak. His
fine linen shirt and sleeveless leather tunic wouldn't offer
much protection if Amaranth didn't retract his raptor's
talons to normal cat claws in time.

A shaft of light off to the right distracted Nimbulan.
He peered in the direction of the next island in the Coronnan River delta. Movement in a pattern contrary to
the passage of wind in the shrubbery betrayed a presence. No unnatural colors revealed a silhouette, only the
movement and the light.

"Someone is hiding over there." Lyman looked through his glass, aiming it at a shaft of sunlight to trigger the magic. "A man, dressed in green and brown and maybe black. I can see his aura but not his face or a signature color."

"Not a magician, then." Nimbulan turned his gaze back to the flywacket.

The light flashed again.

Amaranth screeched and faltered.

Nimbulan covered his ears against the high wail of sound that assaulted all of his senses, physical and magical. But he didn't shift his gaze from the flywacket.

Amaranth grew at an alarming rate. His black fur and feathers paled as he seemed to explode into a dazzling display of silver and purple. All of his black fur and feathers released the light they had absorbed until he reflected the sunshine away from his crystalline skin and hair.

"He's transforming into a dragon!" Nimbulan cried. "Why, Amaranth? Why go back to your natural form?" Once before he'd seen the flywacket burst free from the confines of his familiar shape. He'd flown to join the dragon nimbus as they hovered over the last battle of the Great Wars of Disruption—last Spring.

"He's hurt. He's dropping fast!" Lyman shouted. "The light. It must have been some kind of magical arrow. No normal shaft would penetrate his hide at this distance." The old man began searching the other island, looking through the glass into a wisp of witchfire on his fingertip. "Nothing. No aura, no silhouette, just a ferret running in circles. It's as if the man vanished into the void. Or took the animal's form."

The silvery dragon wings caught an updraft. Amaranth stretched and banked into the soft air, slowing his descent. Only then did Nimbulan see the black spot on his hide, near his heart. The wound spread rapidly across the dragon's chest.

"We haven't time to investigate the assassin. Send Quinnault's guards. We have to take care of Amaranth," Nimbulan said, stretching his arm wide again in invitation.

"They search for one assassin already. Perhaps it's the

same one." Lyman turned back to the trapdoor and called something down the stairwell.

Nimbulan kept his eyes on Myrilandel's familiar. "Easy, Amaranth. Land slow and easy." He turned to Lyman. "Get a healer. Quick. We have to save him. He's our only link to Myri."

"There isn't enough time," Lyman replied, already hastening down the stairs to the wide courtyard in front of the ancient keep. Nimbulan followed.

"Will Amaranth talk to you, Nimbulan?" Lyman cleared the courtyard of guards, servants, and courtiers with a gesture and a stern look.

"I hope so. He knows me. He's my wife's familiar."

"But do any of the other dragons talk to you?" As they emerged into the courtyard, Lyman whistled sharply, encouraging Amaranth to come to him. The noise pierced Nimbulan's ears like dragon speech. "That's right, Amaranth, come to me. I'll help you," Lyman coaxed.

Amaranth seemed to heed the man's advice and aimed for the court. He faltered and rocked.

Nimbulan sensed his pain and uncertainty. "He's losing consciousness. Moments of dizziness, then a brief recovery."

"You're in rapport with him. He'll let you touch his wound. Maybe he'll let you heal him. I'll seek his thoughts." Lyman stepped back as the wind from the dragon wings blasted dust into their faces.

"Do you speak with the dragons?" Nimbulan asked, amazed. He only heard the telepathic communication from the great beasts when they had something specific to say to him.

"My link to the dragons is—different from Myri's," Lyman said. He offered no further explanation.

Amaranth landed bellyfirst, scraping his muzzle on the packed dirt of the courtyard. The almost mature spiral horn on his forehead bent at an odd angle near the blunted tip. Wearily he lifted his nose a little and collapsed, wings half furled.

Nimbulan rushed to the dragon's side. Gingerly he probed with his fingertips to the center of the spreading black spot, over Amaranth's heart. With his left hand, palm up and fingers slightly curved, he pressed under the wing joint, seeking a major blood vessel. Almost instantly his mind moved inward, seeking the source of the wound. Dimly he watched with physical eyes as Lyman placed both hands flat against the creature's skull at the base of his single spiral horn.

This spell has to work. Stargods, please help me do this right.

The silver cord that bound him to Myri sprang to life. It tugged at his heart almost painfully. The hair on the back of his neck stood up, sensing danger. He didn't have time to reflect on its sudden reappearance. Amaranth was dying.

Blackness as deep as the void between the planes of existence invaded Nimbulan's inner vision from Amaranth's wound. He pushed it aside, seeking healthy blood and energy to combat the growing infection. Down, down, he sought a beginning place. He needed a fragment of healthy tissue near the wound to strengthen and begin pushing back against the disease-ridden magic. He hadn't the specific healer's gift, but a lifetime as a Battlemage had taught him much about field surgery for physical and magical wounds.

The blackness raced ahead of him. Propelled by magic, the evil grew thicker as it spread, slowing his probe. He pushed harder. Like wading in freezing honey, he forced his vision forward to the strong wing muscles, hoping the magic would follow him there and stay away from the vulnerable heart.

Thicker and thicker, the black magic encapsulated him, crushing him, robbing him of air. His heart flailed against his chest, fighting against the taint spreading from Amaranth's body into his own.

The void opened before him. Nimbulan searched the black nothingness for a trace of Amaranth. He might be able to separate the essence of the purple-tipped dragon from the magic that killed it, then return them both to their physical bodies.

(The void is forbidden to users of dragon magic.)

Nimbulan ignored the warning. He had to save Amaranth.

A tiny amethyst jewel winked at him in the distance. Purple, like Amaranth's wing-veins and horns. He dived after the spirit-light. It eluded him, always keeping just ahead of him.

Nimbulan concentrated and reached forward with senses that dissipated in the void. Closer. He came closer to the dragon spirit. A black aura surrounded the jewel-toned light. The blackness of evil magic.

He fought his revulsion and tried to push the blackness aside with his mind.

A blinding flash of pure white crystal erupted between him and Amaranth's spirit. Thousands of shards of all color/no color light blasted his senses.

Don't die, Amaranth. Oh, please don't die, Myri's unique mental voice pleaded. Each fragment of crystal seemed to vibrate with her need to save her familiar.

"Break it off, Nimbulan!" Lyman shook his physical body. "Let go of Amaranth. He's gone, you can't help him anymore. Amaranth is dead."

With a jolt that nearly robbed him of consciousness, Nimbulan dropped back into his body. The blackness receded from his mind, a little. Pain exploded from every pore in his body. He pressed his fingertips against his eyes. Starbursts of light appeared on his eyelids. He pushed the pinpricks of light together until they filled his vision.

At last the blackness fled out of him, unable to withstand the light.

"Myri! I have to go to her. She's in the void. I heard her. I have to go back to her."

No. The void is forbidden to users of dragon magic. You have to wait and find her by other means."

Nimbulan shook his head in denial. The movement broke his void-induced thrall. The reality of battle preparations crashed into his frayed senses. The need to stay and protect the city warred with his need to go to Myri.

He prayed to all three Stargods for his wife's safety.

"Amaranth, *Stargods!* What did they do to you?" he cried.

"He lived long enough to tell me something of Myrilandel."

Lyman's words broke through Nimbulan's emotional dizziness. "Where? Where is my wife, Lyman?"

"In Hanassa."

Chill raced up Nimbulan's spine. Hanassa lay deep in

the Southern Mountains, within a dry caldera. There, hidden from the rest of the world, outlaws, Rovers, rogue magicians, and other criminals had built a city. Secret passes and tunnels were said to lead into the heart of the mountain. Few people who entered Hanassa, who weren't invited by one undesirable sect or another, left it alive.

"Myrilandel was twin to Amaranth before taking a human body." Nimbulan shivered in distress. Myri's plea across the void haunted him. "She was happy enough to remain human while Amaranth lived because there could only be one purple-tipped dragon at a time. Now that Amaranth is gone, her instinct will be to return to her dragon form.

"Believe me, I know the instincts that drive her!" Lyman replied. He closed his eyes tightly. The thousands of lines around his eyes deepened.

"I have to find her before she abandons her body and joins the dragons," Nimbulan whispered through his grief. "I have to leave tonight—no, now. There are others who can lead this battle. Myri is in Hanassa. Televarn was headed for Hanassa last year. Maia and her baby are probably with the Rover clan, too."

"*You* have to organize this battle and save the kingdom first," Lyman reminded him. "As much as the dragons need you to rescue Myrilandel, they also recognize your responsibility to maintain peace in Coronnan. You are the only one with the experience and the wits to win this battle."

CHAPTER 6

"Water, the last of the four elements. Equal in strength to its three brothers," Televarn murmured. He stroked the surface of the small pool in the marshy ground of the small river island near Palace Isle. Kardia and Air were feminine elements. Fire and Water belonged to men. He'd rejected Fire as his source of magic today, too obvious, too visible.

The spell he'd put on Quinnault's wine had been Water based—though he'd been wearing the delusion of Maia's face and body at the time. Quinnault should be dead by now. Televarn had delivered the poisoned wine to the understeward over an hour ago.

He chuckled at the image of Quinnault dying. The moment the water in the wine hit the king's belly, it would freeze. The ice would grow so cold it, in turn, would freeze everything around it, growing steadily outward until the entire body was one sold block of ice.

Televarn thought about how he would spend the Kaalipha's reward for Quinnault's death. Gold. One thousand gold pieces to buy mercenaries and bribe the Kaalipha's loyal protectors. Her own gold would be the instrument of Yaassima's downfall and Televarn's rise to power.

Nimbulan would feel less pain than Quinnault from the spell Televarn planned for him. He would have a few seconds to realize that the wall of water engulfing him would cause his death, before life and intelligence vanished in a massive struggle for air.

Nimbulan and the meddling old man had seen him when he killed the flywacket. They knew who orchestrated today's devastation. True to character, Nimbulan had devoted his attention and his magic to the dying animal rather than searching out his enemy. He didn't deserve to be the father of a Rover child.

By Rover law, Maia's son belonged to the Rover parent. Televarn planned to make Myrilandel's child a Rover, too. His clan needed the new blood to expand and grow healthy again. He needed a large and healthy clan to support him when he became Kaaliph of Hanassa. Myrilandel wouldn't reject him then. She'd come back to his bed willingly when he made her Queen of Hanassa.

Televarn cupped his right hand slightly as he swirled his entire hand in the pool of water. The ferret, Wiggles, crept out from his hiding place in Televarn's pant leg and sniffed at the circling water. "Come. Share the spell with me."

Wiggles oozed back toward his dark hiding place.

"Your mistress ordered you to obey me," Televarn commanded the ferret. He clamped his free hand on the animal's neck to keep it from retreating further.

Wiggles plopped down on Televarn's arm reluctantly.

"My name means 'The one who speaks to Varns,'" Televarn muttered. "I was given that name when I rid my clan of its previous chieftain because I am gifted with persuasion. So, why can't I persuade you to cooperate, Wiggles?"

The ferret ignored him.

"I have met true Varns and struck bargains with them, a feat few can claim. You will obey me, beast, as your mistress commanded!" Televarn hated having to remind the creature that its loyalty to another bound it more tightly than his own magic and gifts.

He drew circles in the water with his hand, finding the element more cooperative than the ferret. A small whirlpool followed his movements. He continued the circling motion until he knew he had captured the essence of Water. Slowly he removed his hand from the pool, drawing the swirling vortex up with him. He chanted the ancient words that bound the element to his will.

Water resisted. It did not want to leave the pool where it rested before flowing into the gentle creek, then into the racing river, and finally into the Great Bay. Televarn pushed with his magic; not so easy without the support of his clan and only the ferret to aid him. His family had to remain in Hanassa for now. If they should be discovered in Coronnan, all his plans would fall apart. He'd had enough trouble keeping himself hidden for two weeks while he watched and waited for an opportunity.

Yaassima must not know that he had discovered the dragongate. He had to wait and assassinate his victims after he'd had enough time to journey from Hanassa to Coronnan City by mundane means.

He'd used the time well, observing, planning.

"Come!" Televarn commanded Water. A thin trickle leaped to his hand, trailing back into the pool. Wiggles touched the Water with a tiny paw, bonding with the magic and the element. Televarn took two steps away. Water remained connected to himself, the ferret, and the pool. Two more steps. Water stretched the connection and continued to follow.

"Good." He nodded his satisfaction. Now the hard part of the spell. He had to get the continuous stream of Water into Nimbulan's private bedchamber.

The thought of Myrilandel sharing that chamber with Nimbulan churned acid in Televarn's stomach. His jealousy nearly broke his connection with Water. He forced his emotions down into a cold knot of anger. Water was cold. Water would end the life of his rival.

He walked toward his hide canoe, following the little chirping noises Wiggles made—one chirp meant a step right, two chirps a step left. The ferret instinctively found the easiest pathway.

At the point where the island became more water than Kardia, Televarn steadied his small canoe with one hand; his awkward left hand, not his dominant right where Wiggles clung and they both maintained the thin stream of water trailing back to the pool.

Slowly he levered one knee into the boat. It rocked and slid beyond the reach of his leg. He overbalanced and fell into a cold blanket of mud. Wiggles wrapped tighter around his arm in an undulating wave of fur that mimicked laughter.

"*S'murghit!* Stay still," Televarn ordered the boat and the ferret. He pushed himself up onto his knees and elbows, never letting go of Water or of Wiggles.

Wiggles subsided. The hide canoe bobbed and thrashed under Televarn's hand, more responsive to the buoyancy of the water beneath it and the air above than to Televarn's command.

His fine black trews and shirt looked ruddy brown with the mud. Ruined. His green-and-purple vest embroidered with sigils of power was equally covered in goo. He'd never hear the end of Erda's displeasure for such carelessness. The ancient wisewoman of his clan held too much power over Televarn's Rovers. Power that should be his.

He stilled his growing frustration. Water pulled him back toward the pool of its origin. Perhaps Water had turned the canoe against him.

How to make his tools work with him? What could he promise an element and an inanimate object to pacify them?

(Freedom,) a voice whispered in the back of his head. *(Release them.)*

"Enough," he shouted. "You are mine. You will obey." He pushed more of his waning strength into the binding. Physical contact with Wiggles helped. But the creature wasn't truly his familiar, only borrowed. Their rapport was incomplete. Another annoyance. He'd never been able to bond with a creature so that its senses enhanced his magic and made it totally responsive to his wishes. They'd all escaped his net of control, like Water was trying to do.

The weight pulling his arm back to the pool grew to enormous proportions, then abruptly eased. He nearly fell into the mud again with the sudden release.

The canoe rested easily against its tether. Water remained in his hand.

Not willing to tempt the capricious canoe, Televarn knelt in the mud as he steadied the boat with his hand. More brown-and-green goo soaked through the fine cloth of his trews. He gritted his teeth against the seeping cold and caking stiffness to his vest. Then he slid one knee into his vessel. The canoe wobbled again. He forced it quiet until his other leg rested comfortably in the bottom. He balanced against the mild rocking his entry triggered. Then the canoe subsided, almost with a sigh of resignation. Wiggles slithered off his arm and undulated around the boat, sniffing every fragment. A few drops of Water trailed from the creature's paw back to Televarn's hand.

"Just keep me afloat until I reach School Isle and I'll set you free," he whispered to the boat.

Water quivered, wanting to be included in the promise. Televarn glared at the rebelling element. It stilled. "You'll be free when you complete the task I have for you and not before. Nimbulan won't survive the day. Then Myrilandel will be free of the spell he holds over her and she will come to my bed gratefully—as she did when first we met."

* * *

The darkness of the void faded from Myri's senses. Amaranth's cries faded from her mind. An irresistible urge to leave her body and fly to her familiar made her stretch her arms wide again to catch the wind. But she was deep within the Kaalipha's palace on the leeward side of a volcanic crater. No wind stirred to lift her dormant wings. The elongated bumps on her spine didn't stretch into horns to act as rudders while in flight.

Over and over she relived the moment Amaranth died. His pain and terrible loneliness swamped her awareness of everything, even the cries of her daughter.

"Make that child stop crying!" Yaassima ordered. Her eyes grew wide in growing frustration. Then her tone softened and her eyes narrowed. "You are making us late for the ceremonies assigning commissions to my followers."

Myri only half heard the older woman's verbal caress. *Amaranth!* her mind screamed.

"We must plan the Festival of Naming for your baby. All of Hanassa will rejoice when I name the child my heir." Yaassima clapped her hands together in delight.

How long had she been in the void, unaware of Yaassima's entrance into the common room of the suite? The Kaalipha had obviously been prattling for some time.

Myri fought the urge to transform. She had to stay aware and keep Yaassima away from her baby. Her best defense against the bloodthirsty Kaalipha of Hanassa was to stay out of her way and her thoughts until she found a means to escape Hanassa.

Oh, Amaranth, I'm sorry. I didn't intend for you to fly to your death. When she escaped, would she share the fate of her birth twin?

"Only my husband has the right to name my child," she reminded the Kaalipha of the tradition so old it had become law. Her need to fly faded a little with her efforts to control herself.

Amaranth! How will I live without you. Did you warn Nimbulan?

"We are kin, you and I." Yaassima caressed Myri's unbound hair. "Your husband abdicated his rights to the child when he exiled you. Now I claim the right of kinship and naming. Come to the Justice Hall now. 'Tis your duty to observe how I delegate the commissions and the fees. You and the child must grow into the heritage I give you."

"The rich and powerful of Kardia Hodos come to you only when they need the death of a rival and the disruption of trade." Myri kept her back turned toward Yaassima, hiding the tears that gathered in her eyes.

"I will not deal in death and destruction, Kaalipha." Myri stiffened her spine and her resolve to escape. Amaranth's death would not be in vain. Until then she had to maintain rigid control of herself and her emotions. Grief for Amaranth must wait. She could betray no trace of weakness before Yaassima.

Like a dragon, she must remain invisible while she watched and waited for the best opportunity to escape.

"You are thinking too fondly of your treacherous husband, Myrilandel. I can tell." Yaassima sounded petulant. "He is but a distant part of your past. Better you should think about how to control Moncriith the Bloodmage." Yaassima licked her lips. "I have given Moncriith permission to gather mercenary forces against Coronnan. His planned invasion of your brother's kingdom won't keep him busy long once he learns that you are here. He is so very single-minded in his obsession. I find his rants about blood and fire and the demons *you* control quite amusing."

Myri felt all the heat leave her face. The man she feared most in the world, the one who had stalked her from village to village all her life, lived. Lived here in Hanassa. He wouldn't stop with burning Myri at the stake. He'd murder her baby as well. At least her other enemies, Yaassima and Televarn, wanted her alive.

"Remember this, Myrilandel, if ever you step outside my palace, into the city, I will make certain Moncriith hears about it. He will seize and destroy you. So you see, all your pretty plans to escape Hanassa are for naught. Only I can protect you. Only I can become the family you so long for." She stroked Myri's hair with possessive hands.

Never! Myri vowed to herself. She would have her family back. Her true family of Kalen and Powwell, the baby, and Nimbulan.

But never again would she be able to include Amaranth in that tight circle of love and kinship.

The threat of Moncriith seemed trivial against the loss of Amaranth and the danger to Nimbulan. She had to escape, now.

She needed to fly free, to breathe the sparking clear air of the mountains. The heat haze and dust of Hanassa was all she'd been allowed since Televarn had kidnapped her and brought her to this cursed place.

If only she could fly!

The baby's whimpers kept her firmly anchored to her wingless human body.

"Come, Myrilandel. We mustn't keep my people waiting much longer," Yaassima ordered. Persuasion fled her voice, replaced with deadly impatience.

Myri knew she couldn't ignore the Kaalipha. Yaassima executed those who defied her. She'd executed her consort. Rumor also claimed she'd killed her daughter who had disappeared right after the unlucky consort had lost his head to Yaassima's sharp sword.

Myri caressed the sleeping baby on her shoulder, needing contact with her life to counteract the death that assailed her senses at every turn.

"I have no blood kin, Kaalipha Yaassima. Only my daughter," Myri replied. "I can't claim King Quinnault as kin anymore. He exiled me." Nimbulan had agreed with the edict.

Why had she risked Amaranth to warn Nimbulan? *Amaranth!*

"You should hate your husband for what he did to

you. Yet you cling to his memory as if you expect him to defy his king and join you," Yaassima sneered.

"I love him." He was the missing piece to make her family complete—once she escaped.

"You and your daughter carry the blood of the dragons in your veins," Yaassima reminded her. "That is a heritage that must be perpetuated. Not your paltry emotions toward a treacherous husband and those two grubby children."

"Show me that Powwell and Kalen are safe, and I will not question your wisdom in separating me from *my* children." Myri kept her eyes locked on the blue desert sky above the crater. Clean and clear, untainted by Yaassima's need for blood and destruction. The Kaalipha perverted her dragon hunting instincts, just as her ancient ancestor Hanassa had when he went rogue and deserted the dragon nimbus.

Yaassima twined her fingers in Myri's fine hair. The sexuality behind the gesture made Myri shiver with revulsion. The baby fretted. Myri cooed at her daughter and turned toward her bedchamber, on the inside wall away from the window, without looking at the Kaalipha.

"I rescued you from Televarn's ungentle clutches for the sake of our kinship," Yaassima snarled. "His jealousy knows no bounds. He would have killed your daughter as soon as she was born, rather than admit that the child isn't his. If he let *you* live, Moncriith would have found a way to destroy you. You owe me your life, Myrilandel, as does everyone who seeks refuge in Hanassa."

"I did not seek refuge. Televarn kidnapped me and brought me here against my will."

"Forget the magician who forced marriage upon you. Forget the children not of your body. Only I am your kin. I will protect you as Nimbulan and your brother, King Quinnault, refused to do." Yaassima's voice swelled with pride. As absolute ruler of Hanassa, none of the thousands of criminals who lived in the city questioned her authority.

Myri had been forced to witness three executions in as many weeks. Each time she feared the offender would be fifteen-year-old Powwell or eleven-year-old Kalen, adults responsible for their actions in this vicious society.

After each beheading, Yaassima dipped her hands, with their preternaturally long fingers, into the blood of the dead man or woman. The symbolic gesture, that the death was her responsibility, paled in comparison to the look of nearly sexual glee that dominated Yaassima's eyes for an hour afterward.

Myri sensed Yaassima's hand dropping away from yet another caressing stroke of her hair.

"Let the child sleep, Myrilandel. Put her back in the cradle and come to the Justice Hall," Yaassima ordered.

"She's wet. By the time I change her, she will be hungry, too."

"It is time we found a wet nurse for her. Women of quality do not feed their own children. One of Televarn's women has just lost her baby—Maia, I think, is her name. I'll send for her." Yaassima spoke to the guard outside the door of the suite.

"I will have no Rover woman taint my child!" Especially not Maia, Nimbulan's former lover. "Rovers steal children from their lawful parents."

"Your daughter deserves a name," Yaassima continued without acknowledging Myri's protest. "She needs a name of power; a name that will resound through history as does the name of our ancestor, *Hanassa*. Tomorrow we shall hold the Festival of Naming."

This time Yaassima caressed the baby's hair, only a shade darker than Myri's. Just a trace of silver gilt had appeared in some of the strands with the last few days.

"Dragon hair. We all have it. You, me, the dragons. My daughter didn't have it. Crystal fur on dragons, crystal hair on us. It reflects light away from us so that none may penetrate our thoughts and actions. Mystery is power."

"She's just a baby. Her hair and eye color will change within a few weeks. She will grow into her long fingers and toes. She has no trace of the elongated spinal bumps." Myri denied the kinship her protector pressed upon her daily. "Did you hear me when I said that Maia will not touch my child?"

"I shall present the baby to the people of Hanassa at her naming. They must see that the dragon blood continues. No one will dare oppose me if they know for certain that another dragon waits to exact retribution. They wouldn't have respected my daughter. She was weak, too like her father." Yaassima continued to touch the baby, delaying Myri's retreat to the privacy of her bedchamber. "Her name must be Hanassa."

Never! Myri kept her protestations to herself. She had to persuade Yaassima rather than defy her.

"Rovers steal babies," she repeated. "So few of their babies live that they must rob others of their children to bring new blood into the clans. If you allow Maia near my baby, she will find a way to kidnap her—or substitute her own dead child for my healthy one."

"She wouldn't dare. I am the Kaalipha, and the child is my heir."

"*My* baby is very wet. Do you wish to change her?" Myri asked coyly, knowing fastidious Yaassima would have nothing to do with the rather messy process of rearing an infant.

"Go." Yaassima fluttered her fingers in disgusted dismissal.

Myri dodged around the older woman and walked toward the door to the inner room of the suite.

She waved her hand across a metal plate set into the wall by the doorway. The light panels in the ceiling came to life, activated by some spell only Yaassima understood. The clear panels gave off a directionless glow, like witchlight, but yellow instead of the more natural fire green.

The Kaalipha came no farther into Myri's chamber than the doorway.

"Where is the pywacket?" Yaassima asked. She used the ancient word for a familiar, from a language that had died out from all of Kardia Hodos except here in Hanassa.

"I . . . I don't know," Myri stammered, halting her quest for a clean diaper. Grief nearly felled her again. "Perhaps he hunts rats in your kitchens."

Amaranth! You can't be dead. Knife-sharp pain stabbed her heart and brought tears to her eyes again. The void beckoned for her to follow Amaranth into his next existence.

"Did Televarn kill Amaranth, too?" Yaassima asked. A half smile creased her face and her eyes lit with lustful glee. The Kaalipha didn't read minds often, but when she did, she always found her victim's vulnerability. "I wondered how long that jealous Rover would allow your nasty creature to live. He could never possess it, so it must be eliminated. Just as he will never possess you. I can protect you from him, Myri. But only if you mind your duty to me. I will expect you in the Justice Hall as soon as you clean up the child. You may feed her there. Maia will take over as wet nurse this evening."

"I will not allow another to nurse my child—especially a thieving Rover. Never. And I will not nurse the child in front of your amoral criminals and perverts. Do you hear me?" So much for remaining invisible. But, *s'murghit,* some issues she had to fight.

"My people must see the child and know her for my heir. If they see your breasts and lust after you, all the better. Their uncontrolled emotions give me control over their desires and power over their lives. Just as I have the power of life and death over you."

CHAPTER 7

King Quinnault made his way through the groups of people in the palace courtyard. He didn't have enough to do. Dedicated underlings jumped at every task he created in the battle preparations. As king, he was supposed to be free to make decisions. So far, he didn't even have that chore.

Nimbulan, as the experienced and respected Battlemage, directed the defenses today.

Common citizens filled the courtyard. Quinnault smiled at them as he strode away from the confines of the palace. The corpse of the purple-tipped dragon had been cleared away from the busy courtyard. Later, after the battle, they would hold some kind of remembrance and consign it to the funeral pyre.

Two of the master magicians had fought the formal burning of the dragon body. They needed to study it, dissect it, learn the secret of generating magic. But Nimbulan had insisted. The dragons deserved the same respect as any human—especially Amaranth who had aided in healing King Quinnault last spring. All of the magicians respected Nimbulan enough to bow to his demands.

Quinnault's magical ties to the great beasts went beyond affection. He grieved with the entire dragon nimbus over the loss of the little purple-tipped dragon. Amaranth had been one of his family.

He sorely missed his telepathic communications with the dragons. He'd never shared that level of intimacy with any human. He strongly doubted he ever would.

He moved through the crowd of his bustling citizens, making his kingly, but distant, presence known to them. He couldn't do much else.

Some of the women bent over a huge cauldron, boiling bandages. They paused in their work only long enough to dip him a curtsy. Most of the men acknowledged their king with a nod of the head.

A year ago, he had worked alongside these people building bridges among the islands. Then, he'd been only a lord, the Peacemaker. Now he was king, less useful and more removed from the people he served.

A gaggle of children piled stones together by the gate. Useful weapons, should the enemy manage to attack the palace itself. A five-year-old waddled toward the pile with a stone far too heavy for his skinny arms. He dropped the rock off balance. The entire mound began to spill backward on top of the boy.

Quinnault dashed forward to pluck the child out of the way. He held him against his chest until the rocks stopped tumbling all over the courtyard.

"Can't you stay out of the way, Mikkey!" an older boy scolded. He had been supervising the arrangement of the stones.

"I only wanted to help," Mikkey blubbered.

"We need all the help we can get." Quinnault set the boy down and wiped his tears with the hem of his tunic. "Next time, Mikkey, why don't you give your rock to him and let him place it on top of the pile." He indicated the older boy with a thrust of his elbow.

"Yes, Your Grace." Mikkey executed an awkward bow.

"We're all working together today. No need for bows among battle comrades." Quinnault ruffled Mikkey's hair. The older boy stared at the familiar gesture with wide eyes and dropping jaw. Quinnault reached over to offer him the same rough affection. Then he showed the boys how to arrange the rocks for better balance.

He moved toward the riverbank and the men who wrestled with small boats to float felled trees into the bay. Over half of these people had been refugees from the war a year ago. He expected them to pack up and leave at the first signs of trouble. Instead, they worked side by side with the long-time residents of the islands to defend their new homes—to uphold his kingship.

"All I really wanted was to be left in peace," he said to himself. He turned a full circle, watching all of them work together for a common defense. His heart swelled with pride. He needed to work with them, show them how much their loyalty meant to him.

"Excuse me, Your Grace." Another child tugged at his tunic. "Lord Konnaught requests you attend him." The little girl, not more than five or six, hesitated on her esses but managed to push them out without lisping.

"Where is Konnaught?" he asked her, looking about. The son of his former rival for the crown, wasn't among the workers in the courtyard. Quinnault thought he'd ordered all of his fosterlings to help with the defenses.

"His lordship is in the armory, Your Grace." The little girl bobbed a sketchy curtsy and ran off.

"He should be out here, learning who we fight for." Konnaught had made his belief in his superiority over all of Coronnan well known. His father, Kammeryl d'Astrismos, had claimed kinship to the Stargods and therefore felt he needn't dirty his hands with normal people.

Quinnault had killed Konnaught's father on the field of battle. He owed the boy more than he could repay. But the boy also owed him obedience and loyalty in return for protection and an education.

Quinnault sighed and wondered what kind of temper tantrum would result if he ignored Konnaught's demand for attention.

"Mikkey," he called, waving the rock toter to him.

The little boy relinquished his latest burden almost gratefully and ran the few steps to stand before Quinnault. "Yes, Your Grace?"

"Lord Konnaught is in the armory. Go tell him to bring me a short sword and sheath. Make sure he comes himself and doesn't give you the weapon to carry for him."

"Yes, Your Grace." Mikkey bowed again, a little less awkward this time.

Quinnault ambled over to stand at the foot of the palace steps. The jumble of people cleared around him, giving him a semblance of privacy, acknowledging his separateness. He had no doubt that at least a dozen ears would overhear his conversation with the troublesome young lord no matter where he conducted the interview.

Konnaught approached several long minutes later. He carried a sword far too big and heavy for his twelve-year-old frame. His father's sword. The sword that had nearly split Quinnault in two until the people of Coronnan joined with Quinnault's sister Myrilandel and a purple-tipped dragon to heal the man they proclaimed king.

The weak sunlight of late Autumn highlighted the blond in Konnaught's sandy-colored hair—blond, not the red inherited from the Stargods. Just before his father's death, rumors had abounded that the name of one of the Stargod brothers at the top of the d'Astrismos family tree had been inserted by Kammeryl. The warlord had also dyed his hair to resemble the bright locks of the three divine brothers.

"Why do you demean yourself by consorting with peasants?" Konnaught kept the heavy sword firmly at his own side.

Quinnault couldn't see any evidence of the short sword he had requested.

"You are the king! You should be giving orders from your throne, not out there working with peasants." Konnaught nearly spat the last word.

"The 'peasants' are Coronnan. Without them, I would have no one to rule, and my kingship would be meaningless. We've had this conversation before, Konnaught. I do not agree with your father's views of authority and responsibility," Quinnault said mildly, refusing to let the boy rile him.

"You would have the land. Land is more important than peasants. If my father were king, you wouldn't see him out hugging ruffian babies and hauling rocks like a mule."

"The Stargods did not see fit to let your father be king." Anger began to heat Quinnault's skin. He wanted to turn this malcontent over his knee and spank him.

There had to be a better way to deal with him before he became a bully like his father. Kammeryl d'Astrismos had used pain and intimidation to prove his superior power.

Quinnault refused to do that. He had found a way to bring peace to Coronnan without forcing his followers into submission, with Nimbulan's help. And the dragons. And the help of all those dozens of people working around him.

"Since I am your king, and you are my fosterling until

you come of age, you are required to obey my orders."
Quinnault placed his hands on his hips and glared at
the boy.

Konnaught stood up straighter. He darted glances
about him in alarm.

Quinnault made a decision. He'd allowed his fosterling
too much freedom.

"Konnaught d'Astrismos, you will accompany me on
my rounds today and lend a hand wherever I deem fit.
Come." Quinnault turned toward the battlements. "But
first you must fetch me the short sword I asked for earlier. And put away that weapon. It's too big for you and
too unwieldy for me to carry in a boat."

Konnaught caressed the jeweled hilt of the sword. Reluctantly he returned to the armory, a circular stone
building on the far side of the courtyard. His steps
dragged until he was halfway to his destination. Then he
stiffened his back in defiance.

"You won't be needing a weapon for yourself, Konnaught," Quinnault called.

"A lord must always appear a lord. A sword on his
hip displays his authority for all to see."

"A King must learn other ways to earn his authority,"
Quinnault reminded him—again. "If you keep me waiting, I'll double your time tomorrow studying the history
of Coronnan." Quinnault smiled to himself. That was a
chore he would enjoy, but he knew Konnaught hated
reading and ciphering, thought them demeaning skills.

Today, Lord Konnaught would do something else he
hated.

The boatmen could always use an extra pair of hands
on the oars. Nothing like rowing against the tide all day
to make a man out of an arrogant stripling.

*   *   *

From the top parapet, Nimbulan watched the teams
of men, nobles and common laborers, mundanes paired
with magicians, as they felled trees from the nearest
mainland forest. Every magician carried a few threads
of Nimbulan's formal blue robe, or strands of his hair,
to connect them to him—a trick of illegal rogue magic.
But the mundanes didn't need to know that. None of

the magicians had enough dragon magic left to survive this battle.

Through those connections Nimbulan monitored the sharpness of the blades and the positioning of the fallen trees.

His palms burned with sympathetic blisters. He rubbed his tender hands against his tunic. The new dye rubbed off the worn leather. Now his hands tingled with the coloring chemicals as well as the raw nerve endings.

At least the magic was working. He could keep the channels of communication open and think clearly enough to make decisions. As soon as this battle was over—win or lose—he would leave in search of Myri.

Sighing heavily, he turned his attention back to supervising the defense preparations. He hoped the actual battle progressed more favorably and swiftly than the hard work of the day.

Teams of magicians and fishermen levitated the felled trees into the river where local boatmen guided the untrimmed timber out into the mudflats.

Would they be able to fell enough trees to fill the mudflats with traps? Aching shoulders joined his smarting palms as evidence of their attempt. Nimbulan prayed to the Stargods they had enough time and strength. There wouldn't be much magic left in the kingdom after today—dragon or rogue. But they had to use it all to save the kingdom.

Several nobles joined the numerous soldiers and farmers in the hard work. Quinnault had been among the boatmen earlier along with the arrogant brat, Konnaught. Master magicians and apprentices worked as hard as the men more used to using the strength of their bodies than the power of mind and magic.

Hanic and a few other nobles had suddenly found other places to be—a long way away from the city. Nimbulan was surprised Konnaught hadn't managed to find a way to join them.

Nimbulan was the Battlemage once more, responsible for all the lives that surrounded him. *Never again,* he vowed. He'd sworn the same oath a year ago when he organized the final battle of the civil war that had crippled Coronnan for three generations. *There has to be a better way. If only I can find it.*

"Such a waste of timber," King Quinnault groaned as he climbed the last few steps to Nimbulan's parapet. They watched a fifty-foot tree tilt and smack the ground. "I had plans for those trees, building, export. . . ."

"Books." Nimbulan regretted the loss, too. "Trees will grow again, given time. The cleared area can be plowed and planted. New trees can be started in old, worn-out fields. As long as we save the kingdom tonight, all will work out. Somehow."

"I certainly hope so." Quinnault shaded his eyes and peered out toward the bay.

"I thought you were helping with the trees, Your Grace."

"I was. I got tired of Konnaught's whining. And I thought some of the others would work themselves into heart attacks if I remained down there much longer. They seemed to have to prove they could work harder, longer, and faster than me." The king flashed a wide grin at his magician.

Both men chuckled. A year ago, those same lords were more interested in murdering each other than striving for a common defense.

"They seem to forget, I spent this Autumn hauling loaded fishnets to help feed our growing population. Last Winter I built bridges among these islands. I'm used to hard work. They aren't." Quinnault rubbed his shoulders lightly, more an easing of tightness than a massage of an ache.

Together, they watched two fishermen—and surprisingly, Konnaught—in a flat-bottomed skiff ram the first tree into the mud beside one of the few channels that keeled ships could negotiate. With the help of a magician, they embedded the trunk deep enough to hold it upright against the rising tide. The top branches remained above the waves for now.

Too soon the tide would flood the traps and the fleet would enter the channels.

Too soon. They wouldn't be ready in time. But the sooner this operation was over, the sooner Nimbulan could leave in search of Myri. And Maia's child. How was he going to persuade the mother to allow him access to the baby, help in its rearing, keep Televarn away from it?

"At least you persuaded Konnaught to do more than complain, Your Grace."

"Ordered, threatened, more like. I told him I would try him for treason against his dragon-blessed monarch if he didn't work as hard as everyone else out there. If he whined once more about how his father would have fought this battle, I think I might have strangled him. Spanked him at the very least."

"You'd have to stand in line for the privilege." Nimbulan kept his smile contained. If he'd had his way, Konnaught would have been shipped off to a foreign monastery the day after his father had been defeated in battle.

A large wave slapped at the boat Konnaught rowed, turning the flat-bottomed craft sideways. The log he was towing slipped free of a magician's control.

"If I still had access to ley lines, I could transport the *s'murghing* tree directly into the mudflats," Nimbulan muttered. Dragon magic only allowed levitation, not instantaneous transportation. He was letting the ley lines fuel his magic, but he couldn't advertise that with obvious rogue spells.

A second fishing boat snared the loose log as it towed its own tree farther out into the mudflats. An errant wave caught the sprawling branches threatening to rip it away from that journeyman magician, too.

Lasso it with magic, Rollett. Use your talent, Nimbulan urged the young man telepathically. The tendril of magic connecting them was weak. He'd used too much already today. He'd also thought of Myri too often and lost his usual firm control over the expenditure of power and energy.

Carefully he stilled a special place deep within his belly, preparing it for an influx of magical power. New energy, dragon energy, trickled into the vacancy. Not enough. Not nearly enough.

Were the dragons with Myri, guarding her while he couldn't? They had cared for her and guided her through her entire life. He had to believe they continued to do so. They had to fill the void in her life left by Amaranth's death until he got to her. She'd be so lost and alone, so vulnerable. . . .

Out in the bay, Rollett waved his arms in acknowledgment of the help. Nimbulan relaxed a little. His stomach growled. He'd skipped the noon meal to direct the preparations for battle. Now he was using up his energy stores in surges.

A little girl with muddy brown braids brought a tray filled with mugs of steaming cider and slabs of bread and meat. "Thank you. Please, extend my thanks to Guillia." He bowed formally to the child as he reached for the nourishment. "And would you have someone at the school fetch my text on naval battle strategy from my desk. The door is locked and Master Stuuvart has the key." The book hadn't come with his earlier request.

Nimbulan drank down the spicy brew gratefully, as did Quinnault.

"I'll fetch the book, Magician Nimbulan." The child dipped a shy curtsy, then scampered down the stairs. She looked a lot like Kalen, probably one of the magician girl's numerous sisters. All of the family had been tested for magical talent, but only Kalen seemed to have it— unless one counted Guillia's ability to sense the nutritional needs of every magician living at the school.

Kalen could transport anything. She'd make short work of this chore. But she wasn't here. The now familiar ache of loneliness drove Nimbulan to tear a furious bite from his bread. Kalen had been exiled along with Myri, and he couldn't go find them until the invading fleet from Rossemeyer had been repelled.

"You realize, of course, that the obstacles in the bay won't be enough," Quinnault asked. "Some of the ships will get through." He pointed where some of his men set up a fire pit in the center of the courtyard. Huge cauldrons filled with oil sat nearby, ready to be boiled and thrown on invaders who managed to come ashore.

"What do you suggest?" Nimbulan ignited the kindling with a snap of his fingers without leaving the parapet. He breathed a deep sigh of satisfaction that the simple spell worked. Then he levitated the first cauldron onto the frame above the fire. He controlled it until it was firmly settled. His mind whirled as he withdrew from the levitation. Thirty years as a Battlemage and he couldn't think beyond the first assault. Where was his mind?

(With Myrilandel,) a voice in the back of his head

reminded him. *(Think long. Think like a dragon. Myrilandel is part of the whole.)*

"If we still had some catapults, we could fling burning oil at the ships," Quinnault suggested.

"Witchfire would be better. Only a new spell can extinguish it. It can be guided more accurately than oil and will also give us enough light to pinpoint the ships." Nimbulan's mind started working again. He latched onto familiar patterns of strategy and battle plans. "But we don't have any catapults. We dismantled our siege engines after the last battle. We thought the wars ended, so we used the timbers in the new wing of the palace as a reminder of the devastation we brought on ourselves."

The two men stood in silence a moment, remembering that awful day when Quinnault had been forced into single combat with his arch rival, Kammeryl d'Astrismos. His priestly training hadn't prepared him for the dirty fight that ended with Kammeryl dead and Quinnault nearly so. Only Myri, with Amaranth's aid, had brought her brother back from the brink of death.

Now Amaranth was dead, and Myri was missing. Nimbulan cursed himself for letting his mind drift from the coming battle. He couldn't do anything about Myri until this battle ended.

What would he do once she was safe? She couldn't return to Coronnan. He had responsibilities here. Magicians weren't meant to be family men. He had no precedents to latch onto.

"Some of Kammeryl's engines were abandoned and left to rot," Quinnault mused. "I wonder if they're still usable? Who can you spare to go check? The old man?" He pointed out Lyman's white head amidst the younger men at the edge of the forest.

"Old Lyman might surprise all of us before the day is through. But you're right. He'll be more useful locating a couple of catapults than wearing himself out hauling trees."

Nimbulan checked the level of the sun. The red-yellow orb of light eased past high noon toward the horizon. The turning tide hummed in his blood. His sensitivity to the planet told him precisely how long before the flood tide allowed passage across the mudflats. He looked downriver toward the bay and the line of ships hovering offshore. Dared he waste a little precious magic to check the decks for signs of activity? No. The armada would hoist sail at sunset. Not before.

He watched the waves a moment, noting how high they reached on the mudflats. Each one drowned more of the shore than the previous one.

He and his teams hadn't nearly enough time for all that needed to be done.

CHAPTER 8

"Remove that squalling child from my presence if you cannot control her," Yaassima screamed. The Kaalipha wrenched a handful of her own white-blonde hair, as if tearing it from her scalp could ease the headache the baby's fretful crying caused.

Shyly, Myri covered her breast and rose from her chair at the head of the Justice Hall. She'd endured to-day's Dispensation of Favors for as long as she could tolerate it. Moncriith stood at the back of the former temple to Simurgh, glaring at her while she nursed the baby.

"Whore of Simurgh!" he mouthed a curse at her. The hatred in his eyes dominated all of the emotions swirling about the Justice Hall. Myri's distress at his presence must have reduced her milk and upset her child.

Nursing a baby in public was one of the most natural and proud acts a woman could perform. But the assassins and thieves, including Moncriith, who looked to Yaassima for work and pay, were a hardened lot who viewed any woman's breasts as objects of unbridled lust. Even the women among the outlaws stared at her with moist lips and wide eyes.

Myri wondered how long Moncriith would feign obedience to Yaassima. He didn't usually accept anyone's authority but his own. Unless he wanted to use Yaassima in some convoluted plot before he murdered her. And drew magical power from her pain and death.

Myri had almost reached the stairway leading to the royal suite when Yaassima's words stopped her cold. "Take the child to the wet nurse, then return to help me preside over the Dispensation of Favors."

"Maia's babe has been dead two days. Her milk has probably dried up," Myri said, thinking furiously for a way to prevent separation from her child. She had never met Maia, only knew her from Nimbulan's memory of her and a few rumors the servants had related.

"Maia is a Rover. Everyone knows that Rover women make the best wet nurses."

"Rover women hire out as wet nurses so they can steal the babies and raise them as their own. Will you risk this child to Rover theft?"

"No one steals from the Kaalipha of Hanassa." Yaassima gestured to Myri to withdraw. Then she sat back in a high thronelike chair with a deep sigh.

Myri knew the Kaalipha would wait patiently for her return. *You will have a long wait, Yaassima,* she thought.

Back in the privacy of her own bedchamber, she slammed the door that separated her from the common room. Yaassima's chamber was adjacent to Myri's. A thick wall of stone separated them, but Myri had no doubt Yaassima had spy holes and listening spells to observe Myri.

No one awaited her in the suite. Maia must not have come yet.

"You may watch, but you won't enter this room easily," Myri whispered to the absent Rover. The door had no lock, so she pushed a heavy blanket chest in front of it. The dark wood scraped aside the colorful rugs scattered across the stone floor. The screeching sound reminded Myri, painfully, of Amaranth's cries of distress just before he died.

She blocked the sound from her mind as she stacked two chairs on top of the chest. Then she stood a clothes chest on end in front of the pile. Not satisfied, she shoved the bed against that.

"I will rest undisturbed until my milk comes back," she said to the blocked doorway.

She needed liquid to replenish her milk while she rested. Greedily she drank from the pitcher that always sat on the stand beside her bed. As the water slid down her throat, she tasted copper and salt, different from the usual sulfur tang that permeated everything in Hanassa. Drugs.

The same drugs Erda had given her during the baby's birth. Yaassima must have ordered them, needing Myri docile and obedient.

Myri almost sobbed. She couldn't plan her escape while drugged. This was the last dose she'd take. From now on, she'd test all her food and drink. For now she must rest, must fight the grief that threatened to overwhelm her.

She threw herself across the bed, cuddling her baby close. The infant whimpered, still hungry.

"Soon, Baby. I'll feed you soon," she promised her hungry child.

She pressed both hands into the delicate flesh above her heart. The magical dart had penetrated Amaranth in the same place. Tenderness beneath her fingertips told her a bruise formed there, whether from her own hands or in sympathy with Amaranth's wound, she didn't know.

Tears of loneliness slipped down her cheeks.

Time lost meaning. The baby cried herself to sleep.

Voices in the outer room of the suite startled Myri awake from heavy dreams of crashing to the Kardia from a great height.

"When Televarn returns from his mission, I must send you back to his slave pens," Yaassima said sternly from the other side of the door.

Had Maia finally arrived? Myri wouldn't stir until she knew whom the Kaalipha addressed.

Her breasts ached, too full of milk. Her arms were damp from where her milk had soaked through her shift and gown. It still smelled sweet. How long had she slept? Beside her, the baby cried again. Silently, she reached for the infant, determined to feed her herself. Maia would have no tasks awaiting her.

"For now you may tend to Myrilandel. I fear for her health. Do what you must to get her to open the door and see that the child stops crying." A note of desperation entered the Kaalipha's voice.

"Yes, ma'am." A different voice. One Myri hadn't heard in a long time. Kalen. Her adopted daughter was safe. She would have to open the door to see her. Would Yaassima use that moment to take the baby from her?

She clutched the baby, urging her to feed more quickly. All her latent desire to transform into a dragon and fly away faded as she nurtured her young. Purple dragons had no gender. As a dragon she couldn't care for a baby. This was a task only she could perform. Maia—and through her, Televarn—would never get her hands on this baby.

A loud squalling sound told her she held the baby too tightly. Still, she couldn't let go. If she released her grasp, even a little, *they* would steal her baby. Myri knew that *they* had kidnapped her, betrayed her, exiled her, separated her from Nimbulan and her other children. *They* wouldn't stop until she was utterly bereft and destroyed.

They took form in her mind. Moncriith's face dominated the form, surrounded by the flames he claimed would cleanse her and Coronnan of demonic control.

Vaguely, she knew the drugs clouded her mind.

"Myrilandel, let me in, please. Let me stay with you." Kalen pleaded from the other side of the door. Last Spring, the girl had said the same words to Myri. Kalen's father had disowned the girl when all magicians who could not, or would not, gather dragon magic were exiled from Coronnan.

Kalen's mother had cried out at the girl's expulsion, but would not defy her husband or abandon her other children to stay with the girl.

"Myri, if you don't let me in, I'll have to go back to Televarn. He . . . he's made slaves of Powwell and me. He forces us to . . . he forces . . ." She broke off in a sob.

Kalen was adept at lying and wearing the emotions people wanted to see in her. But Myri had never known her to cry.

"Give me a moment. I'll let you in, but not the thieving Rover woman." Myri began dismantling the barricade. She cursed and muttered under her breath, knowing Yaassima had found a way to force her into the action.

Several minutes later, Myri focused her gaze on Kalen. The little girl stood in the doorway, wringing her hands and looking over her shoulder toward the center room of the suite. The girl's auburn-tinged braids swished with her movements. Concerned gray eyes met Myri's above a small nose with a wide spread of freckles strewn across the bridge.

"Kalen." Myri drew her adopted daughter into a tight

hug. Kalen was safe. The baby was safe. Where was Powwell?

"Yes, Myri, I'm here to take care of you. Can you tell me what happened?" The girl urged her toward the padded rocking chair near the hearth. She slammed the door behind her, putting a barrier between them and the Kaalipha.

"You've grown in the last few weeks. But you still can't keep your hair bound up properly." Myri smoothed a stray strand of hair from the girl's face.

The musky smell of Kalen's familiar was absent. Myri didn't like the weasel like creature that had adopted Kalen soon after they settled in the clearing. "Did your ferret follow you from the clearing."

"I . . . um . . . my familiar isn't in Hanassa." Kalen buried her face against Myri, clinging to her tightly. "Will you brush my hair later? Do you remember the hours you spent brushing it when we lived in the clearing? What made you shove all this stuff in front of the door? Is the baby all right?"

"Her name is Amaranth. My baby must be Amaranth." Myri gently disengaged Kalen's fierce hug and settled into the padded chair, the baby feeding greedily.

Kalen froze. "You'd only allow that if Amaranth had died."

"I felt him die. I almost died with him. The pain. Oh, Kalen, the pain was terrible . . ." Tears gathered in her eyes at last. "We have to find Powwell and get out of here, Kalen," Myri whispered so that Yaassima, safely in the other room, couldn't hear. "We have to keep Amaranth away from the Kaalipha and away from Televarn's people. We have to warn Nimbulan. Amaranth didn't have time to tell him that Televarn plans to kill him as well as my brother."

"Maybe we should let him. What did Nimbulan do for you after he'd seduced you, left you pregnant, and then exiled you?"

* * *

Powwell slipped from the shadow of the cave mouth into the slightly lighter blackness of the open street. The Rover guards dozed before their fire within the cave, seemingly unaware that one of their slaves was escaping. Where could he go? There was only one known exit from Hanassa—a gate controlled by the Kaalipha's magic.

He wasn't certain enough of the way Televarn had brought the captives into Hanassa to be sure there was a true exit beneath the palace.

If he had to resort to drawing blood to find enough magic to open the regular gate tonight, Powwell would—after he found Kalen and Myri.

You have to get me out of here! Kalen had called to him telepathically shortly after the Kaalipha's elite guards had removed her from Televarn's slave pens.

I'll get you all out, Powwell had sent back to her.

Myri's too ill. We'll have to leave her behind. But you have to get me out. Soon, Powwell. Soon, please.

That last message had bothered Powwell. He didn't want to leave Myri behind. He'd promised Nimbulan he'd take care of the witchwoman. He'd promised.

Thorny, he alerted the hedgehog before reaching inside his pocket to pet the miniature hedgehog. The timid creature kept his spines relaxed and soft. Calming energy soothed Powwell's fears and firmed his resolve.

Time had run out. He had to get Kalen and Myri out of Hanassa tonight. This morning he'd watched as two of the Kaalipha's personal guards, uniformed and sober, had slapped chains and a gag on Kalen and dragged her into the palace. Usually such rough handling preceded an execution.

He placed each foot soundlessly in front of him. He'd make less noise if he ran barefoot along the baked mud roadway. Impractical at best, even in warmer weather. No one maintained the roads here. Cracks, stones, and refused littered them, traps for the unwary.

At the next cave mouth, Powwell paused, listening with every sense available to him. Thorny wiggled a little, adding his senses to Powwell's. Light snores filtered through the darkness. Two, no, three people slept within. He peered with his Sight beyond Sight into the interior; an easy spell that didn't require much strength. The fire had burned down to a few shapeless coals. He should be safe crossing in front of the opening. If anyone were still awake, they'd have built up the fire on this freezing night. At least there wouldn't be snow. This high desert rarely saw any moisture at all.

He looked up through the tunnellike opening of the city walls to check the stars. The great wheel had turned past midnight. The guards should be dozing. He ran soundlessly toward the first of seven rock outcroppings strewn across the bowl of the crater that housed the city of Hanassa. Mud huts clustered around each of the outcroppings. The jumble of buildings and pathways created a mapless maze.

The setting moon hid behind the crater walls. Faint starlight glimmered just brightly enough on the minerals embedded in the rocks to show him a rough outline of obstacles. He paused, wrapping the deepest shadows around him like a cloak. He checked landmarks, orienting himself to his memorized path. The escape had to succeed tonight. If he was caught, he'd never get another chance.

He counted his heartbeats. One hundred. The sentry should pass in front of him now. He detected no movement, no sound. Where was the man? The next leg of Powwell's journey across the outlaws' city was the most exposed. He had to wait for the sentry to pass before proceeding.

At last he heard a faint trickle of water. Ah! The sentry taking a piss. Couldn't he use the latrine at the beginning of his patrol route?

Powwell wrinkled his nose in disgust. He couldn't get out of this hole in the mountains soon enough. He'd wasted too much time learning Hanassa and its routines. During those weeks of patient observing, he'd become so frightened by the violence and cruelty of the outlaws that he would resort to blood magic to get Kalen and Myrilandel out of here.

Yaassima had killed her consort because he was *liked* by the outlaws of Hanassa and therefore threatened her control over him and the inhabitants. Then she had killed her own daughter because the girl refused to dip her hands into her father's blood.

He shuddered in revulsion. He'd seen Moncriith in the city yesterday. Moncriith also reveled in blood. If he and Yaassima teamed up, no one in the city would live long.

A little blood magic paled in comparison to the river of death Powwell imagined running through Hanassa.

Thorny puffed up inside Powwell's pocket.

Not you, Thorny. I'd never sacrifice you, he soothed his familiar. *Moncriith is hanging around. He'll slaughter anyone or anything to bolster his magic. But I won't. All I have to do is prick my hand a little.* If he had to resort to blood magic, maybe he should use one of Thorny's spines. Involving his familiar might increase the effectiveness of the hideous procedure.

The sentry burped loudly. Stale ale fumes wafted past Powwell's nose. He grimaced and held his breath until the man responsible for the security of this portion of the city staggered past, hiccuping and bleary-eyed. From his ragged clothes Powwell surmised he must be one of the common road bandits. The patrols were bands of outlaws who paid part of their rent to Yaassima with sentry duty. Rarely did they perform their jobs sober.

After another one hundred heartbeats, Powwell resumed his trek across the city to the palace—which was little more than another jumble of mud huts piled on top of each other on the outside. Rumor claimed the palace had been carved out of a vast cave system and reached far and deep into the ancient mountain.

So far the Justice Bell had not tolled within the converted temple to Simurgh, summoning the populace to witness the Kaalipha's judgment. Kalen wouldn't be executed yet.

Powwell had to arrange the escape tonight. Yaassima preferred dawn executions.

At the seventh and last outcropping of volcanic rock, Powwell waited for the next sentry to pass. The guards were more alert here, members of Televarn's clan. Rovers seldom drank enough to dull their senses. This man had to be neutralized quickly. The sentry's next circuit would take him to Televarn's slave pens where he would make a head count. Any other night the chore would have fallen to a different enclave of outlaws and Powwell could have slipped past his sleepy guards at any time.

He couldn't wait another night. The Kaalipha had taken Kalen.

Using all of his senses, physical and magical, Powwell listened to the sounds of the dirt and rocks shifting and whispering to themselves in the nighttime chill. When he heard a pebble roll and strike another, he knew the sentry approached. Three breaths later a shadow within a shadow shifted.

Powwell rolled his balance to the balls of his feet. The sentry probably weighed twice Powwell's slim adolescent body and stood a full head taller. Powwell needed the advantage of surprise and speed. His magic was too limited in this desert. No ley lines crossed through the ancient volcano, and the dragons shied away from the area. He had no source of power other than his own growing body. Rovers had their rituals, which Powwell didn't know or understand. The Bloodmages drew strength from pain. Powwell would save that for a last resort.

He closed his fingers around a jagged rock he'd tucked into his pocket this morning. With every fragment of strength he possessed, he threw the rock at the passing sentry.

A grunt followed by a thud against the baked mud street told him his aim had been true. Only one more obstacle to overcome, the very alert team of guards at the palace portal.

Powwell paused long enough to thump the Rover more soundly on the head, making certain he wouldn't wake up soon. From the squishy sound of the rock hitting flesh, the guard might never wake again. Televarn would seek revenge. But Televarn was already Powwell's enemy.

Then he grabbed the man's sword and spear. He hefted the weight of each weapon. The sword seemed awkward and heavy in his grasp. It would hinder his stealthy movements and weigh him down if he needed to run. The spear, though, was made of wood, long and slender; just the weight and length of a fighting staff. He ran both of his hands the full length of the shaft, hoping he could imprint it with some of his magic personality through such brief contact. This was a tool he knew how to use.

He pointed the staff at the entrance to the lower levels of the palace, pushing his Sight beyond Sight along the smooth grain of the wood. The fibers within the core of the shaft vibrated in tune with his magic. Details jumped to the fore of his vision. He saw the precise outline of

the cave mouth, lopsided, jagged, obscured outcroppings
that could knock an unwary man senseless. Inside, one
man fed the small fire contained within a circle of stones.
The other paced from the fire to the entrance and back
again, brushing past a gaudy tapestry on the right-hand
wall.

Powwell's instincts told him the tapestry was a blind.
The passageway behind it led to a dead end, possibly
through several lethal traps. A separate cave mouth with
a heavily guarded gate off to the left was the only access
to the inner caves and the palace above. This smaller
cave housed only the Kaalipha's brothel.

While the pacing guard checked the narrow opening
to the brothel, Powwell crept closer. He gripped his
newly acquired staff tightly, channeling his magic
through the wood. A barely visible cloud of gray mist
surrounded him. With luck, he'd be invisible to the
guards. He couldn't tell for sure. He'd never tried this
spell before without Kalen at his side, guiding him
through it.

Holding his breath, he stepped into the cave mouth.
Neither guard stirred. Powwell circled the perimeter,
careful to stay between the guard and the light of the
fire. No sense in betraying his presence with a moving
shadow.

He slid into a short corridor. The sound of soft snores
and restless bodies shifting beneath bedcovers greeted
him. Now all he had to do was find Myri and Kalen
among the dozen women Kaalipha Yaassima kept for
the guards' pleasure, and an equal number of children
belonging to those women. Myri should be among them.
He hadn't seen her since the Kaalipha had removed her
from Televarn's custody three weeks ago. She must have
had the baby the first night here. Would the Kaalipha
send her to be made available to the guards so soon?
She had to be in this dormitory. Except for Yaassima's
private maid, women weren't allowed to sleep in the
palace proper. The Kaalipha surrounded herself only
with men she could manipulate and control.

With his back against the rock wall of the inner corridor, Powwell sidled into the women's chambers. He
dropped the spell of invisibility before it drained too
much of his energy and waited for his eyes to adjust to

the minimal light cast by the still active fire in the central hearth of the cave.

Whoever had built up the fire might still be awake.

Powwell froze, willing himself to blend into the rock wall. He scanned the dark forms upon the scattered pallets for signs of movement or a glimmer of Myri's white-blonde hair reflecting the firelight. One of the figures, larger than the rest, grunted and shifted. The blanket rose up.

A lump choked Powwell's throat. He heard his heart pounding in his ears so loudly the women must surely awaken at the echoes.

"Got to get back to work, love." The rising figure resolved into a naked man. He pinched his partner's bare backside and replaced the blanket. Then, as he reached for his discarded clothes on the floor, his gaze locked with Powwell's. They both froze in place.

CHAPTER 9

"Fifty ships to sabotage and barely one hundred obstacles embedded into the mudflats," Nimbulan pounded the ramparts of the old keep with his fist. "Not enough. Not nearly enough."

Exhausted and filthy with soot and sweat, he watched the small fishing fleet, King Quinnault's poor excuse for a navy, launch into the swollen tide.

Not once during this very long day of frenetic activity had he forgotten that Amaranth had died trying to summon help for Myri. She must be in terrible danger for the familiar to leave her.

He needed to be with his wife, protect her, comfort her in her grief.

Myri would feel Amaranth's death, possibly try to share it. That agony would only compound whatever she suffered in Hanassa. He had to go to her. Then what?

"At least I know she's alive," he reminded himself. The slender cord of silver magic connecting his heart to hers pulsed with life. Amaranth had restored it somehow.

Myrilandel lived, in Hanassa, the hidden city where nightmares were born.

Nimbulan rested his head on his arm. Fatigue weighed heavily on his eyelids. He didn't dare give in to it. In a few moments full dark would be upon them, and he'd have work to do.

Behind him, the glowing sun sank below the rim of the western mountain rage. With the loss of heat and light from the sun, an easterly breeze sprang to life.

Out in the bay, fifty ships hoisted sail, catching the increasing wind that now favored their invasion of Coronnan City and the rich river delta.

Nimbulan focused on the small boat leading the defense of Coronnan. King Quinnault's pale blond head shone in the dying sunlight as he stood in the prow of the boat he shared with Journeyman Magician Rollett and a fisherman, a beacon to rally his people.

Lord Konnaught wasn't in the second boat, as Quinnault had ordered. Where did the brat get to? He was probably tucked snugly into bed with a hot posset on this cold and clear night.

You shouldn't be out there, Your Grace. Konnaught is right this once. The kingdom can't spare you. Nimbulan hoped his telepathic call reached the king. Quinnault had so little natural magic, the chances of him hearing, much less heeding the message, were slim. The dragons were the only ones who could engage his telepathy—and they had left Coronnan.

The Covenant is broken.

Nimbulan hoped he had enough tricks up his sleeves to convince the mundane lords he hadn't yet resorted to illegal solitary magic in order to hold the kingdom together. He hoped he had enough strength, magical and physical, to get through the night.

The fisherman who guided Quinnault's boat rowed eagerly for the rapidly approaching fleet. A large wave lifted them nearly level with a larger ship's deck. The tide neared flood stage; another hour would mark the highest water.

Aboard the looming vessels in the invasion fleet, sailors leaned over the rails, pointing and laughing at the myriad small boats sent to deter them.

Armor, men. Don't forget the armor! Nimbulan ordered the magicians among the fishermen. The threads from his cloak and splinters from his staff kept the lines of communication open since they didn't have any of the communal dragon magic left.

Two heartbeats later, the invading sailors pelted the small boats with ballast rocks, spears, and debris. Much of it bounced off bubbles of magical armor and fell harmlessly into the waves. Two boats wobbled precariously as the flying objects forced men to lose control of their oars.

Nimbulan sent hasty reminders to magicians in nearby boats to protect the faltering ones. They couldn't afford to lose a single man or boat.

The glowing reservoir of witchfire in the cauldron beside him picked out the sparkling magical shields now in place over each of the boats.

One of the foreign vessels listed badly to port as it scraped the first of the submerged trees. Immediately Quinnault, in the lead boat, let loose a flaming arrow into that ship's sails. Dozens more archers followed his lead.

The ship veered off course. The rushing ride embedded the keel in the sucking mud. The ship's captain frantically swung the wheel, trying to regain his course. The rudder jammed and refused to budge.

"One down, forty-nine to go." Nimbulan dropped his arm, and Lyman released the catapult that dominated the keeps' courtyard. A great ball of green witchfire flew through the air, almost faster than the eye could follow. As it sped over the bay, the millions of flamelets that made up the mass separated but did not lose intensity. Sails burst into flame when the witchfire found additional fuel in the canvas sails.

Three ships lost control of their sails in an instant. They, too, ran aground as all hands rushed to douse flames that could not be extinguished by mundane means.

Behind the vessels, half the tiny fishing boats moved close to the sterns of the ships still under control and heading for the islands. Nimbulan watched Quinnault fling a net outward, toward a ship's rudder. The net spread and landed in perfect position to tangle in the steering rod.

The king's long hours of fishing paid off. He hauled the net tight. The ship swung sideways to the waves. The helmsman spun the wheel uselessly, further tangling the net.

Other fisherman weren't so lucky. They needed the extra guidance of the magicians before their nets ensnared more rudders.

Nimbulan signaled for another catapult. Lord Konnaught appeared beside the war engine, seemingly rested, clean, and well fed when every everyone else showed the effects of a long day of hard work. Nimbulan repeated the signal. The boy pointedly turned his back on the magician. He spoke quietly to a grimy man wearing a blacksmith's apron. The catapult remained firmly in place.

Angrily, Nimbulan sent a line of communication to Lyman who monitored the cauldron of witchfire. The old magician limped over to the catapult. He grabbed Konnaught's shoulder with his extra long fingers and forcibly turned the boy around.

"I do not take orders from underlings," Konnaught protested.

Lyman tightened his grip and propelled the rebellious young man to the catapult. Konnaught jerked his hand forward—as if acting only under compulsion—and snapped the trigger. Then he looked up at Nimbulan. Hate filled his expression.

Nimbulan couldn't spare him a thought.

Fire filled the sky. The nearest sail exploded in heat and unnatural light, dropping living flames upon the deck. Sailors and heavily armed mercenaries scrambled away from the blaze. Some jumped ship. A few remained behind, beating uselessly at the fire with heavy tarps and water.

"Witchfire is created by magic. Only magic can douse it," Nimbulan recited to himself. Silently he mourned the men who screamed out their dying agony aboard the ship. Some of the men fled to the sea. They flailed about in the heaving waves. Heavy robes and armor dragged them down. The deepening tide that allowed ships to sail through the mudflats now made the water deep enough to drown the men. The storm that pushed the tide intensified the swells.

The witchfire continued to burn underwater. The few men who managed to shed shields and swords and all-concealing robes couldn't shed the flames that burned clear to the bone.

Nimbulan bit his lip, suppressing his own agony as many men died. Each death diminished him as a man because he was the instrument of their destruction. He'd organized similar scenes too often. There had to be a better way.

Once again he had proved himself the best Battlemage in all of Coronnan. Hundreds of men died at his command.

Enemies, he told himself.

(Men,) a voice in the back of his head reminded him.

"Never again," he vowed. "I will not do this again. Somehow we must find peace from invasion as we found an end to the Great Wars of Disruption. I have to make Battlemages obsolete."

(You need Myrilandel to complete yourself and your work.)

*   *   *

Myri trudged into the Hall of Justice on the ground floor of Yaassima's palace. She stifled a yawn behind her hand. True sleepiness, not a stupor induced by drugs this time. She tucked away the tiny vial of powder she'd stolen from Haanna, Yaassima's maid, before the woman could sprinkle it over Myri's supper. She had substituted plain salt for the drugs. Her meal had tasted vile with too much salt, and she'd been thirsty all night. But her mind was clear of the drugs.

Myri's arms felt strangely empty without Baby Amaranth. She'd placed the sleeping infant into a back cradle while she and Kalen answered the peremptory summons of the Justice Bell. She would never leave Amaranth alone with Maia, who now slept on a pallet at the foot of Myri's bed.

The Rover woman had not roused in answer to the loud bell. She and Myri hadn't exchanged a single word since her arrival.

A sense of dread pushed away the last of Myri's predawn sleepiness. A crowd of men in various states of undress huddled near the doorway, awaiting Kaalipha Yaassima. Their unease became Myri's as she absorbed their fears.

She recognized some of the elite guard who owed loyalty only to Yaassima. The Kaalipha tended to overlook infractions of her arbitrary rules among these guards. The same action from someone else brought swift execution.

Myri's attention centered on a slouched figure in the center of the group. A man on either side seemed to be holding him up by the arms. His head bent nearly to his waist, hiding his face. Myri knew the pain in his belly where he'd been punched with a fist or the butt end of a spear.

Behind her, Kalen gasped and clung for balance to a tapestry wall covering. "Powwell." She mouthed the name.

Myri snapped her attention back to the prisoner. Other than the auburn-tinged hair, she had no clues to the man's identity. Too much of her talent was bound up in her baby to extend beyond basic emotions broadcast by others. She trusted Kalen's instincts.

She had all her children in view. Now all she had to do was lead them out of Hanassa. Getting Powwell safely away from Yaassima would be the hard part.

'What crime did this boy commit?" Yaassima appeared on the dais without warning. She hadn't been there a heartbeat ago. Where did she come from?

The Kaalipha clapped her hands. The torches dimmed. Panels in the ceiling came to life, replacing the flickering green flames with a brighter, more golden glow.

"How'd she do that?" Kalen asked, eyes wide.

"I don't know, and she won't tell," Myri replied, keeping her eyes on Powwell. Other than the ache in his belly he seemed healthy and fit.

Where were the exits? She marked each visible portal into the Justice Hall.

"Tell the man's crime so that I can dispense swift justice." Yaassima's voice swelled to fill the room over and above the babble of fearful men.

"Kaalipha." A man stepped forward and knelt, touching his forehead to the floor.

Myri recognized him as Nastfa, the guard who had carried her to Yaassima's suite that first day in Hanassa. He wore black trews less ragged than some inhabitants of Hanassa, and an almost clean linen shirt. If he dared speak, he must have some authority over the men assembled behind them. Myri already knew that Yaassima trusted him more than most of the elite corps that always surrounded her. Some of them were fully clothed, as if they had just come from guard duty. The others wore bits and pieces of hastily donned uniforms.

"Speak, Nastfa." Yaassima granted him permission to continue.

"The prisoner was found in the brothel. He is one of

Televarn's slaves and has no right to the women there,"
Nastfa said, maintaining his subservient position, with
his backside in the air.

"Who found him?" Yaassima stepped down from the
dais and circled Nastfa. She caressed his upthrust bottom, not with affection, more like appraisal, as if he were
a haunch of pork.

"I arrested the prisoner, Kaalipha." A second man
assumed the position beside Nastfa. He wore only trews
of fine black wool that he'd buttoned so hastily they
fastened askew with gaps.

"Was the prisoner attempting to partner with one of
my women?" Yaassima widened her circle to include the
second man.

"No, I was not." Powwell raised his head as he spoke
and shook off the hands that held him up. He could lose
that head for speaking to the Kaalipha from an upright
position. Just like Yaassima's consort and daughter had.

Myri broadcast caution to him. She didn't have her
husband's easy command of telepathy, only her emotions
to project to another.

"I was searching for my adopted mother, Myrilandel."
He spotted Myri and Kalen beside the dais at that moment. Brief joy lit his face, then he masked all his
emotions.

Kalen took a step toward him. Myri held her back,
uncertain of Yaassima's cruel whims. Safety and escape
lay in avoiding Yaassima's notice.

How could she distract the Kaalipha from Powwell
without drawing unwanted attention to herself and
Kalen?

"Do I understand this report, that you were found *in*
the brothel, rather than attempting to enter?" Yaassima
turned her gaze on Powwell. Her long fingers moved
from the guard's rear end to Powwell's chest. She traced
a glowing design over his heart, her talonlike fingernails
snagging on the rough cloth of his tunic. Myri couldn't
read the design, but she suspected it was a sigil of
control.

Yaassima snapped her fingers. The sigil disappeared
as a knife appeared in her hand. She repeated the symbol with the tip of the knife, slicing Powwell's tunic and
shirt but not his skin.

"Yes, Kaalipha, I was inside the brothel," Powwell answered when the other men looked at the floor and shuffled their feet.

"How did you get past the guards?" Yaassima's eyes narrowed as she scanned the motley array of half-dressed men. Her gaze halted on the second kneeling man.

"I used a spell of invisibility."

The Kaalipha's gaze whipped back to Powwell.

Myri cringed. If she ran and pushed the Kaalipha aside, she might be able to drag Powwell and Kalen through the primary entrance. Where would they go once they were free of the palace?

She didn't have enough information!

"A magician. How lovely. Were you trained by Nimbulan? Or perhaps Myrilandel's Rover lover was your teacher?" The knife disappeared. Yaassima's extraordinarily long fingers flexed and opened repeatedly.

"I received some training from Myrilandel's *husband,* Kaalipha."

"Can you work dragon magic?" Yaassima's voice became too sweet. Myri waited in dread for the vicious blow to follow.

"When there are dragons present," Powwell said.

"Can you work dragon magic now, child?"

"I sense no dragon magic. Nor are there any ley lines near. I have only limited reserves of magic available. I'd rather not waste them on parlor tricks."

"No dragon magic!" Yaassima screeched. "No dragon magic! There has to be dragon magic. I am *The Dragon,* that's what Kaalipha means in the old tongue—dragon. I am descended from dragons. You will take your magic from me. Show me, boy. Show me this dragon magic, or I'll know you for a liar and execute you at dawn for the crime." The torches flared high, adding their green light to the yellow ceiling panels.

"You may have the blood of dragons in you, Kaalipha. But you are not in dragon form. I cannot gather your magic. Nor can I gather Myrilandel's while she resides in a human body."

Yaassima glared at the boy. Color rose in her pale cheeks. Torchlight reflected green sparks off her white-blonde hair. She stood almost a head taller than he.

Powwell had grown these last six moons to be equal in height to some of the men present. Yaassima seemed to swell taller yet. Her arms stretched away from her sides for balance as if she expected them to become wings.

Surprised, Myri stepped forward to watch the Kaalipha more closely. She thought the gesture to be unique to herself. Would Yaassima transform?

Could she transform?

All the men except Powwell backed away from Yaassima, recognizing her posture as a threat.

"I have not the time to test your magic right now. Tell me, though, if you were invisible, how did my men find you? Careful of your answer, boy, your fate resides in my good wishes." The torchlight faded along with Yaassima's temper.

Cold sweat broke out on Myri's back. This was the moment when Yaassima was the most dangerous; when cold calculation replaced hot temper. Life or death. The Kaalipha of Hanassa controlled them both.

"I dropped the spell as soon as I passed beyond the guards. I did not want to use so much of my energy until I had to."

"The guards were in the anteroom and you were in the brothel?" Yaassima turned back to the two men who continued to kneel with their foreheads on the floor.

"One of them was with a woman, Kaalipha. He caught me." Powwell pointed to the second man. The one who had barely had time to pull on his trews.

"You have done me a favor, boy. I must deal with this man's disregard of my rules. I grant you life, Powwell. Today. Guards, take this fledgling magician to the pit. A few moons sweltering in the heart of the volcano will either cure him of his desire to escape or kill him."

CHAPTER 10

Yaassima fluttered her hand in a dismissive gesture. Two fully-dressed guards hastened to haul Powwell away. The other men regrouped in a tighter knot, unwilling to be singled out by the Kaalipha.

Yaassima did not shift her gaze from the kneeling men.

Myri swallowed deeply. No execution for Powwell. While he lived, she had a chance to help him escape, along with herself and her daughters. The longer she delayed, the more dangerous Hanassa became.

"Who was on duty?" Yaassima caressed Nastfa on his buttocks. She reached between his legs and fondled his genitals through the rough wool of his trews. Her palm remained cupped, ready to squeeze with the extra strength of her long fingers. Nastfa gulped. His dark skin paled.

"Bjorg and Evaar, Kaalipha." His voice rose in an unnatural squeak.

Myri smelled his fear and anticipation of pain. She clutched Kalen's arm for support. Yaassima had been known to prolong her tortures when she sensed Myri's loathing, as if she needed to punish Myri, too.

Beside her, Kalen licked her lips. Myri couldn't tell if she moistened them in reaction to her own fear or anticipation. Her swirling emotions bewildered Myri.

"Kalen," she whispered, clutching the girl's arm tighter. "What are you feeling?"

"They betrayed Powwell. They deserve whatever *she* gives them. I want them to suffer for betraying Powwell." This time, Kalen's eagerness to watch the men writhe in pain broke through her armored emotions.

Myri recoiled in disgust.

"There should have been a third man on duty. Who

was he?" Yaassima's grip on the man's balls tightened a little.

"Golin shared the duty, Kaalipha." Nastfa's voice rose again in fear, anticipating Yaassima's grip. His greasy black hair trembled from his reaction. He had nearly Rover-dark hair and skin. But his face bore tinges of yellow and his eyes slanted slightly. He must have been one of the elite assassins of Maffisto before Yaassima brought him into her guard. What power did Yaassima hold over him to make such a ruthless man subservient and quaking in fear?

"Golin, the man who discovered the magician in the brothel, was also on duty?" Yaassima removed her hand. Nastfa nearly collapsed in relief. His companion began to shake, though. "Golin, who was supposed to be patrolling the entrance, shifting the torches every few minutes to cast new and different shadows so an invisible magician would be betrayed by his shadow falling in the wrong place. Golin, who was, instead, naked in the bed of one of my women!" Yaassima slipped her fingers beneath the man's belt. Her long fingernails tore the fine black cloth of his trews. She yanked the fabric with all of her strength. The cloth tore in three straight lines so that the fabric fluttered to the floor in rags.

Golin's shaking increased as the cold night air shriveled his genitals.

"You are not free of guilt yet, Nastfa. You lead this sorry band of murderers. Yours is the responsibility to keep them in line."

Nastfa nodded and maintained his pose. He gulped in air and stared briefly at Myri before dropping his forehead to the stone paving once more.

That one long look spoke of many secrets that had to remain hidden. What did the man try to tell her?

"Tell me, Golin," Yaassima cooed with unnatural sweetness. "In return for refuge in *my* city, you have the duty to protect *my* women certain nights of the moon. On any other night you are free to take one of those women back to your quarters. Yet you forsook your duty to me to lie with one of those women tonight. Do you do this often?" Yaassima placed both hands between his legs.

"You provide for us quite generously, Kaalipha. I had

to make sure the women slept soundly. Kestra couldn't sleep, she claimed she was too cold. She asked me to warm her." Golin stammered.

"Kestra. One of Televarn's women. She dissatisfied him, so he gave her to me as part of his tithe. I should have known a Rover woman couldn't resist a man. Any man, at any time." Yaassima looked up at Myri as she continued to stroke and fondle Golin. He grew with her now gentle ministrations. His magnificent proportions would entice most women.

Myri tried to look away. Something in Yaassima's eyes compelled her to continue observing Golin's humiliation.

"Kestra, isn't she the one who bore a half-caste child two moons ago. I believe the father was a magician from Coronnan, the one who betrayed Televarn. The one who also fathered Maia's baby. He did spread his seed far and wide. What was his name?" Yaassima continued to look at Myri. A malicious grin spread over her face.

Myri swallowed heavily. She knew her husband. Nimbulan, had lived with Televarn's clan for a season before their marriage. He'd been invited to mate with Maia. Televarn had arranged the union and manipulated their emotions with magic. No other woman of the clan was offered to Nimbulan.

" 'Twas Televarn who betrayed my husband, Kaalipha," Myri said through clenched teeth. "Televarn's tales change with the wind. He cannot tell the truth."

Yaassima smiled again. "Nimbulan's infidelity is not the issue here. I could have you castrated, Golin, for neglecting your duty."

Every man in the room blanched. Myri grew hot, then very cold in her mid-region. She knew Yaassima was manipulating her through her empathic talent.

"There is no call for that, Yaassima." She firmed her chin and stared at the woman. She had to stop this. Her own safety paled in significance to the violence that permeated Hanassa. Kalen had already been tainted by it. She had to stop this here and now.

"You wish to deprive me of justice?" Yaassima raised one eyebrow in speculation. Her hands tightened on Golin as a reminder that her attention wasn't totally on Myri's distraction. He shrank again.

Every eye in the room rested on the Kaalipha. Would

she dare perform the torturous procedure with her bare
hands, using her fingernails in place of a knife?

"Golin will be useless to you if he lives. You will
destroy his courage and clear thinking. What good is a
guard afraid to confront men who challenge him?"

"Perhaps, perhaps not. I need loyal men. Men who
know I hold their lives and their deaths in my hands.
Men who know that to fail me will bring worse punishment than my enemies could inflict upon them."

She squeezed Golin harder, then abruptly released her
grip. He groaned and collapsed, clutching his still intact
groin. Yaassima laughed and wiped her hands on the
rags of Golin's trews. "It would be a pity to lose a man
who is hung like a sledge steed in rut. I have a better
idea. Stand up, both of you." She kicked at the two
kneeling men.

Nastfa scrambled to his knees. Golin managed to get
his legs under him but remained slumped over and
groaning.

"For your punishment," Yaassima continued, "both of
you shall stand guard over the women every night for
the next moon. All night. And you shall watch as they
service the guards I send to them, every night. You shall
help undress the women. You shall help them bathe.
But you may not lie with them. If you succumb to the
temptation, and they will tempt you mightily, I will cas-
trate and then execute you both. Do you understand?"

"Yes, Kaalipha," Nastfa and Golin whispered with
relief.

"Louder. I want all of your crew to hear you and
understand that they are to make sure you know what
you are missing." The torches flared again, a sure sign of
her rising temper and a possibly worse fate for the men.

"Yes, Kaalipha," they nearly shouted.

"Good. Then we will begin now. Someone fetch the
women. We will watch the sport together."

Golin bent to retrieve the tattered remnants of his
clothes and his dignity.

"No, Golin. No clothes for you. I need to know that
you suffer torment and understand why you must endure." She rubbed him with her dangerous hand. He
didn't fill it.

Yaassima laughed.

"He's so scared he'll be lucky to get it up again," Kalen muttered.

"Precisely," Yaassima replied. "Come, Myri. You might enjoy this. You haven't been with a man for many moons. Choose a partner, or several, whatever you desire. If you like, I can provide the means for you to play at being raped." Her tone told everyone in the room this was an order rather than a suggestion.

Yaassima clapped her hands. The floor groaned and shuddered. Slowly, the huge altar stone rose from its subterranean hiding place. Stone scraped on stone until the long slab of granite stood a little higher than Yaassima's waist. A metal stake poked up from each of the four corners. Manacles for wrists and ankles dangled from each spike.

Yaassima's victim would rest in the place of sacrifice formerly reserved for offerings to Simurgh. Did Yaassima subject her own daughter to this humiliating torture before murdering her?

*   *   *

"The tide is nearly out," King Quinnault shouted with glee as he bounded up the steps to Nimbulan's post on the battlements. Quinnault cradled his right arm in his left, rubbing the bicep and shoulder.

Nimbulan raised his head from his crossed arms upon the wall. He blinked grit from his eyes. His deep concentration on the individual ships within the battle had also kept him from noticing the world beyond the tangling fishnets, broken hulls, his aching body, and the death of too many men. He had supervised the entire battle and left the throwing of magic to others. Still the exhaustion of maintaining communications dragged him close to unconsciousness.

A gentle tug on his back, a lower pitch to the humming in his ears, a sense of weight in his knees, all told him of the shift in the forces of moon and water.

He sensed no trace of the special stillness in the air that heralded dawn. He longed for the red-gold sunshine to bake the ache from his joints. His eyes were tired of straining through the green light of torches and witchfire.

"You saved Coronnan this night, Magician Nimbulan." Quinnault bowed deeply in respect, still holding his arm close to his body.

"Thanks should go to you and your comrades, Your Grace," Nimbulan replied as he surveyed the wreckage of the Rossemeyerian armada. "Are you hurt?" He reached a hand to touch the injury. Quinnault shied away from him.

"I twisted or pulled something out of place." He shrugged and winced painfully.

"More than a muscle strain, Your Grace." Nimbulan probed the tender spot with insistent fingers.

"Some flying debris broke through the magical armor and bruised it. Then I had to grab the oars in a hurry when Leauman, my boatman, ducked too hastily. The strain pulled something," Quinnault said through gritted teeth.

"I don't think you dislocated anything. Maybe a bruise to the bone. We'll get a healer to look at it. I wish you hadn't endangered yourself out on the bay tonight. If you had been killed, Coronnan would be in dire straits, victory or no. You have no heir to succeed you."

Quinnault dismissed Nimbulan's concern with a wave at the destruction out in the bay. "My people needed to see me leading the charge. They fought harder alongside me than they would have if I'd been safely protected by stone walls—remind me later to reinforce that lesson with Konnaught. I'm tried of his scowls of disapproval."

"Lord Konnaught should have been exiled upon his father's death," Nimbulan grumbled.

"He deserves the chance to grow into his rightful inheritance. I'd rather teach him to nurture the land and the people than punish him for his father's tyranny," Quinnault replied.

The king stared out at the wreckage strewn across the moonlit bay before continuing. "We won't be bothered by Rossemeyer again for a while. Ambassador General Jhorge-Rosse must now respect me as a warrior as well as a peacemaker. We'll present a new treaty to him after we've slept." He yawned hugely, then seemed to shake off his fatigue.

"We should let him cool his heels for a day or two," Nimbulan said. A day or two while he and his exhausted magicians slept and ate and slept some more. "We don't have to make the trade treaty now; we've proved we can defend ourselves. The ambassador must learn that the treaty is an offer of friendship more than trade advantages. We also have many prisoners of war to ransom back to Rossemeyer. We bargain from strength this time."

Fifty ships had sailed into the mudflats of the Great Bay. Perhaps twelve managed to hoist enough sail to catch the wind that shifted to an offshore direction. Thirty-some ships rested at bizarre angles with their hulls run aground on mud and lethal debris. Five had burned to the waterline, their sailors captured as they jumped for the relative safety of the water. Some of the refugees managed to swim toward departing ships and save themselves. Many more died in the pounding waves and the witchfire that continued burning on the surface of the bay. Hundreds of men had surrendered to the crews of the fishing boats.

Nimbulan closed his eyes and concentrated on the flames that bounced and separated with each wave of seawater. When he looked again, all traces of witchfire had winked out. The sudden darkness soothed his eyes but not his soul. He'd cleaned up the last spell of the battle. He could rest now.

"Speaking of treaties of friendship, there are several offers of marriage alliance to consider." Quinnault changed subjects in mid-thought—not uncommon for his keen intelligence. "I'll need your help with a letter to King Lorriin of SeLenicca. I really can't marry his sister. She's ten years older than me and a barren widow. But we have to word the rejection to sound like I am not worthy of her beauty rather than that she is inadequate to be my queen."

"And how old are you, Your Grace?" Nimbulan raised one eyebrow skeptically.

"You know, as well as I, that I'll see my twenty-eighth Winter Solstice a moon hence."

"A mere infant." Nimbulan frowned at his king. "That makes the Princess of SeLenicca thirty-eight. She's been widowed for many years. Perhaps she hasn't had the opportunity to bear children."

"I can't take the chance. I need a young and fertile princess. And I won't have just any well-born lady with the proper dowry and political connections—there are three offers for those. She must be intelligent and have a sense of humor. If she's easy on the eyes, so much the better." Quinnault paced, left hand behind his back, shoulders hunched. With his long face and hair in wild disarray, his silhouette resembled that of a young dragon.

How many of his draconic mannerisms were natural? Some of them could be a result of his magical link to the dragons established at his coronation. Nimbulan didn't know how much of the link remained since Shayla had declared the Covenant broken. King Quinnault didn't talk about it.

Every thought of dragons brought Nimbulan back to his missing wife, Myrilandel. *Shayla, please take care of her for me,* he pleaded with the sole female dragon in the nimbus and Myrilandel's mother. *I miss her more than I thought possible.*

Nimbulan's age and loneliness weighed heavily on his shoulders. He had to convince his king to allow him to leave the capital immediately so he could begin his search for Myri. He'd forsake the much needed rest if he had to. But not his meal. He'd get nowhere fast without food. And soon.

"We'd best get busy. I'm certain General Ambassador Jhorge-Rosse will be demanding an audience at first light." Quinnault turned sharply on his heel at the end of his serpentine route.

"You seem to have a disgusting amount of energy left after a full day of work and a full night of battle, and an injury, Your Grace." Nimbulan surveyed his king. He smelled of salt spray and sweat, of tar and fish. The grin on his face rivaled the setting moon in brilliance.

"I have won a battle on my terms, with weapons I know—the cunning of men and small boats. I respect myself much more tonight than I did when I ran my sword into Kammeryl d'Astrismos' gut." King Quinnault frowned slightly at the mention of that grisly battle. "Time to eat and rest, my friend. Then it's back to work for both of us." He slapped Nimbulan on the back in comradely affection.

Friend, indeed, Nimbulan thought warmly. Surely Quinnault would recognize Nimbulan's need to go in search of Myri and grant him permission to leave. The quest should be his own. No other man had the right—or the desperate need—to find Myrilandel no matter his age or responsibilities in the capital.

Jaanus, the journeyman who had been dispatched on the search for Myri didn't know how to look for the elusive witchwoman. Only Nimbulan could find her. He was sure of that now.

"You must see a healer before you begin reorganizing the world, Quinnault. Coronnan can't afford for you to be laid low by some hidden injury that flares up later."

"I'm glad I made you my chief adviser, Nimbulan. I can't envision governing without you at my side. Why don't you move your quarters into the palace where you are close at hand?"

And under the king's constant eye.

Nimbulan sighed, wondering if he'd have to risk losing the king's friendship and trust by running away. The Commune's influence in the new government had been based upon Nimbulan's relationship with Quinnault.

Surely the new king wouldn't remove the Commune from advisory positions because he was angry with Nimbulan. Quinnault was fairer minded than that. Several of the lords on the Council weren't so generous. Konnaught led a faction that preferred the old way of ruling where personal privilege of the lords was more important than the welfare of the country.

Nimbulan shuddered in memory of the chaos that had run rampant through Coronnan when Konnaught's father had proclaimed himself king.

The ties keeping him in Coronnan were almost as strong as the ties that pulled him to search for Myri.

CHAPTER 11

The Kaalipha and her guard stared at Myri from a frozen tableau. The flaring torches and uncanny yellow ceiling panel lights cast conflicting shadows around the room. An aura of evil followed the shadows.

"Promise me, Kalen, that if Yaassima kills me, you will care for Amaranth. You will keep her from the clutches of the Kaalipha. And if—no, *when*—you escape, you will keep her away from Moncriith and Televarn. Guard her with your life." Myri clutched at her daughter's sleeve. Her long fingers wound around the girl's thin arm, clenching with a grip as tight as the one Yaassima had used on Golin.

"Let me take your place, Myri. They won't kill me." Kalen looked up at Myri with her wide gray eyes, all innocent and trusting.

Behind the familiar mask of naïveté lurked cold calculation. Myri wondered when in the last three weeks Kalen had lost what remained of her innocence. What went on in Televarn's slave pens? Had her virginity been stolen, too? She feared so and grieved that her daughter hadn't had the opportunity to learn joy in sex at an Equinox Festival.

Too early Kalen had figured out that every adult in her life used her—and her talent—for their own benefit. She used her mask of childish trust as a blind while she thrust her own will upon those around her. Myri doubted she had ever been innocent and trusting.

Myri addressed her adversary rather than her daughter. "No, Kalen. This is not about sex or punishment. It is about control. Yaassima cannot control my love for Nimbulan, so she seeks to destroy it by making me feel soiled and unworthy. If I allowed you to take my place,

I would feel even more worthless. I refuse to be manipulated by her."

Yaassima maintained her steady gaze at Myri, saying nothing. A malicious smile crooked one corner of her mouth upward. Her eyes showed no trace of amusement. The manacles lay between them in mute challenge to both their wills.

"But in raping me, or watching you, Kalen, become her victim, my sense of self-worth would shatter. That is not in her plans. She no longer has an heir of her body, and so she seeks one who bears dragon blood to rule this city when she is gone. Dragons are long-lived, but they do die. Sometimes they are killed. Amaranth and I are her only possible heirs. I do not think she will live long enough to see my baby grown and ready to assume the title of Kaalipha. She is older than she looks. She has many enemies who lust for her power, including Televarn and Moncriith." Myri didn't drop her gaze from Yaassima.

"Your logic is very good, Myrilandel, but not perfect," Yaassima said. "Have you forgotten that dragons always mate with three or more consorts? The more fathers, the larger and stronger the litter. I should think you ready to welcome the attentions of these men." She gestured to the incorruptible guards who watched the battle of wills between Myri and Yaassima. None of them had left to fetch the women.

"Dragons can only mate once every two years. If conditions are not perfect, they will wait longer, much longer. They choose their consorts from among the males they can tolerate dealing with day after day. And they never mate while still suckling their young. I will not allow you to control me, Yaassima. Seek your sport with another."

"Your foster daughter is willing."

"Kalen is barely eleven summers. She doesn't know what she offers."

Some of the guards shuffled their feet a little. Myri sensed their embarrassment. Elite assassins they might be, but they maintained their own rough code of honor among themselves. Raping young girls violated even their code.

"I think the child knows precisely what she risks."

Yaassima narrowed her slightly uptilted eyes. An extra lid fluttered down, obscuring the pupil from external view while she looked out on the world from a different perspective. Myri didn't have that extra dragon eyelid. Her body hadn't been born dragon—merely borrowed by a dragon. The dragon personality had forced the body to exhibit some draconic characteristics, but not all. Her spinal bumps were barely noticeable compared to Yaassima's.

"Kalen has been Televarn's hostage for over three weeks now," Yaassima said. "He always samples his female slaves before selling them to traders in SeLenicca within a few weeks of capture. But only after he tires of them. He likes training young girls for life in the brothels. The male slaves, he sells to the mines. But he has not sold this girl, nor her foster brother. Why? What sport do they offer him?"

"Televarn captured hostages, not slaves, when he laid a trap for us among my villagers," Myri replied. "He hoped I would come to his bed willingly in return for their freedom. You thwarted his plans by claiming kinship with me."

Myri closed her eyes briefly, trying to banish the images of the nightmarish day when Televarn had burned an entire village, murdering those who stood between him and Myrilandel.

Yaassima threw back her head and laughed long and loud. The sound rose in pitch and shrillness, echoing around the Justice Hall. Myri was reminded of the deafening sounds made by dragons when they communicated among themselves.

"Your defiance speaks well of your ability to lead the ungovernable filth who inhabit this city," Yaassima said when she gained control of her mirth. "You must be strong of will and ruthless of action to remain alive. I will find another, more willing, victim for my men tonight. Kestra, I think, since she was willing to break my rules to have a man inside her." She waved her hand and the ceiling panels dimmed. The flickering shadows of the torchlight replaced the too bright directionless glare.

The band of guards visibly relaxed. One of the black-clad men slipped out, presumably to fetch the woman.

Stiffly, Myri turned to leave. Wariness overshadowed any sense of relief.

"Tell me, Myrilandel," Yaassima called to her. "Do you reject these men because you loathe them specifically or do you prefer the touch of women?"

Myri froze in her tracks. Truth had served her well so far on this dangerous night. Would it be strong enough to continue to defend her?

She looked over her shoulder at the tall woman with white-blonde hair and unnaturally long fingers and toes. Her instincts told her to find safety in a high dark place, become invisible and slip away unnoticed. Alone.

She couldn't. Baby Amaranth, Kalen, and Powwell all depended upon her.

The sense of belonging to her children banished her lingering thoughts of becoming a dragon. She wasn't a solitary creature anymore and she never would be again.

(Nimbulan must be part of the circle.)

A dragon thought? She hadn't heard the guiding voices in her head since the kidnap. Why now? She didn't have time for questions, only relief that the dragons hadn't completely deserted her.

"No dragon would ask that question, Yaassima. Mating is for the purpose of begetting young. The rest of their lives are solitary, without thought of another of their kind. Why waste the effort of a mating flight on a fruitless passion?"

"Yet Moncriith tells an interesting story of how you murdered his father when you caught him in the arms of your guardia, Magretha. Why would you kill the man with witchfire and permanently disfigure Magretha if not out of jealous rage? You were eleven at the time, the same age as Kalen." Yaassima raised one eyebrow. The gesture often replaced a laugh or a smile.

"Moncriith manipulates history to suit his purpose. *He* threw the ball of flame while waiting in line for Magretha's attention. I was but six and saved the woman who raised and protected me."

Myri clutched Kalen's hand and left before the Kaalipha could think of another dangerous question.

"Do you think she takes women to her bed?" Kalen asked as they hurried back to Myri's bedchamber. Her eyes reflected a fascinated revulsion.

"I do not believe Yaassima shares passions with anyone but herself. In that, she truly is descended from dragons. She loves no one and lives her life alone. But unlike dragons, sex has become a weapon for her, or a tool to control and intimidate people."

Myri slammed the door of her chamber closed as soon as she and Kalen were safely within. She leaned on it, needing to reinforce the barrier between herself and Yaassima. Maia stirred on her pallet to look up at the disturbance. Myri gestured the Rover woman back to sleep.

"I must walk carefully in my defiance of Yaassima. She must believe me under her spell until after I'm gone. Our only hope of escape lies in her belief that no one dares defy her." Myri placed her daughter in the cradle. She lingered there, touching the baby's fine hair and delicate skin.

"I wish, Kalen, you had your familiar, Wiggles, with you now." Myri drew a long breath.

"So do I. I miss him." Moisture gathered in Kalen's eyes in true regret. "But you didn't like him. Why do you want him now?"

"I didn't like his sneaky ways. He stole eggs and hid in strange places. His smell was almost enough to drive me out of the cottage. But if you had him with you now, you could use him to make contact with Powwell. We have to get him out of the pit. Soon."

"I think I can link my mind to Powwell's without a familiar." Kalen's eyes wouldn't meet Myri's, a sure sign she was telling the truth. Only when she turned the wide trusting gaze upward at an adult did she lie. Except for a moment ago when she allowed tears to gather.

"Good." Myri was too tired to figure out Kalen's complicated behavior and motives. "Please, Kalen, find out where he is being held. Tell him not to worry or give in to despair. We'll plan our escape after the next sunset when the guards are sated and sleeping heavily. Yaassima may have done us a favor with that horrible orgy in the Justice Hall." She shuddered at the thought of how close she had come to falling into the Kaalipha's trap and becoming another victim of her "justice."

Powwell stumbled over the rough ground leading downward. Pain lanced through his shoulders as a guard on either side of him grabbed his arms and hauled him along in their rapid course to the pit. The uniformed men before and behind didn't check their stride or look at him.

The pit was death, as certain as the executioner's ax. If the narrowing tunnel didn't kill him first. The lowering ceiling seemed to push all the air out of the cave complex. Powwell thought he felt the weight of several miles of Kardia piled on top of this tiny, tiny cave.

He gasped, willing his lungs to breathe in more air. Each inhale became more painful and shallow.

A blast of heat hit him in the face. Unnatural yellow light glowed along the tunnel walls.

He stumbled again, falling to his knees. Fear set his chin quivering and his limbs shaking. Televarn had led them through the pit from the dragongate to the palace that first day in Hanassa. Powwell remembered only heat and noise and overwhelming despair. No one survived the pit for long.

Not the pit! Not the pit, his mind played the words over and over. *The fire is burning up all the air.*

The people of Hanassa told him of the undead who walked the endless labyrinth of caves deep within the Kardia. They never died, couldn't live, and so they haunted the caves and bled the life from the living guards who were unlucky enough to draw a shift guarding the pit. Hellfires burned day and night. The Kaalipha's magic grew there.

He'd suffocate from his own fears before the undead and the magic robbed him of sanity. He was sure of it.

He was dying already from lack of air. Underground places never had enough air for him. Thorny tried to climb out of his pocket. His ruffled quills poked Powwell's chest. Powwell broke the defeating circle of his thoughts long enough to urge his familiar back into hiding. No one knew he'd brought the hedgehog with him from the clearing. No one suspected that the animal's keen sense of smell might lead him back to the dragongate and home. He had to keep Thorny hidden from the guards.

A guard prodded him with a boot to his lower back. Powwell fell to his knees, careful to protect Thorny. Another boot connected with Powwell's ribs. He collapsed onto his other shoulder and side. The pain barely registered in his mind. Better to die here than face the pit. Thorny could escape and seek out Kalen. She would need a familiar since Wiggles had deserted her about a week after they arrived in Hanassa.

The guards grabbed his arms and roughly pulled him to his feet. Somehow he found the strength to stand on his own. They resumed their march forward to doom.

Take heart! a voice whispered into his mind. The brief contact slithered in and out of his head. He heaved a momentary sigh of relief and filled his lungs with air.

"Kalen?" he asked aloud, wondering if, in his despair, he had imagined her voice. But he had air to breathe. Kalen knew of his problems when underground. Her presence helped his lungs relax and use what little air he found.

"Shut up, prisoner," the guard to his right shoved a fist into his damaged ribs. "You can gibber all you want once we deliver you to the pit." Quickly he unlocked the gate with one of the hollow wands.

Kalen? Powwell cast out with his mind in search of the girl's light mental touch.

Stay alive. At all costs stay alive. I will rescue you!

Definitely Kalen's voice. There and gone again before he could latch onto it.

"How, Kalen?" he whispered with mind and voice.

"I said, shut up." The guards lifted Powwell off the ground and heaved him toward the menacing red glow.

Powwell slammed against the uneven ground. His already bruised ribs exploded in agony. The noise of the clanging gate rivaled the awesome sounds rising from the pit. He barely heard the guards running away, their bootheels echoing along the tunnel walls.

CHAPTER 12

Let's go eat. I feel as if my stomach is wrapped around my backbone," Nimbulan said. "Then I *must* sleep. The ambassador from Rossemeyer and the one from Se-Lenicca can wait until you have seen a healer, Quinnault."

Quinnault looked back across the bay at the destroyed armada. A touch of wonder crossed his face. "I can't say I want to do battle like this again. I want Coronnan to be respected for trade and peace and wise councillors, like you. But I can't see how we can avoid more battles as long as other countries lust after our land and the fish in this bay. I've listened to proposals for dredging a couple of channels to let trading ships in. Where traders can sail, navies will follow."

"What we need is a protected ferry service from the deep waters to the city," Nimbulan mused, following Quinnault's gaze to the mudflats glistening in the starlight.

Midnight, his body told him. The tide would be at its lowest within the hour. Perhaps he'd manage a few hours of sleep before Quinnault and his boundless energy dragged him out of bed at dawn.

Maybe he should leave on his quest for Myri before then. Before the king could once again deny him permission to depart. Myri was worth the loss of a little sleep.

But how far would he get before the depletions of his body stopped his quest?

"There are a couple of little islands out there." Quinnault pointed East with his uninjured left arm. "We could set up loading docks there to transfer cargo and passengers. What I wouldn't give for some Varn diamonds now to pay for building a port city out there."

"Good plan. We'll find the money somehow. The

Varns aren't due to come trading for another fifty years or so. Can we eat now?" Nimbulan took two long steps toward the stairs, dragging Quinnault away from his contemplation of the bay. The king winced as he side-stepped to retain his balance.

"Time for you to see a healer. We'll find one faster over on School Isle. That's where the wounded are being taken." Nimbulan offered a supporting hand to guide Quinnault down the steep stairs.

"I'll row you over to School Isle. We collapsed the bridge in case we were invaded. The old causeway isn't stable since that last series of winter storms undercut it." Quinnault shrugged off any hint of assistance.

Once before, Nimbulan had ventured out in a leaking boat with Quinnault. They'd both nearly drowned before they crawled ashore on Haunted Isle. Now the locals called it School Isle.

"I'll guide you across the causeway. The tide and the river are low now. It's not that dangerous," Nimbulan said.

"You're still a total novice around boats, Nimbulan. You'd rather trust the causeway than a rowboat." Quinnault accused with mock severity. They both smiled in recollection of their first misadventure together—the first in a series of events that had led Nimbulan to the dragons and a kind of magic that could be combined and controlled by the Commune.

"I think we owe the dragons a large thank you for tonight's victory," Nimbulan mused. "We have to do everything in our power to bring them back," he hinted as a prelude to leaving.

"Don't even think about deserting the Commune, or me, Nimbulan. You are much too valuable to retire. As soon as you have a direction to send them in, dispatch every journeyman in the school to search for Myrilandel and the dragons. But you have to stay here. Coronnan needs you too much to risk you on such a dangerous quest." Quinnault cocked his head, listening for any glimmer of communication from the elusive dragons. Myri's gesture.

"Coronnan needs the dragons more than me. My wife is the key to the dragons. *I* must be the one to go in search of her."

"No, it's too dangerous. I can't afford to lose you."
Quinnault replied flatly.

"Even if Shayla herself ordered me to search?"

"Only if Shayla orders it. But none of the dragons
have spoken to me since they broke the Covenant."
Quinnault turned and walked down the stairs toward the
rivergate. Then, looking back over his shoulder, he
smiled a brief apology. "I depend upon you for much
more than magic, Nimbulan. I need your wisdom and
your experience to guide me. I am, after all, only a priest
at heart, and now I find myself a king trying to pull
together a fractious rabble that calls itself a government.
Don't desert me, my friend. Please."

Nimbulan shrugged. He had no words to counter such
an argument. Quinnault had reasons not to trust any of
the lords or other magicians.

In short order, Nimbulan stepped off the rotting
causeway onto School Isle. Two guttering torches provided enough light to see six boats tied up to the adjacent dock. Six boat teams, at least, had returned from
the bay.

"Come, join us for a meal, Your Grace," Nimbulan
invited. "I'm sure we'll find a healer in the refectory.
They, too, will be seeking rest and refreshment between
sessions with the wounded," Nimbulan said as he hauled
his weary body toward the boat dock and the path back
to the school. His knees protested the incline of the path,
and his back didn't want to straighten. He groaned,
pressing his hands against his lower back. The stretch
felt good. He rotated his shoulders and grimaced at the
knots in his muscles. "I'm getting too old for this."

Quinnault whistled a merry tune as he joined him,
pointedly ignoring the last comment.

Nimbulan's spine needed a longer stretch. He bent
and grasped his knees, arching his back before the muscles could spasm.

A thin trail of water caught his attention. No wider
than three drops, but a solid flow. Strange, no rain had
fallen for three or four days. Until three weeks ago,
when the dragons left, the Autumn had been unusually
dry and bright. Why would the puddles and marshy
pools overflow now with just this thin trickle when
creeks drained the water through more normal routes?

His orientation to the spin of the planet, the tides and the cycles of sun and moon told him something was terribly wrong with this stream of water.

"It's flowing uphill!" Nimbulan looked back toward the dock. The line of water ran beside the structure, down the embankment into the water. No clues that way.

In the other direction, toward the school buildings, the water trickled beside the footpath, over hummocks and rocks. He placed his left foot gently on the path, leery of any magic that might spill over from the unnatural trickle. The water continued to move slowly uphill without disturbing his magic.

Quinnault followed him, placing his feet in Nimbulan's footprints. "This reminds me of the first time I rowed you to this island." The king hefted an oar like a quarterstaff, ready to knock heads should anyone menace them. He couldn't seem to grip it with his right hand. He put the oar back into the boat with a shrug of regret and drew his short sword with his left hand. "Good thing I'm Varn-handed."

"Have you ever noticed that a dominant left hand usually accompanies magic talent in a person—even the little talent required of a priest?" Nimbulan mused. "I wonder if the mysterious Varns were also aided by the Stargods."

"Varns are probably myths," Quinnault reminded him. "Wishing for Varn diamonds in return for grain surplus is just that, wishing. But then, we used to believe dragons and flywackets were myths, too."

Both men shrugged at the mystery and turned their attention back to the trickle of water.

"This little Water spell is probably the work of one of my more adventuresome apprentices." Nimbulan rotated his shoulders again to ease the muscles in his back. He automatically checked his store of magic for a counterspell.

Nothing. Until he ate and slept, his magic was as inert as the Water trickle he followed. The spell would have to be triggered by some direct action or word.

Controlling the essence of an element—Kardia, Air, Fire, or Water—was usually a spell that required subtlety and deviousness. Elements didn't willingly allow mortals to chain them. Who in the school had the time and knowledge to practice with an elemental?

He paused in his progress toward the nearby building, picking out the figure of Stuuvart, steward for the school, standing on the front steps. Stuuvart's scowl extended from his face into his posture. His cloak swished behind him with his restless movements, mimicking his attitude. The impatient administrator waved his arms as he shouted orders. Apprentices scurried in all directions at his bidding.

Nimbulan scowled, too. Stuuvart loved his meticulous recordkeeping and full storerooms to the exclusion of his wife and family. But he couldn't send the steward packing without dislodging the entire family—Kalen's family—including Guillia, the cook.

An apprentice ran past Nimbulan. He grabbed the boy's arm to stop his pelting progress toward the unstable causeway to Palace Isle. "What's the hurry, Haakon?"

"Master Stuuvart says we can't afford to feed all the wounded and the peasants. He wants additional stores from the palace, sir. He's madder than a penned lumbird 'cause you sent everyone here after your battle." The boy gasped for breath as if he'd already run to the palace and back over the dangerous passage several times.

"Have any of you boys slept since yesterday's battle preparations?" Nimbulan studied Haakon's face for signs of fatigue. Gray tinged the edges of his flushed cheeks, and his eyes seemed overly bright.

"No time, sir." Haakon shifted his weight as if he needed to continue his errand.

"Have you eaten?" Nimbulan held tight to the boy's sleeve.

"After I've fetched the palace steward, sir."

"It's past midnight! Stuuvart can't expect to refill the storeroom now." Nimbulan suppressed his anger at the steward's obsession. When he could control his words, he said, "All of these people worked very hard to defend this land. Feeding them and caring for the wounded is the least we can do. They have earned their meal and a rest, and so have you."

His mouth watered at the smell of savory bacon and fresh bread emanating from the kitchen wing. Stuuvart's wife always provided just the food that Nimbulan craved most, right when he needed it. The two snacks she had sent him during the battle were all that kept him going now. Guillia mothered everyone at the school. Why couldn't her husband give a little care for their daughter, Kalen? If Stuuvart hadn't disowned her, the little girl might not have gone with Myri so readily.

If Kalen had stayed, Powwell would have as well, her devoted friend and possibly her half brother, and Myri would be alone now—wherever she was. Why did it seem as if what was best for the school, best for his wife, and best for himself were always in contradiction?

The emptiness of his life rose up before him like one of the stone walls of his school. Only a day ago, he had seen a vision of Myri in the bowl of water. Yesterday morning, Amaranth had died, imparting a cryptic message that Myri had been kidnapped to Hanassa. Yesterday, Lyman had told him that Rover Maia had a baby—Nimbulan's baby, the only child he was likely to sire.

Nimbulan pounded his left fist into his right palm in frustration. He'd wasted a whole day that he might have been journeying toward his wife, his former lover, and his child.

Not wasted. He'd helped save Coronnan from invasion. Another contradiction of priorities. When would he ever be able to put his own needs above those of others?

"But Master Stuuvart said . . ." Haakon's protest brought Nimbulan out of his loop of self-defeating thoughts.

"I run the school, Haakon. Now get into the refectory and take your classmates with you. Oh, and have someone fetch parchment and pens from my room. His Grace and I have some plans for ferries and loading docks to organize while we eat." He clapped his hand on the king's good shoulder. He needed to appease Quinnault's enthusiasms, or he'd never take the time to see a healer. Nimbulan wanted the king's health in good order before he left on his quest.

He half smiled to himself, realizing he'd already made up his mind to leave on his quest today. Before dawn if possible.

"I'll bring you the supplies myself, Master Nimbulan."

Haakon ran up the narrow stairs that curved toward the residential wing.

"Wait, Haakon, the door is locked," Nimbulan called to the boy. Stuuvart's younger daughter had never arrived with the treatise on naval warfare so many hours ago when he had requested it. Why not?

Stuuvart had probably found other more "important" chores for the child. More important to Stuuvart and no one else.

Nimbulan eyed the pesky trail of water where it crossed the threshold of the school. Tiny, damp pawprints ran beside the water. Where did the tracks go from here? How long had the water been trickling toward its destination, perhaps filling some unknown reservoir?

A glint of moisture on the stairs told him.

"Haakon, come back! Haakon?" he called anxiously. He mounted the steps without thinking.

A sleek form slithered past him, brushing against Nimbulan's leg. Then, the creature—a ferret?—was gone, so quickly it might have been only his imagination.

A scream split the air.

"Haakon!' Nimbulan rushed forward.

Darkness streaked down the stairs in the wake of the animal. The thin trickle of water swelled to the width of the stairs. His foot slid on suddenly wet stone. A loud roar echoed through the stairwell. Torches sputtered. Darkness filled his mind and his eyes.

The water swelled and rose in a wave, washing over him. He forced himself to relax in the surge of water, as Myri had taught him.

Myri! He couldn't die without seeing her again.

He kicked upward, striving for air. Iron bands crushed his chest. *Only water,* he told himself. *Heavy water seeking its home.*

Air. He needed air. Fight one element with another.

I can't swim. I'll drown. Then his head broke the surface and life-giving air filled his lungs. He almost sobbed with relief.

Hard stone jabbed into his back, nearly knocking the blessed air from his laboring lungs. Walls. Steps. Air. He lay half on the first stair, half in the landing, still breathing. Water exited the building and retreated along the path of the original little trickle.

Nimbulan shook wet hair out of his eyes and waved the torches back to life. He surveyed the damage. Water dripped from every surface, traveling with some urgency back to the primary stream. Every last drop left the stairs and landing. Definitely the work of an elemental.

Nimbulan wiped his face with shaking hands. "Quinnault, are you all right?" The king sat against the wall, somewhat dazed and very damp.

A quick survey revealed the corridor to the refectory remained dry. The trapped element sought only to return to its home, not to spread.

"Haakon!" Nimbulan turned over, ready to crawl up the stairs. "Answer me, Haakon!"

Only then did he become aware of something heavy resting against his shoulders, crosswise on the steps just above him.

Haakon lay there, eyes wide open, limbs tangled, skin pale as the underside of a fish.

CHAPTER 13

"So many deaths. When will it stop?" Nimbulan cried as he cradled Haakon's slack body. In his mind he saw Keegan's face replace Haakon's immature features. Nimbulan had been forced to kill Keegan, his former apprentice, almost two years ago. The boy had run away to become a Battlemage before his training was complete. He had known his new patron would challenge Nimbulan's patron in battle. Keegan had come close to defeating his teacher in that battle. But inexperience had made him more bold than wise. In order to keep the boy's spell-gone-amuck from destroying most of Coronnan, Nimbulan had been forced to kill the boy.

Ackerly, Nimbulan's assistant and childhood friend, had died in battle opposing Nimbulan, the following year, this time from his own spell, not Nimbulan's.

Now Haakon had drowned because some unprincipled magician had chained an element. Water had only been rushing to return to its natural state. The apprentice had been caught in the trap and drowned.

Trap?

Haakon had triggered a trap set for Nimbulan. Under normal circumstances, only Nimbulan would have gone into his private, locked workroom. Why hadn't Stuuvart's younger daughter gone in there earlier when Nimbulan requested the treatise on naval battles? Did Stuuvart know about the trap?

Someone had put Water under a compulsion in order to kill the Senior Magician.

Who? Who had the power to compel an element? He needed to think clearly, not let his grief turn him in circles. If only he had his journal to hand so he could sort his thoughts into a logical order. He didn't have time to sit and ponder, writing ideas and crossing off the scattered thoughts. He needed answers now.

Who? Not one of the apprentices. Dragon magic didn't lend itself to compelling an element. Without the ley lines to power the spell, Water would not comply. No junior magician, dependent upon dragon magic, could have carelessly set the spell to see if it could be done.

That left the master magicians or a rogue. He didn't think any of the men he'd hired to teach at the school bore him a grudge worthy of such complex magic. Besides, they'd all been employed in the battle and its preparations yesterday.

A rogue could have slipped into the school during yesterday's chaos. A rogue who had a different source of magic. Perhaps Moncriith, a Bloodmage who found energy in pain and death, had returned to Coronnan and targeted Nimbulan. Moncriith's body had never been found after the last battle. Could he still be lurking around Coronnan, seeking to destroy the demons he saw in anything he disagreed with? He had preached against Myrilandel as the source of all demons for many years.

New chills raked Nimbulan's spine at the thought of Moncriith pursuing Myri.

Televarn and his Rovers had reasons to hold a grudge against Nimbulan as well. Devious traps were more Televarn's style than Moncriith's. The poison spell on Quinnault's wine yesterday—was it only yesterday?—might not have been the only mischief they organized. Rovers tapped the energy of every living thing surrounding them, including the elements. Their intricate rituals usually required several members of the clan.

Televarn had aspirations to be king of his people. He had tried to kill Nimbulan once before and failed because Myri intervened. Lyman had seen Televarn in the questing vision. Nimbulan had seen Myri.

Myri had admitted to an affair with Televarn. She'd run away from him when she discovered his duplicity. Someone had kidnapped Myri and held her captive in Hanassa. Rovers often sought refuge in the city of outlaws, as did Bloodmages.

"Send out search parties, quickly. Rovers hide in the region. Find them and bring them to the king's hall for justice. Take soldiers with you," he called to the men he sensed gathering around him. "Your murder will be the last, Haakon. I swear it. If I have to follow Televarn all the way to Hanassa, I will stop these senseless deaths." He clutched the limp body to his aching chest. Hot tears gathered in his eyes.

*   *   *

Televarn fed sticks into his little fire, idly watching the green flames consume the wood. If only he dared burn some Tambootie branches, he could watch the progress of the sea battle in the flames with his FarSight. But the aromatic smoke of the tree of magic would alert Nimbulan's people to his presence. This opening in the mainland forest west of Coronnan City was too close to the capital. He couldn't afford to be found. Not until Nimbulan had triggered the trap and drowned in a wall of water. Water should have had time to fill the magician's private chamber to the ceiling by now.

Televarn shivered as a moist breeze rose up from the river. He smelled the richness of the lush forest and the chill ran deeper into his body. "*S'murghing* damp," he cursed the river, the mud, the islands, and the battle that kept Nimbulan from returning to his bed. Televarn needed to be back in Hanassa, breathing the clean desert air, letting the intense sun bake the damp from his bones.

S'murghit! He needed to get back there, monitor Yaassima, and gather his forces to resist her rule. He needed to wrest Myrilandel away from her manipulations.

Perhaps Myrilandel could spy on Yaassima for him and learn the Kaalipha's weaknesses. He had control of one of the Kaalipha's secrets. But he needed more.

How much longer could Nimbulan linger on the battlements? The tide had receded hours ago. If the Senior Magician didn't go home soon, someone else might enter his private chambers and drown instead.

Bare luck had put Televarn in the path of the little girl sent to fetch something from the room earlier in the day. She had the only spare key and knew that no magic seal locked the door. He had pocketed the key and sent her off to her other chores, promising to take the book to Nimbulan himself. He hadn't, of course. He'd left Water alone to do its work.

He checked the section of woods where two trees leaned together to form an arch. That was his exit to safety. At certain times, the dragongate shifted time and distance to open portals to different locations. This was only one of many such destinations. All of the portals led back to Hanassa and nowhere else. During the past night of waiting, Televarn had watched the dragongate open and close once, when the full moon created an arch-shaped shadow between the trees. The interval between access times shifted randomly. He had no way of knowing when the opportunity to return to Hanassa would present itself again. Today, tomorrow, within the next moment? He knew that it would only happen when there was enough light to cast the proper shadows.

He didn't dare leave until Wiggles returned to him. He owed the ferret's owner the return of the smelly little beast. He owed more than he wanted to admit.

A hot blast of wind and a faint tingle of power made the hair on his arms stand up straight. The dragongate was getting ready to open again. His own fire had created enough of a shadow between the trees to suggest an arch.

Where was Wiggles?

If he lingered much longer in this opening, barely two hours' walk from the capital, he ran the risk of being discovered. Should he take the chance of returning without the ferret?

Underbrush rattled off to his left, close to the riverbank. He stood up, ready to kick dirt over his fire and flee the open circle. Once amid the Tambootie trees, with their dormant magic embedded in leaves, sap, bark, and fruit, he could hide indefinitely.

Nimbulan's people would want revenge for the death of their leader. Wiggles might lead them directly here— if they had the sense to follow the creature once the trap was sprung. Perhaps Talevarn should flee now and save himself. Simurgh take the ferret.

The rustling grew louder.

The air between two leaning Tambootie trees shim-

mered. The dragongate wouldn't stay open long. Now—
or wait for the next opening?

Wiggles burst through the thick saber ferns that
marked the path to the river. The animal ran with the
strangely efficient undulations of his kind, tail up, middle
down, shoulders up, nose down. Then his entire body
shifted forward by trading ups and downs. He streaked
across the circular opening in the woods almost faster
than Televarn's sight could follow.

Three men carrying clubs followed Wiggles, barely
two steps behind the ferret. One look at their blue tunics
with the dragon badge over their hearts and Televarn
knew they were Nimbulan's magicians, bent on revenge.

"Come," Televarn commanded the ferret. He snapped
his fingers and the creature leaped onto his leg, clinging
to his trews with needle-sharp teeth and claws. Never
mind the pain and the rents in the cloth. He had to get
back to Hanassa. Now.

The shimmering light between the two trees faded.

Televarn closed his eyes and dove for the remnants
of the strange light just as the first club caught his
hamstring.

*   *   *

"You must hurry, Nimbulan. Quinnault's messenger is
on his way to summon you to court. You must be well
away before he comes or you will never be free to leave
the capital." Old Lyman hastily buckled the straps of
the half-filled pack on Nimbulan's bed.

"I feel strange leaving without the king's permission
and without resolving Haakon's death. I should say the
prayers at his funeral." Nimbulan resisted a jaw-cracking
yawn. He'd snatched a few hours of sleep and a meal.
Other than that, he hadn't slept in a day and a night.

He needed to replenish his reserves. Lyman had
brought food, meat and bread, and a huge pitcher of
water.

He gulped down as much as he could, then hesitated
in the doorway of his private chamber, longing to return
to his bed. All traces of the water that had filled the
room mere hours before had fled when the essence of
the element rushed back to its place of origin.

A few of Nimbulan's books had been damaged. But everything had dried so quickly, so completely, the essence of Water might not have filled the room hours before.

"There are plenty of people who can say the prayers for Haakon." Lyman bowed his head in a moment of silence. "I will say a few for Amaranth, too. The purple-tipped dragon died trying to tell you where Myri is held captive. Will you waste his death in the endless talk that surrounds a government striving for peace?"

Nimbulan recited a brief prayer remembered from his childhood.

"I need my journal. I must record the events and the plots that threaten to disrupt Coronnan and the Commune," he said, searching his desk for the little book filled with blank paper. He cast aside six books from earlier years. He couldn't think straight. Where had he put the new one? He found it open on his desk, the ink from his entries two days ago smudged and blurred from Water's presence. "I must stop the murders of my apprentices. They were like sons to me, Lyman."

"You have a son of your body now, Nimbulan. You must find him and save him from Televarn. But you must leave immediately, before the king and your suffocating sense of duty chain you here for all eternity." Lyman handed him the pack.

"I wish I knew how that man escaped in the woods. Even with fully active ley lines, a magician can't transport a living being. Have an apprentice and a journeyman camp there if they must while they examine every grain of dirt for evidence of magic." Nimbulan shouldered the pack and reached for his journal to tuck into his pocket. His staff jumped to his hand.

"The answers lie at the end of his trail, not the beginning." A far-off look came into Lyman's eyes. He cocked his head as if listening to something beyond human understanding. "Go, quickly. The messenger from Quinnault crosses the bridge as we speak. You can't delay even a moment. Myrilandel and the children are in terrible danger."

"Are you in communication with the dragons?" Nimbulan halted with his hand on the door latch. This revelation might take him on a direct course rather than

chasing in circles after an assassin or running blindly to
Hanassa to rescue Myri.

"All I can say is that a dragon awaits you. A young
one who wants to explore more than he wants to obey
Shayla. But you must hurry or he will fly away with the
rest of the nimbus. You can't afford the delay of walking
to Hanassa. If you do, you will lose Myrilandel forever."

"Be sure you give my letter to King Quinnault. He
deserves an explanation."

Lyman pushed the Senior Magician out the door. "I'll
look after things here, in your absence, but keep in
touch."

"I'm going with you." Rollett, the oldest of the journeymen magicians stood in the doorway. He, too, carried
a pack of provisions, and a journal poked out of his
pocket. His eyes looked hollow and black, as if sleep
had eluded him longer than it had Nimbulan.

"No, Rollett. I can't risk losing you as well. This trip
is dangerous enough." Nimbulan grasped the younger
man's shoulder affectionately, but firmly.

"I'll follow if you don't take me with you. You need
someone to watch your back, Nimbulan. There is treachery here as well as on the road. I am coming."

"Hurry, Nimbulan." Lyman took both Nimbulan and
Rollett by the arm and guided them toward a back staircase. "The dragon won't wait long. Take the boy. He's
right about treachery. Lord Konnaught is with King
Quinnault's messenger. He's planning something. Something dire for you and for the king. Now get out of here
before someone else dies."

CHAPTER 14

Powwell opened his eyes and slammed them closed again in the bright glare. A sharp ache pounded in his right temple and spread to his neck and shoulders, down to his lower back.

A bizarre noise pulsed around him in rhythm with the pain in his head. It sounded like a threshing machine, but louder and harsher. Much louder.

Yeek, kush, kush. Yeek, kush, kush.

Over and over the noise pushed aside rational thought and self-awareness. It smothered him, wrapping him tighter and tighter, until he was the heart of the terrible sounds. Nothing existed but the noise.

He'd heard those sounds before.

"You'll get used to it," a husky voice penetrated the noise and Powwell's mind.

He opened his left eye a slit. If he opened his right eye, the noise and the light would stab it out.

A dirty face looked back at him. Hard to tell if it was a young male or female. The voice gave no clue to gender either. A dirty kerchief knotted over the left ear, Rover style, covered the person's hair entirely.

"Pretty soon you won't notice the noise at all. Even the heat will seem tolerable after a few moons. I'm Yaala." A feminine name. She held out a hand in greeting, palm up. A masculine gesture.

"Powwell." He raised his left hand slowly to place on top of Yaala's. His right arm seemed to be pinned beneath his body. Every muscle in his back and shoulders protested. He winced. Sweat poured off his body in the tremendous heat.

Thorny was in his right pocket! He rolled over, groaning with the movement. He probed Thorny's hiding place with his thoughts and fingertips. His tunic pocket was empty. *Thorny!*

Chip, chip, mmmblr, grmmmblr, came the muffled gibbering reply from nearby. Powwell couldn't understand his familiar's emotions, only that the little hedgehog hadn't been hurt.

"Did they beat you?" Yaala seemed to be squatting in front of him, quite comfortable on her heels.

"Not much." He mentally inventoried the sorest points on his body. The dull ache in his gut and jaw where the guards had punched him to subdue him, and the sharper throb in his right temple made themselves known right away. The rest of his misery seemed to be reaction to those pains.

A small biting irritation on his right calf told him that Thorny clung to his flesh with his tiny claws. The hedgehog must be trying to find a safe hiding place in Powwell's trews pocket. Powwell's discomfort eased a little. His familiar was safe for now.

"Here, drink this." Yaala pressed a metal cup to his lips.

Powwell drank greedily, unaware of his thirst until he swallowed. The taste of rancid eggs fouled his mouth and set his eyes and nose to running. He spat out the tainted water. Some of it sprayed on Yaala's thin shirt.

"Drink. You'll get used to it." She laughed at his discomfort. "It's all you get down here. The heat leaches the sweat from you in no time. You've got to drink a lot or die."

"We're dead already," Powwell grumbled. Cautiously, he sipped at the awful tasting water. He clung to his last communication from Kalen. If anyone could get him out of the pit alive, it was Kalen. He'd have to make the effort to stay healthy and vital until she got here, despite the water.

"Depends on how you look at things." Yaala twisted her legs beneath her and sat on the rough ground. And who's on guard duty this shift."

"Enlighten me." Powwell laid his head back on the ground, urging Thorny into the pocket. The effort of sitting up seemed too much in the oppressive heat. His ribs throbbed painfully. He wanted to bathe them in cold water to reduce the swelling. The hot, red light only aggravated them. He couldn't see any colors, only shades of blacks and grays, overshadowed with the strange red-yellow haze. The light and heat drained everything of vitality and color.

He had to fight the despair that radiated from the pit. Kalen would rescue him. *Come quickly!* he urged her.

"Yaassima never comes down here," Yaala said. "She trusts her elite guards to keep us in line. Not all of her guards are trustworthy."

"That's something positive," Powwell replied.

"The assassins she sends down here either treat us nice or they wind up having an accident."

"They might not kill us, but heat and neglect will," Powwell replied. The feeling of hopelessness wiggled in his gut. Thorny pricked his thigh with his sharp spines, jolting Powwell out of accepting the defeating emotions.

"You'd be surprised how long people can live down here, as long as they remember to feed us." Yaala looked back over her shoulder toward the next chamber. "I make sure they do remember."

Powwell sensed movement in there. He struggled to sit up again. "Is there a chance they'll forget to feed us?"

Kalen had told him to endure. She'd find a way to get him out. But if he starved to death in the meantime . . .

"Not *s'murghing* likely. There are too many of us with family and friends on the outside. They see that we get fed. Besides, Yaassima needs us—me—alive and well." Yaala stood up in one fluid motion. "Drink your water, then I'll show you to your work station."

Powwell shifted onto his left elbow preparing to roll to his knees. As he moved, his shirt stuck to his side where a guard's boot had broken the skin. The coarse cloth prickled against his sweat-dampened back.

"How come you aren't sweating?" he asked. For the first time he realized Yaala looked as cool and fresh as if they were lounging in the clean mountain air of Myrilandel's clearing. Except her clothing was gray. Everything down here was gray or black.

"I guess I'm used to the heat and don't need to sweat now." She shrugged.

Two men wandered toward them, seemingly from the heart of the fire. They, too, looked thin and worn, with dirty sweat masking their features. Their gray clothes hung damp and limp upon stooped shoulders.

"We're ready for the ceremony, Yaala," one of the men said, his voice barely above a harsh whisper. She nodded and started walking toward the brightest point of red light.

"What ceremony?" Powwell asked as he balanced, first on his knees and then on his feet. Thorny poked his nose out of the pocket and wiggled it, rapidly digesting the scents of their new home. He didn't like it and rolled back into a sharp ball. Powwell wished he could do the same.

"You might as well watch with the rest of us. You're one of us now." Yaala beckoned him to follow.

The blinding glare resolved into a single tunnel in a maze of black openings. Powwell spent several moments trying to memorize landmarks—a triangular outcropping here, a rockfall there. Flickers of white movement teased his peripheral vision. He kept looking for the source of those brief glimpses of white rather than for distinctive features.

The heat increased, and he mopped his brow with his sleeve. Maybe the sweat dripping into his eyes blurred his vision. He wished he'd drunk more of the water; as bad as it tasted, he needed the liquid.

"Don't waste time learning the route. All the tunnels lead to one place eventually." Yaala paused where the tunnel opened up into a large cave. She stood at the edge of a precipice. Below them, far, far below them, molten rock churned and boiled, shooting flares up hundreds of feet. None of those huge flares came close to where they stood. A thousand feet or more separated the ledge from the core of the volcano. Still, the roiling lava dominated the scene. The ceiling soared so far above him, Powwell couldn't see the top.

How deep below the crater's surface had they come?

The temperature rose higher yet. Powwell staggered back two steps away from the edge. Vertigo tempted him forward into the boiling heart of the volcano. The Kardia seemed to press heavily against his shoulders. The air left his lungs in long gasps. He couldn't inhale. He imagined all the air was concentrated in the molten rock. If he wanted to breathe, he'd have to throw himself into the next flare that nibbled greedily at the flimsy ledge where he stood.

"Don't look at it. Keep your eyes on the walls." Yaala grabbed his arm and pushed him hard against the tunnel archway. "The pit will eat your soul if you let it. Just as it eats away at Hanassa."

Powwell closed his eyes and absorbed the solid feel of the rock pressing against his back. His feet still tingled with the vibrations of those flares slamming against the ledge. Almost like waves running against a cliff.

Slowly he opened his eyes, keeping his gaze away from the hypnotic fires of the pit. To his right and left people stood in other tunnel openings in groups of four or five. Gray-clad denizens side by side with black-clad guards. All around the immense pit, they stood and waited in respectful silence. Powwell tried counting the faces. He lost track at one hundred and seventeen.

"How many people live down here?" he whispered to Yaala.

"A couple hundred, maybe more. No one counts."

"That's a lot of people to feed without getting any work out of them."

"Oh, we work for our keep. *She* needs us to keep her magical toys active. She also needs us alive as hostages for the good behavior of her followers." A half smile quirked at the woman's mouth, as if she knew something Yaassima didn't.

"Hostages? Can we be ransomed? If there are so many of us, we could break the lock on the gate and charge the guards. It would be easy to storm out of the palace in a group."

"I'm not ready for that." She waved him to silence as two men carried a third to the ledge three tunnels to the left. Silently, they heaved the inert body into the boiling mass below them. The body fell a long, long way, diminishing in size to a pinpoint before it touched the boiling rock. Instantly the internal fires of Kardia Hodos consumed the body.

Powwell's heart leaped into his throat, as he imagined how the flames would burn away his own flesh and dissolve his bones. He knew the man must have been dead before being consigned to the pit. His fears kept seeing himself down there—alive, forever dammed to be eaten alive by the fires.

No one said a word for one hundred heartbeats. Then Yaala raised her voice in a curious ululation, high-pitched, wordless, sad, and triumphant at the same time. Around the pit, the other watchers took up the strange sound until they drowned out the constant roar of the boiling lava and the *yeek, kush, kush* behind them. Powwell's throat worked convulsively. He had to add his own cries to Yaala's.

A curious sense of relief and completion came to him as soon as he let loose the ancient mourning cry. He continued the wail almost eagerly.

At last, Yaala held a single high-pitched note for several heartbeats.

Abruptly, all the inhabitants of the pit fell silent. The absence of sound hovered for a moment, then the roars of the pit rushed back, louder than ever.

As one, the people of the pit turned and walked back into the tunnels.

"For now, that is the only escape from the pit," Yaala said.

*   *   *

Myri pressed her back against the cave wall near the ground level exit of Yaassima's palace. Smooth rock formed most of the corridors, almost perfectly circular tunnels with packed dirt on the floor. Black dirt, black walls, bleak and lifeless. Outside, the crater was filled with redder dirt and rocks—equally bleak but filled with life-giving sunlight and fresh air.

Irregular shadows draped the curving passageway in darker shades of black and gray. Beneath the torches, mounted into iron brackets at regular intervals, the shadows crawled away into a bilious gray green—real fire, burning green as it should. The Kaalipha didn't waste her bizarre magic on light panels in the passageways and rooms where she seldom appeared. She saved her tricks for the times she could make a great show of her power.

A black-clad guard rounded the curve from the direction of the main doorway into the palace. Myri recognized him as one of the men who usually patrolled the interior corridors closest to Yaassima's suite. He whistled a jaunty tune. A satisfied smile relaxed the lines around his eyes that usually betrayed his acute wariness. As he walked, he tossed his belt knife in the air, watched it spin, and caught it again by the hilt. Then he grasped the tip with the other hand and repeated the trick.

All the elite personal guards of the Kaalipha practiced this movement whenever their hands were idle. Few in Hanassa doubted their expertise with the weapons. Those few usually ended up dead.

The guard didn't look right or left as he passed Myri, still whistling, still tossing his knife as if it were a harmless child's toy.

When he moved out of her line of sight, Myri headed toward the main door as silently as she could, letting her soft indoor shoes whisper across the packed dirt-and-stone floor. Kalen was off exploring the kitchens and possible servants' entrances. Myri needed to know the routine of traffic in and out of the main entrance. She had to find a way out of the palace once they rescued Powwell.

Recovering from Amaranth's birth, Erda's drugs, and staying out of Yaassima's way had kept her close to the royal suite for the past three weeks. Without the mind-clogging potions she had found a gap in Yaassima's watchfulness in the suite. But here. . . ?

Myri kept to the shadows beneath the torches. All of the brackets marched along one side of this passageway rather than alternating sides to eliminate shadows. This was a security lapse she didn't expect of Yaassima.

She touched the dark kerchief hiding her hair. In her old leaf-green gown over a simple shift, she hoped to pass as another servant. Any glimpse of her white-blonde hair, so similar to Yaassima's, or the jewel-toned silks Yaassima had given her to wear, would identify her to the regular inhabitants of the palace. She needed anonymity to scout an escape route.

Multiple footsteps echoed loudly around the tunnel walls. A shimmer of reddish orange light signaled the infiltration of sunlight, so different from the green flames of the torches.

Sunlight, air, freedom. She longed to dash forward and experience life once more. She couldn't. Not yet. Not until she knew she could take all three of her children with her.

A side passage opened in the wall opposite her. She dashed across the widening tunnel and secreted herself in the unlit corridor.

A merchant laden with bolts of fabric spilling from his arms staggered past her. A laughing guard walked beside him, picking up brightly colored silk that trailed behind the merchant. New clothes for Yaassima. Good, she would be occupied for several hours while making her selection from the fire-green, bay-blue, and blood-red cloth.

Right on the heels of the merchant and his escort came three women. They wore ordinary sturdy gowns and kerchiefs over their hair. They must be part of the huge staff of servants Yaassima maintained. The Kaalipha never allowed a servant to perform the same chore in the same rooms as the day before, except for Haanna. Yaassima's mute personal maid seemed to love her ruthless mistress blindly. Mealtimes and menus varied widely. No one had an opportunity to detect patterns and routines for laying traps against the only person in Hanassa who maintained any degree of power: Yaassima.

Myri watched a continuous parade of people in and out of the main entrance for a few more moments. Servants, guards, merchants, and outlaws in search of favors all passed through the same portal. Would so many people come this way if there was any other way in or out of the palace?

Her heart sank.

Keep yourself safe from Televarn, Nimbulan. Please be careful. I can't come to you yet. She checked the magical umbilical that connected her heart to her husband's. It appeared stretched and thin, as if the distance between them had grown beyond the physical separation. The pulses of her heart and his counterbeat pushed strongly back and forth, though, with little delay. She wished she understood the nuances of the connection better. The strength of the cord and the heartbeats told her only that Nimbulan lived, and that he loved her.

Was that enough to rebuild their marriage? She didn't know. She'd answer that question when she saw him

again, and gave vent to her anger at his leaving her alone
and vulnerable. First, she had to find a way out of this
horrible city of crime and death with her three children.

She edged closer to the cave opening that formed the
main entrance. If this truly were the only way in or out,
she had to know what security measures Yaassima employed. She kept her eyes on the floor and her extra
long fingers folded within her skirt. No one looked at
her twice.

Through her lowered lashes she watched as the black-
uniformed guards stopped each person entering the palace. Two guards stood to the side of the portal, hands
on their swords. They wore three or four other, shorter
knives stuck into their belts, their boots, and protruding
from their cuffs. Chains crossed their chests and slings
dangled from their shoulders. Two other men carried
metal tubes the length and thickness of one of Nimbulan's small wands, in addition to the multitude of
weapons.

An outlaw swaggered up to the entrance. Myri recognized him as a cutthroat who had stood in line for a job
yesterday in the Justice Hall. Yaassima had denied him
any assignment, especially his request to waylay a cara-
van from SeLenicca bound for Rossemeyer.

The cutthroat flashed a broad smile to the guards, revealing broken teeth beneath his drooping mustache.
Myri knew a moment of recognition. Where had she
seen him before yesterday?

Casually he saluted the guards and stepped into the
cave as if he had every right to enter without scrutiny.

Before he had gone a second step, Yaassima's trusted
men clapped their strong hands around his arms.

"You know the rules, Piedro," one guard growled, not
releasing his grip.

The two men with wands placed themselves in front
of and behind Piedro while the other two maintained
their hold on the outlaw. They waved their wands over
Piedro's entire body.

The wands blasted out an ear-piercing shriek. Myri
clapped her hands over her ears. Every person within
sight froze in place. They remained locked in position
as if the shrill sound had numbed their will as well as
their hearing.

Sweat broke out on Piedro's brow, and he lost much of the high color beneath the dirt and beard shadow on his cheeks.

The four guards shoved the outlaw's face into the cave wall. They stretched his arms painfully over his head. One of them tore the rough black shirt from Piedro's back. He shook the fabric hard. Another guard poked and slapped the prisoner's body. He pressed his fingers into every fold and crevice of Piedro's trews until he came up with a small knife concealed between the prisoner's legs near the groin.

He held up the palm-sized knife triumphantly. Grinning, he slapped his wand twice against a rock by the entrance. The metal chimed against stone but didn't screech as it had earlier. The guard shouted: "Send two escorts. We've got one for the pit."

No humiliating trial in the Justice Hall. Obviously, taking a weapon into the palace meant immediate punishment.

The crowd of people surrounding the entrance began moving again, talking quietly among themselves. A few cast sidelong glances at Piedro, still held hard against the wall.

One serving girl tried to slip outside without being searched. The vigilant guards grabbed her, too. But the wands remained silent, so they let her go.

Two more guards ran up and took custody of Piedro. The criminal screamed pleas and protests as they dragged him roughly into the dark interior of the palace.

Myri turned. They would lead her to the pit. If she remained silent and unseen behind them. She'd spent a lifetime eluding pursuers. The dragons had taught her many things, especially how to avoid detection.

"There you are, Myrilandel," Yaassima said sweetly. She clamped her long-fingered hand firmly on Myri's shoulder.

CHAPTER 15

"You seem restless today," Yaassima said. A satisfied hum followed her words. "Perhaps you should have joined us last night. I found the spectacle of Kestra being raped—invigorating."

Myri turned slowly under her warden's hand, to face her. Yaassima's emotions were dominated by sexual satisfaction. Nothing else reached Myri's empathic talent. Yet she sensed dissatisfaction in the older woman.

"Did you need me for something?" Myri asked. She didn't want to touch on the subject of Yaassima's orgy or Kestra's pain and humiliation.

"You need new gowns. The mother of my heir must appear as regal as I. I thought we burned that hideous peasant gown you're wearing."

The gown had served Myri well for a long time. Most of the people she dealt with in her normal life considered her choice of attire graceful and attractive. Yaassima's clothes were too bright and clumsy for everyday wear.

"The people need to see you suitably clothed. I can't decide between the ruby and the emerald for you." Yaassima started walking toward the interior of the palace. She kept her hand firmly on Myri's shoulder, compelling her to accompany her.

"I prefer the colors of the Kardia to jewel tones," Myri said. She walked slowly, making the Kaalipha adjust her long stride to fit hers.

"Nonsense. You fade into the background. I want you to stand out in any crowd."

Dragons prefer to remain unnoticed. Myri bit her lip rather than voice the thought. Safety lay in making Yaassima believe she took the drugs and didn't have the will to defy her.

"Always remember the tremendous honor I do you in making your daughter my heir." Yaassima threw her hands wide as if embracing all of Hanassa in her enthusiasm. "I think the red for the baby's naming ceremony. Hanassa has such a majestic ring to it. She will grow into the name with proper training.

"My daughter's name is Amaranth." This was something she had to fight Yaassima for. She couldn't allow the Kaalipha to engulf her identify or her daughter's in grandiose delusions. Yaassima had no concept of reality beyond the walls of Hanassa and her own imagination. "If I must wear your fancy silks in brilliant colors, then I will wear purple."

"Nonsense. There are no purple dragons. We wear only the colors of our kind. I have decreed it." Yaassima's eyes narrowed as she glared at Myri, trying to impose her will.

Myri stopped short. Rage boiled within her. "There are no purple dragons now." Amaranth was dead and Myri dared not transform. There would not be another purple dragon until Shayla bred again. Even then, dragonkind might have to wait several generations for another purple.

(Purple dragons have special destinies determined by forces beyond the wisdom of dragons.) Shayla's statement rang through her memory. That special destiny had fallen to Myrilandel. She had become the link between dragons and humans so that human magic could be controlled and used only for the benefit of all.

"I will wear purple, or I will wear my old gown," Myri said. While she remained in Hanassa, she had no other link to the dragons. She must wear purple, the same shade as Amaranth had worn on his wing-veins and spinal horns.

Yaassima stopped on the first step up to their private suite. Her eyes narrowed and her fingers flexed convulsively. "You take your independence and defiance too far, Myrilandel. You will wear the gown I provide or you will wear nothing at all. And the baby's name is Hanassa."

Myri stared into the Kaalipha's eyes, shoulders rigid and jaw set. They were bound together by that gaze for long moments, neither bending to the other's will.

The sound of running footsteps down the steps broke Myri's concentrated defiance. She dropped her gaze but kept her posture. Yaassima looked up, severe annoyance showing in her tightly compressed lips and the deep lines around her eyes.

Kalen skidded to a halt three steps above Yaassima. She clung to the walls of the narrow staircase to keep from falling forward from her abrupt stop.

"There you are, Myrilandel. Amaranth is crying. I think she's hungry," the girl said, out of breath. *I found him,* she sent to Myri telepathically. *I know where Powwell is being held.*

Myri shook her head, wondering how Kalen dared use mind speech in Yaassima's presence. The Kaalipha might overhear.

She doesn't have real magic, only gadgets and toys that make her seem all-powerful. That's what Powwell says.

"I must go to Amaranth." Myrilandel shook herself free of Yaassima's hand that still rested on her shoulder.

"You may watch Maia nurse your child if you must. A monarch does not stoop to such messy, peasant activities."

"Yaassima, you claim dragon heritage in one breath and deny it with your actions. Dragons nurse their own young for many years, until they are old enough and strong enough to hunt on their own. Yet you seek to deny me that same nurturing, instinctive to me. Which are you, Yaassima, dragon or self-serving outlaw?" Had she overstepped the line between safety and strength? Myri pushed away her fear of the older woman.

The Kaalipha's lip curled upward in a snarl. Her fingers flexed as if tearing the flesh of her prey. "You have no need to explore the palace, Myrilandel. You must learn to keep the air of mystery and power, so the *people* we govern don't lose their fear through familiarity. I have set boundaries within the palace. You will soon learn them. Maia and I will take complete control of the care of *my* heir, Hanassa."

Myri looked hard at Kalen, wondering if the Kaalipha had overheard the girl's telepathic message.

"Oh, and, Myrilandel, do not consider defying me on this." Yaassima adjusted her tone to one of mild pleasantries. She pulled a long golden chain from the pocket of her gown. From the chain dangled a dragon-shaped pendant cut from a single crystal. "You will wear this amulet at all times, and I shall know where you are and who you talk to. I have assigned Nastfa and Golin to watch over you day and night."

Curiosity glimmered in the back of Myri's mind. Nastfa and Golin had been humiliated and tormented by Yaassima last night at the orgy. Their resentment toward the Kaalipha might be turned to help Myri escape with the children.

"Nastfa and Golin have a vested interest in staying close to you now, Myrilandel," Yaassima continued. "They entertained me so well last night with their embarrassment that I have commuted their sentence. My women are still forbidden to them, but if you stray beyond the boundaries I have set, they may do with you as they wish. I promise you, they will not be gentle or kind."

*   *   *

"You aren't a very good king," Konnaught d'Astrismos said matter-of-factly.

King Quinnault looked up from a copy of the newly drafted treaty with Rossemeyer to stare at him. The boy returned his gaze, stone-faced and unreadable. But the way he cleaned beneath his fingernails with his belt knife—the small tool every man carried—was too casual. Konnaught sought to pick a fight. Why?

"What brought on this absurd accusation?" Quinnault refused to allow this *child* to unnerve him. But he wanted to just thrash the boy and exile him to the kitchen until he came to his senses, or of age, whichever came later.

Unfortunately, the D'Astrismos line was the closest thing to an heir Quinnault possessed. Konnaught held the grudging loyalty of four of the other lords. They had supported the boy's father and only swore fealty to Quinnault because they were outnumbered by the remaining seven lords. Their oaths came with the proviso that Konnaught be next in line of the throne.

Everyone agreed that an heir must be greed upon be-

fore the death of a king to avoid another contest that
led to civil war.

Until Quinnault found a suitable wife and sired an
heir, he was stuck with Konnaught. He also had to deal
with four disapproving lords on his council who
prompted Konnaught's disrespectful attitude no matter
what discipline Quinnault imposed.

"I thought you had the makings of a real king when
you exiled your own sister as a rogue magician. But
not now."

Quinnault froze. He'd hated exiling Myrilandel. For
Konnaught to hold up that action as laudable revealed
an evil core to his personality. Was there any way at all
to exorcise that evil? He doubted it. He began to wish
he had heeded Nimbulan's advice and exiled Konnaught
the very day his father died.

The boy sheathed his knife and picked at his cuticles
with his free hand. A bad habit Quinnault had every
intention of breaking—if he let Konnaught stay in Coronnan City.

"Don't you have chores or lessons?" Quinnault asked,
keeping a bored edge in his voice. "I don't have time to
listen to your childish fantasies."

"My father would never have allowed Nimbulan to
leave without permission. My father would have locked
him up before he fled."

"What do you mean, Nimbulan has fled?" Disappointment landed heavily on Quinnault's shoulders. He'd told
Nimbulan not to go, confided in the magician how much
he depended upon his advice. The chore of retrieving
Myrilandel from Hanassa should be delegated to
younger men. The dragons insisted only that she be rescued, not by whom.

"Nimbulan has disappeared. I was with the messenger
you sent to fetch him. He couldn't find your chief adviser
anywhere. You should exile Nimbulan now, too. He left,
so he's a rogue now."

*(Do not allow this child to guide your actions. We guard
Nimbulan as we guarded our daughter, Myrilandel.)*

Quinnault lifted his eyes to the open window by his
desk. He hadn't heard a dragon speak to him since Myrilandel's kidnap. And yet . . . was that slight tingle behind

his heart that signaled his awareness of the guardians of Coronnan becoming stronger?

I need Nimbulan, he thought back at the voice in his head.

(You need to put this child in his place.)

"What are you going to do about the outlaw, Nimbulan? He called off the search for the Rover who murdered the apprentice. He's in league with the Rovers. My father wouldn't . . ."

"Your father made the mistake of outlawing Nimbulan when the magician left his protection. If he'd allowed Nimbulan the freedom to pursue magic as he needed, then welcomed him back, Kammeryl d'Astrismos might very well be sitting here now evaluating this treaty rather than me. But your father wasn't all-wise or all-knowing." Quinnault lost a little of his hope that Konnaught could be redeemed by care and good examples. "Your father's mistakes are the reason I am here and you are my fostering—owing me allegiance and obedience. You act more like an exiled rogue than an heir." Quinnault raised one eyebrow at the boy, hoping to intimidate him.

"Dungeons with stout locks were made for men like Nimbulan," Konnaught replied, undaunted.

Quinnault had to make one more try at breaking down Konnaught's dogged hero worship of his misguided father.

Part of him argued that no child deserved to know the depth of evil a father like Kammeryl d'Astrismos had stooped to—the torching and pillaging of his own villages merely to soothe a temper tantrum. Quinnault refused to think of his dead rival's perverted sexual practices that eased his increasing periods of black self-doubt and reinflated his belief in his descent from the Stargods.

Quinnault decided to point out Kammeryl's lack of judgment before he enumerated the man's evils. "There isn't a lock made that a competent magician can't open. Nor a prison they can't break out of if they choose to. Your father underestimated Nimbulan. That is a mistake I shan't make. Now I am through explaining myself to you. You have chores and lessons. I don't want to see you again until they are complete."

Konnaught looked as if he wanted to argue, then turned sharply on his heel and stalked out of the room.

"You'll pay for this, little king. I'll make you pay when I rule this land," he muttered as he slammed the door behind him.

Quinnault vowed to find a wife quickly. If only there was someone else he could name his heir in the interim. Konnaught d'Astrismos must never be allowed to rule, even for a heartbeat. In the meantime . . .

"Guard!" he called the sentry posted outside his door. "Have my steed saddled. I join the search for Nimbulan and for the Rovers. I don't want a stone left unturned anywhere in Coronnan. They can't have gotten far without leaving a trail."

                              *   *   *

"Thank you, Seannin." Nimbulan saluted the young blue-tipped dragon. He rested both hands against the animal's side as his feet reaccustomed themselves to the Kardia.

Nimbulan hadn't wanted to leave Coronnan just yet. There were still clues to be gleaned from that strange clearing by the river where Televarn had disappeared. The little girl who was supposed to have fetched a book for him needed to be questioned. But Seannin had insisted he fly Nimbulan and Rollett away now. The dragon couldn't delay any longer. Shayla awaited him. No dragon dared disobey Shayla.

Few humans did either.

Rollett clambered down from the animal's back, also unsteady. He looked as if he wanted to heave his last meal.

"The flight was gentle, boy," Nimbulan said. He gripped Rollett's shoulder affectionately. "Last time I rode a dragon, we hit a high crosswind. I thought I'd be blown off."

Rollett turned a little green and gulped.

(I can take you no farther, Nimbulan,) Seannin sounded apologetic.

Nimbulan looked down a steep escarpment from the ledge where the dragon had landed. The air was thinner and drier at this elevation than he was accustomed to in the river valleys. He didn't recognize the sparse, lowgrowing vegetation with thick needlelike leaves and tiny flowers.

"You have brought us farther than we could walk alone in a moon or more. For that I thank you, Seannin. You and all of the nimbus of dragons." A moon closer to finding Myrilandel than he was this morning when he left Coronnan City. Hopefully he was closer to some answers as well.

(*You may not thank us when you face Hanassa.*) The dragon bunched his muscles as if eager to be gone from this hostile environment.

"Seannin, why didn't the dragons tell me before this is where Myrilandel was hidden?"

(*You didn't look for her. We will not show you something you do not seek, not even in a dragon dream.*)

Nimbulan dropped his head and closed his eyes. Seannin was right. He'd let Quinnault keep him in the capital for too long before he tried returning to Myri's clearing. Only when Shayla had broken the Covenant between dragons and humans had he actively looked for his wife and their two foster children.

But he'd looked with magic, not with his heart.

Amaranth had died because Nimbulan hadn't sought Myri earlier. If Nimbulan had gone to his wife, might he have prevented her kidnap into Hanassa?

Now he had to make that search his primary quest. He wouldn't rest until he found Myri, Kalen, and Powell. Kings and treaties and magic schools had to wait— or find a new Senior Magician.

Could he willingly give up all he'd worked for just to be with Myri for the rest of his life?

He'd think about that later. After his wife and children were free of Hanassa.

"Where must I go from here?" Nimbulan searched the mountainside for signs of a trail.

(*Follow your heart to Myrilandel. Only you do we trust to save her. The youngling will help you, but only you can find her. We can do nothing more to help. Hanassa is forbidden to true dragons.*)

"I don't understand. Myri was one of you. Dragons can fly anywhere. Why can't you go into Hanassa?"

(*We do not fly over or near Hanassa.*) Seannin bunched his muscles again in preparation for flight.

Nimbulan stepped out of the way of the powerful wings. Seannin launched himself off the ledge and into flight. He thrust down with his wings and rose above Nimbulan's head.

The channel of communication from the dragon's mind snapped shut. Nimbulan felt curiously empty and alone without the few words the dragon had given him. As alone as Myri must feel, cut off from her family and from the dragons.

He turned in a full circle, looking for a way off this narrow ledge and into the hidden city.

"There's a staircase of sorts." Rollett pointed to crude indentations in the cliff wall.

Nimbulan was suddenly grateful for the company of his senior journeyman, a young man he had raised since the age of ten. The bleak mountainside reminded him just how dangerous and lonely this quest would be.

At the same time he feared that he would have to watch this boy die as he had watched so many of his friends, companions, and students pass into a new existence. He clamped his hand on Rollett's shoulder with affection, reaffirming the bonds that had grown between them for more than eight years.

"Looks like someone tried to carve the steps. The intervals are too regular to be natural," Nimbulan replied. Not much of a road, but it was the only exit other than the one the dragon had taken. He peered down the mountain slope once more. Something akin to Myri's dreams of flight invaded his senses. If only he could spread his arms wide and launch himself into the thin air. . . .

"Careful," Rollett warned, grabbing Nimbulan's collar and dragging him backward on the ledge. "After experiencing flight on a dragon, it seems only natural that we should be able to do the same."

Nimbulan shook himself free of the need to fly. That way led only to death. He was not a dragon and never would be. But Myri could be a dragon again, if she wished. Had she transformed in response to Amaranth's death?

Not yet. He'd know if she had. He'd know in his heart.

The silver cord pulsed too strongly between them. His loneliness increased at the thought of losing her. But if that were the only way she could save her life . . .

"Someone must use this route regularly," he commented as he placed his boots along the width of the step. It was too narrow to take more than his toes straight on, so he climbed sideways. The stairs up the mountainside fit his feet better than he'd expected on first glance.

"With these hand notches beside the steps, the route seems almost comfortable." Rollett hauled himself up the steep path.

The magical tendril connecting Nimbulan to Myri pulsed stronger with each step. His heart lifted a little. He climbed higher, taking time to breathe the thin air. No sense in arriving too out of breath to act.

One hundred twenty-two steps above the ledge, Nimbulan paused on a shallow plateau that spread right and left. Rollett crawled up, landing on his belly. He clung to the level area with both hands dug into the sandy soil. "No wonder Hanassa is such a mystery. No one in his right mind would seek this place just to explore," Rollett panted. His eyes were squinted nearly shut, keeping out the bright sunlight and hiding his emotions. His trembling chin betrayed his uncertainty. He never looked down. "I hope there's a different way out. Those steps will be really treacherous on the way down, especially in a hurry."

"Agreed. You are good with detail. Memorize everything, particularly anything that seems odd or out of place." Nimbulan searched the plateau for signs of the trail continuing.

"Something that is repeated too often might be a delusion." Rollett's gaze followed Nimbulan's around the open space.

The plateau measured perhaps fifty long paces wide. The cliff continued to reach for the sky above it. Nimbulan walked a few steps to the right. Around the curve of the plateau, nearly one hundred average paces away, cut into that otherwise impenetrable wall was an archway. Smooth symmetrical sides and the top a perfect half circle proclaimed the opening as man-made. Metal bars filled it with an intimidating crosshatch pattern. Two guards, bristling with weapons, stood on either side of the archway. Two more held positions behind the bars. A long dark tunnel stretched from the barricade into the mountain.

Nimbulan stepped back hastily, out of view.

The guard spotted Nimbulan at almost the same moment.

"What brings you to Hanassa, stranger?" The guard on the right slapped a rock beside the archway with a curious metal wand.

A high-pitched ringing sound attacked Nimbulan's ears. He scrunched his eyes closed in a painful grimace. The sound continued inside his head long after it had ceased vibrating from the hollow metal tube the guard carried. Rollett curled up on the ground—which he still hugged—hands over his ears.

"Have you hospitality for a stranger lost and alone?" Nimbulan recited the formal words accepted throughout Coronnan. The customs of hospitality were ancient and ingrained in the culture.

"Hospitality!" the guard laughed. "No one seeks hospitality here. Who are you, and what do you truly want?" The guard held up the wand, as if he expected it to shoot a debilitating spell from the empty end.

Nimbulan backed up a step, being very careful not to fall off the edge. He kept his hands open at his sides when he really wanted to grab his staff and shoot a counterspell. He'd disguised the staff as a waterskin and lashed it to his pack, knowing it would identify him as a magician. He just had to be careful when he moved, not to knock the long tool against anything that would betray the disguise.

Rollett had accepted the same delusion for his own staff. He looked up as the guard motioned them closer, still holding out the wand. The journeyman magician remained where he was, out of sight from the other guards because of the curve of the plateau. Nimbulan took two steps closer.

The guard slapped the rock again, much harder, with the wand. The high-pitched ringing tortured Nimbulan's eardrums louder this time. He resisted the urge to cower behind his hands.

"Only magicians can tolerate the wand," the guard said when the ringing ceased abruptly. "You are not welcome here. Leave immediately or face the wrath of Yaassima, Kaalipha of Hanassa and Dragon of the Mountains."

CHAPTER 16

"I need your help on Old Bertha," Yaala said to Powwell. Her husky voice was packed with authority. All of the men milling around the central living cavern stopped what they were doing to listen to her, including the guards. Some—the younger and healthier prisoners—glared at her in resentment. The guards showed fear. Most of the others obeyed without question, without thought, incapable of making decisions anymore.

Powwell mopped his brow with the kerchief she'd given him last night. He still felt strange wearing it on his head, Rover style, so he stuffed it back into his pocket. His shirt and trews were soaked with his own sweat. He had no way of knowing how long he'd been down here. A day? Two? He'd survived three work shifts of cleaning and lubricating the giant machines that filled various rooms of the cave system.

Through each waking moment, the vision of the dead man falling and falling into the pit haunted him. While he slept, he dreamed he was the falling man, the heat eating away at his soul long before the fires consumed his body.

He awoke from those dreams shaking with fear. The sense of gaining release and freedom by jumping into the fires frightened him more than pain and thirst and despair.

And overlaid atop those dreams was the sense of being watched by the white wraith that drifted around the caverns, never closer than the periphery of his senses.

Come for me soon, Kalen. I don't know how long I can keep my life and sanity down here.

In the time since the guards had kicked him into the

pit, he'd eaten six small meals of thin gruel. The covered pot of food was lowered down a narrow chute only marginally wider than the pot. When the denizens of the pit had eaten—after much squabbling on the part of the healthier citizens—they reattached the rope to the pot, and it was hoisted back up by unseen hands. Yaala's presence kept the stronger prisoners from gobbling all the gruel, leaving the weaker ones to starve.

Everyone down here acknowledged Yaala as their leader, as above they acknowledged Yaassima as their Kaalipha.

Even with Yaala's supervision, no one got enough to eat. When they weren't working, the men and women congregated in the living cavern, watching the chute for any sign of more food dropping down, kicking and fighting to be first to delve into the pot.

An older man related a tale of many years ago when loaves of bread appeared in the chute every day for a week. He thought a relative of one of the prisoners might work in the kitchen. But the bread stopped coming as abruptly as it started, never to be seen again.

Powwell's mouth watered at the thought of bread—even stale unleavened bread.

The lack of food only hastened the time until he, too, was consigned to the fires at the heart of the Kardia. Since the guards seemed to walk in fear of Yaala, and the accidents Powwell was certain she could arrange for them, maybe they could be coerced into bringing more food into the pit. Maybe . . .

"How do you know so much about the machines?" he asked Yaala as she led him unerringly through the labyrinth of caves and tunnels.

"I hung around the engineers when I was a kid. When the last of them died last year, I was the only one who knew enough to take their place."

"Does Yaassima know that you, a prisoner, are now the—engineer?" Powwell stumbled over the unfamiliar word.

"No." Yaala closed her mouth firmly, refusing to elaborate.

"Which one is Old Bertha?" he asked, just to keep words flowing above and around the sounds of the chugging machines. Each of the monstrous noisemakers had a personality and a name. Yesterday he'd worked on Liise, a small placid machine who only needed a little attention to purr along quite happily.

"Old Bertha is the oldest and crankiest of the Kaalipha's generators," Yaala replied.

The strange name for the machines rolled easily off her tongue. But she'd been in the pit for several years since her imprisonment as well as much of her childhood on a voluntary basis. Powwell couldn't quite form the strange words without thinking.

"What can I do to help?" he asked. "I don't know anything about the machines." He'd been taught to squirt an oily liquid onto various moving parts and wipe up the excess that spilled onto the casing.

"You have a good memory, part of your magician training. I need you to remember where every part goes and what condition it's in when I pull it out and find out why Old Bertha is wheezing and not producing enough 'tricity."

Another strange word, this one for the power that came out of the generators. Magic was much easier to understand.

"You're the only one smart enough to become the next engineer. I'll not trust anyone from aboveground with *my* machines."

As Yaala led Powwell deeper into the cave system, closer to the pit, he examined the tangle of metallic conduits that channeled the 'tricity from the generators to an unknown "transformer" in the Kaalipha's palace. Maybe these conduits were like a staff, and the transformer was a magician who had learned to use this strange power. He'd learned to gather dragon magic to fuel his talent after he'd used the ley lines. This might be another kind of fuel.

The steam that powered the generators came from a lake that filled one of the lowest caverns. Pipes channeled the water above a glowing pit of lava, heating it past boiling into steam. The steam moved inside Old Bertha in some mysterious way, churning out energy that was captured by a turbine—some of the smaller satellite machines. Flexible conduits Yaala called "wires" snaked out of the turbines and disappeared into narrow lava tube tunnels.

Maybe the ley lines were just another kind of wire for naturally generated 'tricity.

Steam from Water becoming Air. Fire from the heart of the Kardia. All four elements were present in the 'tricity. That made it magic. He'd understand how to use it eventually, just as he'd learned to use ley lines and dragon magic. If he lived that long. If Kalen didn't come for him soon.

Yaala ducked beneath a low-hanging slab of black rock within the dim tunnel. The only light came from that strange color-leeching yellow glow produced by the 'tricity. Powwell ducked, too. Behind the slab the roof remained low. He had to crouch to keep from banging his head. Yaala was short enough, so she only had to bend her head. She seemed to know the way and moved adroitly around other obstacles as the tunnel narrowed.

The noise grew louder the smaller the tunnel became. Powwell resisted the urge to cover his ears. He'd almost accepted the noise level back in the passageways. Here the sounds of Old Bertha chugging and wheezing echoed and compounded within the confines of the lava tube.

Yeek, kush, kush. Yeek, kush, kush. The sound assaulted his senses as it had during the trek with Televarn from the clearing. Powwell opened his eyes wider, looking around him for something familiar.

If Televarn had brought them through the pit to the palace, there must be another entrance from outside Hanassa. He turned a circle, peering at everything. Automatically he reached into his pocket to touch Thorny and see if his familiar remembered any of the smells down here.

His pocket was empty. The little hedgehog had found a nest of insects he liked up near the living cavern. He'd left Powwell alone sometime ago while he hunted a meal. Thorny would find him when he'd eaten his fill and napped a little.

S'murghit. He'd have to figure out the connection to Televarn's route by himself.

Yeek, kushshshshs. Yeek, kush, kush.

"It sounds like Old Bertha has a blockage. A big blockage," he yelled at Yaala. He'd learned that much about the generators in his three shifts. The tiniest buildup of mineral deposits from the water supply or rust on old metal created problems.

"I know that. But we've got to blast it clean with this probe before she conks out, or we'll never get her started again," Yaala replied, holding up a long flexible wand type tool. She moved swiftly around an old rock-fall that nearly blocked the passage. "Bertha is *very* old."

Powwell squeezed around the loose debris and nearly stumbled into the largest cave he'd seen down here. He could have built at least two buildings the size of the School for Magicians within the cave. Nearly filling the open space was the largest, rustiest, and loudest machine he'd ever seen.

Encased in black metal, Old Bertha rumbled and groaned and belched steam through rust holes in time with her vibrations. The rattle of the conduits going into and out of the generator gave the impression of a crotchety spider of immense proportions crouching over her latest prey.

Powwell immediately crossed himself in the Stargods' ward against evil as he remembered Moncriith's sermons against demon magic. The Bloodmage had gathered numerous followers to eliminate all magicians tainted by demons, starting with Myrilandel and including every person of talent except Moncriith. If demons did exist, they surely inhabited Old Bertha.

"It's just a machine." Yaala laughed as Powwell crossed himself a second time.

"Then why do you give them all names and treat them as if they were sentient beasts?" Powwell circled the grunting monster, keeping as close to the walls as he could and as far away from the machine as possible.

"Because these machines make Yaassima appear to be a magician. All of her tricks begin and end with them. She can't be overthrown until I know everything about these machines, how to turn them off and how to restart them keyed to a different frequency. She'll be powerless without her toys."

"You mean the lights and appearing out of nowhere? That's magic. My teacher, Nimbulan, could do that." Powwell stopped his circuit when he came to a narrow archway that opened into the pit. The swirling colors of

the molten rock beyond him upset his balance and reminded him of the weight of the mountain pressing on
top of this cave. He kept to one side of the archway.

"But he performed those feats with an inborn talent,"
Yaala argued. "He didn't have to rely on machines he
inherited through fifty generations of Kaaliphs."

"Fifty generations?" Powwell added up the years in
his head, then added them again. "That's nearly a thousand years. These machines can't date back to the time
of the Stargods!"

"Maybe not these machines, but the technology comes
from the time when Hanassa, the first Kaaliph, broke
away from the dragon nimbus and took human form.
He created the city named for him, and it became a
refuge for the scum of Kardia Hodos who weren't welcome anywhere else."

Powwell's brain reeled with that information. Myri
had been a purple-tipped dragon before taking a human
body. Did that make her related to Yaassima in some
way?

"Hanassa used knowledge he stole from the Stargods
to build the machines," Yaala continued. "Maybe he
stole the machines themselves from the Stargods. At
first, the Kaaliphs knew how to replace old and worn-
out machines. Now we can only clean and patch them.
We've lost so much knowledge." Yaala pounded her fist
into her thigh.

She turned her back on Powwell and gave her attention to a quaking water pipe running from Old Bertha
back to the lake. Hot water leaked from the pipe where
it joined the machine's belly. Flaking rust spread outward from the join. "I think there's a blockage in this
pipe."

Powwell walked toward her, ready to watch how she
inserted the probe. The shifting reds and greens of the
pit, visible through an archway, kept drawing his focus.
He looked over his shoulder repeatedly, watching the
play of colors within the frame of the opening. He tried
to break the compulsion to shift direction and walk
through the colors into the pit.

Suddenly he watched not the boiling molten lava
within the heart of the volcano but a secluded glen
within a lowland forest. Tall trees bordered a nearly per-

fect circular clearing with a small campfire in the exact center. A moment later Televarn ran across the clearing and dove into the archway. Two men from the School for Magicians chased him, brandishing clubs.

The Rover chieftain landed in the cave on his belly just as the colors swirled again and changed to the boiling lava in the pit.

Hastily, Televarn picked himself up and limped past Old Bertha. He looked around quickly, but Yaala was on the other side of Old Bertha and Powwell ducked into the machine's shadow. The Rover whistled a jaunty tune as he brushed caked mud from his trews and vest. Then he strode into the nearest exit cavern, dragging his right leg slightly.

"Did you see that, Yaala? It was Televarn, I swear it, he walked out of the pit into this cave."

"Illusions, Powwell. The heat plays tricks on you until you get used to it. Take a long drink, then help me disconnect this valve."

*   *   *

Quinnault cantered slightly ahead of his escort on Buan, his favorite fleet steed. A year ago, he had ridden the length and breadth of Coronnan without a servant or bodyguard. Back then he was merely one lord trying to persuade, coerce, or browbeat the other lords into accepting peace. No one cared if he fell victim to the marauding armies or packs of outlaws that roamed the countryside at will. Today he was king. Many people surrounded him, guaranteeing his safety.

But these mundane guards hadn't stopped the Rover form poisoning his cup. He wished Nimbulan hadn't gone on his dangerous quest. Quinnault didn't really feel safe without his chief adviser and Senior Magician.

Why hadn't Nimbulan told him he was leaving? He hadn't even left a note or message for his king and friend.

Quinnault missed the solitude of his former life. Long rides between strongholds had offered him periods of intense meditation. Now he only found time to ride after supper or when on business as king. He never rode alone. So he kneed Buan into a slightly faster pace. The dozen soldiers who rode behind him urged their own mounts to keep up. But they stayed a discreet two-dozen steed-lengths behind him.

He'd left Konnaught behind with a long series of sword exercises to perform. The brat wouldn't allow him this brief illusion of solitude. What could he do with the boy?

Quinnault wouldn't arbitrarily exile or imprison Konnaught. Execution was out of the question for all but the most violent crimes. He wouldn't allow himself to become the kind of tyrant who made up laws to suit his whims and then broke them when convenient. The new laws required a crime proved to judges before such a sentence could be considered.

Konnaught was too smart to let himself be caught in an active plot to overthrow Quinnault.

The road curved ahead of him, just before it entered a stretch of woodland—a former haven for outlaws. Heedless of possible ambush, he rode without slowing into the evening shadows gathering beneath the trees.

He needed to think, and think hard before full darkness forced him to return to the palace. An apprentice magician rode with the soldiers. He could provide torches of witchlight, but that wasn't enough illumination to ward off predators and light their way home.

He pelted around the next curve, completely losing sight of his escort. The last of the afternoon sunshine dropped into deep twilight. Shadows stretched out to enfold the road in mystery. Buan faltered a step as the road became muddy. Huge clods of the sloppy road sprayed behind him. The sun rarely reached this deep into the woods to dry the trader's road.

Buan slowed of his own accord. Quinnault loosened his short sword as he searched for whatever bothered the steed.

Something light and wispy fluttered across the road. Buan shied. Quinnault fought the beast with knees and reins. He needed all of his skills to stay mounted.

Buan circled and snorted. His skin rippled and twitched nervously. He pranced and circled.

Quinnault curbed him, resenting the concentration required to control the steed. He needed to know what had startled Buan. The now familiar short sword fit his hand comfortably. *Stargods,* how he resented the need to carry a weapon when Coronnan should know peace from violent crime as well as war.

"What is it, boy? You don't usually fuss about a bit of evening mist." He soothed Buan with a quiet voice and a gentle hand upon his glossy neck.

More drifting mist gathered in the woods around him. Short columns of lightness stood in a half circle across the road, spreading to his sides, blocking advance. He kneed Buan to prance in a circle, checking behind him. The road back to his escort remained open.

He turned to face the tallest column that stepped forward from the line of its companions.

"What manner of ghost are you?" Quinnault asked, not liking the slight quaver in his voice. He'd faced the shadowed guardian of Haunted Isle with less uncertainty than he felt now. But he'd had Nimbulan, a powerful Battlemage, at his side then.

Where was the Senior Magician of the Commune now when his king needed him?

"We are not of this world." A deep, melodic voice drifted out of the central ghost. Masculine in timber and authority. His outline fluttered in a slight breeze. "We need conversation with you, King Quinnault."

"You have my attention." Where was his escort? They should have caught up to him by now.

"Your companions await you at the edge of the woods. They are not aware that time passes or that you are not with them. We will restore them when our conversation is finished."

"Are you magicians, that you read minds?" Quinnault's nervousness transferred to Buan. The steed stamped and tried to break free of his master's control.

"Not magicians as you define them. But we have powers similar to them. We seek a bargain with the King of Coronnan. We usually pay in the mineral substance you call diamonds. This time, we trade something more valuable."

"Varns! You're Varns." Fantastic legends surrounded the mysterious merchants who appeared in the marketplaces of Kardia Hodos once each century—always in a year of bounty. They bought enormous quantities of grain and fresh food, paying in diamonds.

Quinnault's grandfather claimed to have met a Varn about forty years ago. They weren't due back in Coronnan for another sixty years or more. This wasn't a year of plenty either.

The king's senses shifted into full alertness.

"Your people call us Varns because we prefer to trade in the city of Varnicia."

"How may I be of service?" A large quantity of diamonds would go a long way toward stabilizing Coronnan's economy after three generations of war.

"Coronnan needs more than diamonds to bring stability, King Quinnault."

Disconcerting how these amorphous beings read his thoughts.

"You need a bride who can give you many heirs. You also need a way of keeping greedy enemies from invading through the Great Bay. We can give you both."

"At what price?"

"We are dying. The tree you call the Tambootie offers the only cure."

"How much will you need?" Quinnault thought of the dragons who used the foliage of that tree for food. Previously, magicians, too, had eaten of the tree to enhance their magic. The addictive qualities of the drug made the Tambootie almost as dangerous as it was beneficial. Now that magicians gathered dragon magic, they had no need of the Tambootie. Dragons were as essential to Coronnan as the promised wife and heirs.

"The new leaves of many acres of the tree will allow us to distill enough medicine for our immediate needs."

"That is a lot. I don't know that we can spare that much." Quinnault sent out a silent plea for advice—permission—from the dragons.

"Raw Tambootie is toxic to humans. What possible reason do you have to hoard it when we need it so desperately?" A note of pleading entered the otherwise emotionless voice.

"Tambootie feeds our dragons. I need the dragons, and the dragons need the Tambootie as much as you do."

CHAPTER 17

Televarn paced the perimeter of the Rover cavern. His cavern. He was *THE* Rover. Every member of the nomadic tribes who dwelt within the city, looked to him for leadership. He controlled their movements, their thoughts, their beliefs.

So why couldn't he find Kalen among them? Wiggles squirmed impatiently inside his vest. The animal sensed that Kalen was near enough that it should be able to join her.

"Be still, beast." Televarn batted at the ferret's paws where it tried to claw through his shirt to his skin. "We'll find her if we have to tear this city apart." The city, not the Kaalipha's palace. He intended to make the palace his home as soon as he deposed Yaassima.

Swallowing his pride and gritting his teeth in distaste, Televarn decided to ask questions when he should have been able to pluck the information from the mind of any one of his followers. Why?

Erda, the old wisewoman of his clan—every clan possessed an Erda, but this one was the oldest, most powerful and *HIS*—shuffled past him into the slave pens. She carried a pot of gruel, the standard meal for captives. As soon as the slaves had eaten, they would be linked together by ankle chains and led to the lush plateau Northwest of the city to work the only fields near enough to Hanassa to provide some food for the inhabitants.

Televarn's obligation to lend his slaves to Yaassima for this work irritated his pride. *He* should make the decision where and when his slaves worked. *He* should be the one running the city and raiding rich caravans for food and other necessities rather than supervising work parties.

"Erda, where have you hidden Kalen?" He grabbed the old woman's sleeve to detain her.

Erda glared at his hand, reminding him of the effrontery of touching an Erda without permission.

Televarn's irritation made him reckless. He left his hand in place.

"Televarn seeks the one who is dangerous. Your death I see in her eyes." She didn't pull away from him, just continued to stare at his hand on her arm, reminding him of his trespass.

Televarn jerked his hand away from her arm as if she offended him, rather than the other way around. "The girl child is important to my plans. Where is she?"

"Seek her where you want her to be," Erda spat at him and continued into the fenced area where twenty hungry slaves awaited their meal.

"What is that supposed to mean?" His words echoed in the cavern. He'd broken the oldest rule of etiquette within the clan by shouting at Erda.

Erda shrugged and plodded on.

"Stubborn old bitch. I'll find Kalen and make her my chief adviser and wizard. There will be no place for old crones who spout nonsense and call it wisdom when I rule Hanassa."

Erda didn't reply.

"Seek her where I want her to be," Televarn mumbled to himself, stroking Wiggles into submission as he paced the cavern once more.

"I want her at my side, reading minds and magically lifting weapons away from my enemies. Kalen isn't by my side. But she might be reading minds and lifting weapons away from my enemies. My biggest enemy is Yaassima, in the palace. Myrilandel is also in the palace. I've waited too long to claim her." He ran his hands through his thick hair, grooming it for his imagined reunion with his former lover.

"Erda, is the witchchild in the palace?" he asked politely.

The old woman pretended not to hear him. He knew she had. She heard everything that happened among the Rovers.

"I can't get into the palace. I don't know that you could either, Wiggles," he mused.

He took a deep breath, reluctant to admit he had only one way to contact Kalen. He had to touch her mind. When she'd first become his ally—back in Coronnan before he'd taken Myrilandel through the dragongate—Kalen had made him promise never to read or control her mind, like he did with all the members of his clan. She had never participated in the rituals designed to bind every Rover to him.

Promises had never bothered him before. Why did he consider respecting this one to Kalen?

Because the child was dangerous. The promise was for his own safety as well as her whims.

He had to risk it. He'd completed the first stage of his plans with Nimbulan's death and the elimination of Amaranth. Myrilandel was now alone and vulnerable, ripe for his plucking. She had nothing left to bind her to her old life in Coronnan. But he had to get her away from Yaassima before he could reclaim his lover and bind her to his will.

Myrilandel had to see him as her rescuer. She had to witness how tenderly he cared for Kalen, her adopted daughter, how he planned to honor the witchgirl and allow her the freedom to maximize her talents—something Nimbulan couldn't do for her in Coronnan where witchwomen were exiled. He expected loyalty from Myrilandel. He knew better than to expect anything from Kalen that didn't suit Kalen.

He and the child were well suited to each other.

He sought his dark and quiet corner of the cavern, way in the back. Years ago he'd scraped away the debris and made a soft meditation nest of furs and pillows. Plain colors, without Erda's distracting embroidery, soothed his eyes and comforted his body. In one fluid motion, he crossed his legs and sank to the floor.

Wiggles squirmed out from beneath Televarn's vest and stretched along the length of his right thigh, head resting on his knee. He stroked the ferret's fur as he breathed deeply.

A light trance settled over him. Resentment churned in the back of his mind. He shouldn't have to work this hard to touch the mind of one of his own. Every member of the clan was connected to him, mind, body, and soul, by the magic rituals unique to Rovers. Only Erda could dissolve bits and pieces of the control.

Kalen had steadfastly remained outside of those rituals for several moons before Televarn laid the trap for Myrilandel. Even Nimbulan had been easier to control than that willful child.

He suppressed his anger before it rent great holes in his trance.

Slowly he released a thin tendril of magic. It resonated against the mineral deposits in the volcanic rocks of the cavern. He heard the magic shift its vibrations until it hummed in harmony with the Kardia. He matched his voice to the solid note. Maintaining the one-note chant, he built a picture of Kalen in his mind. Her brown braids laced with auburn came easily to him. He traced an outline of her hair in the air before him.

Bright green lines followed his finger, leaving a bare sketch of a head behind. He added wide, gray eyes and a snub nose. With tender care he dotted a spray of freckles across her nose. The last detail eluded him. How to draw her mouth and chin? They faded from his memory. All he could see in his mental picture of the girl were her eyes, big, innocent, gazing up at him with awe.

Enough. The eyes were more important in identifying her. They were also a place of entry for his probe. He withdrew his tracing finger and attached his magic to the drawing.

Then he willed the magic to find the one whose image he had drawn.

The magic uncoiled into a slender arrow and darted through a crevice in the cave walls. Wiggles leaped from his lap, following the probe into the depths of the mountain.

"*S'murghit!* There goes my only true link to the girl."

*   *   *

Myri tugged at the heavy necklace Yaassima fastened around her neck, careful to make her movements sluggish. The gold links, each the diameter of her little finger, settled against her collarbones and wouldn't move from there. The dragon pendant rested firmly between her breasts, tightening the fabric of her gown to outline their shape. She started to lift the necklace over her head. A painful whistle sounded deep within her ear.

She dropped the necklace and grabbed her ears, trying to block the sound that stabbed at her mind like a knife.

The dragon pendant glowed brightly.

The whistle and the pain ceased as soon as Myri dropped the gold links. All traces of eldritch light faded from the crystal dragon as the gold links quietly caressed her neck.

An audience of guards and servants paused in their routes through the palace to watch the spectacle of the Kaalipha's favorite receiving an unprecedented gift. Yaassima grinned at them, obviously enjoying her display of power over Myri. Kalen was nowhere in sight.

Myri looked at the pendant where it settled between her breasts as if it belonged there. With one finger she flicked it until it swayed. Her skin burned through her shift and bodice as if pierced by a branding iron wherever the beautiful jewel touched her. The only time she was comfortable was if she ignored it.

"You needn't bother trying to remove it." Yaassima draped Myri's hair over her shoulders, creating a frame for the jewelry. "My great-great-grandfather had it made for his mistress after she tried to run away. The next time she attempted to escape, the necklace kept shrieking inside her mind until blood vessels in her brain burst and she died."

Myri ceased moving, stopped thinking. The purple-tipped dragon, Amethyst, had only been able to take over Myrilandel's body because the little girl was thought dead from bleeding in the brain. The dragon's vitality had allowed the little girl to heal the broken places. Myri's innate healing talent knew the vessels were still weaker than normal. The necklace would kill her quicker than most humans.

"Now that the necklace has found a home on your beautiful neck, Myrilandel, no one will be able to remove it until you die." The Kaalipha let her hand linger on Myri's cheek.

Myri forced herself not to jerk away from the caress. Yaassima had trapped her with a magic-infested slave collar. No matter how beautiful the jewelry, it still branded her the Kaalipha's possession, without freedom or control over her own life. She'd never taste fresh air and open skies again.

She had to. The necklace was just one more obstacle to overcome.

She looked frantically right and left. The gathered servants blocked any route of immediate escape from Yaassima.

"Don't consider killing yourself, Myrilandel, by deliberately crossing my boundaries. Suicide is forbidden by your Stargods," Yaassima cooed, reaching to run her hand across Myri's breast.

The corridor wall pressed against Myri's back. No place to run.

Yaassima squinted her eyes nearly closed. Age lines, spraying outward from her slightly uptilted eyes marred her otherwise flawless complexion. "I think you might welcome my gentleness when Nastfa and Golin finish with you. Just remember, they will do you no harm until you try to escape. And don't try to make friends with them so that they will aid you. Through the crystal dragon, I will hear every word you speak. Don't give me a reason to have the jewelry stab into your brain until you die an ugly death."

The Kaalipha flipped her hand in a quick rotation. She pressed her thumb against the ring on her little finger. The whistle shrieked inside Myri's head once more.

Myri fought to keep from cringing from the pain.

Darkness encroached on her vision from the sides. A white tunnel opened before her eyes. At the end of the tunnel she saw Coronnan, beautiful, cool, green Coronnan. Blue skies invited her to soar free through the fresh air. Her home. Numbulan's home. Freedom!

But she had to transform to win free of Hanassa. Once a dragon, she wouldn't have a human body to come back to. Amaranth would have no mother—only Kalen and a Rover wet nurse.

She allowed the blackness to overwhelm her, praying that Yaassima wanted her alive. Her knees buckled.

Abruptly the whistle ceased. Her eyes cleared. Hot, desert air filled her dry mouth and lungs. Her tongue tasted sour from fear.

"Remember this little lesson next time you defy me." Yaassima stalked back toward the staircase that led to their suite. "Nastfa and Golin are waiting for you in your chamber, Myrilandel."

* * *

Nimbulan hastened away from the gate into Hanassa before the guards changed their minds and arrested him. He searched the mountainside for an alternate route up the steep slope above the gateway. He had to find another way into the city. Myri needed him. Old legends and a few unreliable reports from Televarn said that Hanassa was within the crater of an extinct volcano. The ridge line above him should actually be the rim of the crater. Once up there, he'd try dropping into the city from above.

He spotted a scraped stone next to a prickly bush that seemed to be missing four branches. Upon closer examination, he decided the missing branches had been nibbled off by some browsing animal. The scrape marks came from hooves.

He dug his boot toes into the rocky soil and stood beside the bush. Above it, he saw a line of other plants that might have been lunch for the same animal. He followed the grazing pattern upward, finding footholds that weren't visible until he was almost on top of them.

Rollett angled farther North to see if a better trail existed.

The sun rose higher, more intense here in the desert than it ever shone in the river valleys of Coronnan. Sweat dripped down Nimbulan's back and between his thighs, despite the Winter season. His hands and neck sunburned rapidly in the thin mountain air.

He drank from the waterskin Seannin had made him fill before leaving Coronnan. He wanted more, but the top of the mountain seemed very far away. Perhaps he'd best conserve his supplies until he was inside the city.

Rollett? He sent a query to his journeyman. *Any luck?*

Nothing, came back the reply.

Conserve your water. We may be out here a long time.

They had to remain strong enough to rescue Myri once they managed to drop below the crater rim. And Nimbulan hadn't slept more than a few hours since before the battle. For weeks before that his rest had been troubled by worry over Myri. He wondered if Rollett's more youthful body had rebounded after the grueling battle and the preparations before that. The young man had been almost as depressed over Haakon's drowning as Nimbulan had, further depleting energy resources.

Hopefully the crater's slope into the city would be climbable or not too far a drop to the roof of some building.

Myri. Oh, Myri. I miss you so. Stay safe until I can come for you, he pleaded with every scrap of telepathic talent he possessed.

An hour later, the top of the mountain seemed no closer. Rollett was out of sight around the curve of the slope. Flies pestered Nimbulan's face, crawling into his ears and nose. He swatted at them. Five flew off, replaced by ten more. His pack grew heavier with each step, and he longed to drain the waterskin. He dragged out his staff and used it as a prop to pull himself up one more step.

A small puddle of shade beneath a narrow outcropping enticed him forward. His eyes welcomed the protection from the glaring light, though the temperature didn't vary significantly. The flies continued to plague him as his sweat dried to a salty crust.

Go home. You're too old for this kind of an adventure. Go home where life is safe and comfortable, a small voice in the back of his mind whispered.

"Not without Myri. I won't leave this place until my wife is by my side once more. And not without finding an end to the murdering of my apprentices," he called to the four cardinal directions and the four elements. When he finished this quest, he'd make a home for Myrilandel on one of those little islands in the Great Bay that Quinnault wanted to use as a ferry station and loading dock. That would put her outside of Coronnan and still allow him access to his work in the capital.

He crouched within the shallow confines of the shade until his back protested the unnatural hunch. He sat, curling his legs tightly against his chest and rolling his hips slightly toward the back of the overhang. If he stretched out so much as a hair, the sun beat down, burning him through his clothes. Extremely uncomfortable, he closed his eyes and thought of Myri and the clearing.

He thought about recording his impressions of Hanassa in his journal, but didn't want to waste his energy. His eyes were very heavy and the sun too bright.

He awoke to find the shadows had lengthened. Rollett stood in front of him, hands on hips, trying for an intimidating posture. But the weary sag of this shoulders and neck belied his expression.

"Take a drink, and we'll be on our way, Rollett. Our entrance might be safer after dark," Nimbulan said.

"Cooler anyway. We'll need our cloaks within minutes of sunset. And there isn't much twilight in this desert air." Rollett continued to look around, seeking a way up to the top.

The water refreshed Nimbulan enough that he thought he could finish the climb before full dark. He stretched cramped and aching muscles and stood up slowly.

Thoughts of holding Myri in his arms once more filled him with determination. *A few more hours and I will be with you, beloved.*

Stretching shadows obscured the faint game trail he had followed earlier. Rollett picked it out, feeling for it with the tip of his staff—a trick Lyman had taught the young man—to seek the lingering life-vibrations of the last being who had climbed this way with the sensitive staff. They plodded upward, grasping bushes and rocks for balance as the slope steepened.

Nimbulan dug his staff into the sandy soil as a prop when the bushes weren't close enough. His thighs grew as heavy as his pack, and his head felt as light as the waterskin.

The shadows deepened. The sun set behind the mountain. Chill air dropped dramatically upon them. Stars burst alive in the blue-black sky all at once. The tangy smell of desert plants sharpened in the cool air.

Nimbulan looked up to the rim of the crater. Starlight glimmered against a shiny network running along the crest. He narrowed his eyes, looking for signs of magic. Nothing extraordinary met his gaze. He dragged himself up the last few steps and reached with his left hand, palm outward, fingers curled, for the source of the now sparkling obstacle.

He jerked his hand back, pain stabbing his fingertips. Close inspection revealed tiny punctures where he had met the obstacle. Blood oozed from the cuts He inspected the barrier again, more cautiously, with all of his senses.

A long line of rusted metal fencing, barbed with sharp wires twisted at close intervals, ran the full circle of the crater rim. It stood nearly double Nimbulan's height.

"This fence stretches for miles," Rollett whispered. "I can't sense an end to it, as if it makes a full circle with no beginning and no end."

Two hundred feet below them, down a nearly straight precipice, Nimbulan saw the city. The rising moon, just past full, illuminated the haphazard streets and jumbled huts. Even without the fence he'd not be able to climb down the cliff into the city. Too steep to climb, too far to jump.

The barred gate was indeed the only entrance and exit to Hanaassa.

CHAPTER 18

(When in doubt, stall!)
    The idea persisted in Quinnault's mind. He dismounted slowly, thinking furiously. As he slid down Buan's side, he was briefly out of sight of the Varns. He palmed his belt knife and loosened his short sword in its sheath. He'd never undergone the intense weapons training of a warrior. But he knew the business end of his blades.

His years of studying to become a priest, before his entire family was wiped out by the wars and the plagues and famine that always followed in the aftermath of war, had trained him to negotiate.

"Tambootie has become a valuable commodity since the advent of Communal magic."

The Varn leader turned his head region to the column of fluttering mist on his left. A moment of silence ensued. Quinnault wondered if they consulted telepathically, as magicians sometimes did.

The Varn beside the leader reached up and removed a flowing headdress. Like breaking free of a cocoon, a red-haired woman shook herself free of the coverings. She dropped the elaborate veils to the ground.

That's all the cloaking mist proved to be—many layers of soft, translucent cloth. The woman concealed beneath the drifting draperies seemed to be human.

Quinnault gasped. He'd never seen a more beautiful woman. Her small heart-shaped face was framed by a cap of short curls. A snub nose gave her a look of youth. Big green eyes seemed to sparkle with humor and mischief, another hint of youthfulness. Her full-lipped mouth twitched as if suppressing a smile.

"Am I valuable enough?" Her voice lilted over him

as if she sang a sweet love ballad. Her accent hinted of exotic lands.

Fascinated, Quinnault stepped forward. He needed to be closer to her, make certain she was truly human and real. The heavy swathing veils still hid her figure. Below the neck she could be a many tentacled monster.

He didn't care.

"The ladies of my court will frown at your hairstyle while they rush to mimic it. There will be an abundance of shorn locks for the gentlemen to collect as talismans of luck and favor." He felt himself smiling and wanted to burst out laughing.

"I . . . I am not used to dealing with court ladies." She gnawed at her lower lip with small perfect teeth.

A sense of panic invaded his mind like a telepathic probe from a dragon. He looked at the woman, stunned. No other human had ever been able to awaken his dormant talent.

Are you reading my mind? he asked her.

Not intentionally, she replied. Her eyes opened wide, startled.

He nearly lost his balance gazing into their green depths.

Many of the women in my family have green eyes. It is considered a sign of inherited intelligence. Her mental chuckle told him that she didn't believe the family superstition.

And suddenly he realized that with the lines of communication open in his mind this woman couldn't lie to him. He relaxed a little.

I don't want to lie to you, ever, Your Grace. Please don't lie to me. She gnawed her lip again in uncertainty.

This crack in her composure struck Quinnault deeply. He needed to reach out and protect this woman. He didn't even know her name, and yet he found himself dreaming of long years with her, of children and shared memories.

Katie. The name came to him without a deliberate probe.

The woman shifted her shoulders as if pushing aside her doubts. She extended her hand in a masculine gesture to shake his. "I am Mary Kathleen O'Hara. My friends call me Katie."

So her companions didn't know that he had established a telepathic link, and she didn't want them to know.

"Quinnault Darville de Draconis at your service." He lifted her hand to his lips and pressed a gentle kiss to her fingertips. When he lifted his head, he couldn't let go of her hand. "My friends call me Scarecrow, but don't tell anyone at court."

Scarecrow? The mischief returned to her eyes. "I can think of many names better suited to a handsome bachelor king."

"I haven't been called Scarecrow since I was a teenager, actually, all arms and legs and clumsy as a newborn colt."

"Does that mean you haven't had any friends since?" Concern touched her voice and her smile. *I would very much like to be your friend.*

Quinnault fell in love.

(Offer them half the Tambootie.)

Sense reasserted itself into his brain. "If we can negotiate a treaty, you may have half the Tambootie requested, harvested in thirds. We will deliver the first load when the marriage banns are posted, the next when the marriage takes place, and the final third when our first son is born." He had to keep his eyes closed to keep from giving them everything up front without a thought for the future. If he looked at Katie any longer, he'd give away his entire kingdom without regret.

"We need the Tambootie now," the leader asserted. He tried to push his body between Quinnault and Katie.

Neither of them yielded to him. Nonetheless, Quinnault dropped her hand. "I have a marriage treaty waiting for my signature that promises me a perfectly good princess. My people know her lineage and will welcome the alliance. Her family will secure my entire Western border."

"And leave you more vulnerable to the South and East."

"Do you have a name? Perhaps we could retire to my palace for refreshment. These negotiations could take some time. I will need to consult my Council and my magicians." Quinnault cocked one eyebrow, trying to appear as if his sanity didn't depend upon grabbing Katie's hand again and never letting her go.

"You may call me Kinnsell, Scarecrow. And we can finish this here and now if you are reasonable. Katie could be your wife by tomorrow night."

"You may call me *King* Quinnault, or Your Grace. I rule by the grace of the dragons and I will not hesitate to call them up to dispose of my enemies." He glared at Kinnsell. He didn't need to tell these Varns that no dragon had been seen in Coronnan since his sister had been spirited away.

Behind him Buan snorted as if amused. Quinnault cursed the steed under his breath.

"Magicians and dragons," Kinnsell snorted. "I guess you use the Tambootie to induce hallucinogenic trances that make you see dragons and believe in magic."

"If that is what you believe, then we have nothing to discuss." Quinnault turned on his heel and grabbed Buan's reins. He didn't want to go. Didn't want to leave Katie. But he had to show strength, knock some of the arrogance out of these beings.

"Your Grace, there is no need to go through the lengthy process of banns and an elaborate marriage ceremony," Kinnsell said mildly, almost politely. "A simple exchange of vows is all we require. Your laws do say that when marrying a foreigner the bride's customs prevail at the ceremony."

"But I am a ruling monarch. My people must accept Maarie Kaathliin," he repeated her name with the softer intonation of his people, "as their queen as well as my wife. We must all know her lineage and her dowry." Maarie Kaathliin. The name had a familiar ring to it. Where had he heard it, or read it. Kinnsell, too, sounded familiar. . . .

Kinnsell! the servant of the Stargods. Kimmer, Konner, and Kameron O'Hara. No. The Varns couldn't be delegates of the Stargods. The three red-haired brothers who had saved Kardia Hodos from a plague and given the people justice and magic belonged to the people of the Three Kingdoms, not to the Varns, who hailed from some unknown, unnamed location.

"I assure you, Quinnault," Katie said. "I am the daughter of an emperor, descended from seven hundred years of emperors. I believe you value people descended form your Stargods? My family dates back to them. My lineage is impeccable. We would not press you to hasten our union if the lives of many millions of people did not depend upon access to the Tambootie." She captured his gaze with her own.

He fell into their green depths and knew she spoke the truth.

We need you as much as you need me. But be careful of Kinnsell. He has his own agenda aside from the issue of the Tambootie.

(She will do.)

Quinnault almost laughed at the amused voice in the back of his head. He had no doubt that Shayla eavesdropped on both conversations, spoken and telepathic.

"Half the Tambootie, delivered in two batches—at the marriage and half when our first son is born." He felt an odd reassurance as well as a chuckle of approval behind his heart where the dragons dwelt. "But we must have a public marriage and posting of the banns."

Kinnsell and Katie exchanged another of those meaningful glances. The leader turned away first, sighing heavily.

If this haughty leader bowed to her demands, she must be very strong-willed. Quinnault was glad she was on his side. She couldn't lie to him. He'd know it in his mind and in his heart. So would the dragons.

"You need to protect your shipping channels without challenging your neighbors by building an extensive navy." Kinnsell removed the elaborate headdress of veils and shook his head as if freeing it of the weight. Taller and older than Katie, he, too, bore a head full of red hair, cut short. His complexion and green eyes matched hers. A similarity of jaw and mouth shape suggested close family ties. Father and daughter?

"Agreed," Quinnault said warily. These people knew too much about his situation and he had no bargaining tools other than the unacceptable marriage treaty with SeLenicca. He clamped down on those thoughts lest the Varns read them.

You have the Tambootie. He cannot harvest it without your permission. Our family covenant requires your permission and trade of equal value.

"The mudflats of the bay offer a natural protection for your harbor but prevent shipping into the harbor," Kinnsell continued. He drew the arc of the bay in the ground with a stick. He marked the mudflats with squiggles. "We will build a series of jetties and bridges among the islands at the beginning of deep water. Flat-bottomed barges can transport people and cargo from the port into your city." He finished off the drawing with the exact placement of the four islands.

Nimbulan had suggested the same solution to the problem. It would work. Quinnault forced himself to reply levelly. "Such a venture will take many moons to construct. Possibly years. Plenty of time to post the banns and prepare a great marriage ceremony."

Kinnsell sighed again as if incredibly weary. "We have the technology to build the port in the space of one long night."

"My boatmen will need many seasons to learn the changes in the currents to guide the barges through the mudflats safely."

"We will lend one, I repeat, *one,* of your boatman a device that will show him the shifting currents and channels. Marry the girl tomorrow and while you conceive the first child, we will build your port. But we must have the Tambootie. Three quarters of the original demand delivered in halves."

Can you spare that much Tambootie? he threw the question at whatever dragon might be listening, and he had no doubt they heard every word of every conversation he conducted.

(Not all at once.)

"Two thirds. Half of it this season. The remainder next year. Too heavy a harvest will cripple the trees and prevent them from leafing out properly next year." Quinnault didn't know where that information came from, but he sensed it was true. "If you destroy the trees, you won't have a source for your medicine should your plague break out again."

"You will marry the girl in the morning?" Hope colored Kinnsell's voice for the first time.

"My Western and Southern borders are still vulnerable." How much could he trade for the Tambootie?

"Ties of friendship and trust will protect you better

than anything we can give you. Will you marry Katie in the morning?"

"In the evening. We will have to prepare a gown and a feast." And convince the Council. Soothe the ruffled feelings of the Commune. Placate the ambassador from SeLenicca . . .

A candlelight wedding in an ancient temple. Her mental sigh of delight filled Quinnault with deep satisfaction.

And the fairy tale gown of your dreams, white satin and pearls. He completed the mental picture for her. Seamstresses would have to work all night and all day tomorrow to alter his mother's gown to fit this slight woman.

Katie smiled at him, only for him, and he knew the bargain was worth going to war with SeLennica. The dragons had said she would do. He agreed.

*   *   *

Nimbulan eased behind a tumble of boulders near the gateway into Hanassa. He fished some oddments from his pack for a disguise. Behind another jumble of rocks, Rollett squatted and made similar preparations. No sense in risking a magical delusion slipping if they had to hold the spell too long. Nimbulan loosed his hair from its queue restraint and tangled it into a rat's nest with his fingers. Then he slipped an old black patch over his right eye. The molded fabric was threadbare and ragged around the edges. An equally ragged robe, similar to the one General Ambassador Jhorge-Rosse wore, covered his ordinary shirt and trews. The last item in his pack looked like more rags. He wound these around his head in a slipshod turban. Durt on his face and a stooped posture, dependent upon his staff for support, transformed him into an out-of-luck mercenary from Rossemeyer, seeking employment with the gangs of mercenaries headquartered in the city.

Rollett looked a little firmer of step, but equally ragged in his black robe and disintegrating turban. His own dark beard hadn't been shaved since the morning before the battle and effectively covered the lower half of his face in shadow.

Nimbulan worked his way around the back side of the

boulders so he could approach the gate from the direction of the stairway. Rollett followed silently. The sound of shuffling feet and a mournful dirge sung by a few male throats brought them to a hasty halt.

Nimbulan peered over the cliff edge toward the staircase. Nothing. The sounds echoed in the thin mountain air, defying direction. He extended his FarSight with the few reserves of dragon magic he'd gathered from Seannin.

Around the side of the mountain, on a narrow trail, level with the gate, marched several dozen people. An aura of despair, hunger, and fatigue hung over the marchers. Their emotions beat against Nimbulan's heightened sensitivities. Beyond hatred and anger, they plodded through a routine guided by heavily armed guards.

As the group came closer, Nimbulan saw with his normal eyesight heavy, iron collars around their necks. *Slaves!* his mind screamed in outrage. No one had the right to own another human being. *No one!*

The Stargods had outlawed slavery a thousand years ago, likening it to the horrible human sacrifices demanded of the ancient demon Simurgh.

Outrage and disgust almost pushed him to confront the guards and free the captives. Where would they go in these trackless mountains without supplies, a leader, and a destination? How could he get into the city to free his wife if he disrupted the routine so boldly?

Breathing deeply to calm his rapid pulse, he clung to his hidden position, observing the sentries and their curious wands.

As he expected, the troop of slaves with their eight guards halted abruptly on the little plateau by the gate. The slaves ceased walking in unison, almost as if minds and bodies were controlled by a magician. Televarn's Rover magic could do that. Nimbulan had barely escaped the man's magical manipulation. He'd been looking for it and blocked the spell with his own magic. What could these poor slaves do against so insidious a master?

The rear guards set aside a pile of pitchforks, hoes, and rakes. None of the slaves carried the tools. They might use them as weapons on the march back from the fields. How were they controlled in the fields?

The two sentries with wands slapped the instruments against a rock—the same rock they'd used before. Instantly the high-pitched ringing assaulted Nimbulan's ears. He resisted the urge to hide his head and block the sound with magic. He had to know how mundanes reacted to the noise.

Every one of the slaves froze in place. The guards with the wands moved among them, passing the magical instruments up and down, seeking. Seeking what?

As the guard approached a tall man in the center of the slave group, his wand glowed hot green, as if lit by fire within. The guard's partner searched the immobile slave with his hands, slapping the man hard. He lingered in the region of the slave's waist. Then he pulled a metal belt buckle out from under the man's loose shirt. The wand faded back to its normal black iron color.

Farther down the line, the guards discovered an assortment of metal buttons and eyelets among the slaves' ragged clothing. None of the slave collars or leg shackles reacted with the wands.

Curious. The iron must be specially treated. Nimbulan wondered if he could analyze the shackles and fabricate weapons of a similar material.

"They're clean," the sentry announced. At last the obnoxious humming ceased. The slaves roused from their stupor and shuffled forward, through the gate as if they hadn't been standing frozen in place for several long minutes. Nimbulan longed to dash forward and cross the threshold with them. The sentries resumed their watchful stance. He'd never get past them.

He had to divest himself of any metal not part of his disguise. Reluctantly he removed his glass from his pocket and directed Rollett to do the same. Unwrapping the layers of silk protection, he revealed the large square of precious glass framed in gold. Rollett's journeyman's glass was smaller and framed in bronze. Apprentice glasses were little more than a shard without a frame.

Nimbulan dented the gold rim with his belt knife until he could slip a broken fingernail beneath it. He stripped away the expensive casing, ripping his fingernail further.

The thin rim of gold weighed heavy in his hand. What to do with it? Rollett squeezed his bronze frame into two small coins. With magic, he imprinted them with a fuzzy image similar to the coins of Rossemeyer. Nimbulan chuckled to himself as he formed his gold into three slightly larger coins. What mintage should he mimic? A mercenary from Rossemeyer might have coins from a dozen countries. He settled on the image of the king of Jihab, a country that hired many mercenaries to protect their jewel merchants.

Slowly, Nimbulan counted one hundred heartbeats. Then another one hundred. The slaves were well within the city. The sentries assumed a pose of casual wariness. Rollett offered Nimbulan a supporting arm. They dragged themselves toward the gate, leaning on their staffs, as if incredibly weary.

"Who are you, and why do you approach the Dragon's City of Hanassa?" the first sentry asked when Nimbulan shuffled to a stop in front of him.

"Dragon's City?" he returned the question in a weak and shaking voice. The dragons, the real dragons, had said they wouldn't approach the city. "I hope the dragons inside need another soldier for hire."

"You don't look strong enough to wield a belt knife, let alone a sword." The guard with a wand stepped forward.

"Lost my sword to the bay in the *s'murghin'* battle with Coronnan a few weeks past." It had only been two days since King Quinnault and Nimbulan won that battle, but the guards wouldn't know that. "Had to jump ship to avoid the witchfire. *S'murghin'* unfair of that upstart king to fight with magicians. An honest soldier ain't got a chance against 'em," he grumbled.

"We haven't heard of any battle." The guard raised the wand above the striking rock.

"You'll hear soon enough. King Quinnault wants all of Kardia Hodos to know no one can defeat his magicians and their new powers. . . ." He trailed off and froze his body as the wand and the rock resonated with that horrible sound.

It took all of his willpower to keep from clutching his ears with both hands. His muscles twitched for release as the guard lingered over searching his body for concealed weapons. He didn't even dare flick his eyes toward Rollett, to see if the boy remained as rigid as the mundane slaves.

The guard found Nimbulan's little belt knife—an eating tool more than a weapon. He ran his thumb along the length of the blade, testing for sharpness. It barely creased his skin. Grunting, he returned the blade to its sheath.

Nimbulan sucked on his cheeks to keep from flinching as the guard's hand patted his groin. Did his hand linger overlong? A test or personal perversion?

The guard found another knife, a longer blade inside Nimbulan's boot and a few base coins tucked inside his shirt. Then he searched the multiple folds and pockets of Nimbulan's all-concealing black robe.

"Gold!" The guard's eyes widened as he felt the weight of the three coins.

"A good day's haul. Drinks are on you when we go off duty," the other guard laughed.

"He's clean," the first guard said as he pocketed the coins.

"This one is clean, too," said a second guard, straightening from searching Rollett. The horrible humming ceased abruptly.

Nimbulan wondered if the word "clean" triggered the release. He rotated his shoulders and looked up at the guards. "You gonna search me?"

"Already have. Aander here will carry your knives to the far side of the tunnel and give them back to you there. Enjoy the Kaalipha's protection for two days. After that you have to find a sponsor and join normal work details or leave." One of the guards opened the gate.

Nimbulan moved past the iron bars. A strange tingle snaked across his skin. Some kind of magic, but unlike any he'd encountered in all his years as a Battlemage. He willed his body not to shiver at the alien touch. Nor did he look at Rollett to see if he felt the same tingle. Aander watched them too closely.

A long dark tunnel stretched forward, perhaps three hundred long paces. Lanterns at the far end revealed another barred gate and four more guards. Would they have to go through the same search again? Nimbulan sighed wearily, preparing to ignore the horrible ringing noise and the humiliating search one more time.

The next guard nodded briefly to Aander as he flashed

his wand across the proffered knives. Then he opened the second gate. Apparently the Kaalipha trusted her guards enough to forgo a second test.

At last he stepped out of the tunnel, into the city proper.

"No weapons inside the palace or the tunnel. The wands remember the people and weapons, so don't try sneaking anybody out. You have two days to find a sponsor or get out—the two of you together and no one else with you. Without any other weapons. Other than that there aren't a whole lot of rules in Hanassa. There's lots of hiring of mercenaries right now. You'll find a sponsor easy, if you really want to stay." Aander handed the knives back to Nimbulan and Rollett. Now to find Myri and get her past these vigilant guards and their magical wands.

CHAPTER 19

"**D**o something, Kalen. Oh, please help me get this chain off my neck!" Myri begged her daughter when the girl finally returned to their quarters. She couldn't take a chance that the next time the bizarre whistle stabbed her brain the weakness left over from her infancy might rupture.

Then sun was nearly down and the air stifling. Even sight of the dark blue sky above the crater rim didn't ease her near panic.

Breathe deeply. In three counts, hold three, out three. She remembered Nimbulan's patient coaching from their first days together. He'd been teaching her to trigger a trance. She had to be relaxed before the trance would work.

She inhaled deeply on three counts, trying desperately to still her racing mind and scattered thoughts.

"Don't you want to hear my news first?" Kalen stuck out her lower lip in a good imitation of a pout. Her eyes opened wide and filled with moisture. She hadn't resorted to that expression in Myri's presence for nearly a year.

"News?" Memory of Kalen's errand to discover Powwell's whereabouts broke through her anxiety about the necklace. Hard on the heels of her elation about news of Powwell's whereabouts came awareness that Yaassima listened to every word she said through the dragon pendant.

"I . . . I can't listen now, Kalen. Can you do anything about this necklace?" Yaassima would expect her to try to break the necklace. Myri didn't feel safe telling Kalen about the Kaalipha's eavesdropping. She did look pointedly at the two guards who stood so stiffly by the door, also listening.

Kalen's expression closed. She dropped her gaze with all the innocence and shyness of a normal little girl. "I don't know how to do it." She waved at the offensive necklace biting her lip. "You'll have to free yourself."

Kalen never looked directly at someone when she told the truth. She used her wide-eyed innocence act to cover deceit.

And yet, Myri's magical senses picked up defiance. What was happening inside Kalen's complex thoughts?

She had to trust the girl. They'd been close for a long time. Kalen had learned to trust Myri, though Powwell was the only male she would allow past her defensive barriers. Kalen wouldn't betray Myri, her foster mother.

"I can't break the magical hold the necklace has on me, Kalen. I've tried. It chains me to Yaassima and this place. I have to get it off!" Myri intended to tell the listening woman precisely what she expected to hear and nothing more.

Kalen shrugged and moved toward Amaranth's cradle near the window, rocking it idly with her toe. The baby cooed and gurgled in response. Kalen sneered and turned her head away from the baby.

Myri caught jealousy and resentment from the girl's unbridled emotions. How could she resent an innocent baby?

Because little Amaranth devoured all of Myri's attention. She had little left to give Kalen. "Babies require a lot of attention," Myri said to her older daughter. "But just because my attention is on the baby doesn't mean I love you any less."

Kalen sniffed and refused to look at anything but the blank wall.

Myri reached out to touch the girl, fearful of losing all of the emotional stability they had built together.

Suddenly Kalen looked up, eyes alert, shoulders back and spine stiff. A trance of some sort. Myri had seen the posture often enough in her husband. But she'd never seen Kalen bother with the altered mind state that made a magician receptive to weaving or receiving spells.

"What is it, Kalen?"

The girl remained silent. A streak of dark fur sprang

from a crack in the wall and slithered up the girl's leg, clinging to the fabric of her skirt until it reached her shoulder where it wrapped around her neck.

"Kalen!" Myri shook her daughter's shoulder. She had to break the trance. "Wiggles is back. Wake up and listen to your familiar."

The ferret might very well carry a message of danger. Both Kalen and Myri were vulnerable to magic here in this city filled with Bloodmages, Rovers, and other malcontent magicians. The trance could blind Kalen to magical manipulation.

"Nimbulan is dead," Kalen whispered through stiff lips. Her hand crept up automatically to caress Wiggles. The ferret chirped ecstatically.

"What?" Shock rooted Myri in place. All thought deserted her. "I won't believe it." Kalen didn't know about the magical link between Myri and Nimbulan. No one could see it but themselves.

Kalen lied.

"Believe it. Wiggles brought me a vision. I saw Nimbulan in a great battle on the bay. Drowning. Waves and waves of water. Water pushing him down and down. No air. No strength. Blackness." Kalen barely roused from her trance.

"He can't be dead. I'd know it," Myri protested. Kalen and the eavesdropping Yaassima would expect her to say that.

How had Wiggles observed a battle on the Great Bay when he'd last been seen in the clearing, several days' ride South of any access to that body of water? He had no reason to go North to Nimbulan—whom he'd never met. Myri presumed the ferret had either sought Kalen out or come with her and then gotten lost in the city and the maze of tunnels that made up the palace.

Myri clutched her chest, trying to calm the frantic pulse. But her panic came from the knowledge that Kalen lied and Wiggles was her partner in deceit. She had no reason to grieve yet over the loss of her husband.

The silver tendril pulsed a normal heart rhythm. It grew stronger and thicker beneath her fingers, as if . . . as if Nimbulan had suddenly come closer.

Perhaps Kalen had been misled by her sneaky ferret—could the animal have been tampered with? Not likely.

The bonds between a witchwoman and her familiar were strong and convoluted, but exclusive.

She opened her mouth to ask the girl for details, to find the source of the deceptive message.

The half curl of satisfaction on the right side of Kalen's mouth told Myri more than she wanted to know. Even if she knew the information to be a lie, Kalen wanted Nimbulan dead and Myri lost in grief for him. Why?

*   *   *

Powwell swallowed his fears. Televarn *had* stepped from somewhere else into the tunnels. This was the same route they had taken from the clearing, through the pit and into the lower levels of the palace.

Yaala said it was a hallucination, induced by the heat and dehydration. Powwell knew what he had seen. Knew what he had experienced during the kidnap and his first few moments of awareness.

Thorny confirmed his impression as he waddled up to Powwell and begged to be picked up. As Powwell cradled the little hedgehog in his palm, his familiar replayed scents through Powwell's memory. This tunnel branching off from Old Bertha's cavern smelled different than any other tunnel in the pit.

If Televarn could come and go from this hellhole, then Powwell could, too.

He tucked Thorny into his tunic pocket, letting his familiar's nose work with him. With one hand on the wall and the other extended, palm outward, as a sensor, he crept forward. At each step he stopped and extended his senses as far as he could, looking for something different about this particular tunnel. Thorny had poor eyesight but keen smell. All he could tell Powwell was that this place was different and he didn't like it.

Powwell rotated his left hand, much as Nimbulan did when seeking information or weaving the magic of the Kardia. His palm was sweating, as it had almost continuously since he'd been thrown down here. Nothing else infiltrated his searching senses.

One more step brought him within sight of the heaving lava at the core of the volcano. The churning mass seemed quieter, grayer, less liquid today.

A hot wind blasted his face. Power tingled along the fine hairs of his arms.

Suddenly the view lurched and shifted into a circling vortex of vivid red, green, yellow, and black.

Powwell's head spun. His stomach bounced. He slammed his eyes closed. The Kardia righted. Only his eyes sensed movement.

Slowly he pried open first one eye then the other. Before him lay a desert. Rock and soil—more rock than soil—lay bare in the brilliant sunshine, bleached of color by the bright light. He sensed reds and yellows beneath the glare. Strange arched rock formations sprang up out of nowhere. Mountains rose in the distance, more desert. The only vegetation in sight were stunted grasses growing out of rock crevices in the shade of larger rocks.

Just as suddenly as the view came to him, the scene lurched back into the swirling vortex. The hot wind died and the crackling energy faded.

Powwell grabbed the wall for balance, trying desperately to keep his vertigo in check while he kept the unknown desert in view.

The circles of colors and light faded and the pit returned to its normal place below the tunnel opening.

"Powwell, what are you doing down here? Staring at the pit will only mesmerize you into joining it. That is an honor reserved for the dead," Yaala said from right behind him.

Rather than answer the woman, he examined the edges of the tunnel opening, seeking a spell or other anomaly that would explain the sudden vision of distant places.

"Did you hear me, Powwell?" She tugged at his arm, attempting to draw him back through the tunnel. Behind her, Old Bertha belched and chugged in a normal machine rhythm.

"I heard. I also saw another place. I think this archway is a portal to other places." He didn't take his eyes off the opening.

"Nonsense. I told you you were hallucinating. I saw all kinds of things down here when my . . . when Yaassima first banished me. You'll get used to the heat eventually."

"How long have you been here, Yaala?" Powwell finally shifted his gaze from the portal to her face. Her heavy-lidded eyes masked her emotions, almost fading into her pale skin. He wondered briefly if he would take on the same ghastly pallor after an eternity away from sunlight. Her high cheekbones nearly poked through her skin, revealing a long face with a determinedly out-thrust chin.

No one in the pit was overweight. Most of them were gaunt skeletons, wasted away from short rations, debilitating heat and hard work. Yaala was the healthiest of the lot and by the reckoning of some of the old men, had been here longer than most.

How much of that time was exile and how much her own choice? Powwell was suddenly fascinated with this strangely competent and self-assured woman. Almost beautiful underneath the dust and gauntness. The first stirring of interest tingled in his body.

"What use counting time when there is no sun to mark the passage of days?" She kept those heavy eyelids lowered as she turned her gaze to the boiling lava in the pit.

A spurt of lava flared up. She opened her eyes wide in the sudden red light. Powwell had never noticed the color of her eyes beneath her normally heavy lids. He couldn't see it now. A film covered her iris.

"Are you blind, Yaala?" He touched her back with a gentle hand as he looked more closely at her eyes. She dropped her gaze to her boots and wrenched away from his touch.

The pronounced bones of her spine brushed against his palm. The bumps were much bigger than those of a normal person and sharp, very sharp. He jerked his hand away, then tentatively replaced it, needing to make contact with another human being in this hellhole.

"No, I am not blind." She paused and swallowed heavily. "Come. We have work to do. Old Bertha still isn't working properly, and some of the pipes are corroded. They'll have to be replaced."

"I don't want to stay down here, Yaala. I've got to get out of here. I can't live like this."

"Get used to it. Death is the only escape from the pit,

and you've seen how we dispose of the bodies." She turned on her heel and marched back toward the machinery.

Powwell looked once more to the portal, longing for a vision of the green trees that had surrounded Televarn just before he stepped into the tunnel.

The vortex lurched again, spiraling green, red, yellow, and blue—the blue of a Summer sky above Coronnan. His mouth longed for the taste of fresh, sweet water. His skin clamored for relief from the heat. His heart begged for freedom.

"Look, Yaala. It's doing it again!"

"Hallucination born of desperation. I've seen it before." She kept walking away from the portal, one hand on Powwell's sleeve, dragging him with her.

"Trees! It will take us to Coronnan." Powwell pulled his arm free of her grasp and took two rapid steps toward escape.

Don't leave me alone, Kalen's mental voice pleaded with him. *You have to take me with you. You have to get me out of here. You are the only one who loves me.*

He slumped sadly against the wall. He had to wait.

Come to me soon, Kalen. I can't endure this much longer.

CHAPTER 20

"I will have to lie through my teeth to convince these hidebound lords," Quinnault said quietly. He patted Katie's hand where it rested on his arm. Since the conclusion of the negotiations with Kinnsell, he had been in constant touch with her. He kept a gentle hand at the small of her back, her hand on his arm; he brushed a stray curl from her brow; or brushed his leg against hers as they walked.

At each touch her mind brushed his, and he knew completeness. He didn't know everything about her yet. But he knew enough. She still had secrets from him, but she couldn't lie to him.

If she stepped beyond his reach for more than a heartbeat, or withdrew her mind from his, he felt cold and awkward and terribly, achingly alone.

They paused outside the Council Chamber where the lords in residence had been hastily summoned to approve the royal marriage.

"I was told that your government is new. How can these men be hidebound?" Her humor sparkled in her eyes like green stars. A mature humor despite her childlike stature. The top of her head only reached his shoulder. Her figure was hidden beneath her old-fashioned gown with a long train. The heavy woolen fabric must weigh a ton. And she'd worn it beneath the now castoff draperies. Why wasn't she suffering from the heat generated by the thick cloth?

He wished she'd share the joke with him.

"My lords come from a long tradition of caution. Some of them believe that we have recreated the government by the few for the few. My sense of responsibility for the people and the land is new to them. They will see you as a disruption of their carefully protected privilege. Each has a candidate for my bride. They seek only to bind me closer to them and away from others rather than thinking of the security of the entire kingdom."

"Then we will have to convince them that I am precisely what they want me to be, a foreign princess who brings trade to make them rich and you grateful to them for their wealth." Her full lips pouted, and she bit her cheeks trying to hide a smile.

"They will want to see a signed treaty."

"I will have Kinnsell draw one up in the morning." This time the smile burst through her attempts at restraint.

Quinnault lost contact with the Kardia and his head as he stared at her mouth, longing to kiss her.

"We are to be married tomorrow and you haven't kissed me yet. Isn't it customary to seal a betrothal with a kiss?" She looked up at him, mouth slightly parted, eyes completely serious.

"Did you read my mind again?"

"I didn't have to. Kiss me, Scarecrow. Kiss me and make me forget my fears."

"You are a princess. Diplomatic marriages are expected of the offspring of an emperor."

"Diplomatic marriages among our own kind, among cultures that are similar to our own. Marriages that bring close alliances and the chance to visit home once in a while. You need to know that I will never again be able to contact my family or friends. I have sacrificed myself so that my people can have the Tambootie."

"Your plague must be decimating your people terribly."

"Worse."

"Do you have this mysterious plague?" Caution chilled his ardor. "Will your people bring it here, by design or chance?"

"No. I have been one of the lucky ones. The plague is one of the reasons we have disguised our appearances. The veils have been specially made to act as a barrier for the plague. If I should carry the dormant virus and pass it to our children, I know how to distill the Tambootie for a cure. Your people are safe from us."

"Then your people will be saved by the Tambootie and my people will gain a defensible port as well as a queen. When the succession is secured, Coronnan will finally be able to put aside the fear of civil war, provided our marriage doesn't start a new one. I have worked for this moment a long time. I didn't expect to find a wife I could love and cherish, too."

"Will you kiss me to seal the bargain, then?" She reached up to pull his face down to hers.

He brushed his lips tentatively over hers, tasting the butterfly softness of her mouth. He deepened the contact. Passion exploded in him. He pulled her close against him, cherishing the way she filled his arms so naturally.

"Your Grace!" Lord Hanic exclaimed from the doorway. Shock colored his voice.

"Have the lords assembled at my request?" Quinnault asked, reluctantly lifting his head. He wanted to go on kissing Katie forever.

"Your order, more like," Hanic grumbled. "The ambassador from SeLenicca has come as well. He has that secret smile that tells me he expects you to ratify the marriage treaty with *his* princess." He eyed Katie suspiciously.

"I have accepted a better offer, Lord Hanic. Come inside, I will introduce the Council to my betrothed," Quinnault said. Nervousness assailed him. He'd hoped to break the news to the ambassador in private.

He took a deep breath and felt Katie do the same beside him. Suddenly, he knew that he couldn't tell the entire fantastic story to the foreigners. They'd take it as simply a wild tale made up to explain away an inappropriate passion.

"Whatever I say, Katie, please play along with me."

She pressed his hand in agreement.

They entered the crowded Council Chamber together, arms linked. Quinnault took the high-backed dragon throne, gesturing for Katie to sit next to him, in the chair usually reserved for Nimbulan, his chief adviser.

Five magicians sat among the lords, along with three ambassadors. In the center of the table, surrounding the Coraurlia—the fabulous, magical glass crown provided by the dragons—lay five marriage treaties. SeLenicca,

Rossemeyer, and three lords all had eligible daughters. Clearly, all thought tonight's announcement would confirm one of them.

"My Lords, Master Magicians, may I present to you Princess Maarie Kaathliin of . . ." He couldn't claim she was from Varnicia, the usual trading point for the Varns. The king and his bevy of sons were well known to these men. Where could she be from? "Of Terrania." He named a remote and little known country way to the North of Varnicia.

Katie looked at him strangely. *How did you know?* she asked.

Quinnault didn't respond, sensing mental barriers crashing down between them. He'd have to ask her later about Terrania. Later. He plunged on with his speech, almost babbling in his nervousness. "My Lord Konnaught, I cannot accept your offer of your half sister, the illegitimate daughter of Lord Kammeryl d'Astrismos, as my bride. Five years old is just too young to marry. Coronnan needs a queen now." He handed the rolled parchment to his fosterling. The fragile sheepskin was tattered on the edge, signs of much scraping clean and reuse. The boy probably didn't understand the insult this represented. His sister and the marriage weren't worth a new piece of parchment.

"My Lords Hanic and Balthazaan, I must also decline the offers of your very beautiful and gracious daughters. Either one would make an admirable queen. But we are striving to set up a delicate balance of power here in Coronnan. The twelve lords representing the twelve provinces are equal in wealth and authority. I, as your king, must be a neutral binding force among you, a tie-breaking vote, dependent upon you for revenue and all but the most rudimentary warband. If I marry within Coronnan, the alliance will upset that delicate balance."

The ambassador from SeLenicca smiled smugly and crossed his arms in front of him. He sat back, satisfied. Only a frequent flicking of his gaze toward Katie betrayed any questions he might have.

"My Lord of SeLenicca, please inform His Majesty that I cannot in good conscience marry his sister. She deserves a chance at happiness, to marry the man of her own choice rather than an arranged alliance in which she has no say." He picked up the SeLenese treaty and handed it to the ambassador.

The diplomat's face turned purple with barely controlled rage. He grabbed the treaty out of Quinnault's hands, almost tearing the new parchment. "My king will not be happy about this."

"I am sorry. But my decision is made." Quinnault kept his gaze level, daring the ambassador to stalk out and declare war.

The foreign emissary reclaimed his chair, tapping the rejected treaty against the council table angrily. "Moncriith warned us you would reject us. We are prepared to defend the honor of our princess," he said. His eyes narrowed as he held the treaty out to Quinnault for reconsideration.

"If Moncriith the Bloodmage guides your king and princess, then I have even greater reason to seek elsewhere for my bride." Quinnault stared at the ambassador, challenging him to look away first.

At last the man slid the rolled parchment of the treaty into the wide sleeve of his robe.

Quinnault took a deep breath and continued. "My Lord of Rossemeyer, I must also reject the offer of your king's daughter." Quinnault directed his attention to the next issue. "The Three Kingdoms of Coronnan, Rossemeyer, and SeLenicca occupy this continent in an uneasy peace. If I marry a princess from either of my neighbors, I will again upset the balance of power."

"I understand, Your Grace." Ambassador General Jhorge-Rosse nodded his head graciously. He shot a victorious glance at his counterpart from SeLenicca. For the moment, neither one had won over the other.

"Your Grace!" Hanic protested. "You have just given King Lorriin of SeLenicca an excuse to invade us."

"He will seek war anyway. Making their princess my queen would not guarantee our safety. Read your history—or consult with the Lord Sambol about the number of times his border city has faced invasion."

"Reading is a waste of time for all but priests," Hanic scoffed.

"Reading skills may be reserved for priests and magicians, but it is not a waste of time!" Quinnault replied, holding his own anger in check. "I studied history when

I trained to be a priest. I know that SeLenicca tries to take our resources by force every fifteen years or so. They refuse to nurture their own land and see ours as their rightful pantry when they can't buy food elsewhere. Marrying the Princess of SeLenicca will give us a few seasons of peace, nothing more."

The ambassador narrowed his eyes as if he hadn't expected Quinnault to be so well informed.

"Your Grace, you must marry and get an heir," Lord Balthazaan reminded them all. "Do you remember what happened the last time a king of Coronnan failed to do so? We endured three generations of civil war trying to find a successor!" He stood, leaning his knuckles on the table. His eyes blazed with fear. He had suffered large losses during the war. His lovely dark-eyed daughter was the only asset he had left beside a badly damaged keep and nearly ruined farmlands.

"You have rejected all viable offers, Your Grace. Where do we look for a new candidate?" Hanic nearly screamed. He stared at Katie. Questions and fear swept across his face in rapid succession.

"Her Highness, Maarie Kaathliin of Terrania, will be my bride," Quinnault said quietly.

All eyes in the room turned to Katie. She blushed slightly and lowered her eyes in maidenly modesty.

"The treaty I have negotiated with her father, King Kinnsell requires that I marry her tomorrow evening."

"Your Grace!" every lord in the room protested.

"This haste is most unseemly," Hanic said. His eyes narrowed as he scanned the princess, looking for flaws.

"Forgive the interruption, Your Grace, my lords." Old Lyman stood from his chair near the corner. "I realize that magicians are supposed to be neutral advisers in this new government, but I have some pertinent information."

The lords turned their malevolent glares to the aging magician.

"Senior Magician Nimbulan has been in secret negotiation with King Kinnsell for nearly a year." Lyman looked at Quinnault, his eyes twinkling and his mouth twitching at the obvious lie.

Katie coughed delicately into her tiny hand. Quinnault

recognized her failing attempt to keep a straight face. Were the two conspirators in this lie?

"Even now, Nimbulan is working with King Kinnsell in completing the treaty. This marriage has been planned for a long time. But we feared news of it would jeopardize the rather delicate negotiations. A wedding tomorrow will not be in quite so much haste as you imagine." The old man paused while he swallowed deeply. He cocked his head as if listening.

Who gave him orders?

Quinnault hoped desperately that the dragons spoke to him directly.

"Look at our king, my lords!" Hanic turned his attention away from Lyman's almost plausible explanation. After all, Nimbulan wasn't present to confirm or deny the lie. "He's head over heels in love with the chit. He can't have met her more than once. In love after *one* meeting. She's worked some form of enchantment on him. She's a witch or a demon. Who is to say that the legendary country of Terrania even exists? She's a demon, and we cannot allow this marriage!"

"I will marry Princess Maarie Kaathliin tomorrow," Quinnault said through gritted teeth. "The choice is mine and I have made it."

"We will not crown her queen until she proves she is not a demon!" Konnaught stood up so fast he knocked over his chair. "Moncriith predicted this would happen. He was my father's Battlemage. He warned us all about demons—including the king's exiled sister."

"Moncriith would have been exiled or executed, had he lived, because he refused to gather dragon magic. Moncriith drew his power from blood and pain. We don't know how long he would have contented himself with his own blood and the death of small animals. His next victim would have been human, probably one of us," Quinnault reminded them.

"This unknown, possibly false princess, can't gather dragon magic—no woman can. But she might be a magician working in secret to undermine our peace and stability." Hanic sat down, seemingly calm. "She must prove that she is indeed a princess of Terrania and not a rogue witch."

"How?" Cold sweat broke out on Quinnault's brow.

The magicians couldn't access the void with dragon magic to test her talent. All of the usual witch-sniffers who sensed magic in others but had no other talent of their own had been exiled with the other rogues. Only magicians could survive the other tests for magical talent—fire and water. The only way Katie could prove herself innocent of Hanic's accusation was to die.

He wouldn't abuse her trust or the wonderful gifts from her people by allowing these men to murder her in the name of protecting Coronnan from rogue magic.

"The dragons will tell us if she is the right queen for the king they blessed," Lyman said quietly from his corner.

All eyes turned to the Coraurlia in the center of the table. The glass crown shaped like a dragon head and embedded with costly jewels had been a gift from the dragons as a symbol of their tie to the wearer of the crown.

Quinnault relaxed. The dragons approved of Katie. He knew that in his heart.

An evil smile crossed Hanic's face. "Yes, the dragons. She must face a dragon at dawn. Shayla will eat her alive."

"Dragons don't exist. How can they test me?" Katie whispered. Bewilderment erased the smile from her eyes.

"A demon will become hysterical and flee in its true form when faced by a dragon." Hanic's smile spread with confidence. "If this so-called princess of Terrania can remain in human form in the presence of a dragon, we will accept her as your bride, Your Grace."

But no one had seen a dragon in almost a moon. Shayla had announced to one and all that the Covenant was broken. The amount of magic in the air had dwindled. Would she come in answer to this summons?

If she didn't, would Katie survive another test dreamed up by these superstitious lords?

CHAPTER 21

"Those, 'wires,' as you call them, barely fit through that conduit. How do you expect me to crawl in there and find the broken one?" Powwell asked Yaala. He eyed the narrow tunnel skeptically. He'd just begun to get used to the miles of Kardia above his head and breathe almost naturally within this extensive cave system. The bottom of the conduit rose man height above the cavern where he stood. It couldn't contain enough air for both him and the bundle of wires.

An eerie sensation crawled over his skin; it felt as if he were being watched. He looked hastily in all directions. A flicker of white moved beyond his peripheral vision as fast as he turned his head.

More hallucinations. Or so Yaala said. But she said that Televarn's portal was imaginary, too.

"The conduit is wide enough. I've crawled through it a number of times," Yaala said as she cupped her hands to boost Powwell up.

"You're thinner than I am. And some of the others are narrower in the shoulders than I. Why me?" Powwell kept both feet firmly on the ground, lungs laboring mightily at the thought of entering that tiny tunnel. He'd already discovered that, in the pit, Yaala gave orders and everyone obeyed her without question—except the new man, Piedro, and he'd learn soon enough. Yaala was the Kaalipha of the pit, just as Yaassima was Kaalipha of the city above them.

"You haven't lost your intelligence, so you will recognize the broken wire when you find it," she said, motioning for him to place his foot into her hands.

"You've been here longer than most everyone else. Why haven't you lost your intelligence?"

"Because I haven't given in to my fears and panic.

Because I love the machines. I'd rather live here with them than aboveground with Yaassima."

"Then why don't you go into that conduit? You know these machines—you love these machines as if they were your familiars."

"You will go, Powwell, because I'm training you to know and love these machines as if they were more than your familiars. They are family. The day will come when you will need them. They will need you. I need another engineer to keep things going."

"Yaala!" a man's voice echoed down the corridor from the upper levels of the pit. "Yaala, they need the engineer to fix something above."

Powwell jumped at the words. *"Above!"*

"Coming," Yaala called back. "You'd better come, too. You need to know how Yaassima's toys work." She strode toward the passage out of this small cavern. A very deep cavern. "Oh, and as soon as we get beyond the gate, I'm no longer Yaala. I'm the Engineer. Yaassima doesn't bother with names as long as the job gets done. She thinks I'm dead. I want her to continue thinking that until . . . until I'm ready."

"We're getting out of here? Yaala, if I get out of this place, I won't come back." Powwell could only think of clean sweet air and natural light.

"Yes, you will come back. There isn't anyplace else to go, and I'm not yet ready to kill Yaassima. I have to know everything about these machines before I'll have the power to murder my mother and take her place as Kaalipha."

* * *

"I see that the dragon bitch gave you one of the better pieces of jewelry," Maia sneered as she sorted laundry in Myri's bedroom. "Televarn won't like it."

"I don't care what Televarn likes and doesn't like," Myri replied. She sat rocking in the nursing chair. Amaranth suckled greedily. Her tug against Myri's breast sent a deep wave of satisfaction through her entire being. The faint milky scent of the baby and the smell of fresh sunshine in the laundry almost made her content. Almost.

The weight of the necklace and her own lack of freedom preyed on her mind. How was she to escape if the
necklace killed her as she left the palace? Nastfa and
Golin had already shown their sympathy with her by
escorting her politely around the palace rather than mo-
lesting her as Yaassima promised. They hadn't said anything the dragon pendant couldn't relay to Yaassima.
But Myri sensed their emotions. Nastfa in particular. He
didn't belong here and wanted out as badly as she.

Every time she was with the proud member of the
assassins guild, she had more questions about him than
before. All she knew for sure was that he'd help her
escape if she could break the necklace. If . . . how?

She sent the chair rocking faster to absorb her emotions before the baby sensed her disquiet and became
fretful. The old wood of the chair creaked in time to
her movement.

She and Maia moved around each other in cautious,
untouching circles, sharing the room, the rocker, the
laundry—but never the baby. Maia didn't push the issue
of nursing Amaranth unless Yaassima was present. Since
the Kaalipha had given the necklace to Myri, she left
the two younger women alone a lot.

Neither Myri nor Maia seemed to want to openly an-
tagonize the other. Equally, they were unwilling to
offer friendship.

"Well, you'd better start thinking about what Televarn
wants. He won't leave you here for long. He never gives
up something he claims as his own," Maia said bitterly.
She snapped the diaper she was folding so hard the air
crackled around it.

"Including you and Kestra?" Myri asked. He'd surrendered both women to Yaassima's brothel as part of
his "rent" here in Hanassa.

"We are only on loan until he's ready to reclaim us,"
Maia said weakly. She dipped her head, suddenly very
busy folding a mountain of diapers.

"You don't say that as if you believe it."

"I say what I am told to say."

"Told by Televarn. I know something of the way he
controls your actions and your mind. You don't have to
put up with him."

"You don't know anything." Maia closed her mouth with a snap and turned her rigid back on Myri.

"I know that Televarn has to control everything he touches—including the minds and thoughts of his clan. You don't have to go back to Yaassima's brothel. You have other choices. Other men are not so selfish. Another man will give you a healthy baby. Your baby died because its father was too closely related to you. My husband didn't father your child. Televarn did." Myri repeated the rumors she'd overheard in her exploration of the palace. She longed to say more. The necklace reminded her that Yaassima heard every word spoken in Myri's presence.

"For women in Hanassa, there is no other choice. I accept Televarn's orders or Yaassima's, and they both want me to be the toy of any man they choose. Any other action brings death or the pit." Maia gulped, then firmed her chin.

"As soon as any child I bear is weaned, Televarn will take him from me, just as he took my first son from me," Maia continued. "I thought that Nimbulan was strong enough to change things in the clan, but he deserted me. He deserted you, too. We're both Yaassima's whores right now. That jewelry marks you as clearly as the tattoo she put on my butt." Angrily Maia flipped up her skirt and dropped her drawers enough to reveal the outline of a dragon drawn in blue ink spread across her left cheek. "The dragon bitch enjoyed every scream I let loose. She watched while her men did this to me, and she drooled while they did it. I couldn't sit or lie on my back for over a week afterward.

"Does Televarn know?" Thankfully Amaranth drifted off to sleep, little milk bubbles caressing her puckered lips. The baby wouldn't know the horror Myri felt at the evidence of Yaassima's continued cruelty. Some of her resentment of the Rover woman drained away. They had both been used by Televarn. They were both victims of Yaassima's complicated plans.

"I don't know. He wasn't there when they did it to me. He won't like it if he sees it. It marks me as Yaassima's property, not his."

Myri longed to reassure the woman that she would

include her in the escape plans. She couldn't promise. Kalen, Powwell, and Amaranth had to take priority.

"Neither Televarn nor Yaassima will give up anything they possess," Maia reminded her. "Remember that when you try to escape. They'll kill you rather than give you up. Your children, too."

"What makes you think I plot escape?" Myri asked mildly, remembering that Yaassima listened.

"Because you're a dragon just like the Kaalipha. You have to try, and you will die in the process."

*   *   *

Nimbulan and Rollett wandered into a wineshop—one of a dozen or so scattered throughout Hanassa. So far they'd discovered no inns. People either slept in the cave of their sponsor or sat up all night, drinking and gambling. All of the businesses seemed to be owned by the Kaalipha and run by people loyal to her. How deep that loyalty ran, Nimbulan couldn't tell without a great deal of money for bribes. The guards at the gate had stolen his only valuable coins.

Perhaps they'd get a little information in this hovel built out from the back side of a large rock formation. He assumed that all life within Hanassa took its orientation from the palace which dominated the South wall of the crater. The outcropping stood between the wineshop and the palace. The gate—the only gate into or out of the city—lay on the West side of Hanassa. This place was dirtier and more decrepit than all of the other wineshops combined. The Kaalipha's authority seemed less present, out of sight of the palace.

The stench of unwashed bodies, spilled wine, garbage, and refuse assaulted Nimbulan's senses. He shuddered in revulsion beneath his enveloping robes. He thought he'd become inured to the filth in the city. This shop was worse, much worse than he'd thought. Information might come cheaper here.

Rollett loosened his belt knife. His eyes shifted restlessly in the gloom. Instinctively he stepped behind Nimbulan, guarding his back.

No one seemed to notice their entry. Strangers must not be that unusual here. Nimbulan sat down on a backless stool, the only empty one, near the center of the four-table room. One leg was shorter than the others and he teetered precariously, grabbing the table for balance. The crude planks wobbled when he braced his weight. Five cups of wine already on the table sloshed onto the stained and scarred surface.

Rollett remained standing, wary and alert. Nimbulan had never fully appreciated the young man's ability to observe and absorb detail until now. By the time they left, Rollett would know much more about the people in this wineshop than Nimbulan could have found out in days of conversation.

Five pairs of eyes glared at him with anger and distaste. The owners of those eyes all wore the uniform loose black robes and turbans of Rossemeyerian mercenaries. Dangerous men to offend.

He shrugged and held up his hand to order his own drink and one for Rollett, though he knew his journeyman wouldn't drink it until he had finished observing.

After several long moments of silence, Nimbulan raised his eyes from his cup of rancid wine to confront his equally silent companions. "Where does one find a woman in this town?" he asked.

The man across from him smiled so that the scar running temple to temple across the bridge of his nose whitened. His eyelids didn't shift. "Depends on what kind of woman you want," he replied.

"The Kaalipha keeps the best ones in the palace for her private guards. Our sponsor has a few for his men. Lots of hiring right now. You interested in hiring on?" asked the fair-skinned teenager to Nimbulan's left. His skin wasn't dark enough for him to be a native of Rossemeyer.

Nimbulan schooled his face to keep from betraying his questions.

"How's your sponsor pay?" This was the most information Nimbulan had been able to glean from a night of drinking in every shop in Hanassa.

"One Rosse a day during downtime. Two while on campaign. A share in the loot if we win," Scarface answered. "And free access to his women. They aren't the youngest or the prettiest, but they're all pros and you don't have to tip unless you really want to." He grinned again, revealing several gaps in his teeth.

"What's he hiring for?" Nimbulan asked.

"Big invasion of Coronnan from SeLenicca. Every sponsor in Hanassa is looking for experienced men. Your robes and turbans mark you as veterans."

Nimbulan nodded. "I'll think about it."

"You want to look at the women first?" The teenager laughed and slapped Nimbulan's back.

"I like blondes myself," Nimbulan said.

Everyone in the room stilled.

Nimbulan's heart beat loudly within his chest. What had he said wrong? Rollett shifted his body closer to Nimbulan, so that their backs touched and no one obstructed their peripheral vision.

"Only true blondes in the city are the Kaalipha and her heir," the teenager whispered. He hadn't removed his hand from Nimbulan's back. "Don't talk about them, and don't ask to see them. Kaalipha Yaassima sells all blonde captives within a day."

Nimbulan's skin crawled. How else would one describe Myrilandel's almost colorless hair other than blonde? One of the two women had to be his wife. The vision had shown Myri to be in Hanassa. What was she doing in the palace, the Kaalipha's designated heir? He believed she had been kidnapped by Televarn.

Reluctant babble broke out across the room as the drinkers recovered from Nimbulan's stated preference. He knew the Kaalipha was respected, almost revered, she had the power of life and death over all within Hanassa and dispensed her favors liberally, with conditions. He hadn't known the depth of fear she inflicted upon her people.

"We need the work. Blondes or no blondes in the brothel." Nimbulan decided to change the subject. Maybe he could work his way back to Myri and the Kaalipha later.

"You got into Hanassa, you can't be a spy for Coronnan. Spies get murdered in the entrance tunnel. Our captain needs men willing to commit for a year. His Majesty of SeLenicca put out a call for every mercenary company that's willing. Paying well, I hear. No questions asked. Seems there's to be no restraint on looting and slaves when he wins the war." Scarface's mouth twitched as if savoring a fine delicacy. He placed his hand on the teenager's shoulder. Indirectly, he was in contact with Nimbulan.

Magicians did that to read a stranger's mind. Was he overly suspicious or were these men magicians in disguise? That would account for the pale skin.

Nimbulan gulped back a retort. He had to get back to Coronnan fast. Quinnault needed this information to mount a defense. What had the new king done to precipitate an invasion? Nimbulan had only been gone a few days.

He couldn't leave Hanassa without Myri and Powwell and Kalen. He had to find Maia and her baby, too.

"Moncriith's coming!" a man shouted from the doorway.

Several drinkers scrambled out the door. Rollett took one step away from Nimbulan, as if to follow them. When Nimbulan didn't immediately run from the pub, Rollett resumed his protective stance.

Why not run? Moncriith will recognize you, he asked telepathically.

Nimbulan didn't answer immediately. His senses reeled with this second blow. Moncriith. The Bloodmage who had stalked Coronnan from one end to the other preaching against demons. He saw Myrilandel as the source of all demonic evil in Coronnan.

Our drinking companions look wary but not alarmed, he replied finally. Then out loud he asked, "I heard Moncriith died a year ago. Struck down by King Quinnault's magicians in battle."

"Take more than a dragon to kill that one. Better hide your magic deep, stranger," the teenager advised.

Nimbulan raised one eyebrow in question.

"The dragon bitch has her knickers in a twist about foreign magicians. She gave Moncriith permission to sponsor his own mercenary camp if he'd root out a foreign magician with a blue aura," the young man continued.

Dragon bitch? Myrilandel carried dragon blood in her veins.

"New law announced three or four weeks ago, right after the Rovers delivered the heir to the Kaalipha.

Seems some foreign magician was holding the woman hostage with magic. Most crimes, the Kaalipha gives a man a trial before she lops off his head. For the crime of being an unidentified magician with blue in his aura, it's immediate death and a huge reward to the accuser. That's when we became mercenaries instead of Battle-mages for hire."

"But there's no blue in your auras," Nimbulan protested.

"Why take the chance?" Scarface replied. "Moncriith can't be trusted. He sees auras, the Kaalipha doesn't. He could accuse anyone and she'd be happy to execute the man just to see the blood spill. We're safe as long as we don't work magic in Hanassa. You, on the other hand, radiate blue in all directions."

CHAPTER 22

Televarn tapped his foot impatiently. Wiggles raced around his toes in sympathy. Kalen had sent him a message by way of her familiar to meet her in this narrow corridor near the palace kitchens. She was late.

Why was it that in the outer world women jumped to his command and took no action without his permission? But here, in Hanassa, he did nothing but wait for women to make up their minds?

It was all Yaassima's fault. She'd pay dearly for giving women ideas of power and independence.

Soon. He was almost ready to depose the Kaalipha and yank her dragon throne right out from under her skinny bottom.

He smiled slightly. Yaassima had done him a favor without knowing it. She had placed Kalen in a position of trust within her household.

He had to watch Kalen closely. He'd spent several moons corrupting her before he'd kidnapped Myrilandel into Hanassa. Why the girl had chosen to betray Myri, the only adult who had not used Kalen and her talent for their own ends, he had no idea.

Televarn had promised Kalen power in the new regime. That promise had granted him cooperation—not trust or loyalty.

The girl owed loyalty only to herself and could betray him at the least offense. When she did, Yaassima's retribution would be terrible and swift.

When she betrayed him. Why hadn't he thought "If she betrayed him?"

He expected betrayal, just as Kalen did. Better the snake he knew than the viper he didn't.

Wiggles stopped playing with Televarn's foot. The

creature ceased all motion in mid-ripple. His back fur stood up. Then he darted along the corridor to the next bend. He seemed to flow around the imperfections in the tunnel like liquid fur.

Televarn held his breath. Why had the ferret deserted him? His hand shifted to his belt knife without conscious thought. The fine blade he had stashed at the entrance to the pit rather than risk the searches at the palace gate.

Piedro guarded the growing stash of weapons in the pit. He also sought the secrets of the monstrous machines Yaassima seemed to cherish.

Two heartbeats later, Kalen appeared. She bent to gather the ferret into her arms. A smile lit Kalen's eyes as she nuzzled her familiar.

Wiggles joyfully slithered up to her shoulder and draped himself around her neck like a lover. His needle-sharp teeth chattered perilously close to the great artery in her neck.

A lump of apprehension formed in Televarn's throat. What if the animal had turned rabid? He kept his hand on his knife wondering if he could move fast enough to kill the ferret without harming Kalen.

He pushed aside his concern for the girl. She was a tool. Nothing more. Tools could be replaced.

"You're late," he snapped out his words more harshly and louder than he'd intended. It might be the middle of the night, but the nearby kitchen bustled with activity all day, every day, without stop. The staff never knew when the Kaalipha might order a meal for one or a hundred. Anyone of them could spot him talking to Kalen and report to Yaassima.

"I don't have the freedom of the palace like some people," she returned, just as harshly.

"Where is Myrilandel, and will she help us overthrow Yaassima?" He started pacing, pointedly not looking at the little girl. She'd grown in the two weeks since he'd seen her. Her body was losing its boxy shape and had started showing signs of the curves she would eventually develop. But she was still a little girl and he was not interested in her. Myrilandel was the only woman he lusted after.

"She will help. I have made certain of that. But she refuses to believe Nimbulan dead. Tell me again how you accomplished it so that I can give her the grisly details. Maybe then she will accept my word as truth," Kalen ordered. She continued to caress Wiggles rather than direct her gaze to Televarn.

Televarn looked at her through narrowed eyes, resenting her lack of respect for him. He had to play his hand carefully with her or trigger betrayal.

He turned his thoughts to the problem before them. Myrilandel had to be convinced that her husband had died. She would never become his queen as long as Nimbulan lived. She'd made vows before a priest, vows that could only be broken by death. Once released from her miserable husband, she would welcome Televarn again as she had for a brief time a year ago.

"I didn't see Nimbulan die," he admitted.

"What do you mean, you did not see him die? He has to be dead!"

"I set the drap. Wiggles was part of it and returned to me when it was sprung. Ask him how the magician died." Televarn resumed his pacing. A niggle of doubt thrust its way into his brain. Nimbulan had to be dead. Wiggles had slithered under the sealed door. But he couldn't leave the magician's private quarters until the door opened—the magic of the spell bound him there as it did the Water. The Water had supported Wiggles, kept him from drowning. Nimbulan had the only key to the door.

"Someone drowned in your trap," Kalen muttered, gazing deeply into the ferret's eyes. A look of rapt joy softened her features while she communed with her familiar. Hints of adult beauty—cold and austere—showed in the planes of her face and the luster in her clear gray eyes.

The only other time he'd seen her look so happy, so vulnerable was . . . never. Televarn wondered when she had become so bitter.

"Wiggles ran past a male, with Water following close behind in an angry wave. As he exited the building, he brushed against two more males, taller men. They smelled mature. The first one's scent wasn't as strong." Kalen looked up, startled. "Nimbulan might not be dead. The male who triggered the trap was just a boy."

"*S'murgit!* That man has more lives than a cat. What do I have to do to kill him?"

"Nothing. All that is important is that Myri believes he is dead and that Yaassima ordered the assassination."

"The Kaalipha put out a contract, and I accepted it. But she won't pay up until I can prove he's dead." He slammed one fist into the palm of his other hand. He needed that money to pay men to storm the palace. Hundreds of men fighting alongside every Rover he could secretly gather into Hanassa. They wouldn't do it without money. A lot of money.

But if Myrilandel or Kalen could be coerced into killing Yaassima first, his plan would prove much easier to carry out.

"Tell Myrilandel what you know. Tell her how Wiggles witnessed the death of the only person who could open Nimbulan's sealed door. Remind her that Yaassima controls the reward for the death of Nimbulan and Quinnault. Tell her whatever you have to so that Myrilandel demands revenge. Revenge by her own hand. Yaassima will die and Myrilandel will be my queen. I will give her children she can adore, children who have no connection to the magician who enslaved her for her talent."

"If either woman lets you live long enough to rule." Kalen smiled sarcastically with one corner of her mouth. She continued stroking Wiggles.

*   *   *

"I've never heard of a magician hiding his talent before," Nimbulan said around a very dry throat.

"Then learn to do it in a hurry." Scarface grabbed Nimbulan's wrist on the table. "I'll take you into a trance and show you where to look."

Nimbulan didn't have time to ask why these men were cutthroat mercenaries in Hanassa when they might be employed as honest magicians elsewhere. The void opened before his eyes as Scarface breathed deeply in the first stages of trance. Nimbulan followed him, sensing the urgency. Rollett moved closer, placing his hand on top of Scarface's. Nimbulan wasn't certain if his companion joined the trance or merely monitored it.

Three deep breaths brought him into rapport with

Aaddler, Scarface. The void revealed true names, ideals, and faults. Nimbulan scanned his companion carefully, seeking a source of trust. Before he could examine more than the constant pain behind his eyes from the old wound, Aaddler said, "Nimbulan, I know you from old. We faced each other as Battlemages. I know you to be honest and true to your oaths. Trust me. Look into your heart's aura. Look for the beacon."

Nimbulan had never heard of an individual organ having an aura, he'd always looked at the layers of energy that enveloped the entire body. Those layers had to begin somewhere.

Another's colors were always easier to see than one's own. He searched Aaddler in the region of his heart. Sure enough, a tiny flare of dark green light pulsed there. Dark green suited Aaddler—suppressed fire hiding behind logic and reason. He remembered him now. They had fought to a standstill fifteen years ago. Both patrons had withdrawn from the battle. Aaddler had saluted Nimbulan in respect for his talent and retreated honorably.

Find your own beacon. This is the core of your magic. The beginning and the end. Find it quickly.

Do it! Rollett added. *I sense Moncriith is very close. His thoughts revolve around destroying every magician he encounters.*

Nimbulan looked deep within himself. He knew his signature color was blue, had identified it long ago when still an apprentice. The layers of his own energy flared and blinded him.

Follow the life-cord backward! If a mental voice could hiss, Aaddler hissed. *I can't afford to be caught with you, Nimbulan. Your guilt will become my guilt. You are the magician Yaassima seeks to eliminate. You are the husband of her heir and the only person who can take the heir and her baby away.*

The news of a baby slid into his awareness. Did Yaassima have control of Maia's baby as well as Myrilandel?

With a deep breath, Nimbulan found the blue-and-silver umbilical that trailed from his corporeal body into the void. Wrapped tightly around it was a crystal-and-pale-lavender umbilical. *Myrilandel!* He'd found her at last. If he followed her umbilical, he'd be beside her in an instant. But only in his mind. Living bodies couldn't traverse the void.

He traced the umbilical back into his own body. Each layer of energy was thicker, more resilient. He pushed harder until he faced a blazing blue light like a thousand sapphires sparkling in sunlight.

There. Now grasp the beacon and place it atop the physical table.

Nimbulan followed instructions. The pulsing blue energy didn't want to leave his body. His magical talent had defined his life for so long it had become entwined with his very soul.

Yank it out. Now. We haven't time to waste. The Bloodmage enters this abode, Rollett ordered as his own blue-and-red beacon slid into the wood grain of the table's surface.

Reluctantly, Nimbulan thrust the beacon out of his body. Once free of his personal energy, the light dimmed. He needed all of his willpower to keep himself from rejoining with his talent. His body was but an empty shell without it.

Drop the damn thing onto the table. Aaddler nearly deafened Nimbulan's mental hearing.

He obeyed. His talent spread out into a gentle puddle with clearly defined edges. His talent filled a space shaped like a hand, fingers slightly curved—the gesture he used to gather magic. Aaddler's puddle took on the shape of an open mouth, tongue tasting the air. Rollett's looked like two eyes connected by a furrowed brow.

Let your talent merge with the wood. The Bloodmage can't find it embedded in an inanimate object. Good. Now lighten your trance so that you are aware of your body and the room around you. You will have to react to Moncriith as if he is no threat. Aaddler withdrew slightly from the rapport he and Nimbulan shared.

"Don't take your hands off the table." Scarface nudged Nimbulan's knee with his boot beneath the wooden surface. "You have to stay in contact with your talent, or you'll lose it forever."

CHAPTER 23

Nimbulan kept his eyes glued to his wine cup. He waited for the hair on the back of his neck to bristle as a warning that Moncriith approached. His body remained inert. The faint sensory tingles on his skin that told him much of what happened around him evaporated with the removal of his talent.

Colors faded before his eyes. A general numbness began to creep through his body. He bit his lip to control his panic.

He pressed his hand harder against the table where his talent lay. The wooden surface contained six other puddles. None of the five mercenaries, nor Rollett, seemed overly concerned with the separation from their talents.

Nimbulan's knuckles turned white where he gripped the table.

"He'll leave soon enough." Scarface grinned in sympathy. "He's single-minded enough to ignore anyone without an obvious talent."

"He could get us into the palace, Nimbulan. He has the Kaalipha's ear," Rollett whispered.

"I won't risk becoming his ally," Nimbulan replied. "He's too dangerous."

Nimbulan heard footsteps behind him. Heavily booted feet. He couldn't detect any other clues to the man's identity and nearly panicked. He needed his talent to survive.

Moncriith would sense the talent and condemn him on the spot.

"Stand up, soldier," Moncriith ordered. He pressed a knee into Nimbulan's back as a prod.

Nimbulan resisted the urge to turn and look at the man, see how he had changed in the last year. He

wanted to demand how the man dared survive the last
battle in Coronnan when Ackerly, Nimbulan's assistant
and oldest friend, had died. Instead, he said defiantly,
"You ain't my officer."

Scarface nodded ever so slightly in acknowledgment
of the tactic.

"Yaassima, Kaalipha of Hanassa, gave me the authority to sponsor my own troop of mercenaries. Lorriin,
King of SeLenicca, marches into Coronnan as soon as I
have gathered my forces. I can gather soldiers any way
I choose to. I choose all of you present."

"You'll have to debate that with our captain,"
Scarface said. "We have signed blood oaths to follow
him to the death."

Nimbulan gulped back a protest. He couldn't sign an
oath like that. He had no intention of staying with these
men any longer than he had to. As soon as he found
Myri, he would leave and never return.

"Your captain fell to my blade less than an hour ago,"
Moncriith boasted.

All heads turned to stare at a man's severed right
hand. Two rings glinted on the lifeless fingers. Blood
dripped from the stump onto the floor. Even if the
owner of the hand lived, he'd never wield a sword again.

Moncriith held his bloody trophy up in his left hand
while he twirled a long knife in his right. Traces of blood
lingered on the blade.

"I'm surprised he didn't bring the man's head,"
Scarface muttered bitterly.

"The head would involve an instant kill. No more
pain. As long as he has the hand and the victim lives,
he can fuel his magic with the pain," Nimbulan replied.
Outrage at Moncriith's casual dismissal of life boiled up
from his gut.

Briefly, Nimbulan noted the new scars that creased
the Bloodmage's face and arms. He hadn't given up his
vile magic that required blood and pain for fuel. If he
was recruiting mercenaries, his war would be a crusade.
With the new invasion of Coronnan by SeLenicca, Moncriith could carry his demon hunt right back to the dragons that now protected King Quinnault and the
Commune of Magicians—presuming they would return
now that he actively searched for Myri.

What had he said? King Lorriin marched when Moncriith was ready! Who organized this campaign, the king or the Bloodmage?

Stargods! he had to get back to the capital soon, with his wife, Kalen, and Powwell. He didn't know either of Myri's adopted children well, but he'd not leave behind anyone she loved.

"By your oaths in blood you must now follow me, the man who defeated your captain in single combat." Moncriith kicked the stool out from under the teenager to Nimbulan's right. The boy lurched sideways, keeping one hand on the tabletop.

Nimbulan bit his lip to keep from crying out. The boy's fingers had slipped away from the puddle of his talent. He darted a look to Scarface to see if this condemned the boy to a mundane life or not.

Scarface replied with a tiny shake of the head, then lifted his chin ever so slightly toward the teenager's puddle. It had spread within the grain of wood to reach his fingertips.

Nimbulan relaxed a little. As long as he touched some portion of the table, his talent was safe.

"By my vision from the Stargods and the authority of the Kaalipha, I claim your loyalty. I have the power to make you obey me." Moncriith touched the partially coagulated blood on the hand and chanted a string of unrecognizable words.

Even without his magic, Nimbulan recognized the spell the Bloodmage wove—a compulsion to follow him blindly.

"We have to get out of here, fast," he whispered to Scarface.

"Not without my talent. If I grab it and run past the Bloodmage, he'll know me for what I am."

"Is there another way out of here?"

"Not unless you want to dig a hole through solid rock into the volcano."

"If we let him capture us, we'll get into the palace. We can turn on him once we're inside," Rollett reminded them.

Moncriith increased the volume of his chant. All around them, men's faces took on glazed looks. Already the need to obey pushed at Nimbulan. He willed it aside.

"On my count of five, grab your talent and run for the door, don't try to attack the Bloodmage, and don't look back," Nimbulan murmured to the men closest to him. "Whatever you do, don't touch Moncriith or that bloody artifact. If you do, you will be marked by magic, and he'll be able to follow and command you anywhere."

Five men nodded. Nimbulan kept his eyes on Moncriith, waiting for the crucial moment between partial awareness while he set up the spell and a full trance when he had total command of everyone within reach of his aura.

"One . . . two . . . three, four, five!" Nimbulan closed his eyes, wrapped both hands around the tiny sapphire beacon on the table and dashed for the door.

Moncriith ended his chant and spread his arms to gather the auras of all the men in the room.

Nimbulan ducked and rolled past the Bloodmage. Moncriith's hand brushed his shoulder. He opened his eyes wide, fully aware.

"Nimbulan! There. Grab the foreign magician. Yaassima will reward us greatly for his head!" Moncriith shouted.

Rollett stumbled into Moncriith, knocking the heavier man off balance. He fell against the table Nimbulan and the others had just vacated. The bloody hand flew out of Moncriith's grasp and landed flat against Rollett's chest.

The young man's eyes glazed over. His mouth gaped slightly. He turned and faced Moncriith, obedient and docile.

In unison with the men in the wineshop, Rollett unsheathed his sword and marched after Nimbulan.

*   *   *

Sweat broke out on Televarn's brow and under his arms. His legs twitched restlessly beneath his sleeping furs. He flung out his arms seeking his bedmate. His mate. His bride.

Myrilandel.

He clutched only cold air within the Rover cavern in Hanassa. Thirty-three days she had been his in that secluded cove on the Great Bay. His, body and soul. Over a year had passed since he had possessed her unconditional love.

Over a year since she had deserted him. Myrilandel, the only woman who had ever left *him*. He couldn't rest until he bedded her again and wiped the memory of Nimbulan from her mind.

Enough! He thrust his sleeping furs into the corner. He'd not wait another day to wrest control of Hanassa from Yaassima's hands. By the time the sun set again, he would claim Myrilandel as his wife, and together they would dip their hands in the Kaalipha's blood.

"Get up." He kicked his uncle in the small of the older man's back. "Marshal all of our people and give them weapons. We storm the palace from within and without at dawn."

"Where are you going?" Uncle Vaanyim groaned and pressed his hands where Televarn had kicked him. Then he sat up and rubbed his eyes sleepily.

"To claim some favors a scar-faced mercenary owes me."

"What about the slaves, do we arm them, too?"

"Why not? We need numbers of people to overwhelm the guards before they can slap their wands and freeze us all."

"The slaves may turn on us and try to escape."

"So what? They will cause more chaos at the gates. Arm everyone you can find. If you run out of weapons here, you know where we have stored the extras in the pit." Another advantage of the dragongate. Over the past two years, he'd brought in large numbers of swords, spears, and clubs from outside and hidden them in the rabbit warren of tunnels that led beneath the palace to the pit. The means of the Kaalipha's destruction had never passed her guards with their detection wands.

He reminded himself to force the secret of those wands from Yaassima before he lopped off her head with her own execution weapon.

"Televarn, tell Scarface to bring all of his magician companions." Uncle Vaanyim rolled stiffly to his knees. "We'll need them to neutralize the wands at the palace gate."

*   *   *

What to do with the loose talent in his hands? Nimbulan wondered as he ran from the filthy wineshop.

His table companions ran past him, also holding their
magical abilities in their hands. They all needed a moment of quiet privacy to reabsorb the talents.

Rollett. What had the boy done with his talent? Nimbulan needed his magic to break Moncriith's spell upon
the journeyman magician. But his talent made him an
easily recognizable target.

The sound of marching feet behind him spurred Nimbulan to run faster in his companions' wake. He stumbled over an imperfection in the ground. His knee
twisted under him with an audible crack. He resisted the
urge to brace his fall with his hands. His face met the
Kardia. A sharp rock stabbed his chest. Fire ran up his
leg from the wrenched ligaments in his knee.

"Spread out, men. Bring me that magician alive!"
Moncriith ordered.

The Kardia reverberated beneath Nimbulan's body
from the force of the men marching in unison. Probably
thinking in unison, too. Televarn's spells did that to his
followers as well.

Nimbulan turned over, still cupping his hands around
his talent. He needed a place to hide it and himself. An
inanimate object he could hold.

His staff! Where in Simurgh's hells was the thing?

As he thought about his valuable tool, a long stick
rolled toward him, resting against his hands where he
held his talent. The staff had found the magic talent that
had molded the grain and shaped the knobs and bends
in the once straight tree branch.

Quickly Nimbulan thrust the tiny blue beacon into the
staff, a nearly inanimate object that Moncriith should
not sense.

He still had to break the Bloodmage's hold upon
Rollett. Perhaps there was a mundane method. What?
Villagers used them all the time to break curses, real
and imaginary. He'd never paid enough attention to the
lives of people outside the army and the training of
Battlemages. Myri would know.

The footsteps came closer. Nimbulan tucked his miserable knee beneath him. He bit his lip until he tasted
blood to keep from crying out in pain. Awkwardly he

scrunched into the nearest shadow. His staff seemed to melt into the darkness with him.

A blazing light illuminated the stretch of path he'd just measured his length against. He stared at the bloody hand that held aloft the witchlight. Moncriith. The Bloodmage had slashed his own palm to fuel the light.

Nimbulan ducked his face deep within his folded arms to keep the light from reflecting off his pale skin. Through his closed eyelids, he sensed more light. Had Rollett added his own abilities to Moncriith's?

Stargods, he wished his talent was intact. But Moncriith would seek it out. Slay him on the spot and collect a huge reward for the deed.

More light crept through his closed eyes. Moncriith must be flooding the area with balls of witchlight. The glow dimmed as the Bloodmage's spell faded.

He heard a cry, and the light blazed once more. Nimbulan winced in sympathy with whichever man suffered the slash of Moncriith's wickedly sharp knife for the sake of a little more magic light. He had to rescue Rollett before he became a victim.

If ever Moncriith's compulsion on these hardened mercenaries fell apart, they'd turn on him. Nimbulan didn't have time to wait for that, nor the privacy and peace to set a counterspell to Moncriith's terrible compulsions.

The footsteps moved on, more slowly as the men searched for Nimbulan with mundane senses. Or were they searching at all? Maybe only Moncriith looked. The mercenaries could be just following him. In which case, the Bloodmage would use his magic to seek Nimbulan's magic. That brief touch in the wineshop had given Moncriith a glimpse of Nimbulan's magical signature, all he'd need under normal circumstances.

But Nimbulan's magic was now embedded in the staff, not his body.

Slowly he stood up, using the staff to brace his painful knee.

"I'm getting too old for this kind of adventure," he muttered as his back resisted straightening and his shoulder revealed another wrenching injury.

He limped in the direction Scarface had taken. He

needed help finding Myri and getting out of here. The magician mercenaries seemed his only chance.

"There, grab that man! He was with the magician we seek," Moncriith commanded ahead of Nimbulan and to the left.

Nimbulan swallowed back his instinct to run in the opposite direction. He couldn't. He needed Scarface. The man had befriended him with cooperation and an important lesson in magic. Battlemages weren't known for sharing anything magic. If Scarface could gather dragon magic, he'd make a valuable contribution to the Commune.

If they could escape the city. If they found Myri.

He limped forward as quietly as he could. One hundred paces from his hiding place, he encountered the backs of the men from the wineshop. They stood in a half ring around Moncriith. Rollett stood in the exact center of the lineup. Backed up against the wall of a small building, Scarface and one of his compatriots defended themselves with their staffs. They batted off the fireballs and truth spells Moncriith flung at them.

Nimbulan ducked one of the repelled balls. He almost smiled at the image of turning this bloodsport into a game. He presumed the magicians had also embedded their talents into their staffs. How else could their tools combat Moncriith's magic so accurately?

A crowd of noisy gawpers drifted closer. Nimbulan needed to get his new friends and Rollett free before the locals realized the reward attached to his capture. He had no doubts any of them would gladly sell him, alive or dead, to the Kaalipha.

Nimbulan tapped Rollett on the shoulder. He took one step to his left. Nimbulan slipped into place beside him, directly behind Moncriith. The Bloodmage didn't take his attention off Scarface and his comrade.

From this new vantage point, Nimbulan surveyed the faces of the mercenaries standing shoulder to shoulder in a near perfect half circle. Their faces remained blank and unresponsive. A few revealed muscle twitches of resistance in their shoulders and fingers. Nimbulan didn't need his talent to recognize their reluctance to remain in thrall to Moncriith any longer than necessary.

Despite the danger, Nimbulan felt a small smile flicker

across his cheeks. Without bothering to weigh the consequences, he hefted his staff in both hands and swung with all his strength at the back of Moncriith's head.

The Bloodmage crumpled to the dirt. The mercenaries raised their swords over their heads as one.

Rollett's blade pressed sharply into Nimbulan's spine.

CHAPTER 24

"Swear loyalty to our new captain!" Scarface shouted to the assembled mercenaries as he lifted his sword to join the others in salute to Nimbulan.

"What?" Nimbulan looked right and left in amazement. He'd been prepared to flee or defend himself against the trained warriors. Instead they looked to him for leadership.

"Moncriith defeated our old captain. You defeated Moncriith and broke his spell over the men. Therefore you are our new captain," Scarface said with a wide grin. He prodded the Bloodmage with his toe.

Moncriith groaned and tried to raise his head, but he collapsed onto the ground again with a sickening splat that meant a broken nose. Blood gushed over his face.

All traces of blank enthrallment had left the men's faces, including Rollett's. The dark-haired young man grinned.

"Before you wake that piece of bloody garbage," Rollett said, holding Scarface back from kicking Moncriith again. "We need a plan. He can get us into the palace. He has the ear of the Kaalipha. He can get us all past the guards and their wands without a search."

"He'll have to think he's taking Nimbulan to Yaassima for justice," Scarface added. "You willing to risk that, Captain?" He looked at Nimbulan, eyes wide with speculation.

"I'll have to. I have to rescue my wife and the children. I presume Powwell and Kalen are with her. She wouldn't willingly separate from them."

"After that, these men and I will decide what to do with our lives. There's always the invasion of Coronnan. You can take on our sponsorship, Nimbulan, and collect the money from SeLenicca's recruiting agents. They leave at dawn and plan to launch the first strike within a week."

"No." Nimbulan cast about for ideas. He had to either stop that invasion or get word to Quinnault fast. What had the boy done to precipitate a major invasion in only a few days?

But he couldn't leave without Myri.

"Quickly, Moncriith is coming around," Rollett ordered as if he were the new mercenary captain. "Scarface and Nimbulan, on the ground. The rest of you, put those blank looks back into your eyes."

"Some of you will have to secure the gate so that we can escape later. Drift away now, before Moncriith knows you are gone," Nimbulan added.

"If we all work together, with magic and mundane weapons, we have a chance. But we won't be able to hold the gate long," Scarface replied.

"Then take a moment to reabsorb your magic." Nimbulan held his staff upright in front of him while he anxiously took the usual three deep breaths. He'd been without his talent too long. He felt diminished, half a man. He lost sight of his quest to free Myri while he reached to restore the lost talent.

The staff shimmered in the moonlight. A pulsing double aura spread outward from it. Deep in the core of the wood grain lay a throbbing blue light, dimmer than what he remembered it should be.

He willed the blue light to return to his heart where it belonged. Slowly, too slowly, the blue crept out of the staff into his hands. It found his veins and merged with the blood flow returning to his heart.

A sense of completeness pushed up his arms like the taste of cool water after a long day in the hot sun. His fingers tingled with renewed sensitivity. The ache in his wrenched shoulder and scraped knee faded. His heart beat faster, truer, more powerfully. Awareness of every cell in his body returned.

The beacon of light settled into place with a satisfied wiggle that felt like a sigh of relief.

Scarface pointed to Nimbulan's left. "There's a commotion at the gate. Maybe something we can take advantage of."

Two men faded into the shadows in the direction of

the gate. Nimbulan had no doubt they'd return shortly with a report. He and Scarface stretched out on the ground as if Moncriith had felled them with his last spell.

Almost as if cued by their preparations, Moncriith raised himself up on one elbow and shook his head clear.

Nimbulan watched him through half-closed eyes. As the Bloodmage rolled and heaved his body upward, the prominence of his bones was sharply outlined beneath his bright red robe. For all the breadth of his shoulders and squareness of his shape, the man was not well fed. Or something ate away at his innards. Disease or fanaticism?

"Bind those two with magic and mundane means. We will take them to the Kaalipha for judgment," Moncriith grunted before he was fully erect.

"There is a disturbance at the gate, Captain," one of the mercenaries said in a monotone as he slipped back into line. "There is information to be gained, sir."

Moncriith looked into the eyes of each of the men who surrounded him, then back to the inert bodies of Nimbulan and Scarface. "Bind them and bring them along. I would know who disturbs the Kaalipha's peace." He shuffled off in the direction of the gate, confident that his men would follow. He shook his head repeatedly, as if trying to clear his muddled thoughts.

By the time they reached the solitary portal into or out of Hanassa, Moncriith had regained much of his poise and his habitual confident stride.

Nimbulan kept his head down. Impatiently, he tested the ropes Rollett had placed around his wrists. They slipped easily over his hands. He pushed them back up again before Moncriith could turn and test them.

When a milling crowd around the gate came into view, Moncriith halted his men. They stopped moving in unison, continuing to stare straight ahead without expression. Nimbulan had no doubt they saw everything.

A troop of twenty palace guards stood squarely in front of the gate, swords drawn, wands aimed at the crowd. Behind them, several figures crouched by the slapping rock.

"Hey, butt-licker, them wands don't work without the slapping rock. Can you defend yourself without them?"

a slightly built man taunted from the depths of the crowd.

"Get some good use outta that there rod. Ram it up the Kaalipha's butt instead o' ours," a drunken woman yelled. She threw an overripe fruit at the rigid guards. They didn't flinch.

"Ain't seen you fight with those swords before." A half-dressed woman swiveled her hips and bent forward so the guards could see the fullness of her breasts. "They're stiffer than the ones you usually wield on the Kaalipha's orders."

The guards didn't move. Their sword tips remained at the ready.

The crowd oozed forward one step.

Someone else lobbed a sulfurous smelling egg at the unmoving wall of guards. The bloody yolk splattered against one man's clean, black uniform. He didn't flinch.

The milling people pressed closer yet to the lethal sword tips and hated wands.

"Do my eyes betray me, or are they in some kind of trance?" Nimbulan whispered to Scarface.

"I believe they are being controlled by a magician. They are well disciplined and very loyal, but I've never seen them so unresponsive before," the mercenary magician replied.

Moncriith whipped his head around, silencing them with a glare.

"I'd like a closer look at the slapping rock and what those people are doing to it," Nimbulan whispered.

Rollett surreptitiously nudged Nimbulan with his confiscated staff. The journeyman grounded the butt of the staff and leaned it against Nimbulan's hands, without shifting his gaze or moving his body. In full contact with the staff and the Kardia, Nimbulan called his TrueSight up from the depths of the little bit of dragon magic left within him.

The shape of the slapping rock jumped into his vision in precise detail. The brown lump, so unusual in this black and gray landscape, lay on its side, revealing a deep hollow place inside it. A tangle of hair-fine tentacles grew from the middle of the rock. But it wasn't a true rock.

What kind of strange creature is this rock? Surely it

must be alive in some manner. No natural mineral grew
appendages. The wands responded to the sounds it
made, like dogs trained to a whistle.

"Look at the girl crouched beside the rock." Scarface
pointed to the figure closest to the creature. His tones
couldn't reach much beyond Nimbulan's sensitive ear.
"That's Yaala, Yaassima's daughter. Everyone thought
she was dead after the Kaalipha killed her consort—the
girl's father—when she tired of him. Made the girl
watch. When Yaala refused to wash herself in her father's blood, Yaassima threw a fit and condemned her,
too. Said she didn't have enough of the dragon in her.
I wonder how she managed to stay alive. She seems to
be doing the chore of the Engineer, the only one Yaassima trusts to work on the wands and the slapping rocks.
Maybe she's been hiding in the pit."

Nimbulan's blood froze in his veins. Myri had a lot of
dragon spirit within her. What did the Kaalipha have
planned for his wife?

The young woman removed one of the long red appendages inside the "rock." She pulled an identical
snakelike piece from inside her tunic and placed it where
the discarded one had been.

"Wh . . . what is the pit?" Nimbulan kept his eyes on
the young woman and the other person in ragged and
filthy clothes who handed her metal tools upon command. Something seemed familiar about the shape of his
skull and the way he braced his legs . . .

"The pit is the heart of the volcano. Yaala is the only
person other than the Engineer I've ever seen leave it
and live."

"What about the young man beside her?"

Scarface shrugged. "I've never seen him before."

Just then, the young man turned his head to scan the
crowd. His eyes lingered on Nimbulan, then opened
wide in recognition.

"Powwell!" Nimbulan breathed the name, barely loud
enough to hear. "My foster son. He must have come
here with Myrilandel and . . . and Kalen. I've got to
rescue all of them." His heart turned over at the sickly
pallor of the boy's skin, the shoulders bowed in defeat.

The young woman, Yaala, rolled the rock back into
place. She stood and dusted the knees of her trews. All

of the guards relaxed from their enchanted vigilance. Six of them broke away from the half circle and prodded Yaala and Powwell in the back with the wands. Reluctantly they trudged back toward the palace and the pit.

Nimbulan took one step as if to follow.

"If you go after him into the pit, you'll die, too," Scarface said.

*   *   *

Myri carefully untangled her legs from her sheets. She moved slowly so the soft mattress wouldn't shift and awaken Kalen who snored softly beside her. Baby Amaranth cooed and blew bubbles. Myri lifted her from her cradle, automatically checking her diaper. Nearly dry for once.

Maia shifted on her straw pallet at the foot of the bed but didn't awaken. She slept with her arms pressed tightly against her breasts. The front of her shift was wet and smelled of sour milk.

Myri's empathic talent shared the aching pressure of too much milk with no child to suckle. She hugged her own baby tightly, cherishing Amaranth's life. Maia had only memories of the children she had lost.

Myri left the bedchamber rather than think about Maia's loss. The door to Yaassima's room remained firmly closed.

Singing softly to Amaranth, Myri wove her way around the heavy furniture Yaassima favored to the window in the common room. Dull light glowed behind the ceiling panels, never totally extinguished. Tonight, they didn't seem to give off as much of a glow as usual.

As she did so many nights, Myri stared out at the dark sky above the bowl of the crater, longing to fly to freedom. If she transformed into her dragon form, would the necklace choke her to death before it destroyed her brain, or would she break free of Yaassima's bondage?

She blinked back the moisture that filled her eyes. For the sake of the baby in her arms, she didn't dare transform. But she had to put her half-formed escape plans into action tonight. Kalen had fallen prey to the vices of lies and deceit so prevalent in the city. The girl had to be taken away from here now or she'd be lost forever.

Powwell, too, was in terrible peril in the pit. Yaassima's demands for the baby chilled Myri to the bone.

How to subdue Yaassima long enough to steal the trigger for her necklace? The questions spun around and around her brain, a lot like the dancing harlots in the streets below.

No one in the city seemed to sleep tonight. Crowds of people gathered around pubs and wineshops, or danced serpentine patterns around the city, shouting and singing with a kind of desperation Myri couldn't understand. She'd heard Nastfa and Golin say that this kind of revelry only happened the night before large companies of mercenaries left the city on campaign. Tomorrow Hanassa would be nearly deserted. Fewer crowds for her to hide among.

Myri had caught an emotion of regret from Nastfa. He needed to leave the city, but not with the mercenaries. His roots and his heart belonged elsewhere. His need to be gone was reaching the point of desperation.

Would Moncriith leave with the soldiers? Now that he knew Myri resided in Hanassa, he might elect to stay and seek a way to destroy her. He'd hounded her for as long as she could remember, driving her from village to village. His preferred method of execution of witches was burning.

Why did villagers always believe his sermons against the demons only he could see and not the healing and helping she gave them?

Only the nameless fishing village near her clearing had resisted Moncriith. She missed her friends there. She missed her home nearly as much as Nastfa did.

"I want to go home," she sobbed.

First she had to get herself and her children out of the palace. Then out of Hanassa without Moncriith or Yaassima seeing her.

A disguise for herself and the children as mercenaries perhaps. Could they walk out with the armies?

Suddenly the silver cord of magic that connected her to Nimbulan glowed brighter with a more rapid pulse. She looked from the cord tugging at her heart out the window to the closest knot of men, near the gate.

One figure stood out among them. He stood tall and proud, a long twisted staff in his left hand, a faint blue aura gave him an air of command. She didn't need to follow the cord to know her husband.

I come, beloved, he called to her with his mind.

Your daughter and I await you! she nearly shouted back to her husband in triumph. *Be very careful, Lan. Yaassima binds me with magic and mundane traps.*

Nothing will separate us once I reach you. Not even the terrible Kaalipha of Hanassa, Nimbulan replied.

She breathed a deep sigh of satisfaction. She had known he would come for her eventually. The silver cord wouldn't let them remain separated too long. She was so relieved at his appearance she couldn't resent his delay.

He'd need help getting them out of the palace. She thought she could trust Nastfa and Golin. How far would they go in their revenge against Yaassima? Or would their own fears restore their grudging loyalty to her?

Her mind refused to think beyond holding Nimbulan in her arms again. She drank in the sight of him. The men around him began to take on individual characteristics in the wild torchlight that filled the city tonight. That could be Rollett standing to Nimbulan's left and slightly behind him. Another teenager and a middle-aged man also stood nearby. Then her gaze lingered on the back of the man that seemed to be in front of the group. He turned his face to glare at Nimbulan.

Moncriith. She'd know him anywhere.

What was her husband doing with their archenemy?

The hairs on the back of her neck prickled a warning before she heard a soft footfall. Carefully she shut out the telepathic communication from Nimbulan. All these weeks as Yaassima's pampered prisoner and she still wasn't sure of the extent of the Kaalipha's powers.

A heavy hand rested on her shoulder. Not Yaassima. She turned her head to look at this new companion.

Nastfa, her constant guard, stood beside her. Golin slept somewhere else in the suite. Nastfa held one finger to his lips to signal silence.

That brief moment of physical contact told her more about Nastfa. He had never been loyal to Yaassima. He'd only used his position among the elite guards as a way of saving himself when he found himself trapped

here. When he'd completed his spying mission for the
King of Maffisto.

Myri nodded her head once in compliance, eager for
this man's help. She shot one more glance out the window. Moncriith still stood with Nimbulan. She had to set
her escape into motion by herself.

The senior guard squeezed her shoulder gently, reassuringly. He held both hands together and rested his
cheek on them, pantomiming sleep, then he pointed to
Yaassima's private chamber. Abruptly he looked up, almost startled. A moment later he laid his face back onto
his hands.

The Kaalipha slept lightly.

Myri nodded again, uncertain what the man wanted
of her.

Nastfa fished a small vial from his pocket. The enam-
eled metal tube was sealed tightly with wax. He pointed
again to Yaassima and pantomimed a deeper sleep.
Gently he placed the vial into Myri's hand and closed
her fingers around it.

The moment of physical contact relayed his emotions
to her empathic talent. He hated the Kaalipha as did his
king. Even before Yaassima's humiliation of him in the
Justice Hall the other night he had hated her. But he
feared her also. Feared that if he tried to kill her himself,
he would fail. He didn't know where the loyalty of his
men lay. His years of entrapment had eaten away at
his confidence.

"When?" Myri mouthed the word, lest Yaassima
awaken and overhear through the dragon pendant.

A tiny bell rang within the Kaalipha's bedchamber.
Myri looked toward the sound, startled. The door to
Yaassima's room opened and her sleepy-eyed maid—
the only servant Yaassima trusted near her regularly—
shuffled out, headed for the carafe of wine and cups that
always sat on the side table.

Yaassima must have drained the carafe by her bed
already. Most nights the wine was all that allowed her
to sleep. She frequently ordered Myri to bring the wine
so the Kaalipha could regale her with bloodthirsty tales
of her dragon ancestor Hanassa.

"I'll take the wine to Yaassima. Go back to sleep,

Haanna." Myri waved the woman back to her pallet in a tiny alcove.

She could trust only herself. She had to get the children out of Hanassa tonight.

Haanna flashed Myri a grateful smile and stumbled back to her bed.

With shaking hands, Myri poured the bright red wine into a goblet of fine porcelain. She stared at the vial a few seconds, indecisive.

Yaassima rang her bell again. "What keeps you, Haanna. I'll send you to the pit if you don't hurry," the Kaalipha called querulously.

Smiling slightly, Myri pocketed the vial and withdrew powders left by Erda to make Myri docile and obedient. She hadn't taken any drugs for days. There should be enough here to send Yaassima to sleep for days. Or forever.

CHAPTER 25

"There is nothing of import happening here." Moncriith signaled the mercenaries to follow him. "Back to the palace. The Kaalipha will want to be a part of the execution of these foreign magicians."

The troop of mercenaries wheeled as one man and marched back toward the palace. Nimbulan and Scarface had no choice but to follow them. They needed Moncriith to get them into the palace without a search for weapons or magic.

"I have to find access to the pit, after we rescue Myri," Nimbulan whispered as they neared the palace entrance.

"You'll have to give the boy up for dead. No one survives the pit. You saw how pale and wasted he looked. He won't live long even if you could get him and yourself out," Scarface replied.

A line of dancers snaked out from a side path. They alternated men and women, each holding the waist of the person in front of them. The lead reveler was too drunk to stand on his own. He swayed and stumbled into Moncriith.

Moncriith backhanded the man across his face. Blood spurted from the man's nose. He fell backward, throwing the entire line off balance. "*S'murghin'* wastrels. I'll sacrifice you one and all before I let you join the ranks of my army!" Moncriith screamed at them.

A woman burst out laughing at the Bloodmage's posturing—too drunk to be afraid. Her ragged red gown drooped off her left shoulder, revealing most of her breast. She caressed herself, taunting Moncriith to join her.

Moncriith turned back toward the palace. His deliberate path took him through the line of mercenary magicians. He shoved Rollett out of his way. The journeyman magician stumbled and fought for balance. His flailing arms and shifting steps broke the blank expression of numb obedience to Moncriith.

Nimbulan gasped silently. Every one of the mercenaries stopped and slid silent hands toward their swords. *Don't break rank! Keep your weapons sheathed until HE orders you.* Nimbulan directed his warning into the mind of each man. The Bloodmage had to believe himself in control of this troop until they were well within the palace.

The dancing woman sidled in front of Moncriith, continuing her drunken taunt. He slammed his fist into her face. She fell backward over the jumble of collapsed dancers. Her leg twisted under her as she fought for balance. With an audible crack, the bone broke. She stopped laughing abruptly. Her jaw quivered and pain filled her eyes. But she didn't cry out. The drunken dancers found this hilarious. Insults to the woman joined their off-key song of celebration. Nimbulan caught a few derisive comments about Moncriith as well.

"Doesn't anyone in this city sleep?" he asked Scarface out loud. Moncriith whipped his attention back to the magician and away from the revelers.

"Not the night before half the town leaves for a major war." Scarface spoke a little too loudly, demanding Moncriith listen to him and not be sidetracked by the dancers.

"Silence, demon spawn. You won't live long enough to join these people in the glorious campaign to stamp out the demon-led king of Coronnan," Moncriith said. He raised his fist as if to slam it into Scarface as hard as he had the drunken woman.

"You like preying on helpless victims, don't you, Moncriith. People who can't fight back and prove just how weak you really are," Nimbulan sneered. He inserted his bound hands between his new friend and Moncriith.

The Bloodmage's face darkened with rage. "I don't have time to waste trading insults with you, Nimbulan. I shall have my revenge when Yaassima and I both dip our hands in your blood. I shall carry your severed head into battle as a symbol of the end of the demons that control you."

The troop of mercenaries stepped forward as if pro-

pelled by a single will. Nimbulan ground his teeth together trying to keep from ending this charade and
murdering Moncriith there and then.

Rollett nudged Nimbulan with his staff, reminding him
to keep his thoughts under control as well as his actions.
Nimbulan forced his frustrations away from the front of
his mind.

The palace loomed ahead. The jumble of buildings
piled on top of each other spread across a good portion
of the Southern arc of the crater. Four guards stood in
front of a smoothly rounded arch, just broad enough to
admit two men walking side by side, very close together.
Off to the right of the gate was another opening, less
regular, shorter and narrower yet.

Nimbulan touched Scarface with his elbow and tilted
his head in the direction of the smaller entrance.

"The brothel for Yaassima's guards. It doesn't lead
into the palace," Scarface replied under his breath.

Nimbulan wondered if he should look there first for
either Myri or Maia.

Two guards stepped forward, challenging Moncriith's
right of entrance. The Bloodmage spoke a few words in
an ancient language and wove his hands in a complex
sigil. The eyes of the guards glazed over.

"No need for your wands and your searches," Moncriith said smugly. He waved aside the first two guards.
They stepped back to their accustomed sentry position.

"The Kaalipha has given me the freedom of the palace, and I vouch for my men. None of them would betray me."

Moncriith turned and glared at the phalanx of men
behind him.

All of them thrust a clenched fist forward in salute.
"Death to all demons. Long life to Moncriith the demon
slayer," they chanted as if in thrall.

The guards nodded acceptance.

"Alert the Kaalipha. I have found the foreign magician she seeks and brought him here for justice," Moncriith ordered. The guards nodded again in compliance.

A long tunnel widened inside the entrance. Torches
placed at random intervals along one side of the rock
walls lit the way. They rounded a curve and marched

into a side tunnel. A particularly long stretch of shadowed darkness stretched before them.

The palace gate and the four guards were out of sight. This walkway seemed deserted.

Nimbulan grabbed his staff away from Rollett's custody. Scarface retrieved his own staff from another mercenary.

"Now!" Nimbulan shouted. His bonds fell away from his hands.

Moncriith turned to see what disrupted his march forward. Seven men held swords at the ready, all aimed at his gut.

"You won't get away with this, Nimbulan," Moncriith warned. He flicked his wrist. A long knife slid down his sleeve and into his palm.

"I think I will." Nimbulan leveled his staff to counter any spell the Bloodmage might weave.

Moncriith took a step back as his hand closed around his naked blade. The Bloodmage flinched slightly as his sharp knife sliced his palm. Blood dripped onto the weapon.

"Watch him, he's got the power of blood to fuel his magic," Rollett warned.

Nimbulan matched Moncriith step for step, pushing him toward the shadowed wall. The other men pressed closer. Eagerness to end Moncriith's tyranny showed in their bared teeth and determined grip on their weapons.

A bubble of armor draped around the Bloodmage. Nimbulan could barely sense it with his own diminishing reserve of magic. Moncriith stepped back again and ran into the wall.

Nimbulan closed his eyes and brought forward the last of his dragon magic. Rollett placed his left hand on Nimbulan's shoulder. Power swelled and multiplied within him.

Quickly, before the reservoir of magic was used up, Nimbulan pierced Moncriith's armor with the end of his staff. He flipped the tool horizontal again and rammed it across Moncriith's throat.

The Bloodmage's face turned dark with rage. He grabbed the staff with both hands and pushed against the magic and the staff with all of his might.

Nimbulan pushed back with the amplified dragon magic.

"You can't do this!" Moncriith croaked.

"I just did it," Nimbulan replied. "You are no match for communal magic. Take his weapons and bind him with mundane and magic ropes."

Carefully, he kept his enemy pinned to the wall with the choking staff while Scarface and the other men bound Moncriith.

"You're going to leave him alive?" Scarface asked.

"If Yaassima has enough magic to control this city, she will be able to sense his death. We can't afford to alert her to our presence." Nimbulan clenched his fist and rammed it into Moncriith's jaw. The Bloodmage slid to the floor. "Hide this trash in the next alcove. Add another blow to his temple to make sure he's out. Then wrap him in armor so he is invisible to mundane guards. We have to find Myrilandel before the guards alert the Kaalipha that we are in the palace."

*   *   *

Quinnault paced the long corridors of the new wing of the palace. He couldn't sleep. Every time he thought about tomorrow, his heart raced, heat filled his veins and his head felt like it floated.

Tomorrow he would wed Katie.

After she passed judgment by the dragons.

After the Council recognized this marriage would benefit the entire kingdom.

The palace was quiet tonight. Usually someone was about at all hours, checking torches, using the privy, raiding the kitchens. He met no one on his prowl past Katie's bedchamber. If only he could see her, watch her sleep for a while, he might be able to relax enough to snatch a brief rest before dawn.

He eased closer to her door. No one stirred within. He pressed his ear to the heavy wooden panels, hoping to catch the sound of her soft breathing. A murmur of voices, anxious and intense rose behind the panel.

Who? Who had invaded Katie's bedroom in the dead of night?

He reached to lift the latch, barge in, and demand explanations. Shouted words stopped him.

"I am in charge here." Katie's voice rose, became shrill.

Quinnault backed away. He bumped up against the protruding alcove wall that masked this corridor's join with the older, central keep. He smiled. His architects had incorporated older tunnels and hidden passageways into the new building. Escape routes in case the keep fell to invasion or treachery, they had insisted.

The secret panel yielded to the pressure of one hand and slid inward on recently oiled hinges. Cold, damp river air gushed out of the tunnel. He stepped inside and closed the door behind him.

He kept his right hand against the wall, counting stones until he reached the twenty-seventh. He identified it by tracing its outline, rougher and larger than its neighbors. At the bottom right-hand corner he found an extra knob, no larger than his little fingernail. He turned it three times to the right. Half the wall swung inward a narrow slit. He stepped through and found himself behind a full-length tapestry between a wardrobe cabinet and the inside corner of the room.

The loose weave of the wall hanging allowed him to see the majority of the room. Princess Maarie Kaathliin paced anxiously at the foot of the four-poster bed. The bed hangings were thrown open to reveal rumpled sheets and blankets. Katie was fully dressed in her heavy woolen gown. She kept her hands folded inside the full sleeves and hunched her shoulders as if warding off a chill.

A large fire blazed in the hearth, heating the room well beyond what Quinnault thought comfortable. Kinnsell stood before the fire, warming his hands above the flames.

"I am still your father, Mary Kathleen O'Hara, and you will obey me in this. We owe it to the Empire."

"I will not discuss this. We do it my way or not at all." Katie ceased her pacing abruptly. "And stop trying to break down my shields. Isn't it bad enough their magicians will be playing games with my mind and my memories tomorrow."

Kinnsell stood firm, staring at his daughter with fierce concentration.

"Get out of my mind and this room, Kinnsell. Get out or I call the guard, and all of your fancy weapons and technology won't get you out of their dungeons. I'll see to it." Katie matched him stare for stare. "Go back to Terra, Daddy, and make a new desert. You are very good at that."

Kinnsell stalked out of the room, back rigid. The cords on the back of his neck stood out from the tension in his jaw.

Katie slammed the door behind him.

Quinnault shifted his balance to his toes ready to flee or dash forward, whatever seemed called for. Unsure of what he had just witnessed, he braced himself with one hand against the wall and breathed deeply. Dimly he was aware of Katie wrapping a brick from the hearth in a wad of cloth. She placed it beneath the covers on the rumpled bed and climbed in, fully clothed. He could hear her teeth chattering and wondered how hot the climate of her home was—truly Terrania?—that she found this warm palace so cold.

Katie tossed and turned for several minutes before curling up in a ball and drifting to sleep.

Quinnault waited several more minutes before stirring. He longed to stand closer and watch his bride. He hesitated, unsure of what he had witnessed between Katie and her father and if it boded ill for his kingdom.

His mind spun furiously. He hadn't found contentment watching Katie, only more questions.

The latch clicked. Quinnault pressed his back against the wall. Katie didn't stir.

He watched the door inch open, half expecting Kinnsell to reappear with some new argument. A Rover-dark man of medium height and lithe build crept into the room. He looked all around and closed the door behind him. It didn't latch.

Before Quinnault could catch his breath and leap out to question the man, the intruder moved forward with three long strides. He pulled a long cord from his pocket and wrapped it tightly around both hands.

Quinnault dove out from behind the tapestry as the Rover tightened the cord around Katie's slim neck.

CHAPTER 26

Where is Scarface hiding tonight? Televarn asked himself. He'd already checked the wineshops the magician haunted. The man spent a lot of time drowning his physical pain in wine. Tonight he seemed to be occupied elsewhere. No one had seen him.

Some of the shopkeepers were lying. Scarface had been there, but wasn't there when Televarn looked. He checked with magic as well as mundane senses.

Lacking the magician, Televarn decided to return to the palace and alert his spies to the impending revolution. He'd also get Piedro out of the pit with the huge stash of weapons. Piedro was a good man to have watch the Kaalipha's apartments. He was patient and ruthless. He'd enjoy killing anyone who went into or out of Yaassima's private quarters without permission.

I'll have to warn him not to touch Myrilandel or Kalen, Televarn reminded himself. Piedro was as dangerous as he was useful.

The palace guards searched Televarn with efficient speed and sent him on his way. The Rover chuckled to himself. He'd had several blades made of the special iron the Kaalipha used on slave chains. The wands were not tuned to that substance. He had enough weapons on him to murder all four of the guards at the gate and they never found them.

Just inside the main tunnel, he ducked into a dark side passage that would take him to the Justice Hall and then down into the pit. He stumbled over something large and inert. It groaned and shifted away from his boots.

Televarn stared at the crumpled figure lying prone on the ground, hands bound behind his back. Dim torchlight reflected off scar tissue on the man's face.

"Are you alive, Moncriith?" he asked. Best if he keep his distance until the man was fully awake. One blast of a defensive spell thrown when the Bloodmage was half awake could kill any innocent bystander.

"Of course, I'm alive. Nimbulan didn't have the guts to kill me or even do me serious harm," Moncriith said as he spat dirt from his mouth. "Untie me."

"Nimbulan?" Cold raced up and down Televarn's spine. Kalen had been right after all. The Water spell had claimed a different life from the one intended.

"Yes, Nimbulan. You failed in your assignment. I don't intend to disappoint the Kaalipha in mine. Untie me!"

"I can't. He's wrapped magic into the rope that binds your hands and ankles."

The knots were very professional, the work of a mercenary and a magician. Scarface wasn't the only magician disguised as a professional soldier, but he was the best of the lot. If he had allied himself with Nimbulan, there was trouble brewing this night. More trouble than Televarn could invent.

His plans began to evaporate. Maybe he should just grab Myrilandel while she slept and flee through the dragongate.

No. He'd worked too long and too hard to depose Yaassima. Everything was in place. He just needed to rearrange his plans. Maybe he could use the chaos created by Nimbulan's rescue attempts.

"Use your magic to break the bonds," Moncriith ordered. "If we time it right, Yaassima will execute Nimbulan for us."

"Yes. He will try to free his wife. I can arrange for Yaassima to discover him," Televarn replied. He continued to examine the knots, but didn't try to release them.

"You can turn Myrilandel's anger toward Yaassima to your advantage," Moncriith coaxed.

"What will you gain? You want to kill Myrilandel, too." Televarn didn't trust Moncriith. No one did.

"I want revenge against the Commune of Magicians and I want the Crown of Coronnan. I can't successfully invade with my mercenaries as long as Nimbulan lives to guide Quinnault. If you keep the demon Myrilandel here in Hanassa, I have no need to seek her death."

"I thought you were recruiting on behalf of Se-Lenicca." Televarn began working on the knots. The spell on them was hastily constructed and easily broken down.

"I'm using SeLenicca just as you have been using Yaassima."

"We'll need to coordinate our plans. Timing will be everything. Nimbulan has to be dead before we attack the palace. But Yaassima has to still be enthralled with his blood. She's usually senseless for half an hour after an execution." Televarn sat back on his heels, thinking.

"I will sense his death." Moncriith licked his lips as if savoring the taste of death already.

Televarn resisted warding against evil with gestures and spells. Moncriith would interpret them as fear—or worse—cowardice. Televarn had no intention of appearing weak and therefore vulnerable to this very dangerous Bloodmage.

"Nimbulan's death will be my signal to dismantle the slapping rock at the palace gate. I saw the girl Yaala work on it earlier. This is the first use the girl has been since Yaassima refused to execute her when I ordered it. Yaala showed me how to put the rock to sleep without knowing it. You must hurry, Televarn. Nimbulan has had enough time to make his way through the palace to Yaassima's quarters with Scarface and the other mercenaries."

"Scarface owes me his life. He will have to help us. I have weapons stashed inside the palace. I'll kill Yaassima while she's still in thrall. You'll come in with your mercenaries and my Rovers. Hanassa will be mine."

"Ours."

* * *

Quinnault grabbed the intruder by the wrists, forcing him to release the pressure on Katie's throat. He gritted his teeth, putting all of his strength and leverage into his efforts. The Rover only leaned back, pulling the corded silk belt tighter about Katie's neck.

Her eyes popped open, and she clamped her fingers around the garrote. The fibers were too fine and slick for her to get so much as a fingernail between it and her vulnerable throat.

The Rover laughed at her efforts. Quinnault shifted his grip. If he could only find the one vulnerable nerve beneath the man's arm. He closed his eyes, remembering the trick taught him by his tutor in the monastery. Sometimes a priest had to defend himself without weapons. He fought the loose folds of the man's black shirt and the thick embroidery on his vest, seeking, probing. Pressing.

There.

The Rover's hands went limp.

Katie rolled out of the bed and away from her assailant in one panicked movement. She gasped and pried the cord away from her throat.

"Call the guard," Quinnault ordered as he shifted his grip once more. This time he captured the Rover's head with his left arm and controlled his right wrist with the other.

"Your name," he demanded.

The Rover laughed again in response.

"I'll have your name now or by torture later." He twisted the man's arm back and up. A grimace of pain crossed the man's face but he kept silent.

Quinnault twisted harder. Another fraction of an inch and the arm would break.

"My chieftain calls me Piedro," the intruder said through gritted teeth.

Quinnault relaxed the pressure on the arm a fraction. Dimly he was surprised at his lack of revulsion in causing the man pain. His priestly training to preserve all life seemed to have fled the moment Katie was threatened.

"That tells me that you answer to another name." Quinnault reasserted the pressure on the man's arm.

"Don't we all?" Piedro shrugged within Quinnault's tight grasp. A desperate gesture to twist free. Quinnault didn't let him. One of the small bones of Piedro's wrist slid out of place under the fierce grip.

Piedro dropped his head. His defiant pose melted. But the tenseness in his thighs belied his acquiescence.

"Who sent you?" Quinnault gestured with his head for Katie to call for help.

She just stood there, the bed between herself and her

assailant. She held her tiny hands to her throat, gently probing for injury. She stared straight ahead, wide-eyed, mouth working silently.

"Katie, get help. I can't hold him forever." At the same moment he pushed upward on the arm he held while pulling back on Piedro's throat.

"Yihee!" Piedro screamed as his shoulder dislocated.

Katie moved at last, staggering slightly as she hastened to the door and yanked it open. "Guards!" she croaked. Then she swallowed deeply and repeated her call, louder, more confidently.

"I estimate you have less than one hundred heartbeats to tell me who sent you before I turn you over to my very efficient guards. They were not trained as priests and have less respect for life and pain than I do." He tightened his grip on the man's throat.

"Can't talk if you throttle me," Piedro said calmly. Too calmly.

"I'm not letting go. Who hired you? I don't think you are smart enough to think up this plot on your own."

"I have my reasons for killing your bride with the belt to your own dressing gown, Your Almighty Supremeness."

"Cut the sarcasm. I know who would profit from such a plot to bring down my kingdom." Too many people. "Which of them hired you?"

Piedro laughed as the sound of heavy boots pounding in the corridor foretold the entry of the household guards. "Oh, they are properly embarrassed that you captured me in the middle of the crime. You who they are pledged to protect. They never suspected I walked right past them."

"A magician. I know how to control you now. Throw him in the dungeon. Have three magicians working together seal the door. I'll interrogate him myself. When I have time. In a week or two. If you think of it, you can feed him in the interim. That will give me time to import a professional torturer from Maffisto." Quinnault stared at the wall, fighting his urge to become as vengeful and violent as Kammeryl d'Astrismos had been. He would not succumb to his base urges and destroy the peace and harmony of Coronnan with his own bad example.

Piedro put up a little resistance as three burly guards

wrestled him through the doorway. He dug in his heels. "There isn't a dungeon made that can hold me, Your Supreme Loftiness. I am a Rover."

"Make sure three magicians seal the dungeons. And don't leave him alone until they do," Quinnault returned. "Tell them it needs to be a spell that even Nimbulan couldn't break."

"You'd best look to your own house before you start throwing accusations far afield, and trusting every magician, lord, and peasant in the land," Piedro called over his shoulder.

"What does that mean?" Quinnault grabbed a handful of Piedro's thick black hair and yanked backward.

Piedro laughed. "All of your tortures are nothing compared to what my chieftain doles out every day. I have no reason to blab."

*   *   *

The tunnels within Yaassima's palace wove an intricate pattern through the ancient mountain. Nimbulan could never be sure how many times they doubled back on themselves. All of the passageways seemed to lead back to the large hall that had once been a temple to Simurgh. He shuddered with residual pain and terror every time they neared the place.

Finding Myri was proving more difficult than expected. His heart cord pulsed strong and true but gave no indication of which direction led to his wife.

Few guards patrolled the corridors. The first one they encountered, a dark man in an ill-fitting uniform, turned Nimbulan around and pointed back the way they had come, without being asked for directions. "The Justice Hall is along that tunnel, take the first left then the second right." He moved on his rounds without checking to see if they complied. Obviously, if they had gotten into the palace they weren't considered dangerous.

The next guard, also Rover-dark and uncomfortable in his clothes, gave them the same directions.

"Some transgressor must have been caught. There will be a trial and execution shortly," Scarface whispered.

"We have to find Myri and the children, my children, fast." Nimbulan paused at the first turning. He savored the taste of those words, *my children.* Firmly he pushed aside his need to stop and wonder at the beauty of such a simple phrase. Since his brief mental contact with Myri he'd finally come to believe in those words. "My Children."

"I don't know where the Kaalipha's apartments are," Scarface admitted.

"We need to split up. But we'll keep a light telepathic contact all around." He directed the gathering of mercenary magicians to follow three different tunnels. "Rollett, I need you to dismantle the slapping rock at the main gate."

"Easy." Rollett grinned. "I can disrupt the magnetic fields with mundane tools and no magic."

The observant young man had sensed more about the slapping rock than Nimbulan had.

"I trust you, Rollett, to be thorough and remain unobserved."

"With pleasure, sir. I'll have an exit ready for you." The young man's white teeth flashed through the accumulated dirt on his face. He stepped backward and faded into the shadows, a trick Nimbulan had taught him.

Nimbulan and Scarface took a fourth tunnel that he could have sworn they had not tried before. Within two dozen long strides they found themselves back at the still empty Justice Hall.

"How long a march to the staging area in SeLenicca?" Nimbulan asked to keep his mind off the memories embedded into the rock walls of the Justice Hall. Myri's empathic talent would center on this horrid room and trap her in a useless whirl.

"A week at the most. We're scheduled to march through an obscure pass in the Southwest while King Lorriin advances through the pass at Sambol at the same time. Rossemeyer will try a new invasion of the bay." Scarface gestured them forward along a major passageway.

"Rossemeyer tried the bay a few days ago and lost the battle. I don't think they have enough ships left to try again."

"That was last week. The summons spells have been flying fast and furious for two full days. Rossemeyer is itching to avenge their reputation as the fiercest fighters in all of Kardia Hodos. They will find more ships and mercenaries even if they have to buy them from the Varns."

Nimbulan chuckled briefly. The mythical Varns weren't due to appear in the port cities for another fifty or sixty years. Even then, no one ever bought anything from them. The Varns bought food, vast quantities of grain, produce, and livestock. The only currency the mysterious beings recognized was diamonds.

Rossemeyer wasn't likely to find a source of shipping from the Varns—or anywhere else.

One less worry. He still had to get back to Quinnault and avert this new threat to Coronnan. After he rescued Myri.

"You said that Yaassima appears magically upon the dais after everyone is assembled?" He prowled around the stage, carefully avoiding the hideous altar in front of it.

"One minute the space is empty. The next moment she appears in all her glittering cold beauty."

Nimbulan pressed against the tapestries covering the back wall. His first encountered resistance long before he expected. He stepped back and examined the perspective of the woven pictures of a mountain meadow ringed by mountain cliffs. A waterfall seemed to tumble over a pile of boulders near the center.

He'd been there before. That was the meadow Shayla, the female leader of the dragon nimbus, had chosen to educate Nimbulan and Myri into the mysteries of dragon magic.

Something was wrong with the angle of the water spilling down into a creek that meandered along the meadow.

He touched the threads depicting the water with a single sensitized finger. Harder to do that now. His reservoir of dragon magic was gone. He had only the strength of his body to fuel his inborn talent. His stomach growled, reminding him he needed more fuel, and soon.

The silvery threads of the tapestry parted as he thrust his finger, then his entire hand through the weaving. He stepped back in surprise.

"Come look at this," he called to Scarface. He plucked at the loose threads hanging free of the woven picture. They parted to reveal another tunnel snaking up a spiral staircase.

"I bet this leads to Yaassima's private quarters," Scarface said. A grin twisted the straight line of the scar.

Nimbulan looked at his heart cord. No clues. "Up those stairs," he whispered.

Scarface shrugged and hurried toward the narrow staircase. The steps were shallow and well worn, the edges rounded and slippery. They spiraled sharply around a metal center post. Damp residue clung to the black metal. It had been in place a long time. The passage became narrower and each step higher.

"Are you sure this is the right way?" Scarface asked. his low tones echoed in the confined space.

"Yes." The silver cord tugged at Nimbulan now, urging him to climb faster. Myri awaited him at the end of that cord.

He remembered the days right after she had partially healed him, almost a year ago. The cord had sprung to life, keeping them close together and dependent upon each other. They had both resented the bond, thinking it sprang from the other as a means of control. Gradually Myri had recovered from the draining healing spell. Nimbulan had healed enough to function on his own. The cord hadn't evaporated, merely stretched. They had found love then, and the cord strengthened each day as did their emotional bonds.

Until it snapped moments before Shayla announced the covenant with dragons was broken.

That must have been the moment Televarn kidnapped Myri. Despite Nimbulan's wrenched knee and aching shoulder, he increased his pace, taking the stairs two at a time. He stretched his legs and his love to reach forward to his wife.

He rounded the final curve. A long corridor with many doors stretched before him. One door at the far end was taller, broader, than all the others. Heavy bronze panels, embossed and hinged with gold, blocked the entrance to an important suite. In front of the majestic door stood a grim-faced guard in black. Nimbulan counted at least six knives, and a cudgel on him.

The guard hunched his shoulders and widened his stance a fraction. His hands flexed, ready to grab a weapon.

Nimbulan stopped abruptly, holding his staff ready to

focus whatever defensive spell came to mind. If he had the strength to throw it.

That's Nastfa, Scarface whispered in his mind. *He was kicked out of the assassins guild in Maffisto. Then Yaassima recruited him to lead her personal guard.*

He probably knows six dozen ways to kill us before we get close enough to launch a spell, Nimbulan replied.

So close. He'd gotten so close to Myri. If he could just get through this one last obstacle she would be in his arms again.

Nastfa smiled. His full set of white teeth shone in the yellow light of the dim ceiling panels.

Nimbulan's heart leaped to his throat. That grin could only mean that Nastfa enjoyed killing people. Why else would he become a professional assassin?

Slowly, Nastfa raised his hand.

Nimbulan blasted him with paralysis.

Nastfa's grin froze. His hand remained poised over the hilt of a small throwing knife.

Nimbulan took one step forward. Nastfa didn't move.

The door behind Nastfa creaked open a slit.

Nimbulan saw Myri's incredibly long fingers curve around the panel.

"Careful, that's the Kaalipha!" Scarface said, aiming the end of his own staff at the door.

"No, that's my wife," Nimbulan asserted. He pushed past Nastfa and yanked the door open.

"Lan!" Pale and beautiful, Myrilandel stood framed in the light of the ceiling panels. Her nearly colorless hair reflected the strange light in a halo of gold.

"Myri!" Nimbulan threw caution to the wind and rushed forward. She came into his arms, fitting against him as living water.

Her sweet smell filled him—different than he remembered, better. His heart beat stronger, truer. More completely than rejoining with his talent. A sense of rightness washed over him. He bent to kiss her, tasting her differences and her familiarity. Her curves molded against him with the ease of belonging.

He came up for air, then bent to claim her mouth once more. He seemed to have waited all his life to hold her this close.

A resounding slap stung his cheek before he could complete his kiss.

"What was that for?" He reared back his head in alarm and found himself staring into Myri's livid eyes. Normally very pale blue, they'd lost more color in her anger.

"That was for forsaking Powwell and Kalen when you promised to aid and guide them. And this . . ." She slapped him again, "is for deserting me and leaving me vulnerable and never even coming close enough for me to tell you about . . . about . . ." Tears pooled beneath her eyelids, bringing the iris closer to their normal color.

A soft whimpering sound drew his attention into the room behind him. Kalen stood, dressed and ready to flee, with a baby in her arms.

Nimbulan cocked one eyebrow upward. "Do you have Maia's baby?" he asked. His task would be much easier if he didn't have to go looking for yet one more person.

"*We* have a daughter, Nimbulan. I have named her Amaranth. I hope you approve," Myri snarled. "Maia lost her baby son—Televarn's child, not yours. She sleeps soundly in the other room. We mustn't let her betray us to Yaassima—if the Kaalipha ever wakes up from the drugs I gave her—or to Televarn."

Nimbulan kissed her again, long and hard, before speaking again. "We must be on our way immediately." He had no doubt that Televarn, Moncriith, and Yaassima would follow them with murderous intent.

"We have to get Powwell out of the pit," Myri reminded him.

He snatched another quick kiss from Myri to keep him from doubting the outcome. He trusted Rollett to secure the gate. Once beyond the city, Myri could call the dragons. Shayla must restore the Covenant then.

"How sweet. The lovers reunited just in time to die together," Yaassima said, coming into view from one of the rooms within the suite. Televarn stood beside her, holding the sagging woman up with one arm around her waist. His other hand held a beautiful goblet of delicate porcelain.

"You really should have used some of your own magic in the sleeping potion, Myrilandel. My mixtures are so easy to counteract," the Rover chieftain said. His wide smile nearly interfered with his words. "Scarface, relieve the magician of his weapons and wake up the traitorous guard. We're going to have a party in the Justice Hall."

CHAPTER 27

Televarn continued to hold Yaassima up on the long
trek from her apartments to the Justice Hall. The
bell clanged harshly again and again, summoning the entire city to witness judgment. Maia stumbled behind
them, while Scarface and the guards herded Myri, Nimbulan, and Kalen ahead of them. Why was Scarface still
holding Nimbulan's staff? He should have discarded the
powerful tool rather than keeping it close to the magician. So close that Nimbulan could grab and use it in
a heartbeat.

Scarface honors his debts. Especially a life debt to me,
Televarn reminded himself. *He won't dare betray me.*
Stop worrying. Still he wished the staff had been discarded elsewhere. He needed someone to intervene between Scarface and Nimbulan.

The guard, Nastfa, was still frozen by Nimbulan's spell
and useless to Televarn's plans.

He'd known the guard was a spy for the king of Maffisto since he arrived in Hanassa six years ago. Why
Yaassima hadn't discovered this truth remained a mystery. Maybe she believed Nastfa had switched allegiance
to her. Maybe her own arrogance blinded her to the
possibility of spies and traitors within her ranks.

Nastfa was immune to the promise of a route back to
his home country in return for his group siding with
Televarn and the Rovers in the rebellion against Yaassima. At least he was until he awoke from the trance.
The offer couldn't be made in front of the Kaalipha
either.

Patience, he reminded himself. Everything was falling
into place. *Patience.*

Yaassima stumbled frequently on the route to the Justice Hall. She cursed at each false step. By the time they

encountered the back door to the circular room, she could almost stand upright by herself. Televarn kept his arm around her, needing her weak and dependent.

"I'll reward you for delivering Nimbulan to me, Televarn. But I won't reward you with the woman as you requested. She defied my laws. She must die with the man she calls husband." Yaassima struggled to stand upright on her own two feet.

Televarn adjusted his grasp to keep her off balance. She was so tall—taller than Myri, who stood eye-to-eye with him—his shoulder felt dislocated by her weight.

"What of the babe?" Televarn asked casually, as if Myrilandel's life or death meant nothing to him. He shifted his stride, keeping it uneven so Yaassima would have to concentrate on her steps and not her plans.

"Hanassa is my heir. I will raise her properly to control the power bequeathed to us by the dragons. I see now that Myrilandel would interfere too much with the raising of the child. She must die." Yaassima shrugged off his arm and straightened her long, bumpy, back. She glared at him, as if she knew his intentions. But she didn't reprimand him. "Open the door for me, Televarn. I must confront my people with justice."

Hundreds of people would witness the execution. Televarn had made certain his agents prepared the populace and the palace denizens while he crept into Yaassima's bedchamber by a secret route. Some of the tunnels he had crawled through, not even the Kaalipha knew about. Certainly, she wasn't aware of the opening in the interior wall of her bathing chamber. The laundry bin covered it. Maia had discovered it when she overturned the bin in a fit of rage just yesterday.

Maia's uncontrolled thoughts were easy to read at a considerable distance.

"Nimbulan must die first, Yaassima." Televarn tried to keep the begging quality out of his voice. "Myrilandel must watch him die and know that she brought this on herself."

"Yes. She must suffer by watching him die. I give you the privilege of holding her head so that she may not turn away." Yaassima shook off the last effects of the sleeping potion.

Televarn smiled to himself. Little did the Kaalipha

realize that the drugs and spells he'd used to counteract the potion had left her mind open and vulnerable to his suggestions. The enthralling ecstasy she always experienced after an execution would seal her doom. A true Bloodmage, like Moncriith, drew power from blood and death. Not Yaassima. She used them like sex to satiate her bizarre appetites. When she dipped her hands in Nimbulan's blood, she'd be powerless to defend herself from Televarn's poison-dipped blade.

Yaasima stepped through the narrow bronze door— miniature duplicate to one of the panels that sealed her private suite. The lights blazed as the doors swung forward. Smoke swirled and thunder clapped. The audience hushed, then gasped in awe as the Kaalipha of Hanassa, descendant of dragons, stepped through the tapestry and appeared as if by magic.

"I'll wrest the secret of that trick from her before she dies," Televarn said as he followed Yaassima through the doors. He watched with the crowds as Scarface and a cortege of mercenaries escorted Myrilandel and Nimbulan through the other door, below the dais. The couple held hands and looked proudly ahead of them. Kalen stumbled behind them, weeping loudly. She hugged the baby to her chest, clinging to the squalling form as if her life depended upon never letting the infant go. But no tears marred her innocent looking face. Wiggles wrapped his nearly boneless body around Kalen's neck like a fur collar. Only his nose twitched, seemingly investigating the baby Kalen clutched so tightly—a sure sign that the animal communicated with Kalen. They were followed by members of Yaassima's private guard, dressed in black and keeping their eyes glued to the floor. Was that Nastfa hidden in their midst? The head of the elite guard wasn't where Televarn had left him, behind Nimbulan and Myri. No time to worry about him.

Maia slipped in behind them, eyes searching the shadows of the huge Justice Hall. Televarn doubted that Yaassima saw her. The Kaalipha's eyes were riveted on Myrilandel in pure hatred.

"Nimbulan, Magician of Coronnan, you conspired to steal my most precious possession from me. My heir and her child," Yaassima said. "Myrilandel, you conspired with this foreign magician to abandon your true heritage.

I took you in, treated you like a daughter, made your child my heir!" She screwed up her face in anguish.

Televarn wondered if any of her outrage and sense of betrayal were real. Yaassima didn't give in to emotions that couldn't benefit her.

"Do either of you have anything to say before lawful execution by beheading?" Yaassima recovered her poise and glared at her prisoners.

"If I swear in blood to be your obedient heir and raise my child to follow the dragon heritage of Hanassa, will you allow my husband to live?" Myri held her head high, proud and defiant.

Televarn had never wanted her more. Her strength and courage were worthy of the Rover Queens of legends. With her by his side, he could rule the world.

"No, Nimbulan must die!" Televarn hissed into Yaassima's ear. The magician had to die once and for all. Otherwise Moncriith wouldn't know when to launch his attack. Myri would never be his while her marriage vows bound her to Nimbulan.

"Myri, are you sure you want to do this?" Nimbulan asked. He tilted her face toward him with a gentle finger. She seemed to melt into his touch.

"I will do anything to spare your life, beloved. I'm still angry that you deserted me and the children, but I do love you." Myri kissed his palm. Her bottom lip trembled and tears overflowed her beautiful eyes.

Angry heat flooded Televarn's face and chest that she should express so much sentiment for *Nimbulan.* Nimbulan, the aging magician who forsook the power of his Commune, refused to lead Coronnan, and stood behind a king when he could have been king himself with more power than any three monarchs in the rest of Kardia Hodos.

"He's a sniveling weakling, Myrilandel. Why waste your love on him when . . ." At the last minute, Televarn closed his mouth over the words that would proclaim his intentions.

"You love her, too!" Yaassima's eyes grew round and wide; their colorless depths took on a dark purple shade that did not bode well for him.

"As do you, Yaassima. You want her body in your

bed as much as I want her in mine. Kill Nimbulan, and we can share her."

"An excellent idea. But I do not share what is mine, Televarn. Send the magician to the pit and take Nastfa and Golin with him. I see them hiding behind their friends. I want to know that they suffer a long time before they die."

"Never! Nimbulan must die now," Televarn screamed. "All my plans are for naught if he lives. Kill him." He thrust his knife into Yaassima's back, waving for his followers to do the same to his rival.

*   *   *

Two dozen Rovers cast off concealing cloaks and hoods. They drew swords in unison. Yaassima's guards reacted quickly, extending their own weapons in mute challenge.

Shouts and cries and the clash of weapons wielded in anger erupted throughout the Justice Hall. Myri grabbed Amaranth away from Kalen, desperate to know the child was safe. Her head spun with the rapid shift of emotions and her knees nearly buckled with relief when she saw Yaassima sag under Televarn's knife. At the same time her healing talent burned within her, trying to drag her to the victim and heal her.

Between two ribs. Not mortal. Televarn's aim was off. The painful wound evaporated from her consciousness. Yaassima would survive without Myri's attentions.

"Run, both of you," Scarface directed as he tossed Nimbulan his staff. He blocked an attack from a Rover with his own staff. Three quick moves sent the dark-haired man reeling backward. He fell over one of the elite guards. Their limbs and weapons tangled, bringing more men into the heap.

Myri's talent relayed the pain of the blow from one man's chin to her own jaw. She had to blink hard to keep her balance. She shifted forward to keep from falling.

Nimbulan fended off another Rover with his staff and his fists.

The blow to the side of his head sent pain pounding into her temple. She clutched the baby tighter, trying to block her talent. Her jaw ached as she ground her teeth together. She concentrated on biting the insides of her mouth rather than thinking about the chaotic pain generating emotions around her.

Nimbulan wrapped one arm around her waist, holding her up. The warmth of his body and the strength of the cord that pulsed between them gave her a measure of new strength and stability.

On the dais, Televarn and Yaassima struggled. The Kaalipha raked the Rover's face with her talonlike fingernails. At the same time, Televarn pushed against her jaw, trying desperately to keep her from gouging out his eyes.

Myri cried out in pain as he twisted the blade in Yaassima's back—the same way he had twisted the knife in Nimbulan's wound over a year ago.

Life and death hung in the balance. The void stretched wide before Myri. She held back. Saving Yaassima would not gain freedom or peace for the children or herself. She had to deliberately turn her back on a life that needed healing.

Suddenly the Kaalipha wrenched the bloody knife from her own side. She thrust the blade into Televarn's throat. Her gleeful laugh rose shrill and piercing above the chaotic noise of dozens of other individual brawls. Triumphantly, she withdrew the knife, twisting it. Then she plunged it deep into Televarn's heart.

"You need more than a poisoned knife to kill a dragon, Televarn," Yaassima sneered.

Breath left Myri's lungs in a sharp spasm as her talent changed focus from Yaassima to Televarn and back again.

She had to get out of here before someone died and took her with them into the void.

"Bring me my child. Return Hanassa to me!" Yaassima screamed to any who could hear.

A guard lunged for the precious bundle Myri carried.

She whirled sideways and back out of his reach. He took two running steps closer, stretching his arms to grasp the baby.

"No one will take my baby away from me!" Myri cried as she pivoted and kicked. Her foot landed squarely in the man's stomach.

"Ooof," he grunted, expelling air as he stopped short in surprise.

Protective triumph replaced Myri's empathic sharing of the man's pain.

"This way." Kalen pulled at her sleeve. "We have to save Powwell." Her eyes lost the feigned wide-eyed innocence she'd been portraying since Myri had awakened her. Only desperation shone through. Her ferret chittered anxiously on her shoulder.

"Lead the way, Kalen." Nimbulan knocked a black-clad palace guard senseless with his staff. With his free hand he herded them toward the interior doorway.

"Not that way," Scarface called behind them. "Rollett has dismantled the gate. We can get out of the city." He gestured toward the exterior of the palace.

"Not without our son," Nimbulan said. He saluted Scarface. "Tell Rollett we'll join him soon." With a few swipes of his staff, he cleared a passage for Myri and Kalen.

Scarface shrugged and followed. Maia grabbed his arm. "You've got to protect me. My people will kill me if I do not bring them the child," she panted as she ran to keep up with him.

Myri reluctantly nodded to Maia, knowing the truth of her statement. But she'd have to watch the woman. She couldn't be allowed the opportunity to steal Amaranth.

Scarface blocked an overzealous Rover as he shifted the aim of his throwing knife from Nimbulan to Maia. "Come, then, but if you betray us, I'll kill you myself," he grunted as he tripped one of the black-clad guards.

Pain and fear receded as Myri separated herself from the two dozen or more individual fights in the Justice Hall. No one seemed to know who to fight for or against.

She'd last seen Nastfa and Golin and some of the other black-clad guards fighting with the Rovers against Yaassima's more loyal followers. Moncriith and his followers entered the fray, surprising Nastfa from the rear.

Good-bye and thank you! Myri thought toward her valiant ally. *Escape by the gate if you can. Ask for Rollett. He'll let you through.*

She ran with her companions through the twisting interior tunnels. Her senses insisted the way was familiar, but she'd never been in this portion of the palace before. Or had she?

No time to wonder. She had to find Powwell. She had to get out of Hanassa. Now. Before the guards organized themselves and closed the gates.

Down. Down into the heart of the volcano. The heat increased.

Nimbulan was sweating, too. Amaranth fretted, kicking at her blankets.

Darkness pressed against Myri's eyes. Nimbulan lit the end of his staff with soothing green witchlight.

Kalen seemed to know the way. In this matter, Myri trusted her. Kalen loved Powwell as she loved nothing else in this life.

The tunnels took on an unholy red glow. Myri stumbled and caught her balance against the rock wall. Heat seeped through her clothes from the living stones.

Pressure on her back told her of a dozen or more men who followed her. Desperation pushed them to stop her flight before Yaassima's rage turned on them.

Myri ran faster. Down. Hotter. Her mouth went dry. The baby slept, whimpering with discomfort.

At last, light appeared at the end of the tunnel. Red light, pulsing and flaring brighter, then dimming a fraction. Myri felt like she was staring at the sun after the darkness of the tunnels.

"That's the beginning of the pit," Kalen said. She pointed to a massive gate of crossed iron bars straight ahead. Footsteps and shouts echoed against the tunnel walls behind them. Many men, heavily booted. Their anger twisted inside Myri.

"They mean to kill us," she gasped.

They stumbled forward. Nimbulan and Scarface fumbled with the lock. Finally a blast of magic from Nimbulan's staff broke the latch.

"Rollett was right. Disrupt the magnetic fields and everything falls apart," Nimbulan said with a wry smile.

They all ran forward. Nimbulan closed and latched the gate behind them with more magic. Myri hoped the spell would hold against whatever bespelled keys Yaassima's men had.

Another dozen steps forward and around a bend in

the tunnel, a broad cavern opened. They all stopped short.

Dozens of people, clad in filthy rags, turned to stare at them. Some held bizarre metal tools. Others dipped water from a sulfurous smelling stream. A few lounged against rough pallets made of more rags, staring listlessly at an empty pot that sat in a niche with a rope attached to the handle.

Six black-clad guards sat in a far corner of the cavern, playing a game of dice. They looked briefly toward the newcomers and returned to their game.

In the background a loud chugging noise beat against Myri's physical senses. Pain lanced from her ears across her eyes. She felt Nimbulan and Scarface wince, too. Amaranth whimpered, too exhausted from the heat to cry loudly.

Maia seemed to accept the heat and noise as natural. Had she been here before? How and when? No one had been known to escape from the pit and live.

Hopeless resignation weighed heavily upon Myri. The people who had been consigned to the pit trudged through their days waiting for death to release them from the heat and the drudgery. The guards didn't care about anything except the end of their shift. They feared something down here almost as much or more than they feared Yaassima.

Myri stretched her senses, counting the lives she encountered. Hundreds of despairing personalities blurred together. Her talent couldn't sort them.

"I can't sense Powwell," Kalen cried. "I can't find him anywhere in the pit!"

CHAPTER 28

The shouts and clanging of men beating their weapons against the gate echoed down the tunnel. Nimbulan only hoped the lock would hold against them.

"Powwell!" Kalen darted off into a side tunnel, calling anxiously.

Myri set off in a different direction, stretching her senses as far as she could.

"We can't afford the time to aimlessly search." Nimbulan pulled her back. "We have to do this right or we'll never get out of here. Kalen, Myri, come back. We'll do this with a plan!"

"I fully intend to get out of here, if for no other reason than to make you pay for deserting the children and me, love," Myri replied. A half grin mocked the severity of her words.

Kalen returned grumpily, frowning at Myri's gesture of affection.

Nimbulan had no doubt he'd hear about his intense sense of duty for the rest of his life. In that moment he vowed to make up for every slight he'd given her since their first meeting. "I love you, too. Now stay with us, both you and Kalen, and let's get on with the business of escaping this hellhole."

"Where are Powwell and Yaala?" Nimbulan addressed the prisoners in the command voice he usually reserved for the battlefield.

All of the denizens of the pit turned back to whatever they were doing, without bothering to answer. The guards cowered deeper into their private thoughts and fears.

"The Kaalipha has been stabbed. There's a riot in the Justice Hall. You are free. We can open the gate for you," Kalen added.

Two men near the entrance who rubbed oil onto strange metal tools looked up again. A flicker of interest crossed their eyes. Two men darted furtively up the tunnel toward the gate.

"Armed men are coming closer with every heartbeat. Tell us where we can find Powwell, and we'll help defend you," Nimbulan added.

Some of the people heard him. Dully they shifted toward the interior cavern. The guards looked up with a spark of interest and . . . and hope?

"*Powwell!*" Kalen screamed.

"Pwl, pwl, pwl," the caverns called back to her.

"Follow those people into the next cavern." Scarface gestured with his staff. "We have to find a hiding place. Those guards will break the lock any minute now. They don't usually go beyond the gate. This time, I think they will."

"Did anyone see what happened to Golin and Nastfa?" Myri asked. "They helped me. If they lead those guards, we'll be safe."

"They are hardened assassins, Myri. Their fate is their own and not your concern," Nimbulan said, drawing her farther away from the entrance.

He tied his ratty black robe into a sling for the baby. The heat building in his skin knew a moment of relief. They'd all be shedding layers of winter clothing before long.

As he draped the carrier around Myri's neck, he glanced at the tiny red face drawn into a whimpering pucker. A sense of wonder nearly paralyzed him. He'd helped create this tiny morsel of life.

He traced the line of the child's cheek. Amaranth turned into his caress, seeking comfort and nourishment. She waved her tiny fists in delight.

A wave of possessiveness engulfed him. "My daughter. We have a daughter." Finally he looked into Myri's eyes for confirmation that this was indeed his child. His wife smiled and time stopped around them.

"You also had a son," Maia said defiantly. She crossed her arms across her breasts, drawing her shoulders down. "But he died before he had lived a full moon. He might have lived if you had taken me back to the city with

you. There are plagues in Hanassa that kill the innocent
and leave outlaws and misfits untouched."

Nimbulan pitied her. She was as much Televarn's victim as Myri was.

"Neither of you told me about my children," he said.
A bit of anger crept into his tone. "I couldn't meet my
responsibilities to them if I didn't know they existed."

Did either woman consider him fit to help raise the
babies? His shoulders felt tremendously heavy with
the conviction that Rollett was the only young person
he had successfully helped raise—he'd only had a few
moons with Powwell and no time at all with Kalen. He
hoped Rollett was managing at the gate and could hold
it long enough for Nimbulan to get back there with this
motley group.

Quickly he sent a telepathic message to his journeyman. His mind met only confusion, no specific identity.
Perhaps the depth of the cave system and the configura-
tion of the rocks blocked his talent.

"You weren't around to tell about babies or anything
else," the women replied in unison.

"I would have been if I'd known."

"Hmf," Myri snorted and centered her attention on
her squirming child. Maia turned her back on them.

"I promise I'll protect you both," Nimbulan said to
the women. "You and the children." Possessive protection welled up in him.

"Time enough to play proud papa later," Scarface
nudged him forward. "We've got to get out of here.
With or without the boy you seek."

The chugging sounds grew louder as they passed
through a low, narrow tunnel to the next cave. Nimbulan
resisted the urge to cover his ears. He had to absorb
every sound, lest he miss some trace of Powwell.

Beyond the threshold of this cavern lay a huge black
metal monster, chugging and belching. *Yeek, kush, kush.
Yeek, kush, kush.* Long, thick tentacles ran into the beast
from the floor and out of it into tiny tube tunnels high
up on the wall. He was reminded of the mass of wire-
thin lines within the hollow slapping rock.

"What's the fuss?" The woman Scarface had called
Yaala approached them from yet another cavern, deeper
and lower into the volcano.

An older man of scarecrow proportions gestured mutely toward the gate and the guards. Yaassima's men were scrambling to their feet, pretending to look alert and concerned as the noise from their approaching comrades increased. Yaala lifted her eyes to the newcomers. Puzzlement crossed her face.

"Are you new prisoners? I've never known Yaassima to send a baby down here," she said approaching Myri.

"We flee the Kaalipha." Nimbulan addressed her. "But we can't leave without Powwell."

"You can't escape Yaassima." She shrugged one shoulder and turned back toward the inner cavern.

"Yaassima is dead," Kalen insisted. "We saw Televarn stab her with a poisoned knife."

"Truly?" Yaala turned back, interest animating her face. Nimbulan noticed the draconic characteristics then, in the long straight nose and high forehead. But her fingers weren't overly long and the strands of hair that strayed below her knotted kerchief were darker, more yellow. Her eyes were a definite blue, not the pale, nearly colorless orbs of Yaassima and Myri. He wondered if she had the pronounced spinal bumps of the vestigial dragon horns like Myri did, or if that trait was tied to the long fingers and nearly transparent skin.

Myri looked as if she was about to protest Yaassima's death. None of them knew for certain who lived and who had died in the Justice Hall.

"The child speaks the truth," Myri said. "We saw Televarn stab Yaassima and twist the knife as he pulled it out."

"We must hurry," Nimbulan added. "We don't know how long the guards will be disorganized and allow us through the gates." *Rollett, are you safe? Did you succeed?*

No answer.

"I . . . I'm not ready to take control of Hanassa. I don't know how to use all of Yaassima's toys. I need more time!" Yaala looked anxiously from the noisy monster to the chain of passageways back to the surface.

"Hanassa isn't worthy of you, Yaala. Come with us." Powwell entered the cavern from the same interior room Yaala had come from. His skin had taken on a ghastly gray pallor that didn't bode well for his health. He touched the woman's shoulder affectionately, staring at her.

Myri reached out a hand to him. Powwell grasped it and pulled his foster mother into a tight hug, baby and all. Then he reached to gather Kalen close, too. The little girl edged between Myri and Powwell, effectively breaking their embrace.

Through the cord connecting him to his wife, Nimbulan sensed her need to touch the young man with healing and strength. Strength she couldn't spare until they were all safe. He also sensed her puzzlement over Kalen's obvious jealousy.

"There isn't time to waste arguing," Nimbulan intervened. "The guards are close on our heels. We don't know their loyalty. We have to hide, then sneak past them."

"They won't cross the threshold. They'll barricade it and starve us out rather than risk ambush in the pit. I've seen them do it before, the first time I organized a rebellion," Yaala said bitterly. "Now I know better. There is no escape from the pit until I know how to shut down every machine and deprive the Kaalipha of her so-called magic and her weapons. But I also have to know how to restart them, so I can take control away from her. I'm not ready!"

"Machines?" Nimbulan stepped forward, curious. He needed to examine the chugging black monster. His fingers itched to sketch the machine and record it in his journal. Only the Stargods could have built so fantastic a device that gave an individual the power to mimic magic.

"Yes, machines. Yaassima doesn't really have any magic. It's all tricks, powered by 'tricity," Powwell explained. "I know how to stop them. And I know another way out, if you are willing to trust me." He looked Nimbulan squarely in the eye; no longer a boy, hardened into a man, making a man's decisions.

"I trust you, Powwell," Nimbulan replied. "I always have."

Rollett! Answer me, boy. We're going out another way. Escape now, while you can.

No answer, nothing but the confusion of a dozen minds in chaos.

He'd just have to come back for Rollett. It wouldn't

be easy, but he couldn't leave his journeyman. He'd lost too many friends, students, and colleagues.

But he had his wife and children back. His quest was partially complete.

"I'm sorry to deprive you of your staff, but I need it. And yours, too." Powwell turned to Scarface, holding out his hand for the tool.

"No, Powwell," Yaala screamed. "I can't let you destroy them!" She launched herself at the young man's back, fingers flexed as if trying to claw him.

"You can't stop him!" Kalen stepped between Yaala and Powwell. "We have to get out of here. The only way to do that is to destroy the Kaalipha's power." She clenched her fist and slammed it into the woman's jaw.

Yaala teetered in her tracks, disoriented and confused. Scarface rushed to catch her.

Sounds of a scuffle broke out in the cavern behind them. Shouts of triumph and pain rang out louder, then the clash of iron weapons against stone. Screams of terror echoed through the cavern system. Underneath the sounds of battle, the rhythm of the machines beat discordantly.

Flickers of movement, a wisp of white, caught Nimbulan's attention. He looked right and left and saw nothing. The guards wore black, not white. The prisoners' clothing was mired in gray filth. Who watched them?

"This way," Powwell called to them as he retreated deeper into the cave. He looked over his shoulder, shuddered slightly, then crossed his wrists and flapped his hands—an ancient ward against evil. What did he fear?

"We don't have to destroy all the machines, only Old Bertha," Powwell said. Determination hardened his jaw. "She is the key to all the little ones that feed power into the palace network of wires."

"No, not Old Bertha. If you shut her down, we'll never get her started again," Yaala protested weakly. "Bertha is sick. I have to take care of her." She rolled her head against Scarface's shoulder, then her eyes closed and she went limp.

"I'll carry her," Scarface said. "I want out of Hanassa as badly as you do. I've had enough of thieves and cutthroats and rule by terror." He gestured with his chin for Nimbulan and the women to follow Powwell.

They passed through four more caverns, each containing a machine identical to the first one they had encountered. The sounds of fighting behind them faded. Nimbulan breathed easier. Powwell stopped looking over his shoulder.

Nimbulan wished he had time to stop and examine the exotic machines. Powwell pressed on through an empty cavern and then into the largest chamber they had yet encountered. Here resided a monstrous machine, easily four times the size of any one of the others. Arrhythmic coughs and wheezes accompanied the regular chugging he had almost become used to. Clearly, this machine was sick. Possibly dying.

"Well, Old Bertha, time to put you out of your misery," Powwell addressed the black monster. "You've served the dragon lords of Hanassa and that white wraith well. Now it's time to rest." Grimly he took Nimbulan's staff and thrust it deeply into the machine's belly, through an open panel.

Old Bertha whirred and clanged. Bright green sparks shot out from the open panel. The lights around the cavern flickered and dimmed.

A curious emptiness tingled in Nimbulan's right palm where he usually carried the now dead staff.

Powwell thrust Scarface's staff into a second opening. More sparks, louder whirring and bright flashes of fire belched from the dying machine.

"This way," Powwell called, indicating a narrow tunnel. "She'll explode in about five minutes, just about the time the guards arrive to kill us."

Nimbulan hurried behind Powwell. He herded Myri and Maia before him. He had no need to direct Kalen, she stuck closely to Powwell's heels, making certain Myri and the baby never came in contact with the boy. Scarface flung the unconscious Yaala over his shoulder and brought up the rear.

At the end of the short passage, Nimbulan saw the roiling mass of fiery lava and no other exit.

CHAPTER 29

"Let me get this straight. I have to face a dragon, and if I don't freak out or transform into a demon, then your Council will consider me human?" Katie asked Quinnault. She turned her big fire-green eyes on him.

Residual fear lay behind her innate humor and optimism. And her mind remained firmly closed to him.

Quinnault searched for signs of bruises on her lovely throat. Only a little redness lingered to remind them of the assassin.

The Rover, Piedro, was safely confined to his dungeon cell. Quinnault had checked only a few moments ago to make certain his prisoner hadn't slipped away.

He knew how to deal with physical danger to himself and Katie. He didn't know how to ask what had transpired between Katie and Kinnsell before Piedro had entered her room. They would have to discuss it before the wedding. First he had to make sure there would be a wedding.

"The dragon will determine if you are fully human and worthy to be our queen," he replied, not knowing how to address the other problems facing them.

The maids had dressed her in a simple white shift that hung lightly on her body. The fine linen fabric revealed tantalizing hints of curves. He could see the outline of her legs and wanted more.

"One of your magicians is going to create an illusion of a dragon, to make me think I face a monster worse than that assassin last night," Katie continued, mulling over the problem. "I can deal with that, though I don't like other people messing with my mind." She shook her beautiful head, the soft curls bouncing and catching glimmers of torchlight.

Only you, Scarecrow. You're the only one I trust with my thoughts.

Then let me in. Let me see what truly frightens you so that I can combat it for you.

Her mind snapped shut once more.

I can't let you see my secrets until we are wed, until you can't send me home.

"I've seen into your mind, Katie. You have secrets, but that doesn't make you a monster. I know that you are good, and kind, and honest. You care for me. What more do I need to know?"

A tear touched her eye, and she blinked it away quickly.

"Kiss me, Scarecrow. Quickly before I lose my courage."

He bent his head, savoring the warmth of her trembling mouth. She stood on tiptoe to bring him closer yet, clinging to him with a kind of desperation. He enfolded her into his arms, keeping her close to his heart.

"I won't let anyone hurt you, Katie. Not my people, or your father, or the dragons."

"I can deal with your monsters, Your Grace. I expected primitive plumbing and no central heating. Assassination and kidnap are facts of life for the nobility of my world as well as yours. What bothers me is the lack of privacy. Am I never going to be allowed to be alone?" She gestured with her head to the bevy of maids who stood behind her, respectfully looking away from their new mistress. The almost smile was back in her eyes.

When he had left her last night, Quinnault had ordered two of them to sleep in the room despite Katie's protestations. They should have been there before the Rover tried to strangle her. But Katie had sent them away. Had she wanted merely to guard her privacy or to have a moment to argue with her father? And how had Piedro known she would prefer to sleep alone? Most noblewomen always kept a maid in their beds if their husbands were not there to warm them.

"Servants, courtiers, and pests are a way of life for nobility on this world, I'm afraid." Quinnault spoke quietly into her ear so that none of the hovering servants, courtiers, and pests could overhear. He didn't trust his telepathy to penetrate her barriers. A few more kisses and no barriers would stand between them. Not even their clothes. "There will be moments we can steal away from them, but not often. All these people are a sign of respect for my authority as well as part of our security."

Assassination and betrayal had been a way of life for three generations in Coronnan during the Great Wars of Disruption. He liked to think he'd eliminated those factors. True power lay in maintaining peace not imposing war. But, he knew, many people—including some of his Council—hadn't accepted that premise yet.

Piedro had made it clear that he intended to end Quinnault's reign by making it look as if he had murdered his own betrothed.

But Piedro hadn't acted alone. Who had hired the Rover?

Quinnault checked the shadows for signs of unwanted intruders. There were a lot of shadows. 'Twas barely dawn outside. The interior of the keep was still dark and damp with night chill. Quinnault shivered inside his heavy tunic and cloak. Katie must be freezing in the simple shift that symbolized purity and her maiden status.

His thoughts jerked to a halt. He hadn't thought for a moment to inquire about previous lovers. Somehow, it hadn't seemed important until now. Customs might be different in her land. Some societies didn't value virginity. Coronnan seemed strangely ambivalent on the subject. Festival in the more remote regions initiated youngsters into the joy of sex by the age of twelve or fourteen. A population depleted by war made the begetting of children more important than virginity at marriage. Noble lords sheltered their offspring, enforcing sexual innocence, to artificially inflate their value in the marriage market—insuring there were no bastard children to claim titles and lands.

Quinnault had refrained from joining with a woman throughout his teenage years while he studied for the celibate priesthood. Once he assumed the leadership of his family and responsibility for his lands he indulged in the random partnering of Festival, but so far had not found a woman he was willing to repeat the experience with.

Somehow, he knew that life with Katie would be different. With her in his bed, he wouldn't need to think about any other woman.

"Uh . . ." he heard himself make noises, but he'd forgotten what she said in his speculation about the wedding night to come.

If the dragons found her worthy.

If the Council accepted the decision of the dragons.

"I know how to block illusions if I have to, but I suppose that would be impolitic," she repeated.

"The dragons are not delusions cast by the magicians, Katie. They are real. They are wise. And they won't hurt you, no matter how frightening they are the first time you encounter one. I remember the day they arrived at the School for Magicians. I thought my heart would stop beating before they ate me." He almost smiled in memory of that fateful day when magic in Coronnan changed for all time. "Now I know better. Dragons are meat eaters, but they don't like the taste of humans. And they like their meals cooked. Why else were they blessed with fiery breath?" He grinned, trying to relieve her fears.

"Your magicians must be very good indeed, to fool the entire populace." She smiled and tucked her little hand into the crook of his elbow. "Come. Your 'dragons' await us. Or should I say, the Council and the magicians await us."

"Katie," Quinnault said as he halted in mid-step. "You have to understand the dragons are real, now, before you see them and run away screaming in fear."

"Princesses from Terra—Terrania—are made of sterner stuff than you think. I have faced worse terrors than an illusory dragon." Impatience crossed her face, erasing the humor that normally danced across her features.

Suddenly, Quinnault feared for her life as well as their future—more so than when he wrestled Piedro into submission. Dragons had made a pact never to willfully harm a human so long as humans did no harm to the dragons and offered the tithe of Tambootie and livestock to the creatures. Shayla had announced the end of the compact more than three weeks ago when Myrilandel had disappeared.

What if Katie, with her strange Varn powers and technology took it into her head to harm the dragon? The pact would be shattered beyond mending and communal magic would dissolve forever with the loss of the dragons. Quinnault's reign of peace would be more effectively ended than if Piedro had succeeded last night in implicating the king in murder.

"Your Grace," a page greeted them as he hurried up the corridor to fetch them. "The Council awaits in the Grand Courtyard." The boy bowed deeply, sneaking a peek at Katie as he bent his head.

"We haven't time to argue about the reality of dragons, Katie. Just stand still and let the dragon judge you."

"I don't like the idea of being judged by an imaginary beast." She set her jaw determinedly, an expression she had assumed when confronting her father. She'd won that argument.

"You are as stubborn as my sister," he muttered. "I hope you aren't as foolish and earn the condemnation of my lords."

"I didn't know you had a sister. When will I meet her?"

"Most likely you won't." He clenched his teeth together, firmly closing the issue of Myrilandel and why she couldn't be a part of his life.

Thoughts of his brief reunion with the sister he thought had died at the age of two, brought him to Myrilandel's husband, Nimbulan. Why had the Senior Magician of the Commune defied orders and gone in search of Myrilandel himself, without so much as a note of explanation? A younger man would have a better chance of succeeding. Nimbulan should be here now to guide Quinnault and Katie through the coming ordeal.

And prevent complex plots involving Rovers and traitors close to home. If anyone could ferret out the hidden motives and traps in the Varn's offer, it was Nimbulan.

His Senior Magician had a lot of explaining to do when he returned.

He wouldn't think about Nimbulan not returning from his dangerous quest.

A blast of cool air from the open doors of the palace onto the Grand Courtyard sent lumbird bumps up Quinnault's arms. Katie shivered slightly beside him. He patted her hand in reassurance, but couldn't look at her.

Not now. One look at her skeptical face and he'd drag her back inside the palace, away from the ordeal by dragon.

Seven of the Twelve Lords awaited them, standing in a rough circle around the edges of the circular paving. None of their ladies had joined them. By their own choice or a decision of the Council? Quinnault didn't like the implication that the women needed to be protected from this ceremony.

Master magicians from the Commune filled in the spaces between the lords. Every man in the court looked grim and unforgiving. The walls and risers intended for this outdoor arena hadn't been constructed yet. The dais, left over from Quinnault's coronation last Spring, stood in the exact center of the circle. Only Old Lyman stood at the foot of the dais.

Quinnault looked up into the lightening sky for signs of a dragon. He wished he knew which one would answer the summons put out by the magicians last night. He'd prefer docile old Ruussen, the red-tipped male who viewed all humans as beloved children to be coddled and indulged with humor.

"There is still time to change your mind, Your Grace," Lyman said as Quinnault and Katie approached the dais. "The ambassador from SeLenicca is prepared to send messages of reconciliation to his king if you renounce this woman in favor of the princess of SeLenicca."

"I suppose he sent messages by magician last night, authorizing an invasion?" Quinnault stared at the top of the Western wall, wondering how long a reprieve from invasion such a reconciliation would buy him.

"Every magician was busy last night, sending messages through the glass to all interested parties. I intercepted a particularly interesting one aimed at a *Bloodmage* in Hanassa," Lyman replied. The last statement was almost whispered.

"Moncriith," Quinnault said through clenched teeth. "I wonder who really rules in SeLenicca, King Lorriin or the Bloodmage? Is their drought so terrible they will engage a Bloodmage to win a few acres of grain from Coronnan?"

"I fear it is so, Your Grace," Lyman replied sadly.

"Food is short all over Kardia Hodos. Our rain and the acres left fallow during the Great Wars of Disruption incite jealously and greed among those whose bellies are slack and whose children are dying of hunger."

"I feel for them. But I cannot feed the world. If they invade, I won't be able to spare the men to plow the extra land to provide food for those in my own country let alone theirs."

Katie squeezed Quinnault's arm, reminding him of the instant rapport they had shared. "I can give you a few new seeds that will multiply your yield per acre. But it will take time for those seeds to grow and produce enough more seeds to sow all your fields. The rest of my dowry must be enough to defend Coronnan for now," she whispered.

Quinnault looked out over the bay, a sight that would be obscured when the palace and this courtyard were finished.

"Use your FarSight, Lyman, and tell me what you see on those distant islands." Quinnault pointed to the small dark specks that were just barely visible on the horizon.

Lyman's eyes crossed slightly as he took the regulation three breaths to trigger the spell. "I see a great many men on four small islands. They are very active, but I cannot tell what they do."

"Kinnsell and his crews," Katie said. "They uphold their part of our bargain, Quinnault."

"And I must uphold mine. Summon the dragon, Lyman. Katie, my love. You must stand in the center of the dais, alone, and wait for your destiny." His heart in his throat, Quinnault disengaged her small hand from his arm and stepped back into the circle of nobles and magicians who waited on the judgment of a dragon to determine their future queen.

*   *   *

"Wait a moment. The gate will open soon. I can't control it," Powwell said. In a few sparse sentences he explained his observations to the others.

Nimbulan nodded slowly with each sentence. His hand came up, palm outward. Scarface peered at the opening through squinted eyes as if testing the truth of Powwell's statements.

Powwell hoped, desperately, that the portal chose that circular opening in the forest of Coronnan as its next destination. Too many of the scenes he'd viewed wouldn't support life for long.

"Yaassima!" Myri choked. She grabbed her ears, scrunching up her face in agony. The crystal dragon pendant glowed eerily in the dim cavern. Powwell thought he heard a high-pitched whistle in the back of his head, but couldn't be sure.

She stumbled closer to the tunnel entrance, relaxing a little as she put some distance between herself and the pit—or did she move closer to the palace and Yaassima's controls?

Nimbulan grabbed for the pendant. He jerked his hand away from it as if burned.

"Televarn threatened me with a necklace like that if I didn't spy for him in the palace." Maia slunk away from Myri in fear. "I didn't want to be chained to him. It's bad enough that he's in my mind all of the time."

"Yaassima is the only one with the key to that necklace," Kalen said matter-of-factly. "Myri can't take it off while the Kaalipha lives. Nor can she set foot outside the palace perimeter and live." A small secret smile crept over her face.

Powwell looked at her, alarmed at her attitude, almost as if she wanted Myri dead, or to remain Yaassima's captive. He didn't like the way that smile lit her eyes with mischief, nor the fact that she kept shifting her expression from eyes wide open and innocent looking to hunched over and closed. She only did that when she was plotting something more drastic than her usual deviousness.

"What do you know?" he whispered to his foster sister, the one anchor in his rootless life.

She turned that false smile of hers on him, as bright as the sparks that had shot from Old Bertha.

A blast of hot wind rose up from the churning lava.

"It's happening," Scarface announced. "Amazing. The gate is opening!"

They all looked at the arched opening as the boiling red-and-yellow lava turned to a vortex of red and green and black and white. A lot of white—like the wraith that haunted the caverns. Powwell shuddered in cold fear.

A vast arctic plain, covered with drifting snow and frozen grasses stretched before them. The shadow of a massive ice flow at the edge of the plain formed an arch. Beyond it stretched miles and miles of frozen wasteland without a hill, shelter, or sign of people.

"We can't go there," Nimbulan said.

Myri moaned as she pressed her fingertips against her temples. Her pale skin blotched with purple flushes high on her cheekbones and deep on her throat, spreading downward onto her chest.

"What kind of spell is this?" Nimbulan wrenched at the necklace. All color drained from his face.

"It's Yaassima's magic. Myri can't leave Hanassa as long as both she and the Kaalipha live," Kalen repeated. "This is proof that Televarn failed . . ." She turned as if to flee the tunnel. Powwell grabbed her around the waist to stop her.

"Yaassima doesn't have real magic," Yaala said from where Scarface had sat her inert body against the wall of the narrow tunnel. "Every power she mimics begins and ends with the machines. When they explode, so will the necklace."

"Then how does she control the necklace?" Nimbulan turned on her. Anger brought color back into his face. "We have to get if off Myri before it destroys itself and her with it."

"If the necklace lives, then Yaassima does, too." Yaala seemed to crumble in on herself. "She'll kill me this time, just like she killed my father. Then she'll dip her hands in my blood and taste it as if it was the sweetest ambrosia. My own mother . . ." She shuddered and shook herself as if ridding herself of the hideous memory. "I might have a key to the necklace." Yaala levered herself up from the ground.

"The gate is closing!" Scarface said. The hot wind from the pit died with the gate.

"Wait a few moments. It will come around again to a different location," Powwell reassured him. "The wind comes just before the swirling colors."

Yaala peered closely at the clasp on the back of the

chain and the crystal pendant on the front. "Can I have more light?" she asked.

"The guards are very close," Powwell reminded her. "Light will alert them to where we are. Right now, they are stumbling around half blind. Torchlight doesn't go very far in these caves." He peered out into the larger cavern.

A man with a torch rounded Old Bertha. Strange shadows danced around the flames. Powwell ducked back into the cavern. "Hurry. They are close," he whispered harshly. His throat nearly closed on the words. He hadn't seen the wraith, but the hair on his arms and the back of his neck stood up as it did when it was near.

Yaassima would kill him this time. She'd kill them all without a trial or explanation or anything.

Yaala pulled a small black box out of her pocket. "Motes work on the wands and the slapping rocks. Yaassima has several of them stashed in her pockets and hidden in her jewelry. That's how she triggers her special effects. This one might work on the necklace, if it's connected to the same frequency." She pressed the box against the clasp.

A soft whirring buzzed around the tunnel followed by a loud rattle. The necklace fell into Nimbulan's hands. Myri nearly collapsed against him. She rested her head on his shoulder.

"Gate's opening again," Scarface whispered.

"Hurry, the guard is coming." Powwell risked a quick peek into the cavern. The guard investigating Old Bertha and the two staffs jammed into her innards looked up at the sounds from the 'mote.

"It's a desert this time. Hotter than the wind portending it. Weird arching rocks," Scarface said, disappointed.

"I've counted one hundred heartbeats between cycles," Nimbulan said.

"They aren't regular," Powwell told him. Sometimes faster, sometimes slower. I've counted ten different locations and they don't come in the same order every time. The snowscape is new to me."

"We've got to get out of here. There are twenty men with torches out there, coming this way!" Kalen wailed.

"I think Televarn is dead." Big tears rolled down her cheeks.

Kalen never cried. Powwell's heart felt too heavy to stay in his chest. His beloved Kalen cried for a murdering Rover when she wouldn't cry for anyone else.

"Stargods, I wish I had a dragon," Nimbulan whispered. "I wish Rollett were here, or would answer my calls. Can anyone else reach him?"

Scarface and Myri both shook their heads.

"Wish all you want, we have to take the next gate out. No matter what the location," Powwell whispered, moving away from the tunnel opening. Kalen remained, peering out. She dried her tears with her sleeve and stared grimly at Old Bertha.

"There they are! Get the Kaaliph," a guard yelled. His words echoed around the cavern. His footsteps sounded like thunder as he ran toward Kalen at the tunnel entrance.

"Gate opening," Scarface sighed at the first puff of the wind.

"Pray for green trees or a dragon," Nimbulan tossed the necklace into the still visible pit. The portal seemed to explode in a shower of every color in the spectrum.

Green trees materialized before their eyes. Trees and rough grass and round mountain peaks behind. More slowly, the outline of a shimmering dragon flickered into view.

"Go, go, go," Powwell shouted. He grabbed for Kalen's hand to pull her through the gate with him.

"Wiggles!" she screamed and pulled free of Powwell's grasp. She chased after her familiar as it scampered into the main cavern.

"Kalen!"

"No, Powwell, we have to leave, now. She made the choice." Nimbulan grabbed his arm. His teacher dragged him away from the cavern opening. Kalen disappeared into the darkness beyond.

"Kalen," Powwell called. "I can't leave you."

"You must. We have to escape now. She made her choice," Nimbulan insisted. "She'll follow us when she can. If she wants to. She's a survivor."

The constant whining coming from Old Bertha raised

in pitch to the intensity of a dragon scream. "Kalen, get away from the machine!" Powwell yelled.

Metal screamed against metal as pieces ripped free. A single boom and thud that shook the ground beneath them. Red fire, brighter than the pit, blazed within the cavern. A fissure opened in the wall, running horizontally from the pit into the cavern. Lava glowed behind it. Then another explosion was followed by the screams of dying men.

Blazing lava flared from the pit through the vision of the gate's destination.

Nimbulan yanked him harder. Powwell felt as if he were flying. . . .

"Kalen," he sobbed.

The hot wind followed him, a sure signal that the gate closed behind him. Cool green caressed his eyes while a fresh breeze smelling of Tambootie ruffled his hair.

CHAPTER 30

Nimbulan shook his head and blinked his eyes several times. The Kardia didn't boil and move beneath his feet. Fresh green grass, trees, and blue skies replaced the sense-destroying landscape of the gray tunnels beneath Hanassa. Cool air caressed his face. Air that smelled of life and dragons. Instinctively he gathered dragon magic. Like taking a deep gulp of air after holding his breath underwater for a long, long time. How many days ago had he nearly drowned in Televarn's Water spell. Two? Three? It seemed a lifetime. How long ago since he'd filled himself full of dragon magic without fear of depletion?

"We're free of Hanassa," he said. "But I don't know where we are."

He let Powwell collapse against the ground, stunned and crying over the loss of Kalen. The boy needed some time alone. Nimbulan turned his back to give Powwell privacy while he checked his companions and indulged in his own grief over Rollett. If only he'd thought to keep his journeyman close beside him . . . If only he'd tried a little harder to reach the boy.

A journeyman must travel alone to complete his quest.

Can you hear me, Rollett? he broadcast the message far and wide in all directions. He could focus it better if he knew where he was.

Nothing responded to his call. *S'murghit, Rollett, answer me!*

Still nothing.

He decided to concentrate on those he could help and guide. He trusted Rollett in many things. He'd just have to trust him to take care of himself. But he ached to return for the boy. Young man. He's a man now. On his own.

The dragongate remained firmly closed.

Yaala plopped down beside Powwell, not intruding on his grief, just there if he needed her. A valuable friend. Maybe more, in time.

Rollett had been a valuable friend as well as student and assistant. Almost more a son than Powwell whom he and Myri had adopted but he'd never had the chance to get to know.

Myri stood beside Nimbulan, a small smile spreading across her face. "I'm free!" she whispered, as if she couldn't quite believe it. "My baby is safe."

Nimbulan reached over and brought her tight against his side, where she belonged. She snuggled into him, filling the emptiness he'd lived with for too long. He lowered his head to kiss her once more. He'd never get enough of her. He pushed aside thoughts of Rollett, so he could appreciate the warmth of his wife.

Amaranth fretted once more and Myri lifted her from the sling onto her shoulder. "I think she's hungry. It has been a long night."

"It has indeed," Nimbulan replied. The first glow of false dawn shimmered on the frosty hilltops. A bird chirped a sleepy query to the sun. At least it wasn't raining or snowing. "I'm hungry, too. We need to find food and shelter. Warm clothes. *S'murghit,* where are we?"

"Uh, would you care to greet our host?" Scarface stammered through clenched teeth.

Nimbulan looked ahead of them to the emerging outline of a nearly transparent dragon. The growing light reflected off of wing-veins and spinal horns in an iridescent display of all color/no color.

"Good morning, Shayla," he greeted the only female dragon in the nimbus. "I have rescued Myrilandel. I hope this restores the Covenant between humans and dragons. Can you tell us where we are, perhaps take us back to Coronnan City?"

The dragon dipped her head.

"She returns your greeting," Myri said. She cocked her head as if listening intently. "She wants to meet the baby. She doesn't say anything about where we are or taking us away." Myri separated herself from Nimbulan's embrace and walked over to the crouching beast.

Shayla stretched her neck to peer at the infant clutched in Myri's arms.

"Do you trust that monster with your child?" Scarface took a step forward, alarm radiating from his body. He clenched and flexed his fingers as if ready to launch a defensive spell.

"Of course I trust her. No dragon would deliberately hurt a human, especially children. They adore children."

"If you say so." Scarface's expression betrayed his inborn fear as well as his attempts to master it. "Damn cold out here. We need help."

Maia didn't look reassured at all. She backed up until she stood within the arched shadow cast by a rock outcropping. Her hands beat at empty air as if pounding on a firmly closed door.

The dragongate didn't open.

"So that's what Yaassima wants to be—wanted me to be," Yaala whispered. She turned her eyes away from the beautiful dragon to look at the grass.

"Yaassima didn't understand true dragonkind," Powwell replied, still wrapped in his grief. "She created a myth in her own mind and then tried to change reality to fit her version. She failed." He kept looking to the place where they had emerged from the pit. The shifting vortex of time and distance remained closed.

Nimbulan knew he'd have to go with Powwell if the boy decided to return for Kalen. But he had to get back to the capital, too. He had to take care of Myri and her baby. He probably owed something to Maia as well. She had borne him a son, though the baby had died. His responsibilities weighed heavily on him at the moment.

Rollett would understand. Wouldn't he?

Ah, Rollett, what have I done to you?

"Ask Shayla again where we are, Myri. I need to get back to Coronnan City and warn Quinnault of the impending invasion," Nimbulan said. He kept looking at the round tops of the hills that stretched into the distance. "You might ask when we are as well. Those hills look much older than the sharper peaks of Coronnan."

"I don't think I want to hear this." Scarface held his temples and sat heavily on a nearby rock. He began gathering loose sticks and branches, piling them into a fire stack.

A mental chuckle invaded Nimbulan's mind. The humor behind the brief communication was definitely draconic in nature.

"Shayla says we are in the time you expected to be. The dragongate folds distance not time." Myri straightened her neck and peered at the dragon with a touch of concern creasing her brow.

"Something calls her. She must leave." Myri looked around, rapidly shifting her focus from the nearby trees and grass to the far hills.

Shayla bunched her shoulder muscles and spread her wings in preparation for flight.

"Where are we?" Nimbulan asked hurriedly. His transportation was leaving. "We have to get back to the capital! We need warm clothing and food."

"Shayla says to beware of the massing men in the valley below." Myri's words were nearly drowned out by the downthrust of mighty wings.

"Massing men?" The sense of many lives pressed against his mind. "Hundreds, no thousands of men," he gasped.

"Angry men," Myri echoed his tone of concern.

"The army of mercenaries, preparing to invade Coronnan from SeLenicca," Scarface added. "We're in one of the mountain passes between the two countries."

"Mercenary patrols there, to the West with arrows nocked and swords drawn," Yaala gasped, jumping up and pointing.

"The gate is opening," Powwell shouted. "We can go back for Kalen." He jumped up and pointed to the rapidly shifting colors within an arch shaped shadow between boulder and tree.

"No!" Nimbulan stared at the partially opened portal. Moncriith is there waiting for us."

A hazy vision of the people behind the gate kept shifting out of focus, never solidifying. Blood pounded in his ears at the sight of Moncriith pushing Yaassima and Kalen into the pit. Huge tongues of lava reached up greedily to enfold them.

"Kalen!" Powwell rushed forward to catch the little girl.

The gate dissolved before he reached them.

CHAPTER 31

Myri ran downhill as fast as she could. Nimbulan carried Amaranth. Yaala dragged a reluctant Powwell away from the dragongate.

Soldiers followed them, close on their heels. She sensed more men running beside them. Still others moved to cut off their retreat.

Nimbulan and the others stopped short before the barricade of soldiers that appeared in front of them without warning.

"Don't move." One of the mercenaries stepped forward from the dozen men who aimed weapons at the party of refugees. He held his arm straight out in front of him.

A witch-sniffer. He'd followed the scent of dragon magic to capture Myri and Nimbulan and the others.

Myri looked from the drawn swords to the eyes of the soldiers holding the weapons. Their fanatical hate nearly blistered her empathic talent. "They are Moncriith's men," she whispered to Nimbulan, choking back her fear of the Bloodmage who had stalked her nearly all her life.

She wouldn't allow her fear to keep her from protecting her children and her husband.

"Moncriith?" Yaala mouthed the name without sound. "He helped persuade Yaassima to murder my father and exile me. He always meant to take over Hanassa. Now that he has killed the Kaalipha, he can." Her words were soft and bitter.

"Be quiet. Bind them." The mercenary leader gestured for his men to come forward. They hesitated and shuffled their feet.

"We have to get out of here, Nimbulan," Scarface said under his breath. "Moncriith is smart enough to follow us through the gate." He deepened his breathing in preparation of a spell.

"Not yet. We have to know the battle plans," Nimbulan said harshly. "Then we have to relay the information to King Quinnault. We can't fight King Lorriin if we don't know his tactics."

Myri gripped his arm with both hands. Her long fingers clenched and released spasmodically. The swordsmen fumbled with ropes that hung from their belts rather than approach magicians.

She absorbed and understood their hesitation. Moncriith wasn't there to protect them from magic they didn't understand. The archers wavered in their aim a tiny fraction. Their uncertainty could make them release their arrows without thought or true aim. She retrieved Amaranth from her husband. The baby's best protection lay in keeping Nimbulan's hands free to work magic.

Maia tried to slink behind the nearest tree. Another soldier with nocked arrow met her at the side of the tree trunk. She backed up, joining the troop of refugees.

Myri deliberately gathered the soldiers' malice and compounded it with uncertainty. When the negative emotions churned in a heavy knot in her gut, she swallowed her misgivings and broadcast them back on a tight line to the aggressors. Her talent rebelled, bouncing back to her, compounding the negative emotions within her. She wanted to whimper and cower behind any cover she could find.

She had never used her empathy for anything but healing. This attack was against everything she had ever hoped to achieve with magic.

To protect her children, she swallowed the rebounded emotions and added fear to her broadcast.

At the first sign of wavering arrows, she turned, putting the baby between herself and her husband.

"Demon magicians!" The lead soldier hissed through his teeth. His still outstretched arm shook slightly. "Lord Moncriith ordered death to all demons." He raised his arm to signal the archers to fire.

"Wait!" Nimbulan commanded.

Myri had heard that tone of voice before—on the battlefield when an entire army and the full Commune of Magicians looked to him for leadership. She dropped her replay of bad emotions. The lead soldier's hand wavered in the up position. Myri held her breath.

"When I left Hanassa, Moncriith had just hired my band of mercenaries to join your ranks," Nimbulan said. "Kill us and you risk the wrath of your leader."

Myri peered closely at Nimbulan's face and aura. Untruth flickered around the edges of his statement. Not a total lie, but not the truth either.

"*Lord* Moncriith don't hire no magicians," the soldier averred. "And where's your band if you be a true captain? Women and babies can't fight a war."

"We merely seek shelter for our families before we join our band." Nimbulan dismissed the man's misgivings.

The witch-sniffer didn't look as if he believed Nimbulan.

"What makes you think we are magicians?" Nimbulan asked in a reassuring tone. "We carry no staffs, nor do we wear the blue robes of the Commune, *Lord* Moncriith's true enemy." He held his arms out to his sides, palms out, as if inviting trust. At the same time, his arms came in front of Myri, urging her to seek protection behind him. His fingers curved slightly over his palms, he prepared a spell with that habitual gesture.

Myri sensed no ley lines in the immediate vicinity. Had Nimbulan gathered enough dragon magic when Shayla was here to neutralize the dozen or more men? She looked at Powwell and Scarface. They also prepared to defend with magic but waited for Nimbulan's lead.

Yaala and Maia huddled together as far away from the magicians and the mercenaries as they could. Carefully they inched toward a tree that might give them cover. If the mercenaries didn't stop them.

"You still haven't told us where to find your band of mercenaries. If you truly have one, *magician,*" the sergeant accused. He looked back down the path he had recently traversed. No reinforcements seemed to be approaching.

"You didn't answer my question, sergeant. Nor did you salute a captain. Insubordination. I could have you flogged." Nimbulan's voice turned iron cold. Myri shivered from the implied menace behind his words.

"I smell the demons in you." The sergeant looked right and left hastily, betraying his nervousness.

"Moncriith makes witch-sniffers sergeants over men with better leadership qualities," Scarface mumbled under his breath. Then louder he said, "Hanassa is rife with incompetents like him stumbling over their own feet, changing orders almost as fast as they make them. Any true mercenaries Moncriith hires will be demoralized and in disarray by the time they get here."

"I am a good leader!" the soldier protested. "I earned my rank."

"Did you truly?" Nimbulan pushed doubt into his words. He lifted his hands, still palm outward, still holding his magic tightly bound.

Beside him, Scarface did the same with a gesture of fluttery finger weaving. Powwell eased himself to stand next to Nimbulan. The toe of his boot touched the Senior Magician's foot. Their auras combined as did their magic.

Myri sensed the doubt growing in the archers. Their bow strings lost a little of their tension. The men holding swords dropped the tips a fraction.

Nimbulan and Powwell built upon the results of Myri's emotional attack.

Amaranth opened her eyes, focusing on her mother's face. The baby's emotions came through to her clearly. She feared the death of the men.

Your daughter is an empath! Myri screamed mentally to her husband. *Kill them and you will kill her.* Carefully, she clamped down on her own talent. She had the closest ties to the baby. Amaranth would know everything she felt, everything she absorbed, everything she broadcast— for good or for evil. All of the turmoil and chaos of the past night must have awakened Amaranth's talent early.

What of you, beloved? Nimbulan asked. The silver cord between them raced with their combined heartbeats.

I will survive. I have control over my talent now. The deaths of these men will hurt me, but not slay me. Our daughter will follow them to the void if they die violently in her presence.

*   *   *

"What do you mean to do with us?" Nimbulan asked evenly to the soldiers who still confronted him. "You're renegades, out to kill all strangers rather than save your energy and your weapons for the campaign you were hired to join."

Before the mercenaries could react, Nimbulan pointed the index fingers of both hands at the men. Faint blue sparks sizzled along his skin, shooting out of his fingernails. He directed the compulsion magic to engulf the mercenaries in a cloud of glowing blue sparkles. The cloud spread over the entire patrol.

He couldn't have commanded that much magic on his own. He nodded his thanks to Powwell for the boost to his magic.

Scarface aided him with his own spell, binding the men in place while Nimbulan questioned them.

The sergeant stared straight ahead, eyes glassy, barely breathing. His men froze in place. The blue sparks caught their expressions of horror.

Amaranth wailed as if stuck with a pin. Myri shied away from the freezing pain that bound the men's muscles in knots.

"Get this over with. Quickly, before Amaranth stops breathing," she ground out through her nearly paralyzed jaw. She edged over to Yaala and Maia, putting a little more distance between the baby and the paralyzed men.

Nimbulan nodded briefly to his wife. He forced down the panic of haste. He'd only be able to complete the task safely if he mastered his own emotions.

"When do you march across the border into Coronnan?" he addressed the mercenaries.

"Tonight, as soon as word arrives that King Quinnault has married the Princess of Terrania," the sergeant replied in a monotone.

Terrania! Was Quinnault totally insane?

"What about the troops coming to join you from Hanassa with Lord Moncriith?" Nimbulan forced out the words while keeping his rage and fear under control. If he vented his emotions, his daughter would suffer.

"They will have to catch up with us in Coronnan."

"Why not wait?" Nimbulan asked coolly. Through the silver cord, he sensed Myri using his emotional control of his magic to counteract the overwhelming fear within the mercenaries. Her muscles relaxed a little. Amaranth's breath continued uneven and difficult.

"We raid and pillage randomly. No pitched battles until we confront Quinnault's army near the capital. By then he won't have a populace to draw troops from."

S'murghit, how did one fight dozens of small battles without a single man directing the whole. Nimbulan needed masses of men to direct in an overall plan. He had no skill interpreting battle on the level of a single patrol.

"King Lorriin, when does he march?"

"He takes the city of Sambol tonight. Then he sails down the River Coronnan to take the capital, raiding as he goes."

"S'murghit!" Nimbulan said aloud this time. Guilt began to creep upward from his gut to his mind, clouding his thinking. "When did Quinnault have time to woo a princess and sign a marriage treaty? I knew I should have sorted through the offers for him before I left the city."

"The marriage negotiations took place in secret over many moons, led by Nimbulan, the king's magician," the sergeant replied as if the question had been addressed to him.

"That is interesting news to me." Nimbulan raised one eyebrow, biting his cheeks to keep from laughing at the ridiculous rumor. Nervous laughter.

"Quickly. We have to leave now. I don't like Amaranth's breathing." Myri bounced the baby in her arms, trying to break the empathic link between the infant and the men.

"Yes, we will leave. Scarface, can you arrange a delayed release from the thrall for these men? Powwell, set up a summons to Lyman at the Commune."

Powwell looked at his feet. Red tinged his cheekbones.

"I'm sorry, Powwell. I forgot you never mastered that spell before Televarn kidnapped you. I'll do it, as soon as we are away from here." Nimbulan, too, looked at his boots. If Powwell had been able to work the spell well enough to keep in contact with Nimbulan during the first few moons of Myri's exile from the capital, Nimbulan would have known of her pregnancy. He would have broken away from his responsibilities in the capital to be with her.

Instead, he had deluded himself that all was well with her because he did not hear otherwise.

That thought sobered him. Did he love her enough to sacrifice his work in the capital and with the Commune to be with her for her own sake, or only for the child of his own body he had wanted so desperately?

He'd waited until Shayla had broken the Covenant between humans and dragons to seek out the cause.

"Maybe the gate has opened again," Yaala said, still staring at the grouping of rocks and trees that had been their portal from the heart of the volcano. "I've got to find out what happened to Yaassima. Hanassa should be mine, not left to whatever riffraff decides to step in."

"The sequence and the timing of the dragongate are random," Powwell said harshly. Embarrassment at his failure to work a basic communication spell still tinged his face. "It needs an arch shape to solidify—even if only a shadow. Maybe the sunlight changed the opening. Maybe Kalen fell into a different location when the gate couldn't open here." Hope brightened his eyes.

"We have to get safely away before these men recover," Nimbulan reminded him. "I have to get this information back to Quinnault immediately, before he enters into this disastrous marriage. I won't leave you behind like I left Rollett. It's a long walk back to the capital." He stretched his arms as if gathering his little band into a herd.

"You won't leave me behind, but you'll desert Kalen. You'll let her die because you won't budge to help her. Just as you deserted Myri when she was pregnant and needed you most," Powwell said bitterly.

CHAPTER 32

Quinnault watched Katie march up the three steps of the dais, rolling her eyes in disbelief. His gut turned cold in despair. Visions of his solitary life stretched before his imagination. Having given his heart to her, he couldn't imagine marrying anyone else. Without this marriage he'd lose the port, he'd lose his credibility with his Council. He'd lose the stability of an heir.

She had to pass this test. She had to survive and become his wife!

He had fended off assassins last night. He only wished he could intervene with the dragon for her.

"Where is Nimbulan, Lyman? He should be here, presiding, advising. Helping," he whispered into the old magician's ear.

"He's off being a daddy and restoring the Covenant with the dragons. We'll know if he's done that if a dragon responds to my summons."

"Myrilandel had a baby? Why didn't Nimbulan tell me he's a father? I'd have given him leave to go to my sister moons ago. But I need him here now." Joy for the new life warred with his irritation that no one had told him.

"He didn't know himself until after he left." Lyman continued to scan the skies.

"Then why didn't you tell me? You seem to know more about it than Nimbulan. You always know more than you tell."

"It wasn't my secret to tell." The magician shrugged enigmatically.

"You also seem to know more about the dragons than anyone, including Myrilandel—who is half dragon—and myself with my magical bonds to them through the Coraurlia. How, Lyman. Tell me now." Quinnault studied the old man.

"Because of Myrilandel, you know that purple-tipped dragons have special destinies. They are always born twins but only one may remain a dragon, the other must seek a different form to fulfill its destiny. My twin deserted dragonkind and sought his own life path, forever separated from dragonkind. It was left to me to live both lives."

"You were born a purple-tipped dragon!" Quinnault stared with his mouth half open. Quickly he recovered and checked the ring of lords and magicians to see if any of them had heard the astonishing confession.

"Look. There. Nimbulan must have succeeded in saving Myrilandel and her baby." Lyman pointed eastward, toward where the sun rose over the Great Bay.

"We will discuss this later, Lyman," Quinnault said, also looking across the bay.

A small shadow blocked the growing sunlight for a moment, then the light burst forth brighter, shimmering with rainbows. A dragon approached.

Quinnault shaded his eyes with his hand and looked toward the East for signs of the huge beasts that had blessed his coronation by flying over this courtyard at the moment the priests placed the Coraurlia on his head. His eyes slid right and left, dazzled by the light. He breathed a sign of satisfaction that warred with his concern for Katie. The dragons were as much a part of him now as Katie.

"There, look!" Lyman pointed higher than the rising sun on the stretch of the bay. "Lords of the Council, you should be able to see the dragons now."

Gradually the rainbows faded and revealed a vague outline of wings and spinal horns. All colors swirled into no color around the outline. The male dragons sported a primary color along their wing-veins and horns. This, then, must be Shayla, the female leader of the nimbus. Quinnault's eyes wanted to slide around the flying form, giving the dragon an illusion of transparency.

At this distance she appeared no bigger than his sister's flywacket. But Quinnault knew Shayla would fill the courtyard. Her head was as high as two sledge steeds and her body as broad as two more.

A harsh judge who had announced the breaking of the Covenant. Quinnault knew the heat of guilt. He had exiled his sister, Myrilandel, the chosen intermediary between dragons and humans. Did Shayla hold a grudge?

He shifted his gaze to Katie. She, after all, was the point of this demonstration. She stood in the exact center of the dais, slim and tiny against the larger backdrop of the unfinished courtyard and the bay beyond. The morning breeze pressed the thin fabric of her pure white shift against her body, outlining her breasts and legs. She seemed unconcerned by the immodest revelations of the simple garment. Her gaze wandered across the bay, not focusing on the dragon even after she shaded her eyes with her hand.

She probably couldn't see the rapidly approaching dragon because she didn't yet believe in Shayla's existence.

Resentment rose in his throat against the men of his Council who had arranged this test to satisfy their own lust for power. Quinnault recognized their motives now, not caution against an unknown princess, but the desire to prove their king in error and thus increase their own power within the Council.

The assassin must come from a different source— someone less subtle, more desperate.

Who stood to gain from the death of this unknown princess?

He dragged his gaze away from Katie to survey the reactions of the men in the court. Lyman, still at the foot of the dais, seemed unmoved by the approach of the dragon. Indeed, a small smile played across his ancient mouth as if this entire exercise was a big joke. The other magicians smiled, too. But differently. They experienced a great joy at the sight of Shayla, much as Quinnault did. They almost swelled with pride and happiness as they filled with dragon magic. He'd seen them do this before whenever a dragon was present.

The Lords of the Council reacted differently. Most with the slight cringing of men faced with their fears but too prideful to run. Some closed their eyes and mumbled prayers. None of them reacted to the dragon with joy— though they had called Shayla to preside over this test.

Slowly, as if moving in a world that measured time

differently, Shayla dropped into the courtyard. The bulk of her massive, crystallike body barely fit between Quinnault and the dais, yet somehow she managed to land gracefully with only a minor breeze to ruffle the king's hair. Lyman scuttled adroitly out of her way, moving much more quickly than a man of his years should.

Good morning, Shayla, Quinnault greeted the dragon. *I hope the demands of my Council did not disrupt your day too much.*

(The selection of your queen is important, Quinnault Darville de Draconis. Unlike dragons, humans are not meant to live alone.) Shayla dipped her head in greeting to him. Then she turned her steedlike muzzle toward the small woman on the dais.

Katie stood stiffly, unmoving, as if frozen in time. Her mouth hung partly open in awe. Quinnault saw her perfect white teeth and pink tongue caught in mid-gasp. He was enthralled by her vulnerability. He hadn't recognized that quality in her before. Her small frame was filled with so much strength and humor there shouldn't have been room for this weakness. His heart swelled with the need to protect her.

(So, this is the thing you humans call love,) Shayla chuckled in the back of Quinnault's mind. *(My daughter possesses almost too much of it. I can no longer expect her to live the solitary life of a dragon. You must not force this on her.)*

He wanted to smile with the shared emotion. He didn't quite dare. Katie was still vulnerable to both Shayla and the Council. *I will do what I can to make sure that my sister, your daughter, is no longer alone.* Why had he promised that? He had no idea how he could reverse the edict of exile for Myrilandel and not other rogue magicians.

(Tonight, I will mate with my consorts as you mate with yours. The nimbus will be strong once more. 'Tis the wrong season, but a necessary symbol of our ties to you.)

What I feel for this princess is more than lust of the body, Shayla. I need her at my side every day of my life. I need to share the big decisions and the small daily trivia with her. My life is incomplete without her.

(It is the same, King Quinnault. I am no longer a solitary dragon, but part of a greater whole. Without my con-

sorts and my children, I am less than I am now. Myrilandel has taught me this.) Shayla cocked her head as she examined Katie.

Quinnault sensed puzzlement in the dragon. Then, Shayla turned her attention to Lyman.

"Princess Maarie Kaathliin of Terrania," Lyman said in a stern and commanding voice.

Katie shook herself free of her paralysis and flicked a glance at the old magician. Her eyes returned quickly to the dragon before her.

"Princess, the mental armor you have erected to block out any chance of illusion is very strong. If we cannot poke holes in your barricades to communicate with you telepathically, then we cannot create an illusion for you. The dragon is real. Touch her and know the truth."

Katie paused indecisively a moment, shifting her gaze from Lyman to the dragon, over to Quinnault and back to the dragon. After an interminable moment, she lifted her hand and stretched it forward, stopping a finger's length from Shayla's muzzle. She bit her cheeks and closed her eyes. Then, resolutely, she stretched the extra distance. Her fingertips brushed the soft fur, then jerked back as if burned. She opened her eyes wide and collapsed into a heap of white linen and tangled limbs.

Quinnault leaped for the dais. In two strides he crossed the distance, shouldering Shayla out of the way. Mutely he lifted Katie's limp wrist.

His hands shook so badly he couldn't find her pulse.

*   *   *

Powwell stumbled over a tussock walking backward. He had to keep watching the portal to see if Kalen found her way through it. Nimbulan watched it as well, as if he expected Rollett to walk through it, too. The gate should reopen again soon. The air remained still, without trace of the hot blast from the heart of the volcano.

Ahead of him, the others walked close together, hurrying away from Moncriith's mercenary patrol.

Myri and Maia pointedly ignored each other. Myri strolled at an easy pace. Her longer legs kept her physically closer to Nimbulan than the Rover woman. Neither of them ever got close enough to the Senior Magician to allow him to touch them, or help them over the increasingly cold and rough path.

At least they'd been able to take warm clothing and a few supplies from the patrol. They would survive in this low pass through the Western Mountain Range. If they stayed ahead of Moncriith's men.

What about you, Kalen? Where are you now? Do you live? Powwell prayed that the dragongate had sent her elsewhere at the last minute. He couldn't forget the sight of the hungry lava burning through the bones of a dead man his first day in the pit.

No, Kalen. I won't believe that happened to you.

He turned his gaze back to the top of the hill where the trees leaned together to form an arched shadow with the pile of weathered rocks. The sun continued to rise, shrinking the shadow to a slim line.

He stumbled again. Moisture gathered in his eyes. Even if Kalen escaped the pit, she couldn't come here until the sun rose again in the morning to create that arch. Desperate to get away from the boiling lava, she might plunge into one of the hostile environments of desert, storm-tossed sea, or frozen wasteland and perish before she could get back to Hanassa.

His mind kept shying away from those last moments in the dark and close tunnel. He didn't want to think of the weight of the Kardia pressing on his shoulders or of the way Kalen had run after her familiar, finding the smelly ferret more important than her own safety. He forced himself to remember all the details, as if he memorized a spell he had read in one of Nimbulan's many books. He reached for Thorny, forgetting to speak to his familiar before touching. The hedgehog hunched in startlement. His spines pierced Powwell's hand. Five drops of blood oozed onto his palm. He sucked at them, letting the sting draw more tears from his eyes.

"Just before we stepped through the portal, the guards said 'There they are! Get the Kaaliph.'" He muttered quietly, dredging the memory out with difficulty along with all of the others. "He said 'Kaaliph,' not 'Kaalipha.' Yaassima must have been captured or killed by Moncriith." This time he let the others hear his words.

"I think I would have felt her death," Myri said, stopping abruptly. "Hers or Televarn's. I . . . knew them both very well. I watched the pit engulf her in that vision, and I sensed nothing."

"Moncriith as Kaaliph of Hanassa," Nimbulan said, tasting the words as if seeking poison in them.

Myri lost all color in her normally pale face. She shuddered.

Kalen! he shouted through the void to his friend. *Kalen, please live. You have to live.*

No one answered. A cold ache started in his throat and spread outward. "I have to go back! I have to know what happened to her." Powwell started running back up the hill toward the portal. Scarface blocked his passage. The strange magician held his shoulders tightly, preventing him from going any farther.

Powwell beat at him with clenched fists. Desperation turned his breath to sobs. The hands on his shoulders remained firm but gentle.

"The gate is closed and the patrol is waking up, Powwell. You can't go back through the dragongate." Scarface shook him slightly, forcing him to think beyond his immediate desire. "I know what you are going through. I lost my family during the wars. They were attacked by the troops of our own lord. He suspected we harbored an escaping soldier from the enemy. Their Battlemages made me watch, wouldn't let me help my family. I was spared because I was too valuable as a magician. Later I escaped to Hanassa. It's a pain you never get over, you just learn to live with it."

"I can't leave Kalen in Hanassa!" Powwell added mental blasts to his attack on Scarface.

Scarface only shifted his hold to encircle Powwell's throat from behind.

"Think, Powwell," Nimbulan soothed. *Think with your head, not your heart. Getting yourself killed won't help Kalen."*

"She loved that damned ferret more than me!" Powwell cried. All of his strength dribbled out of his limbs. "And Wiggles got her killed by Moncriith."

"You know the bond between a magician and a familiar is very special, Powwell," Myri said. "Imagine how you would feel if Thorny left you for more than a few moments. Kalen must have been separated from Wiggles for all the weeks since we left the clearing, until yesterday. The ferret wasn't with her while we were in the village and was still missing when she came to me in the palace. He found her yesterday. Those special bonds brought him through hundreds of miles of mountains to reclaim her. Her sanity might not have survived another separation so soon."

Powwell stopped his struggles, aghast at Myri's words.

"What do you mean, she and Wiggles were separated?"

"He wasn't with her when Yaassima first brought Kalen to me, right after . . . right after Amaranth died and I was so distraught I couldn't care for my own baby. Kalen must have felt much the same when she first arrived in Hanassa without Wiggles to comfort her."

"She had the blasted ferret tucked into her sleeves when Televarn pushed us into the dragongate near the village. Wiggles was with her the first week we were in Hanassa. I didn't see him again, but you know how he hides." Every muscle in Powwell's body froze with fear. Fear that what he had perceived as the truth was false. Fear that Kalen had indeed deserted him by choice.

Thorny gibbered at him from his tunic pocket. Powwell couldn't understand all of the rapid ripples of emotions broadcast by the hedgehog. He did catch a sense of being told to run, *Run quickly, back the way we came.* Then the memory of being dragged through the dragongate.

Silence echoed in Powwell's ears.

He fought the conviction that Thorny had heard Kalen tell her familiar to run away so she could avoid leaving by way of the dragongate with Powwell and Myri and Nimbulan—her family.

"Where . . . where was the ferret when Kalen came to me? She said Wiggles wasn't in Hanassa." Myri, too, seemed afraid to move lest she discover an ugly truth.

"I don't know." Powwell shook his head in denial of the entire issue. But Kalen's duplicity wouldn't go away.

"When I first discovered evidence of Televarn's Water spell, I saw tiny pawprints beside the trickle of water," Nimbulan said. His left hand came up, palm out. The habitual gesture told Powwell that he sought information. "A moment before the trap crashed over me, I saw a small animal dash past me. At the time I thought it one of the rat-catching ferrets Quinnault keeps in the palace who was running from the wall of Water. Later, the guards searching for Televarn also reported a ferret in the clearing with the Rover. They disappeared together."

"Kalen and Televarn? I won't believe it." Powwell cringed inside, wanting to run far and fast—run from the idea of Kalen corrupted by the slimy Rover.

"I caught Kalen in a terrible lie at the moment Wiggles returned to her. She told me Nimbulan had drowned." Myri clutched at her husband's hand as if to reassure herself that he lived indeed.

"Kalen hated Televarn. She hated Hanassa and . . . and . . ." Powwell choked on the next thought. "And yet she thrived there. I watched her daily as she blossomed. I wanted to believe it was womanhood coming upon her and her love for me."

"The brat thrived on power, not love," Scarface added, spitting into the dirt. "I saw her often enough in the city. The first week you arrived, she was always with Televarn. Even after the Rover chieftain left the city on his assassination commission, she never went out to the fields with the work parties, but she carried messages for the Rover clan."

"What do you know about it? You never met her!" Powwell wrenched free of the magician's now gentle grasp. Anger exploded in his mind. He needed to slam his fist into something. Scarface's ugly visage was the nearest satisfactory target.

Scarface caught his wrist easily, restraining his blow.

"Televarn used the girl as a messenger. She came to me and my men several times. I owed Televarn—some favors, favors that I resented and he never let me forget. I watched the girl manipulate people with words and with magic. She inflated men's self-esteem with promises of sex with herself or the Rover women. She hinted at influence with Televarn and Yaassima's growing dependence upon the Rovers. She was using Televarn's plans to depose Yaassima to elevate herself to a position of power in the new regime."

"I loved her," Powwell said. Defeat weighed heavily in him. He knew Scarface spoke the truth. He had watched Kalen's manipulations. She had told him that she wanted to be in a position so that no one could use her for their own gain. Her parents had sold her talent for food and shelter. Ackerly, Nimbulan's former assistant, had tried to sell her talent for gold that he kept himself. She had pleaded with him to forget his plans to help Myri. She was jealous of the baby, thought Myri had deserted and betrayed her by having another child, as she thought her mother had betrayed her for staying in Coronnan City with Kalen's brothers and sisters.

"She wanted to be in control of herself and everyone around her." Powwell didn't realize he'd spoken until her heard his own words. "I thought it merely a childish dream. No one has that kind of power over people."

"Yaassima did," Yaala said in her deep voice, so husky he could never tell if she verged on tears or not.

"Kalen and Televarn would make quite a pair." Nimbulan shook his head sadly. "With his ambition and her plots, they could have ruled all of Kardia Hodos in time."

"If either of them lives," Powwell added. He didn't think Kalen was dead. But where could she be and still live? Their bonds had been close before they had been kidnapped with Myri. After that she had changed, and the closeness, the whispered confidences in the slave pen, the shared tears, holding each other to keep out the cold and the terror, were all a sham. On her part. "I love her. I would have taken care of her. I wanted to marry her as soon as she was old enough."

"You do realize, Powwell, that Kalen was your half sister? The physical resemblance between you is too strong to be coincidence," Nimbulan said.

"She wasn't!" Powwell screamed. "She couldn't be. I won't believe it."

"I doubt that Stuuvaart sired her," Nimbulan continued. "He has no trace of magic in him, neither does Guillia or your mother. I believe a magician seduced both women and then abandoned them. Not an uncommon occurrence in the war years."

Powwell took a deep breath and released it. Stuuvart, the self-serving steward at the School for Magicians, was the last man he wanted to acknowledge as his long-lost father. But who? He didn't want to think about it. Was afraid to believe it.

"The physical resemblance between you and Kalen is

too remarkable," Myri reinforced her husband's statement. "Your speech patterns and gestures are also too similar. It is right that you should love each other and be friends, but you can never be intimate with her, never make her your wife."

"You have no proof that Stuuvart isn't her father."

"When we get back to the School, I will find a way to prove it to you, Powwell," Nimbulan said, resuming his trek Eastward, toward Coronnan. "Now would be a good time for the dragons to return."

"That won't stop me from finding a way to go to Kalen."

"Somehow, I don't think your sister will appreciate your efforts, any more than my brother will welcome my return to Coronnan," Myri mumbled.

CHAPTER 33

Shayla! Myri called into the vastness of open sky.
Her mind and her heart remained empty of the
dragon's presence. She huddled closer to Nimbulan and
the small fire they allowed themselves while she nursed
her baby and they all ate of the dry journey rations. The
absence of the dragons left a chill deeper in her heart
than the winter wind that whipped through the pass.

"I can't hear Shayla at all!" Myri tried again to summon a dragon—any dragon. "This is as bad as when I
was in Hanassa. I can't hear the dragons." All her life
she had listened to the voices in the back of her head,
guiding her through life when no one else cared for or
trusted her.

She understood they would not go near Hanassa in
any way, even to reassure one of their own trapped
within the boundaries of the volcanic crater. Their vows
of separation from the stronghold of the renegade
dragon, Hanassa, who had taken human form, had lasted
for centuries. Dragon memory was long.

She wondered briefly if Old Lyman who had been, in
his previous existence, the last purple-tipped dragon before Amaranth and herself, had known Hanassa.

This emptiness was something more than the dragon's
avoidance of Hanassa. The dragons roamed free over
this land. Shayla had been calmly munching on a stunted
Tambootie tree when Myri and the others emerged
through the dragongate. Almost as if she expected Myri
to emerge there and wanted to make sure her daughter
was safe.

Now Shayla shunned her call for help and reassurance.

"I can't raise Lyman at the school," Nimbulan said,
staring into the fire. He held his glass, minus the gold
frame, before his eyes, magnifying the flames and his

spell. "We have to get news of the invasion to Quinnault before he marries the temptress. I wonder where she really hails from and who planted her in Coronnan. I have a lot of questions about the princess who appeared as soon as I had left the capital."

Myri looked closely at his bland expression. He had locked away his emotions from her gentle probes since Powwell's terrible accusation.

"Talk to me, Nimbulan," she pleaded.

"I just spoke to you about the summons spell." He continued to peer into the fire through his glass.

"You said words, but you haven't talked, haven't reacted to the terrible hurt Powwell dealt you with his words."

"He didn't hurt me. He spoke the truth. I hurt myself with my regret and my guilt."

"You won't heal, Lan, until you talk to me."

"There is nothing to talk about. I valued my apprentices above you and Kalen. 'Tis my shortcoming. I must learn to live with it."

A chill ran through Myri. "Do you mean to abandon me again? Me and Amaranth, your daughter."

"I don't know what I will do after I get word to King Quinnault about the invasion. I don't know if I'm capable of loving anyone enough to . . ." Without another word, he traded his glass for a journal and began writing with a black stick he kept tucked inside the book.

Myri looked at the intricate marks on the page, wondering what he recorded. She'd never learned to read and hoped Nimbulan would remain with her long enough to teach her.

"Why do you ask where the princess comes from, Lan?" Myri asked. I've heard of Terrania in old legends."

"Do you remember the landscape of the desert with red sand we saw through the dragongate?"

Myri nodded.

"That is Terrania," he replied grimly. "No one has lived there for many thousands of years. Quinnault's bride is a fake." He returned to his journal.

Scarface watched from the edge of the rock overhang that sheltered them in a mountain pass from any mercenaries patrolling in the area. The ones they'd left behind should have recovered by now. They had no way of knowing if the witch-sniffers would pursue revenge for the massive headaches the paralysis spell would leave with them and the loss of their cloaks and food, or if they would retreat to nurse their injured emotions and minds.

"Could Televarn have planted the princess?" Yaala offered. "He thrives on convoluted plans. He sold his women to the brothels for politics as well as money. Perhaps he plotted with this woman for the purpose of inciting a war. If he can create enough chaos, then he can step in and take over for lack of leadership."

"That sounds like Televarn," Myri agreed. During the moon she had lived with the Rover more than a year ago, he had proved false in his protestations of love and loyalty.

"Televarn doesn't need to be sneaky. He just needs to read your mind once, and he'll never leave you alone," Maia said bitterly. "He uses people like candle stubs. When they are used up, he throws them away."

"I left him before he could discard me. So he has to pursue me. No one else may possess me until he decides he is finished with me." Myri added.

She checked the now sated and sleeping Amaranth rather than dwell on the Rover chieftain. Satisfied that the baby was safe from the blazing emotions that had run rampant a few hours ago, she shifted her attention to Powwell. The boy sat, sullen and staring into the distance. He systematically stripped a long stem of grass, then plucked another, stripped it, plucked another. Myri wondered if he knew what occupied his hands.

"Maybe I can summon Kalen," he said quietly. "She was always receptive to communication spells, though she hated sending them." His words barely reached across the fire to Myri.

"Even if she answered, Powwell, we can't help her yet. We need to get to the capital, fast," Nimbulan said. He stood abruptly and scanned the skies. "But I promise you, as soon as I have arranged for the safety of my king and the kingdom, I will return to Hanassa for Rollett and Kalen. Maybe if we join our magic, Powwell, we can catch someone's attention in the capital."

Powwell stood up, lethargic, his attention still on the distant hilltop and the dragongate.

"I would be interested in this new magic," Scarface said.

"Before I can even test you to see if you can gather dragon magic, I must have your life's oath of loyalty to the Commune, Aaddler."

Myri raised her eyebrows at Nimbulan's use of the man's real name. Involving a real name among magicians seemed a gesture of intimacy or intense seriousness.

"I understand." Scarface nodded his acceptance. "I must think on this. A lifelong commitment like that cannot be taken lightly."

"I respect that more than a hasty agreement that might be regretted later. I find the fellowship and ideals of the Commune easier to live with than the constantly changing rules and loyalties of solitary magicians and rogue mercenaries," Nimbulan replied. He turned his back on the stranger as he took Powwell's hand in his own.

By some unspoken agreement, Scarface also turned his back on the two communal magicians, continuing his watch of the low mountain pass—a narrow but easy passage from SeLenicca into Coronnan.

Myri observed, through the magic cord that bound them together, Nimbulan's preparations for the next attempt at a summons. Desperately she hoped that this time she would comprehend the secret of dragon magic. If she could figure out how to gather and use the special energy. Then, and only then, could she return to Coronnan legally with her husband, never be separated from him again.

Once again the elusive process passed by her so quickly she missed the essential ingredient. Once again she was shut out of the special bond of communal magic.

She sank back onto the ground beside Amaranth and Yaala. The need to open communication with someone prompted her to speak to the young woman. "Why did Yaassima exile and disown you? You seem like a woman who could lead."

"I don't look like a dragon." Yaala shrugged and shifted uncomfortably. She pulled her back straighter, away from the hard rock surface they had been leaning against. Her light blonde hair had more color than Myri's or Yaassima's. Broken nails and encrusted dirt on her fingers couldn't hide their slender length. But they weren't extraordinarily long like Myri's or Yaassima's. Or baby Amaranth's.

"Do you have the spinal bumps?" Myri asked.

"Very prominently." Yaala wiggled her back again, trying to find a comfortable position.

"Mine aren't very obvious," Myri volunteered. "I borrowed a human body for my dragon personality. Myrilandel was blonde and long boned already. My fingers and toes grew to accommodate Amethyst's instincts to grasp and climb. I guess Amethyst also bleached the color from my hair and skin. But I couldn't grow the extra eyelid that protects dragons from dust and the super brightness of the sun in the upper atmosphere."

Yaala stared at the flames, much as Nimbulan did to work the summons. A light film dropped over her eye.

"Which person are you, Myrilandel or Amethyst?" Yaala shifted slightly, putting a few more finger lengths between herself and Myri.

"Both and neither. Myrilandel was only two when her human body was on the verge of dying. Amethyst gave her the vitality to use her natural healing ability to correct the weak blood vessels in her brain. The two personalities were so strong that they compromised on forgetfulness, neither of them dominant, until I met the dragons and found a husband who loved me enough to let me explore my past without prejudice. I like to think I developed a personality all my own." Unique, worth preserving. Yaassima had forced her to fight for what she held important in life rather than running away. Did she have the strength and will to continue the fight for Nimbulan's love?

Yes. She had to. Her family wasn't complete without him. She wasn't complete without him.

"Yaassima can't allow anyone that kind of freedom and individuality." Yaala pushed the words out through clenched teeth. "She has to control every thought, every gesture, every moment of their lives. I fought her. My father encouraged me. That's probably the real reason she executed him and exiled me to the pit."

"And yet she is very lonely," Myri whispered. "She

needed to love you. Since you didn't meet her expectations, she transferred her need to Amaranth and me. If only she had recognized that the strength you found to fight her was the strength you need to rule Hanassa, you . . ."

"But she did recognize it. She hated it and saw me as a rival rather than a partner." Yaala stood up, ending the conversation. "I think the summons is working."

Myri felt Nimbulan's growing excitement through her talent. The silver cord vibrated in tune with the magic pulsing through the glass.

"Lyman, you have to warn the king," Nimbulan said into the glass. He looked tired and hungry from his efforts to contact his friend at the school.

"Not now, Nimbulan. We're all very busy." Lyman's voice was so strong they all heard the message. "Shayla says you are safe. That is enough for now."

The communication ended abruptly, leaving them alone on the vulnerable mountain pass.

CHAPTER 34

"Get a healer!" Quinnault bellowed. He lay Katie flat against the wooden platform of the dais and began breathing into her mouth.

(She will be difficult to live with, Quinnault. Are you sure you wish to mate with her for all time?) Amusement tinged Shayla's voice.

"Be quiet, I'm trying to save her life, Shayla."

(She lives. Your efforts are redundant.) Again that irritating chuckle invaded his mind.

Beneath his hands, Katie stirred. Relieved that the dragon was correct, he raised his head enough to glare at Shayla. "The shock could have killed her."

"It very nearly did," Katie whispered. Then she raised her right hand and slapped him soundly across the face.

"What was that for?" He reared back, dropping her back to the dais with a thump. He fingered his right cheek delicately. He'd be lucky if it weren't bruised for the wedding ceremony and banquet. Not a good precedent to set for the beginning of a lifelong commitment.

"That was for every man in my life who presumes to know what my duty is and what is best for me. And since my father and brothers, and esteemed royal grandfather aren't here to collect their share, you get it all." She sat up, pushing away from his hovering presence. An angry flush replaced the paleness on her cheeks.

Some of her fears leaked through to his mind—the chill morning breeze against her nearly naked body, and the hostility of the lords and magicians surrounding her. He smiled, realizing that only he stood between her and all those terrible things. Things he could protect her from.

Shayla pushed her enormous muzzle closer.

Katie slapped her away—somewhat more gently than

she had Quinnault. "Go away. I told you I don't like
other . . . beings mucking about in my mind. That goes
for you too, Daddy!" She directed her last words toward
the islands in the bay. "Telepathy made me special back
home. Here, it's a nuisance. I don't want any more of it."
Anger banished all those fears. But the faintest tremble
touched her lower lip.

Quinnault wanted nothing more than to kiss it back
into stubborn firmness.

"She's a magician. We can't have a rogue magician
for a queen. The marriage treaty is voided!" Lord Hanic
shouted across the courtyard. The other lords pressed
closer, along with the magicians to look more closely at
the angry princess.

"You can't break a dragon-blessed treaty, Hanic,"
Lyman reminded the Council member. "Nor can you
depose a dragon-blessed monarch. You wrote that law
and forced it upon the Council."

Lord Hanic glared at Lyman, standing his ground. He
opened his mouth to issue another pronouncement.
Shayla turned her gaze on the man before he said anything. Quickly he closed his mouth with an audible click
of his teeth and backed away from the dragon.

"I'm not a magician, and I don't want to be one. I
can read minds a little, and that's too much,' she retorted. "For seven hundred years, the only telepaths
we've been able to find in my—um—country are in my
family. Kinnsell wanted to take some of your magicians
home to study them. I wouldn't let him. Telepathy is a
curse. From now on, I swear to keep my thoughts to
myself and stay out of everyone else's!" *Except for you,
Scarecrow. I couldn't keep you out if I tried.* "I'll take
drugs to suppress my talent if I have to."

Quinnault sat back on his heels, amazed at the transformation of his gentle princess into this spitting spotted
saber cat. Some of Shayla's humor spilled over into him.

"You are the most beautiful woman in the world!" he
laughed uproariously.

"Stifle it, Scarecrow, before I pack my bags and run
far, far away from this dirty backwater."

He ended her tirade with a kiss. She pummeled his chest
with her fists. He captured them and deepened his assault on her full lips, savoring the taste of her on his

questing tongue at last. Slowly she relaxed her struggle but did not respond. He enfolded her in his arms, pulling her into his lap, twining his fingers in her silky hair.

Her mouth opened a fraction as her arms stole around his neck.

Heat invaded every pore of his body, filling him with passion.

"Are you two going to come up for air?" Lyman asked.

"No." Quinnault stole a quick gulp of air and renewed his kiss.

(Are you certain you wish to spend the rest of your life with this headstrong woman and no other?) Shayla asked.

Quinnault looked the dragon in the eye as he breathed deeply, trying to control his raging passion for the woman in his arms.

Shayla's penetrating gaze made him squirm as she examined his motives. He looked from the dragon to the islands in the bay, back to Katie, then returned once again to the port, thinking furiously all the time. He had so many questions. Was his love for her enough to overcome them?

Katie drew his eyes like a lodestone to iron. Finally he had his emotions under control and could speak in a normal tone of voice.

"I have no choice, Shayla. I have to marry her."

Thwack! Katie slapped him again as she squirmed to be free of him.

"I thought I didn't have a choice either. But I'll be damned if I put up with this. I thought we could care for each other, but you are as selfish as every other man in my life." She fought his grasp with fists and kicks.

He clung tighter to her, desperate to rectify the misunderstanding. "Katie, I meant that you are the only woman I want. I can't choose another after meeting you." He put all of his feelings into his eyes, staring at her. Willing her to believe him.

She glared at him. He held her gaze. Gradually the truth penetrated her stubborn mind.

"Oh, Scarecrow," she sighed and kissed him as passionately as he had kissed her only moments before.

(You have my blessing, King Quinnault Darville de Draconis. Enjoy!) Shayla bunched her muscles, took two

running steps, and launched herself into the sky. *(To-night I shall fly with my consorts as will you. We will both conceive, though the seasons are not quite right. The future of Coronnan and of the nimbus is assured.)*

"Where are you going, Shayla? Won't you stay for the wedding?" Quinnault asked. He kept a tight hold on Katie, afraid she'd disappear in a puff of smoke now that she was his.

(I have my own celebration to attend.) The dragon blasted their ears with a high-pitched screech that announced her triumph and her passion. As she circled the courtyard, the outlines of five male dragons joined her.

Quinnault picked out red, blue, green, yellow, and orange along the wingtips and veins of the consorts.

"The more fathers, the big and stronger the litter," he quoted.

"Not for this princess, King Quinnault. You are the only one allowed in my bed," Katie retorted. She reinforced her statement with a resounding kiss that left him light-headed.

"Well, at least wait for the nuptials and some privacy," Lyman laughed. "Don't we have a banquet to prepare?"

"Go ahead. We'll be right with you," Quinnault waved them away and pressed his mouth to Katie's once more.

*   *   *

Nimbulan walked closer to Myri, slipping his arm around her waist, a subtle support before she stumbled again. She didn't lean into him, but she didn't pull away either. He was too tired to think about the tangled mess he'd made of his personal life.

Maia still presented a big problem.

What to do with her? He owed her a home. She'd never be allowed to return to her clan. Without them, she had nothing. Unless Televarn was still manipulating her through his mind link.

How far away must Maia be to get beyond Televarn's reach? Had the Rover Chieftain survived the knife thrust?

He turned his mind back to watching his steps rather

than thinking about how much women complicated his life. The bachelor life of most magicians seemed inviting.

But if he hadn't married Myri, loved her so desperately, he'd not have his daughter. His very beautiful daughter.

"Let me take the baby, Myri. She must be very heavy for you." He lifted the tiny bundle of life out of her makeshift sling.

Myri's hands grabbed for her child, resisting separation. Nimbulan saw her emotions play across her face even as he sensed them. "You won't lose her if you let me hold her for awhile. I'm not Yaassima. And I'm not a Rover who will steal any child for the sake of new blood in the clan," he reassured her. He refused to look at Maia while he spoke. Did the Rover woman still seek to kidnap Amaranth for the benefit of the clan and Televarn?

Myri relinquished the burden of the baby's weight reluctantly. As he cradled Amaranth in the crook of his right arm, he draped his left around Myri's shoulders. The sudden warmth that filled his soul almost stopped him in his tracks.

In many ways, Nimbulan was an unknown to her. Their courtship and marriage had been brief before her exile.

He had allowed her to become the victim of an edict that put the fears and prejudices of the Council above the needs of the individual. *He* had become so involved in politics he hadn't followed through with the sporadic communication with her and Powwell.

He kept walking, trying to figure out his emotional upheaval. He thought again of the four islands in the Great Bay. He'd take Myri there, and they would live together for the rest of their lives. He couldn't leave her again.

But he couldn't tell her about his plans in case they came to naught. There had to be a way to keep her close without breaking the laws of Coronnan.

The low mountain pass twisted and turned back on itself a dozen times, leading into box canyons and across surging creeks before descending the hills into Coronnan. Nimbulan didn't know how to use the terrain to

their advantage. He needed a broad plain with two opposing armies. That he could plan for.

They'd walked for hours. They were all tired and hungry. They all watched the sun march progressively closer
to the horizon and the time for Quinnault's wedding.

Lyman and the other magicians continued to ignore a
summons spell. Without a dragon to carry them to the
capital, Nimbulan had no hope of preventing the union
of his king and the false princess before the invasion.

"We need to stop and eat," he said though his mind
urged him to continue forward.

What had gotten into Quinnault that he would risk
his fragile peace? Where had the Princess of Terrania
come from? More important, who was behind the plot?

"I'm sensing a mass of people behind us," Scarface
replied warily. "I don't think this is a good time to stop."

Nimbulan scanned the canyon to his left. A small
creek joined a slightly larger one at the mouth of the
opening. He guessed the easy game trail led into yet
another dead end, hopefully one that offered numerous
hiding places, possibly caves where they could light a
fire and rest.

Powwell turned automatically up the trail, without argument. He'd been so depressed since leaving Kalen behind that Nimbulan wondered if the boy was capable of
independent thought.

Yaala trudged after the boy, bound to him by their
shared experiences in the pit and yet apart from them
all.

Myri reached to take back the baby.

"Please, Myri, let me carry her a little longer. I know
I don't deserve this special blessing, but . . ." How did
he make amends for all those lonely moons of exile that
made her vulnerable to Televarn's kidnap and Yaassima's cruel imprisonment of her?

She nodded slowly, maintaining eye contact with him.

"Our daughter is very precious. I vow before you and
the Stargods that I will never do anything to harm her
or you again." He touched his heart, then hers to seal
the vow.

Myri rewarded him with a weak smile. Her hand lingered tentatively on his as he supported Amaranth

against his shoulder. Yet he feared every moment she would withdraw from him.

Maia's face turned bronze-red beneath the olive tones of her skin. "I was your first love. I gave you a *son*. You never promised me anything."

"Myrilandel is my love and my wife. I will provide for you, Maia, do what I can to protect you from Televarn and the rest of the clan. But I do not love you, I doubt I ever did. We were both victims of Televarn's manipulations. We did not enter that union of our own free will."

"They're getting closer!" Scarface hissed, urging them into the rugged canyon. "Can't you feel their malevolence beating against the rocks? They want blood. Our blood."

Cradling Amaranth in one arm, the other supporting Myri around the waist, Nimbulan increased his stride. He left Maia to Scarface's ministrations. Yaala guided Powwell.

They needed a hiding place, someplace with wood where they could separate from their talents. Only then would they be safe from the witch-sniffers.

"Not that way, Lan. I feel people up this canyon. Lots and lots of people!" Myri held him back.

Nimbulan turned to retreat. Two dozen archers faced them, arrows nocked, bowstrings taut.

"So we meet again, Nimbulan. This time on my terms, on my battleground, without any of your dragon demons to defend you or your witch," Moncriith said mildly, working his way through the ranks of soldiers to face Nimbulan.

CHAPTER 35

Doubts nagged at Quinnault. He didn't have enough to do to keep them at bay. Katie was closeted with the women, preparing for the wedding. His servants and stewards bustled about the palace, preparing for the ceremony and the banquet to follow. Even the magicians all seemed to be occupied, looking for omens in arcane spells and rituals.

More often than not, he was in the way—just like the day they had prepared for battle. This time his chief steward and the senior ladies of the court had become the Battlemages.

He chuckled at the idea of viewing a wedding in the same light as a major battle.

Memories of Katie and her argument with her father came back to haunt him. *I am in charge,* she had said. They'd do it her way or not at all. Do what?

Kinnsell had left, accepting her edict that the Varns would harvest the Tambootie, build the port, and leave, never to interfere with Kardia Hodos again. What rare qualities of leadership did Quinnault's bride possess that allowed her to command meek obedience from her father?

Quinnault wondered if she'd order her husband around with the same authority. The telepathic bond between them meant that she could manipulate him with a thought. Would she? Or would she keep her vow to suppress her talent? He didn't know if that was possible. He'd never heard of any drugs that effectively masked a talent without putting the patient to sleep for days on end.

And what about Kinnsell's plot to kidnap magicians for study? Katie claimed that was the core of their argument last night.

Quinnault had no doubt that Kinnsell had the means to remove several powerful magicians from Coronnan without detection. Would he obey Katie's edict or appear to accept her orders and then do precisely what he wanted later?

Kinnsell hadn't been seen all day. Would he come for the wedding? As Katie's father, he had every right to participate in the ceremony.

Too many questions and no answers.

Too many people rushing about the Great Hall, including Lord Konnaught. Quinnault's fosterling stood in the center of the dais, hands on hips, lower lip thrust out belligerently. No one paid him any attention.

Quinnault decided he'd ignore the brat, too.

Since he couldn't talk to Katie or her father, Quinnault decided to talk to someone else. Piedro, the Rover assassin. He'd feel a lot better about the ceremony if he knew who had hired Piedro. Nimbulan had told him often enough that Rovers were incapable of independent thought, all were manipulated by the clan chieftain who was always the dominant mage. He wondered if last night's attempt to strangle Katie and place the blame on Quinnault was part of the aborted poison plot arranged by Televarn.

"Bessel," he called to the journeyman magician who directed apprentices on the placement of witchlight torches around the great hall. "I need your assistance."

The young man detached himself from the younger students almost eagerly.

"Do you know who sealed the dungeon cell last night?" Quinnault asked as he guided Bessel toward the cellars.

"Gilby and I did it, Your Grace, along with Master Maarkus." Bessel thrust his shoulders back proudly.

"Can you undo it by yourself?"

"I can let you in and out of the cell, sir. But since the three of us set the spell, only the three of us can break it and allow the prisoner out. Do you wish to interrogate the prisoner now?" Bessel loomed back over his shoulder at the hectic preparations for the wedding.

"Yes, now. Before his employer tries something else." Quinnault signaled two guards to follow them.

Together they wound their way through a series of

cellars, then down another spiral staircase into the chambers cut from the bedrock of Palace Isle. A long corridor broken by the doorways of a dozen cells stretched before them. All the doors except one stood ajar. Quinnault hadn't jailed anyone but Piedro in years.

"Are you going to torture the prisoner now? Can I watch?" Konnaught asked as he hurried down the steps behind Quinnault and Bessel. He pushed his way between the guards who followed the king everywhere. The men stepped away, hands on the hilts of their swords, eyes wary.

"This is none of your concern, Lord Konnaught. Return to your lessons at once." Quinnault stood firmly in place, refusing to move any closer to Piedro's cell until the boy had left. With a flick of his head upward he gestured for the guards to remove the pest.

"But I must know how this is done when I am king." Konnaught glared at him, mimicking his hands on hips posture.

"I have no intention of dying prematurely so that you can be king. Tell me, did you arrange this assassination so that I would?" Quinnault grabbed the boy by the neck of his tunic. He wanted to shake the brat but restrained himself, as a king must.

"I'd be more direct, if I were to do something so stupid. And I'd hire a more intelligent assassin," Konnaught snarled back, not intimidated by Quinnault's superior size or his barely restrained anger.

"Then why are you here?" Quinnault asked. He kept his eyes focused on the stone steps behind him rather than the boy who incited such anger in him.

"Because I want to watch the Rover-scum squirm under torture."

"Did you ever watch your father beat his lovers until their faces were bloody pulps and they bled from the inside?" Quinnault bared his teeth as he moved his face closer to Konnaught's, maintaining his fierce grip on his collar.

Konnaught shook his head. He closed his eyes and gulped.

"What about the times your father pillaged and burned entire villages for no reason other than to soothe his temper? Did you watch then as innocent men and women burned alive? Did you enjoy watching their skin melt away and their hair becoming torches as their lungs clogged with smoke?" Renewed anger at the depredations of his now deceased rival burned within Quinnault. In this moment he put aside his regret that he had wielded the sword that killed Kammeryl d'Astrismos, Konnaught's father.

"No—no, Your Grace," Konnaught stammered and sagged within Quinnault's grip. Then he stiffened. "But they were peasants. . . ."

"They were innocent *people*. I refuse to argue with you anymore, or put up with your insolence and your idolization of your father's evil. Pack your possessions. You sail at dawn for the Monastic School in Sollthrie."

"You don't dare exile me. I—I'm your only heir. I—I hold the allegiance of three other lords who think your view of government is stupid. And I think you are stupid," Konnaught blustered. But his chin quivered as he spoke.

"Then you must learn to think differently. I know of no better place to do that than Sollthrie."

"But . . . but there's nothing there!"

"There is the finest school in all of Kardia Hodos."

"But no one ever leaves there. They . . . they stay and become celibate priests."

"Precisely. I should have sent you there last Spring, but I was too kind and expected too much from you. Guard, take him back to his room and supervise his packing. He won't need much."

The guard on the left took Konnaught's elbow, somewhat more gently than Quinnault had grabbed his collar, and led him back up the stairs.

"Now, Bessel, let us see what this Rover knows." Only a tiny bit of regret niggled at Quinnault's brain. He'd failed with teaching Konnaught responsibility, justice, and concern for others. Maybe the boy was incapable of learning such concepts. Mostly he felt a tremendous relief at having made a decision.

He turned to face the sealed prison door.

"I'm afraid we are too late, Your Grace," Bessel said, peering through the slitted window of the heavy wooden cell door.

"What do you mean?" Quinnault shouldered the young journeyman aside to look himself. The cell appeared empty. "He was here this morning. His guards reported him screaming to let him out not an hour ago."

"He's gone, Your Grace. The Rover has escaped and left my seal and the mundane locks in place."

*   *   *

Powwell nearly jumped out of his skin at Moncriith's words. He'd been so preoccupied with his own misery he hadn't watched his steps until he nearly stepped on the Bloodmage.

"Where's Kalen?" he blurted without thought.

"Silence, demon spawn!" Moncriith intoned, raising his hands in the same gesture priests used to denote a benediction.

Blood dripped from Moncriith's fingers and a gash across his forehead. Behind him lay the corpse of a man wearing the black uniform of Kaalipha Yaassima's personal guard. His throat had been slit. His mouth was frozen in a scream of horror.

"Nastfa!" Myri choked at sight of the man.

"I name him traitor," Moncriith replied. "He fell victim to the seduction of the demons within you, Myrilandel. He had to die. What better way than as sacrifice to give me enough magic to stop you once and for all?" He cocked his head and smiled almost amiably.

The Bloodmage was insane, Powwell realized. Moncriith had murdered a man and mutilated himself, again, to fuel his fanaticism.

"With my head and my heart and the strength of my shoulders, I reject this evil." Powwell signed the cross of the Stargods. Beside him, Yaala did the same.

"The Stargods can't protect you. They are with me," Moncriith proclaimed. "Prepare to die!"

Nimbulan's hand landed on Powwell's shoulder. The familiar blending and surging of power pulled the last remnants of dragon magic out of Powwell. He fought the light-headed emptiness. He had to stall while Nimbulan prepared a defensive spell. The dragons wouldn't allow an attack fueled by their magic, only defense.

But an attack might very well bring a dragon to them posthaste. He hoped Nimbulan realized this or read his thoughts. He had to stall.

"Where's Kalen?" Powwell asked again. "You came through the dragongate in Hanassa. Kalen was the only one left there who knew its secrets."

"She and Yaassima died opening the gate for me. Their deaths shifted the vortex to take me directly to my troops. I was the last person through before the tunnels and caverns collapsed behind me. The *demon's* gate is closed forever."

"You bastard!" Powwell launched himself at the Bloodmage. Rage turned his vision red. Vaguely, he heard Nimbulan protest the separation between them and the division of the magic.

He didn't care. The only thing that existed for Powwell was Moncriith and the need to kill the Bloodmage. Fingers flexed, he aimed for Moncriith's eyes. Soft skin squished beneath his jagged and dirty fingernails. He felt a satisfying gush of hot blood against his palms.

Inside his tunic, Thorny hunched. Sharp spines penetrated Powwell's clothing to prick his chest. His emotional contact with the hedgehog strengthened his anger and his determination to kill Moncriith.

He kicked back at the men who tried to pull him off of Moncriith. He heard screams and closed his ears to them.

Someone pressed a dagger against his throat. He didn't care. Moncriith had killed Kalen. Moncriith had to die. Powwell would gladly die with him as long as the Bloodmage died. Painfully. Messily.

"Powwell, no." Myri's quiet command penetrated the red blur of pain and fury. "He's not worth murdering."

Powwell didn't release his grip on the now screaming Moncriith. Thorny relaxed his spines. Powwell refused to follow his familiar's lead.

"Amaranth isn't old enough to separate herself from the victims around her. Kill Moncriith and you kill the baby." Nimbulan reminded him quietly. "Do you want my daughter's death on your soul as well as his?"

Moncriith roared triumphantly as he broke Powwell's grip on his face with a mighty thrust. Powwell flew backward, landing on his butt with a harsh jar that sent his head spinning.

The note of exultation in Moncriith's pain shook Pow-

well more than Myri's words or the spine numbing fall.
How could the man revel in the pain?

Then he knew. As soon as Moncriith's blood had
touched his hands, Powwell had felt a surge of strength
and power. His own pain from the prick of Thorny's
spines added to it. He had tapped blood magic without
thinking. The rage drained out of him. His stomach
twisted into a knot.

"To me, Powwell. I need your magic," Nimbulan
called. His hands rose up, palm outward, fingers curved,
to catch the magic hurled by Moncriith.

Powwell struggled to get his feet beneath him. They
wouldn't cooperate. Yaala's hand grasped his belt and
propelled him in Nimbulan's direction. He landed face-
down in the dirt, one hand touching his teacher's
scuffed boot.

Tingles worked their way up from the ground, through
him. He lay across a ley line that begged him to tap
its energy.

Useless.

Nimbulan couldn't combine with ley line energy. They
needed dragon magic. Powwell's store was empty.

Nimbulan faltered in his defense. His own store of
magic must be dangerously low as well.

Where were the dragons?

Moncriith yelled something in the old language as he
hurled a massive ball of witchfire at Nimbulan and Myri.

Nimbulan extinguished the flames before they reached
the band of refugees.

Powwell pressed his face deeper into the dirt. He had
never taken an oath to the Commune to forsake all
other forms of magic. Nothing prevented him from drawing the ley line into himself. He could throw some kind
of barrier between Moncriith and his friends. He had to
protect them, make up for his lapse in tapping blood
magic.

A barrier. He needed a barrier. He dredged a half
memory up from somewhere. Nimbulan had thrown a
wall in front of Moncriith's attacks on Quinnault's army
a year ago. How had he done it?

Powwell didn't have time to remember. In his mind
he created a picture of a brick wall rising up from the

ground between himself and the Bloodmage. He pushed the magic outward with all of his strength.

Moncriith's next volley of magic darts, meant to enter the mind through the eye and destroy all thought and memory, crashed through Nimbulan's defenses.

CHAPTER 36

"Open that *S'murghing* door, Bessel," Quinnault ordered. "Guard, fetch Old Lyman. Carry him here over your shoulder if you have to. I don't care what he's doing or which dragon he's talking to, I need him here. Now."

"I don't know how Piedro could have left without a trace. No one can transport a living being from place to place and live," Bessel protested.

Quinnault recognized the young man's deep breathing as preparation for a trance. He stepped out of the way to let him work. Questions whirled through his mind. He drew his belt knife just in case the assassin was somehow hidden in the cell and planned to rush them as soon as the door opened.

"Maybe we should wait for the master magician," he suggested.

"Yes. That isn't my seal on the door," Bessel said. His eyes crossed in puzzlement. "I don't recognize the signature or style of the spell. No one from the School set it. I know all of them." He sounded almost relieved.

"We are dealing with rogue magicians as well as Rovers and assassins. On my wedding day! Piedro warned me to look to those I trust for his employer. Who? I wonder if I dare go through with the ceremony until I know for sure who wants me not only dead but discredited as a murderer."

"Lord Konnaught?" Bessel offered.

"I doubt it. He doesn't have the forethought or the money to plan such a thing."

"The style of magic will tell us much," Lyman said, bustling down the steep stairs. He rubbed his hands together in excitement. "An interesting puzzle. I love puzzles almost as much as I love books. Wonderful treasures, both. They make a man think."

"You didn't have time to be summoned from School Isle unless you flew or transported," Quinnault growled, ready to suspect anyone of Piedro's escape.

"Of course not. I was in the Great Hall helping arrange tonight's entertainment. We have five apprentices who are quite talented with delusions and fireless lights. They'll put on quite a show during the banquet," Lyman replied. He bent to eye the lock on the cell door without further ado.

"What do you see, old man?" Quinnault pressed him.

"Not as much as Nimbulan would. These eyes are aging and less interested in detail than I could wish." Lyman frowned as he straightened to peer through the slit window.

"Which is another complaint I have with the world today. I wish Nimbulan would get back here. He never should have left. Not even a note," he bemoaned.

"But he did leave a letter of explanation. I gave it to the messenger you sent to fetch him." Lyman looked around the dank dungeon as if he expected to find the errant courier hiding there.

"I never received it!" Quinnault barked. "Guard, bring me that courier!" Heat stung his cheeks and his fingers tingled with the anger building inside him.

Nothing was going right. Bad omens for the wedding ceremony and his life ahead with Katie.

"Unnecessary, boy." Lyman looked at Quinnault as if the king were indeed an errant child. "Lord Konnaught was with the messenger that day. Who told you that Nimbulan had departed on a personal quest?"

"Konnaught." None of Quinnault's anger dissipated. "That demon spawn child deliberately interfered with a royal messenger. More reasons to exile him. Guard, Konnaught is to be confined to his room and watched. He is not to attend the wedding or the banquet. See to it immediately."

One of the men retreated. His haste up the slippery stairs suggested he was happy to remove himself from target distance of Quinnault's temper.

"Open the damn door, Lyman. I'm getting tired of this. I want explanations now, even if I personally have to break every bone in Piedro's body. Nimbulan has a lot to answer for when he gets back. He'd have known a way to make sure this Rover didn't escape."

"All in good time, my boy. Nimbulan's errand was necessary. You'll see that when he gets back."

"Which will be. . . ?"

"When he gets back."

"Stop with your riddles, Lyman. Who released the Rover?" Quinnault began to pace, hands behind his back, shoulders hunched. He couldn't think standing still.

"Not any magic I know firsthand," Lyman replied.

"Varn magic, perhaps?" Quinnault had to ask the question that had been hovering in the back of his mind since he'd witnessed the argument between Katie and her father. He trusted Katie, but not her father.

"Closer to home, I think," Lyman said. He pulled his glass from a deep pocket of his blue robe and looked closer at the entire doorjamb.

"How close?" both Quinnault and Bessel asked.

"Kardia, Air, Fire, and Water are present. Smell the urine? That's what he used for Water." Lyman wrinkled his nose.

"That sounds like a Rover spell. Piedro must be a clan chieftain, so he can't be working with Televarn," Quinnault mused, as he continued his pacing.

"Perhaps. Perhaps not." Lyman wiggled his fingers in an arcane pattern. "Bessel, help me with this." He signaled the journeyman to come closer. The young man placed his hand upon the old man's shoulder. Together they took three deep breaths.

Quinnault sensed the power building between them. But he didn't have enough magic on his own to see their auras merge and expand.

"The original seal was broken from the outside and reset from the outside. Our Rover had help. Someone who could come and go without question. Your guards wouldn't let just anyone down here, would they? I wish Nimbulan were here. He knows more about Rovers than I do." Lyman continued his trance as he lifted the latch on the cell door and pushed it open. The empty room showed no signs that anyone had been there in many years.

"Whoever helped Piedro had to have Rover blood in him," Quinnault mused. "Nimbulan told me that much. That's the only way their magic works is in combination with other Rovers. Someone close to me, someone trusted, with Rover blood. Who could that be?" He stopped pacing as stared at the empty cell.

"Nimbulan is the only person I know with Rover blood. Some distant ancestor. That's how he learned about Rover magic," Lyman whispered.

"Nimbulan?" Quinnault didn't dare breathe. "I refuse to believe that Nimbulan was part of this conspiracy." But the evidence suggested the possibility.

*   *   *

Powwell's ears roared with the strain of pushing the wall to intercept the rapidly flying magic darts. The roar grew louder. He needed to cover his ears. He wanted to throw up.

The roar increased, ululating up into a screech so high-pitched he barely heard it.

A wall of flame split the ground between himself and Moncriith. Instinctively Powwell pulled himself into a fetal ball, protecting his face and neck from attack.

Moncriith screamed in frustrated rage. His magical darts dropped to the ground, repelled by Powwell's wall of flame.

Something heavy shook the ground beneath Powwell. He risked peeking in the direction of the vibrations.

Another body joined Moncriith's sacrificial victim. This one still breathed, though its eyes stared sightlessly upward and the mouth hung slack. Gender and personality were lost in hideous burns across half the face and burned clothing hanging on the frame in tatters. All trace of hair had been burned away, leaving a naked skull. The straight nose, high cheekbones and thin mouth were marred by the oozing raw meat of massive burns. The person curled and shrank against the cold air of the mountain pass.

"Kaalipha?" Yaala gasped.

Powwell raised his head a fraction higher. "Where did she come from? Where's Kalen? If Yaassima survived the pit, then Kalen might have, too. Where were you?"

Hope blossomed inside his chest. Kalen might still live.

"She was in the void," Myri whispered. "Tssonin brought her out."

Powwell looked further. A young dragon—red-tipped but still silvery along his wing-veins and horns—perched on an outcropping halfway up the canyon walls. He breathed steam. Outrage swirled in his multicolored eyes.

"What does Tssonin say?" Nimbulan asked Myri.

"He says he found Yaassima in the void alive and still anchored to this existence. She is not welcome there. The secrets of past, present, and future lives do not belong to such as she. She hasn't the magic or the wisdom to use the information. She must die in this existence before entering the void again." Myri's words took on confidence as she spoke. She cocked her head slightly, listening to the telepathic commands of the dragon that only she could hear.

"Impossible!" Moncriith spluttered. He poked a finger toward the still flaming line that encircled Nimbulan and Myri and the others. "I threw her and the witchchild into the boiling lava before the gate fully formed with the landscape of hills just above the main camp of my army."

"We know," Nimbulan replied. "We watched through the partially open gate. Where is Televarn?"

"I killed the traitor," Yaassima croaked. "I killed him with the knife he poisoned for me."

"He can't be dead!" Maia screamed clutching her head between her fists. "He's still whispering in my mind how he'll punish me if I don't tell him everything that's happening."

"Another mystery we cannot solve," Nimbulan said.

Powwell crept a little closer to Yaassima. He needed to talk to her, find out what happened to Kalen. The wall he had erected blocked him. He dismantled the spell. The wall of dragon fire remained, a clear line separating Moncriith's people from Nimbulan's.

"See her burns?" Moncriith continued to rant. "They are her just punishment from the pit. No one could live through that inferno. I watched her hair and clothing ignite. I drew power from her pain."

The thought of Kalen suffering the agony of that fire hot enough to melt rock, while still alive, nearly made Powwell ill.

"If Yaassima survived, where is Kalen? Tssonin, where is Kalen?" Desperate hope propelled him upward to face the dragon. "You've got to tell me what happened to her."

"Tssonin says that he only found Yaassima because she doesn't belong in the void. If your sister remains there, then she is fated to learn something important from the life forces that shroud her from dragon senses."

"What does that mean? Tell me what that means." Powwell turned on Myri. All his frustration and anger and fear pulsed in his throat. He needed to lash out at something. The dragon was an easy target. Suicide to try.

Tssonin opened his mouth and breathed fire, renewing the wall between Moncriith and the refugees. Powwell shrank away from the evidence of the dragon's power.

"We don't know what Tssonin means, Powwell. Dragon communication is usually cryptic." Nimbulan placed a gentle hand on his shoulder.

Powwell shrugged it off. "I have to go find her."

(That route is dangerous. You have much to learn before you can enter the void and learn with safety.) A young blue-tipped dragon joined Tssonin on the ledge above the canyon. *(Seannin,)* the dragon announced his name.

The dragon's words rocked within Powwell's mind. A headache pounded behind his eyes. "Then teach me what I need to know," he demanded. "I have to find Kalen."

Moncriith raised a mundane bow and shot an arrow through the dragon flames that separated him from his quarry. Wood, metal, and feathers penetrated where magic couldn't.

Seannin breathed a new stream of green fire. The spinning shaft exploded and dropped to the Kardia in a flutter of ash.

"We seem to be at an impasse, Moncriith," Nimbulan said. "The dragons protect us from you. But they do not protect Yaassima. We will depart."

"Seannin and Tssonin, will you fly us to the capital?" Myri asked politely.

"We may still be in time to stop the wedding," Nimbulan said, heading toward Seannin, dragging Myri and Yaala with him.

"It's already too late," Moncriith called. "King Lorriin will invade anyway. We want more from Coronnan than just a marriage treaty. He needs your arable land and farmers. SeLenicca can never be nurtured by any but the Stargods. I intend to give him what he needs—for a price—once I rule Coronnan as the Stargods dictate I must."

Tssonin breathed a new ring of flames around Moncriith and his men, preventing them from menacing the refugees as they clambered aboard the dragons.

                    *   *   *

"Do you suppose we really conceived a child this night?" Katie asked, pressing her hands against her flat belly.

Quinnault looked at the pale skin beneath her hands. An occasional freckle enticed his eye, beckoning him to search her entire body for more. He'd found most of them in the hours since midnight, after the wedding banquet.

"If we haven't made a child tonight, we'll have to keep trying until we get it right." He couldn't stop smiling. He felt like an idiot, grinning until his face hurt. Loving Katie was the most natural, satisfying thing he'd ever done. The casual liaisons he'd indulged in paled in comparison to the joy he knew with Katie.

Questions and problems of kingship faded whenever he thought of Katie. Her father had arrived for the wedding, suitably clothed as befitted the Crown Prince of Terrania. He hadn't renewed his argument with Katie. When asked about progress on the new port he had nodded curtly and replied, "Before dawn." He hadn't said much else the entire evening.

"I never thought I'd be lucky enough to have a child," Katie said wistfully.

"Why not?"

"Pregnant women and small children are particularly vulnerable to the plague that attacks my people. It comes in waves every few generations. Usually it goes away, naturally, after three or four years and tens of thousands of deaths. This time it has lasted ten years and doesn't look as if it's waning. Any woman healthy enough to have children is afraid to have them. That is why we need so much of the Tambootie. We have to get the plague under control before our population dwindles to nothing."

Quinnault kissed the smooth skin just above where Katie's hands still pressed against her stomach. "Your people will have as much of the tree of magic as the dragons can spare. The plague will be stopped," he promised. A delicate quiver across her skin followed his trail of caresses upward. She reached to bring him higher, matching his passion in yet another long kiss.

Her response to him delighted and awed him.

His Katie.

He released a satisfied sigh. "Wherever you come from Maarie Kaathliin, you belong here now, in Coronnan. With me."

"I never thought I'd be happy calling any port home except where I was born. But this certainly feels like home now." She rested her head against his shoulder.

For a moment they lay silent, enjoying the contented closeness. Her mind brushed his in a momentary deepening of their mutual joy. Then she withdrew, slowly, as if drifting into sleep, not the quick closing of a barrier.

"I feel as if I've known you all my life," Quinnault murmured sleepily. It had been a long day.

"One day can be a lifetime," she replied softly.

He drifted on the edge of sleep, reluctant to give in to the clouds that pressed against his brain, lest he awaken and find Katie a mere dream.

"I'm cold, Scarecrow. I'd like to get my shift." She squirmed away from him.

Reluctantly he let her go. The room seemed no cooler than usual for this time of year. "There's an extra quilt in the wardrobe cupboard." He rolled to his side, one arm draped across the empty space where Katie had been a few moments ago. Her scent lingered on the sheets. He inhaled deeply, anxious for her to return, too sleepy to follow her movements about the dim room.

"Mind if I blow out the candle?" she asked from behind the privacy screen that led to the water closet.

"Mmmmm . . ."

The soft rumble of voices hovered just below his hearing. He shut out the brief annoyance. The palace never slept. Servants found chores and duties at all hours of the day and night.

The rumble came closer, louder. A touch of anger colored the tones. He should get up and see what the fuss was about. No one was supposed to disturb him tonight, except for the most dire emergency. He'd had enough of those yesterday to last a lifetime.

He half-opened one eye, willing the disturbance to go away and Katie to come back again. The tiny night lamp didn't cast enough light to see her moving about. He hadn't heard the wardrobe door open or close, nor the curtain to the water closet swish on its sliding rings, only the distant but angry voices. Kinnsell again? Where was Katie?

He sat up, suddenly alert and alarmed.

The voices grew louder, more insistent.

"You can't go in there!" the steward protested.

"I must. The kingdom is in dire danger." A new voice. One he hadn't heard in several days. Hoped not to hear again until he had some answers. Nimbulan.

"Open the door, Your Grace!" Fierce pounding followed the magician's words.

"Gently, Lan. We need calm and wisdom now," a feminine voice soothed. A voice he barely recognized. But only one person alive used Nimbulan's childhood nickname. A woman who had no business being in Coronnan at all.

His exiled sister, Myrilandel.

Nimbulan had broken the law by bring the witch-woman back to the capital. He'd been implicated in attempted murder and conspiracy. He'd deserted Quinnault when the king needed his advice.

The door nearly buckled under fierce pounding.

"Wait a minute, Nimbulan," Quinnault yelled back angrily. He reached for his robe. "Katie?"

She didn't answer.

"Katie?" he asked a little louder.

"Just a minute, Scarecrow. I'm . . . um . . . busy." Her voice came from his dressing room. Not hers. Not the water closet.

"*S'murghit,* Katie what are you doing?" He swung his legs over the edge of the bed.

"This won't wait!" Nimbulan replied as the cross bar on the door flew across the room, toward the shuttered window. The door crashed to the floor. Light spilled into the room from the corridor revealing Katie leaning over a strange black box no bigger than her tiny palm, tapping a code into the bizarre apparatus.

CHAPTER 37

The door to Quinnault's private chambers, in the center of the old keep, had landed on the stone floor with a resounding *thunk*. Nimbulan stared at the offending barrier with a glimmer of satisfaction. Some of his frustration echoed down the spiral staircase with the collapsing door.

Some. Not all.

The entire day had been one thwarted plan after another, followed by a series of long delays. Seannin and Tssonin had been the engineers of many stops along the journey to the capital. Granted, they were young dragons, unused to carrying the heavy load of six adults. Grated, they had all needed a bath and meal while the dragons rested. Granted, Nimbulan had benefited from an aerial view of King Lorriin's troops hidden in the mountain pass near the border city of Sambol.

But each stop and detour had pushed them past the time when Quinnault would wed the false princess from a non-existent country. Now he had arrived too late to prevent the marriage, or the consummation of that marriage.

He needed to smash something. The door hadn't been enough.

"What is the meaning of this?" Quinnault asked in outraged tones. His gaze flicked back and forth between Nimbulan and the princess—queen now—crouched over a strange black box.

"That looks like one of my 'motes." Yaala pushed past Nimbulan and crossed the room to the other woman in six long strides.

" 'Motes?" Quinnault and his bride asked in unison.

"Yeah, they turn 'tricity on and off. The Kaalipha uses—used—them all of the time," Yaala said with unusual enthusiasm. She hadn't shown so much animation since Powwell had sabotaged the monstrous machines that powered Hanassa.

" 'Motes and 'tricity . . ." Queen Maarie Kaathliin murmured. "Remotes and electricity!" Her eyes brightened. "You have generators and remote controls? That's impossible. The family covenant forbids technology on Kardia Hodos."

"If that was indeed what the Kaalipha of Hanassa possessed, they work no longer," Nimbulan reminded them. He didn't understand what the queen talked about. Maybe he could use her arcane knowledge to discredit her and end this marriage. "What were you doing, Your Grace?" He pointed at the black box.

"This is none of your concern, Nimbulan," Quinnault said sternly. His kingly dignity was severely impaired as he flipped the sheets back across his lap. "But there are several questionable matters that you need to answer for." He stretched for a dressing gown, just beyond his reach on a nearby chair, while trying to keep himself covered.

Beside Nimbulan, just inside the doorway, Myri sucked in her cheeks to keep from giggling.

"The security of this kingdom is my concern, Your Grace," Nimbulan said, trying very hard not to yell at his king. "I have reason to believe that your bride is a spy planted here by your enemies."

"This breech of . . . um . . . protocol is almost enough for me to label treason, Magician Nimbulan. On top of the charges of willfully bringing an exiled criminal within the borders of Coronnan. And suspicion of several charges of conspiracy and attempted murder." The king glared at his sister, Myrilandel. The harshness of his gaze softened as his eyes lingered on her face, so similar to his own and yet different, changed by the dragon spirit that inhabited the body. Then he caught sight of the bundle she carried.

His mouth opened slightly, and he almost reached to see the child.

"My only crime, brother, is that I was born female and unable to gather dragon magic," Myri said softly.

"The presence within my borders of magicians who cannot or will not gather dragon magic is a danger to my government and the peace we are trying to build.

And so all solitary magicians had to be exiled or executed. I cannot make exceptions for you, sister. I fear you must leave Coronnan."

"I know that. And I will, as soon as you are safe from the invasion that threatens you." Myri bowed her head in acceptance of her fate.

"An invasion prompted by your marriage to this woman, Quinnault," Nimbulan said. He looked again at the woman in the corner. He didn't know what conspiracies Quinnault was talking about, so he chose to ignore them in favor of threats he could unravel. "Terrania is a desert wasteland that hasn't been fit for human habitation in thousands of years. Even the lizards and flies have abandoned it. She cannot be the Princess of Terrania."

"You may leave, Steward. This discussion must remain private." Quinnault nodded to the servant who still stood in the doorway. He had followed Nimbulan and the others, wringing his hands and protesting disturbing the king on his wedding night.

The steward sidled past Scarface and Powwell, eyes wide, feet reluctant to move him out of earshot. He stopped in front of Maia and pointed to the mole on her cheek just to the right of mouth.

The woman in the vision spell questing the source of poison had a mole in the same place. So much had happened in the last few days, Nimbulan had difficulty remembering how short a time ago that was.

Quinnault nodded acknowledgment gestured the man out of the room. "These other people are not necessary to this discussion either, Nimbulan." Quinnault nodded toward Yaala who still peered over the bride's shoulder, trying to examine the black device, and Scarface and Powwell who stood by the door in a guarding stance. "The Rover woman will have to be questioned regarding her relative who tried to murder my queen last night with the tie from my dressing gown."

A sly smile that Nimbulan didn't like at all stole across Maia's face.

"Maia's clan is all in Hanassa, Your Grace. I don't see how any of them could be involved," Nimbulan said. "Unless . . . Maia, were any of your people sent to the pit?" He whirled to face the woman.

"Piedro?" Powwell interrupted. "A Rover-dark man

was sent to the pit right after I was. He never did much, just wandered around like he was lost in a dream."

"That was the man's name!" Quinnault said. He almost jumped up, then remembered why the sheet was tangled around his hips and sat back on the mattress again.

"When was the last time you saw him, Powwell? Did he know about the dragongate?" Nimbulan asked.

"Maybe. I think he was part of Televarn's gang when they kidnapped us and took us from the village into Hanassa. He looked like the man who had Amaranth in a sack over his shoulder," Powwell replied. He stroked something just inside his tunic pocket as he spoke.

"Televarn again. He must have followed Piedro and helped him escape my dungeons. Lyman said that Rover magic opened the magic seal from the outside." Quinnault eyed the dressing gown, just out of reach.

"Televarn couldn't have done it," Myri said, dropping her head to stare at the floor.

"Don't defend the man, sister, just because you lived with him for a while," Quinnault said harshly.

"I am not defending the man who betrayed me twice." Myri raised her head to glare at her brother. Her eyes lost most of their color as her emotions tumbled across her face.

Nimbulan touched her arm before she broadcast all of her fears and anger into their daughter. She relaxed a little at his touch.

"Televarn did not leave Hanassa," Nimbulan informed his king. "We saw him last with a poisoned knife sticking out of his throat. If he survived, he was in no condition to follow us. Moncriith was in charge of Hanassa by then. He is dead, isn't he, Maia?" He whirled to face the Rover woman who cowered near the door.

She nodded mutely, too frightened to do more.

"Who is in your mind now, Maia? Which Rover has picked up Televarn's reins of manipulation?" Nimbulan pressed her for an answer.

"I don't know," Maia wailed. "A voice, a control. The same as always. It could be Televarn. It might not be. We are all so closely related, many times over-related, its hard to tell one slave master from another."

"If not Televarn, then who? Lyman insisted the magician who opened the cell door and resealed it had to have Rover blood. You are the only magician I know who has a trace of Rover blood in his heritage,'' Quinnault accused.

Nimbulan's face went hot, then cold. His frustrations returned and he wanted to plant his fist into someone's face. Right now, his king looked to be a fine target.

He took a very deep breath in an effort to control himself. "Your Grace, every one of my relatives carries the same remote trace of Rover blood. That makes them vulnerable to mind manipulation by a Rover mage. I think I know this Piedro from my days in the Rover camp. He had the makings of a powerful mage if he ever broke free of Televarn's control. He could easily have used the dragongate a number of times to subvert my cousins or brothers, or a number of others with a tiny trace of Rover heritage. He could have been working in Coronnan for moons, or years.''

"The same way Televarn subverted Kalen,'' Powwell whispered.

Myri shifted her attention from her brother to Powwell, taking the boy into her arms and his grief into her heart. They would both heal in time.

Time they might not have.

"You have not explained this 'dragongate,' Nimbulan,'' Quinnault reminded him.

Nimbulan briefly explained the strange vortex created by the combination of heat and pressure within the volcano. Their escape from Hanassa, the vision through the partially open dragongate, and their encounter with Moncriith took only a few more sentences. He didn't consult his journal. The events were embedded deeply in his memory now.

"All these refugees risked much to help me rescue Myrilandel. I only wish I had had time to fetch Rollett, too. I'll have to go back for him. Soon.''

"We have nothing to fear from them, Scarecrow,'' the queen said proudly. She continued to tap the device with her right index finger.

"Scarecrow?'' Nimbulan lifted one eyebrow.

Quinnault met him stare for stare with no further explanation. But his gaze kept flicking to the black box held by the queen.

"For the Stargods' sake, allow the man some dignity.''

Myri rolled her eyes and finally tossed the king a silken robe from the chair near the bed. Her cheeks worked in and out, but she couldn't suppress the grin on her face.

Nimbulan was glad to see her sense of humor returning after the dramatic events of the past few weeks.

"It's nice to see that your legs are nearly as long and shapely as mine, brother," she said around her smile.

Quinnault gave her a brief smile of thanks and returned his attention to the false princess from Terrania. His mouth clamped shut on a question. He was probably waiting for privacy before questioning her. Nimbulan had to shatter the man's illusions now, in front of witnesses, before the royal bride subverted the king's mind further.

"Your wife is probably a foreign agent planted here in order to precipitate an invasion," Nimbulan reminded Quinnault. "I have learned that King Lorriin leads an invasion of Sambol as we speak. He's been poised for weeks, waiting for an excuse to seize valuable farm land to feed his people."

"I know about Lorriin. The marriage treaty with his sister would not have kept the peace between us beyond Spring planting." Quinnault shrugged into the robe. He turned his back briefly as he stood and belted the garment. "I knew it when I agreed to marry Maarie Kaathliin and give her people half a ton of new Tambootie leaves in exchange for a port city and jetties built on the bay islands."

"A half ton of Tambootie? What strange magic requires that much of the weed?" Nimbulan's mind spun with the possibilities. His entire Commune wouldn't use that much of the fresh leaves bursting with essential oils—if they used Tambootie any more, which they didn't. The trees were reserved for the dragons. "A half ton will strip many trees to the danger point. They may never recover enough to feed the dragons. Dragons are more necessary to your peace than a precipitous marriage just to get an heir."

"My wife's father assured me they will spread their harvest across all of Coronnan and take the leaves in two batches so they don't endanger any of the trees. Besides, Shayla personally approved of our marriage."

"Shayla?" Myri asked. "She left us in a hurry before

she could carry us to safety. Did she come here? She wouldn't respond to my call afterward."

"I faced your dragon at dawn." Maarie Kaathliin shuddered and finally ceased her tapping. "Then she flew off. We haven't seen her since."

"I had a message from your dragon, sister. You are not to worry, she will be with you after she rests from her . . . er . . exertions." Quinnault flicked a shy glance to the bed.

"Oh!" Myri clasped a hand over her mouth. Then she cocked her head as if listening, a sure sign that the dragons spoke to her and her alone. "No wonder Shayla ignored me. Only two of my brothers, barely half-grown dragons, could be spared to fly us home. All of the adults were—engaged. Congratulations, brother. You'll be a father by the Autumnal Equinox."

"Really?" the queen stepped closer to Myri, hands pressed against her belly as if seeking confirmation.

"You still haven't told me what kind of illegal magic your wife's people intend to work with the Tambootie. I can't believe the dragons would willingly give up so much of their necessary food supply.'"

"Not magic," the queen said, clutching her husband's arm. Her voice carried a note of desperation that made Nimbulan want to believe her. "My people need the Tambootie for medicine. A plague threatens our very existence and the leaves of the Tambootie provide the only cure."

"Why should we give this valuable drug to your people? We might need it later ourselves. Plagues travel wide and unpredictably. Your very presence could infect us all," Nimbulan said.

"This plague will not attack you. I guarantee that." Maarie Kaathliin stood straight and defiant. Her small face suddenly looked much older and jaded than Nimbulan first thought. "As long as we keep the machines out of Kardia Hodos, the plague has nothing to feed on."

Quinnault draped an arm about her shoulders and pulled her close. His gesture clearly signified that they belonged together. The top of her head barely reached his armpit. Granted the king was tall compared to the majority of his people. But a woman's average height was closer to that of the average male. Maarie Kaathli-in's head should reach the king's chin, at least.

"How can you guarantee that a plague will not come to us in a trade ship, or on the back of a steed wandering in from SeLenicca, or on the khamsin wind from Rossemeyer? How can we trust you when you say you come from a land that no longer exists?"

"She didn't say she came from Terrania. I did," Quinnault said. Then he turned to face his wife, hands on her shoulders "Why did you confirm the idea I pulled out of the air?"

"There has been a misunderstanding of my origins. I hail from Terra, not Terrania."

"Terra is not a land I have heard of. Why would you claim she hailed from a barren land that has not been inhabited for many hundreds of years?" Nimbulan searched Quinnault's face for signs of the lie he knew must come.

"Because she is a Varn. Her father is a Varn. Her grandfather is emperor of the Varns. Try telling my Council that and make them believe it."

"No one living has ever seen a Varn. Legends. They always appear a hundred years ago. Never now. And they never reveal their true form."

"Because we cannot allow you to learn our secrets. You would destroy yourselves and create the same environment that breeds our plague before you realized the dangers of our technologies," the queen insisted.

"Machines? You do everything with machines?" Yaala tugged at the queen's sleeve. Her passion for her machines was written all over her face. "Can you help me repair my machines? Can you make Old Bertha live again?"

"Old Bertha?" Both Quinnault and his bride stared at Yaala.

"The largest of my machines, the key to a network of littler generators and transformers that powered the lights and gadgets that imitate magic."

"Bertha was the name of one of my ancestors. A strong-willed woman who never married, took numerous inappropriate lovers—they got younger as she aged— and voiced her volatile opinions quite loudly," the queen chuckled.

"That sounds like our Old Bertha," Powwell said from the doorway. "A cranky and willful old lady who worked at her own convenience and no one else's." For the first time since leaving Kalen behind, he showed some levity.

"How old are your machines?" Maarie Kaathliin turned to Yaala with a new animation.

"Very old. Older than any records. Legends claim the machines go back to the time of the Stargods," Yaala replied.

"Impossible. The three O'Hara brothers established the covenant that protected Kardia Hodos from intrusion by any but a few carefully selected representatives of the family. They forbade technology powered by anything but water, air, or fire. They didn't let you have the wheel and isolated reading skills to a very few."

"But that doesn't answer our questions, Your Grace," Nimbulan tried to bring the subject back to his present concerns. "We have to stop this invasion and the conspiracies you have uncovered in my absence."

"You must destroy the machines!" Maarie Kaathliin urged Yaala. "They contain the seeds of the plague. I pray that no other machines powered by fossil fuels exist. The tainted air that comes from them will lie dormant for centuries waiting for the right mix of pollution and sunlight variance to grow and breed."

"The machines are already dead," Powwell volunteered. "I killed them to give us time to escape." He turned away and muttered under his breath, "Unless the wraith fixes them."

The queen breathed easier. Obviously she hadn't heard the last comment. "Then the generators must stay dead, and isolated. We can never allow technology to taint your air as it has my home's."

"That still doesn't tell me what we can do about the invasion. We haven't time to gather an army and march it to meet King Lorriin." Nimbulan clenched his hand, longing for his staff to help him think. But Powwell had used it to kill the machine. He needed another.

"We need a wall to keep them out. Just like the Kaalipha used the walls of the crater to keep out strangers," Scarface said, his face brightened with ideas. "Powwell had the right idea when he blocked Moncriith's attack with a wall. We need a wall. A magic wall."

CHAPTER 38

"Do you know how much magic would be needed for such a feat?" Nimbulan stared at Scarface, gape-mouthed. It could work. They'd need a very large focus to concentrate the minds and talents of every member of the Commune—masters, journeymen, and apprentices combined. Something like a magician's staff.

His old staff had been shaped by his magic, finely tuned over many years to work with him. A staff was too individual. For the combined might of the Commune they needed something else, something common to them all.

"A temporary wall at the passes . . ." Scarface shrugged.

"That will only work at the passes we know Lorriin's using *this time*," Quinnault said. He didn't pace as he usually did when he thought. The new queen seemed to quiet his restless energy. "King Lorriin will just find different entries and port cities. He's desperate for arable farm land and men to work it. A lot of Kardia Hodos is. A drought rages into its third year across the Northern continents. Lorriin can't buy food there, and he has some strange belief that SeLenicca can't be worked."

"You're saying we need a magical wall all around Coronnan?" Scarface whistled his amazement at the audacity of the proposal.

"Except for the bay," Nimbulan corrected. "The mudflats and your new port city will give us protection there. A massive chain across the port of Baria and towers with armaments on either side of the entrance will protect that harbor by mundane means. Most of the North coast is crumbling clay cliffs, impossible for heavily armed men to climb. So that will reduce the size of the spell by one coastline." He began to pace, his mind

working furiously—as Quinnault used to do. He needed
a focus. A big focus.

(A focus made of glass.)

Yes! He paused, looking up at the ceiling as if the
idea had come from there. *Why glass?* What properties
did glass have that existed in no other compound?

Clarity. Glass magnified and enhanced the vision.
Made from all four elements, glass gave the magician
access to the power of any one or all of Kardia, Air,
Fire, and Water to wrap around his spell without being
warped or changed by the spell. Wooden staffs shaped
themselves to an individual magician. Glass would remain impervious and accessible to many not just the one.

Yes. The focus must be made of glass. The most precious and rarest substance in all of Kardia Hodos.

"Droughts follow nine-year cycles on this planet,"
Maarie Kaathliin offered. She moved forward, too, back
under Quinnault's arm, as if she needed contact with
him to maintain life itself. "The wall must last at least
another six or seven years to prevent war until the climate shifts again."

"Could your father build us a physical wall to block
the passes?" Quinnault asked Maarie Kaathliin.

"Not in time. The jetties, bridges, and docks at the
islands will use up most of our resources. I've just signaled him that he may depart as soon as he is finished.
Your part of the bargain is complete, love." She held
up the little black box.

Yaala tried to grab it from her for examination. The
queen pointedly tossed the box into the hearth fire.
Flames engulfed it, glowing hot red and yellow around
the black. A strange smell permeated the smoke.

Nimbulan wrinkled his nose. No one else seemed to
notice the smell. But Yaala stared at the hearth as if she
could will the device back into her own hands, intact
and working.

"The islands?" Nimbulan returned to the subject at
hand. "You've made all four of the islands into a port?
Already?" Nimbulan's heart sank. Now he couldn't ap-
propriate one of the islands as a home for himself and
Myri. "Do you really need all four islands?"

"Yes," Maarie Kaathliin said. She continued speaking,
dismissing the question. "Kinnsell needs to get back

home with the Tambootie as soon as possible. He can't spare any more time than it takes to complete the port. Besides, a physical wall would hamper peaceful trade. I presume you plan on establishing this 'wall' or force field or whatever to have gates and such?"

"We'll have to post magicians at each known road and trade route to do that." Nimbulan forced his disappointment to the back of his mind. He had to tackle one problem at a time. "We don't have enough magicians at the moment to cover every known road into Coronnan, even if you count all the apprentices and journeymen. Presuming we can get the wall up." Nimbulan held his hands up, palm outward, fingers slightly curled. The habitual gesture for weaving magic wasn't enough anymore. As he paced, he looped one arm through Myri's and drew her to his side. Together, they paced. Together, they discussed and defined the necessary elements of the massive spell. Together, their minds worked and built upon each new idea.

He couldn't exile her again. He needed her close by. All of the time.

"We have to use the years of the drought cycle to grow as much surplus as we can to help feed Kardia Hodos," Quinnault mused as he joined them in their pacing, bringing his bride with him.

"Don't forget a way to store reserves for our own drought which will probably follow," the queen added.

"We should sell food at minimum tariff and profit to keep our neighbors from becoming desperate," Nimbulan said.

"Hopefully when they recover from drought and we fall prey to the weather, they will be willing to help us in turn," Quinnault finished the thought. "I'll need strong trade treaties. We'll all meet with the ambassadors first thing in the morning."

"Overseeing the production of all those extra acres will also give your lords an occupation so they don't have time or inclination to plot another civil war, or assassination." Scarface chuckled.

"Aaddler," Nimbulan addressed his new friend. "This is a matter for the Commune, using communal magic. Solitary magicians must be excluded. It is more than the law. It is the only way we can enforce the peaceful use

of magic for the benefit of all. You have proved yourself
a valuable ally. But I must have your oath to the Commune, Coronnan, and King Quinnault before you involve yourself any further." He couldn't look at Myri.
His statement effectively sent her in exile once more.
She dropped his arm as if his touch burned her.

Slowly he turned to face her, one hand resting on her
shoulder, the other caressing the baby in her arms. "And
when the spell is complete, I will resign my place in the
Commune and join you in your clearing. We won't be
separated again, Myri. Ever."

"Not even in death, beloved," she vowed, kissing
him softly.

"What if I can't spare you, Nimbulan?" Quinnault
asked under his breath. "Will you break your oath of
loyalty to me?"

* * *

Powwell watched Scarface solemnly approach King
Quinnault in the little reception room. Soon it would be
Powwell's turn to face his king and the Commune. Quick
tests, moments before, had proven Scarface's ability to
gather dragon magic.

"I, Aadler, do solemnly swear to abide by the laws of
the Commune, and to defend the Commune against solitary magicians. I promise to use my magic, gathered only
from dragons, for the benefit of all Coronnan as directed
by the lawful king, anointed by the people and blessed
by the dragons. And if I should stray from this oath,
may my staff break, and the dragons desert me,"
Scarface recited the oath of the Commune, holding his
new staff horizontally in front of him with both hands.
Beneath the staff rested the softly glowing Coraurlia, the
dragon crown. It sat upon its velvet pillow at the king's
feet on the dais of the throne room. Its soothing all
color/no color light engulfed the staff and the magician
in an aura of truth that could not be broken.

As the last words fell from Scarface's lips, the new
staff began to twist a little, three strands beginning to
braid.

Powwell gulped back his fears and tried to fade into
the walls.

"Now it is your turn, Powwell. You left Coronnan before we could determine the necessity of this oath for all those who gather dragon magic," Nimbulan said. He placed a hand on his shoulder, urging him toward the dais.

"I'm only an apprentice, and poorly trained at that. Shouldn't I wait to see if I have the ability to become a full magician?" Powwell protested.

"No, Powwell, we can't wait. We need every magician available for this spell. They must all be confirmed members of the Commune," King Quinnault said from the throne. He and the queen had taken a few moments to dress before presiding over this brief ceremony.

None of the refugees had had a chance to rest or eat since arriving in the capital. Now they would plunge headlong into the defense of Coronnan. Powwell needed time to think.

He looked at the assembly of sleepy-eyed master magicians crowding near the throne. They all stared at him, needing the oath-taking complete so they could get on with the business of creating a massive defense spell. No help there. He had to take the oath.

Once taken, never broken.

Taking a deep breath he stepped forward to face the king and the glass dragon crown. The queen sat beside Quinnault, avidly curious, not missing a single detail that might slip past the weary magicians.

Someone handed him a staff, as newly cut as Nimbulan's and Scarface's. He opened his mouth to recite the words. Nothing came out but a cough, dry as the dust of Hanassa.

He swallowed deeply, thinking hard, and finally croaked out the words.

"I, Powwell, do solemnly swear to abide by the laws of the Commune, and to defend the Commune against solitary magicians. I promise to use my magic gathered only from dragons, *while in Coronnan,* for the benefit of all Coronnan . . ." He continued with the oath as prescribed. Only the queen, with her avid curiosity and attention to detail raised an eyebrow at his insertion. Once he left the borders of Coronnan, he would be free to follow Kalen with whatever magic tools presented themselves.

"Good. Now we must get to work. Is the map table ready?" Nimbulan asked, easily assuming authority over the Commune and Powwell.

*   *   *

"I don't think we will have enough power," Nimbulan said, resigned to the fact that the border of Coronnan was just too long.

"Can we leave gaps over the impassable parts of the mountains?" Quinnault paced around and around the three-dimensional map built into a sand table. The map of Coronnan measured as long on each side as two tall men—large enough for details of rivers and hills, towns and forests.

Nimbulan rubbed his eyes wearily. The women had gone to bed. Most of the magicians as well. Once the strategy and details of the spell were worked out by Nimbulan the Battlemage, and his king, the others would rise to support them.

He wished Myri could be a part of the spell. Her subtle healing touch just might finish off the rough edges, make it a wall to preserve peace rather than a mere deterrent to war. Life versus death. Love of Coronnan rather than hatred of their enemies.

"Without a focus, we can't do more than push back the enemy for a day, maybe two. *With* a focus we could barricade the border with SeLenicca but not the Northern coast or the Southern border with Rossemeyer." *And the pass that leads to Hanassa where Moncriith claimed the title of Kaaliph.*

"What if we randomly rotated the wall so that invaders never knew where it would or would not be?" Quinnault offered.

"Too time and energy consuming. All my magicians would be engaged in doing nothing but maintaining the wall. We wouldn't be available for healing, communication, soil fertility—nothing but border patrol. That would defeat the whole purpose of the Commune, to make magic available to all of Coronnan for the benefit of all of Coronnan."

"The dragons are waking. Maybe they have a solution." Quinnault cocked his head, like Myri did, listening.

"I need them to fly over the border and tell us precisely where each of the armies is at the moment we set the spell. Presuming we can."

"Shayla is landing in the courtyard of the school." Myri wandered in, rubbing sleep from her eyes and yawning. She hadn't slept much either.

Nimbulan welcomed her into his arms. He rested her head against his shoulders as she fought sleep.

"Why is Shayla coming here?" he asked as he kissed her forehead.

"She has a gift," Lyman said as he bounced into the room with a disgusting amount of energy. "She says she found your focus."

"Glass. The dragons have made something of glass." He remembered the whisper across his mind last night as he pondered the problem.

"That would be my guess,' Lyman smiled. Age lines dissolved from his face.

"Are you getting younger, old man?" Nimbulan peered at his friend.

"I wish," he replied and winked at Myri. "I have too many lifetimes to complete for that to happen. Come, come, we mustn't keep Shayla waiting. She's anxious to get on with this business, so she can get to the work of building a nest for her next litter. A new litter of dragons. I remember the last one, over twenty years ago. . . ." He looked sharply around at the others to see if they had noticed his reverie.

"You were there at the birthing," Myri said, eyes alight. She didn't show any surprise that a human had been allowed to view Shayla's babies when man-made magic had injured her and caused her premature labor and subsequent stillbirth of fourteen of the young. Myri and her familiar Amaranth had been two of the six survivors—asexual purple-tipped dragons with a distinct destiny separate from the dragon nimbus.

"Of course, my dear. I gave you and Amaranth your names."

"What is he talking about?" Nimbulan whispered to Myri. "Why was he there?"

Myri smiled obliquely. "Dragons have to have some secrets, Lan."

"Enough reminiscence." Lyman clapped his hands with enthusiasm. "Shayla commands our presence." He ushered them out of the palace and across the bridge to School Isle amid a growing throng of citizens. Wide-eyed and gape-jawed people stumbled over each other as they watched the sky rather than their feet.

Nimbulan realized that dawn had come around again and he hadn't slept more than a few hours in the last four days. Why did dragons always insist on presenting their surprises at this awful hour?

"Because the light makes them appear more spectacular," Myri answered his unvoiced question.

"I must be tired to lose control of my thoughts." Grimly he scrubbed his face with his palm, hiding a yawn behind it. At least he'd eaten his fill every few hours, restoring some of his energy.

"Your thoughts are always close to mine, Lan. You can't hide anything from me." She squeezed his arm affectionately.

"Apparently, your anger toward me for leaving you alone so long has evaporated. I wish my guilt would fade as quickly. I have a lot to make up for." He held her tight against his side, glad to have one complication removed from his life. "As soon as this is over, I will send journeymen on quest to rescue Rollett and Kalen. This time I will stay by your side."

"A good plan, Nimbulan. Keeping my family together is more important than venting my anger."

"I'll remember that you are listening if I should ever be stupid enough to look at another woman."

"You'd better not even think about it." She punched his arm affectionately.

He winced. His nerves were worn thin and everything hurt—her reminder of their problems, her punch on his arm, and the glare of a dozen rainbows streaming from the sky into the courtyard of the school. The courtyard that at one time had contained the well of ley lines.

"What ails you, Lan?" Myri caressed his arm with healing touches.

"I'll be all right when I have eaten again and slept a bit," he said, distracted by the sight of six adult dragons cavorting through the air like dandelion fluff. They soared high, dove with incredible swiftness, turned in a tail length and flew loops around each other. Their play contained an element of deep satisfaction and joy that he'd never seen in them. The males seemed to glow brighter along their colored wing-veins and horns, the primary colors pulsed deeper and truer, not fading into obscurity with the rest of their crystal fur.

Shayla was easiest to pick out in the happy antics. Every color in the spectrum rippled along her fur in constantly shifting prisms. Waves of deep satisfaction washed over the dragons, spilling into the crowd of human onlookers.

Nimbulan remembered a day when he, too, had felt like that. The day he first made love to Myri.

His need for sleep vanished, replaced with a deeper need. He wrapped his arm around Myri's shoulders, pulling her closer, tucking her warmth against his side, inhaling her sweet fragrance.

"No time for sleep." Lyman handed him half a round loaf of bread and a hunk of cheese. "We've a spell to work and an invasion to repulse."

"I don't know how we're going to do it," Nimbulan mumbled around a huge bite of bread. Soft and warm from the oven, it nearly melted as he chewed. Energy began to creep back into his veins. "Did the dragons find us a focus?"

"I believe so." Lyman pointed to the center of the courtyard, nearly bouncing in his enthusiasm.

There, atop the mortar that obscured from all senses the ley line well, rested a huge black table. Round, sitting on a single pedestal. Gleaming black, the rising sun glinted off the seamless surface.

"It's made of glass! *Black* glass," Nimbulan shouted, running to examine the treasure more closely. "Black glass forged by dragon fire! We can work the spell."

CHAPTER 39

"I am frightened of this spell, Shayla," Myri confided. *(You have done this before, daughter,)* Shayla replied as she rose on a thermal above the courtyard

Myri looked at the large glass table, a wondrous treasure, rather than at the dragon who had given birth to her spirit but not her body. Only one or two sources of sand clean enough to produce usable glass existed in Kardia Hodos. Man-made fires didn't burn hot enough to use the other sands. But dragon breath did.

(You must be the eyes of the magicians. They cannot view the placement of their wall otherwise. You must let your mind fly with us.)

"When I flew before, it was always with Amaranth, my twin, my otherself. I knew his mind better than I knew my own. We blended easily and he always returned me to my own body afterward." She knew this task was essential to the success of Nimulan's spell and the safety of the kingdom. She knew it. And yet she feared the outcome would change everything she held dear.

The outcome or the process? Dread hung around her like an unwelcome ghost.

(Now you are alone in your fragile human body. Blend with me, and we will soar through the clouds. Trust me to know when the time is right to end the joining.)

"How will I feed the images we see to Nimbulan?" She looked to where the Commune placed chairs around the table, crowding them together to accommodate all of the masters, journeymen, and apprentices. An aura of power began to pulse stronger and stronger as the chain of magicians grew. Like heat waves on the desert sands, the power spread. It pushed outsiders away from the table, the joined magicians, and the spell.

Nimbulan sat in the place closest to the center of the school buildings. Lyman sat on his right, Scarface to his left, and a timid Powwell sat close by. Yaala, bathed and clothed in a fine gown of pale green, stood with Quinnault and his foreign queen. She looked like Yaassima's daughter now, a princess in exile rather than the scruffy desert rat who haunted the chambers of the pit. Maarie Kaathliin held Amaranth so that Myri would be free to link communication between the dragons and the magicians. The new queen cooed at the baby and played with her lovingly, absolutely enchanted with the child.

Maia remained inside the school where she couldn't spy on the proceedings. Mundane guards made sure she didn't contact Piedro or any of her clan.

Myri need not concern herself with her companions and family if something should go wrong with the spell. She knew in her heart and her head that something would go wrong that would change the life path of all those involved in the spell.

(The silver cord that connects you to Nimbulan will channel your visions to him. Do not fear, daughter. We will guard you well on this spirit journey.)

Myri knew that. She recognized her questions as a stall. If she released herself to the dragons, she might never come back to her own body.

Yes. She finally recognized the human frame as *her* body. She was Myrilandel, a unique blending of the dragon Amethyst and the human girl. She wanted to remain human, to live with and love Nimbulan, to raise her daughter and bear more children.

Flying with the dragons would jeopardize her anchors to this life.

(There is no other way, Myrilandel. Nimbulan needs you to be his eyes.)

"I know." Myri placed her hand on Nimbulan's shoulder to physically link herself to him. The power building around the table parted slightly, as if a living being with a consciousness, allowed her hand to penetrate only as far as her husband. No magic or love in all of Kardia Hodos could link her to the swelling communal magic.

Unconsciously she shifted her feet until she found a comfortable stance. Awareness of the ley lines beneath the paving tingled through her feet. Nimbulan said he couldn't sense the power within the Kardia any more. She enjoyed the contact with the ground—a solid and firm anchor to the land and her life. He relied on the ephemeral power drifting in the air that she couldn't sense at all.

Their magic centers had shifted. A year ago, she sought flight with the dragons, and he found his magic rooted in the Kardia.

(Now.)

Myri closed her eyes and concentrated on the thoughts of the dragon mother of the nimbus. A continuous patter of gossipy comments about the weather, the taste of last night's meal, and the beauty of the clouds dribbled into her mind. With the words, came pictures, wonderfully vivid pictures. Gradually the words faded, and the pictures came to the front of her vision.

Her focus tilted and spun as her mind gazed down upon the wide stretch of bay glittering in the morning sunshine. Her perspective shifted to an aerial view, and she realized that she looked down upon the string of islands that made up the capital city.

Shayla flew lower. In their shared eyesight, they saw individuals with recognizable features and auras. A circle of lives around the wonderful glass table. Magic inhabited the men and spilled into the table, growing by leaps and bounds like a living thing.

One life stood out, separate from the others and the magic and yet . . . connected.

Suddenly, Myri realized she looked down upon herself, standing beside Nimbulan and the Commune. Beside, not amid.

Acknowledgment of her separation from the men severed her last mental contact with her human body. She and Shayla flew West, upriver, toward the trading city and the mountain pass where an invasion had already begun.

*   *   *

Nimbulan settled into his trance as he focused on the pattern of sunlight on glass. Waves of different colors and textures of black evolved before his eyes. His magic-heightened senses became aware of all the different minerals that made up the glass. He felt the fire that melted them together into a new, cohesive substance. The dragon flames transformed them into something new, bigger and more interesting without damaging his unique individuality.

He recognized that communal magic was like dragon fire on sand. Each magician remained an individual, yet bonded and changed into something more powerful and cohesive than a single man. The dragons had given humans a wonderful gift with this new power.

The first blending of magic always impressed him with this tremendous sense of belonging. All his years as a solitary Battlemage hadn't prepared him for the sensation. Almost better than sex.

At that moment he sensed Myri's hand on his physical shoulder. A different kind of touch than Lyman's, or his own connection to Aadler. His longing to draw her into the wonderful circle of communal magic almost broke his trance and connection to the other magicians.

The safety of Coronnan depended upon completion of this spell. He needed all his concentration, all his experience, all of his power and more to complete the barricade.

He breathed deeply. The essence of Tambootie in the air invaded his nostrils, changed, mutated into power. The energy of dragon magic filled every crevice inside his body and his soul.

(Now.) Now he was ready to create a wall that would protect Coronnan and give the war-ravaged land and people a chance to build a peaceful, cohesive government—as cohesive as the magic that sang through his blood, picking up harmonies from the other men in the circle until they grew into the most beautiful music ever experienced.

"Where?" He heard and felt his question through every sense—born and acquired—within him.

(Here.) Myri's voice whispered across his mind. Myri's voice and yet different. Multiple Myris. As he was a multiple within the circle of magic.

His mind opened to a distant vista. He saw the rolling hills that grew ever taller until they became the old mountains that separated Coronnan from SeLenicca. Streams cut ravines through the hills. The ravines became wide passages through the physical barrier. He imagined a wall, twenty feet tall, immeasurably thick and powerful, yet invisible to the casual eye, along the highest ridges.

(No. Closer. See the armies.)

Hundreds of men crawled along fifteen of those passages, almost to the end. Almost into Coronnan. If he set the wall along the ridge, the armies would be trapped inside Coronnan, free to raid and pillage at will.

He shifted his imagery lower, at the eastern end of the mountains, deep into the foothills.

The men marched closer. Half a mile away.

(Now. You must drop the wall now.)

He dropped the wall across the center passage, where the men were closest to their target. A satisfying *thunk* reverberated through the Kardia, sensed through his whole body. The vibration must have traveled along a ley line to the well beneath his feet.

From Myri's aerial view he surveyed the wall. It looked solid and complete. A deep breath restored his perspective. He began stretching the wall North and South. The magic thinned. The power glowing within the black glass focus dimmed.

His connection with the Kardia, through Myri, told him the wall shrank to knee-height. The first wave of attackers stumbled, then stepped over the invisible barrier.

*   *   *

Myri watched the magnificent wall expand lengthwise, pulling substance from itself to follow the full length of the border. In horror, she watched as it shrank in height with every stretch outward. Nimbulan pushed more and more power into the wall. It continued to shrink. He didn't have enough power at his command to build the new barrier as high and as strong as needed.

Coronnan would fall to invasion and renewed war. Memories of her brief time in the healer's tent after a battle churned inside her physical stomach as well as her soaring mind.

Wounded men had screamed in agony. Their pain became her pain as she tried to heal a few. For every one

she helped, three more appeared. There was never an
end to the terrible wounds inflicted by other men. The
numbers of the dead mounted with each breath.

So many men cut down in their prime that the villages
had no more men to plow and hunt and sire new babies.

Nimbulan had helped bring peace to Coronnan. The
people had not had enough time to recover from three
generations of civil war and consider peace a way of life.
A few new lives had been conceived to replace the dead.
Not enough. Never enough.

She grieved for the bleak future that stretched thinner
than the wall. Tears tracked her physical face as well
as her dragon mind. The Kardia trembled beneath her,
sobbing for the new assaults on it, rich farmland turned
into battlefields, orchards reduced to firewood for massive armies, widows and orphans left to starve. . . .

The Kardia trembled again and the human Myrilandel
felt the quake through her feet. Ley lines filled with
power trembled beneath her. She knew how to tap the
web of lines that crisscrossed Kardia Hodos like the
mesh of fine lace and turn them into magic. She could
channel the power of the Beginning Place into Nimbulan's spell.

Whatever fate awaited Myri lay in this well of power.

She relaxed her physical body while viewing it from
afar, above, and beyond reality. The energy flowed upward, through her receptive muscles and bones. Fire
heated the Water in her blood. Air expelled from her
lungs. The Kardia in her bones and muscles joined with
the other three elements.

The heat of her power continued to build within her
body, beyond her ability to contain it. She breathed
flame and still the fire grew. So did the magical wall.

Her hand clutched at Nimbulan's shoulder, needing to
feel his skin one more time before she gave herself up
to the elements. She moved her hand to his, where it
rested on the table that organized and focused the spell.

The power burned through her, burned up her fragile
humanity. Only a dragon body could withstand the enormous heat she pulled out of the living Kardia.

She couldn't remain human and survive to finish the
spell. Coronnan and her family needed the new barrier
at the border, desperately.

With love and regret she looked at her husband, felt his love being returned to her through the magical cord that would always connect them, no matter which body she used. Then she looked toward her baby. Queen Maarie Kaathliin cuddled her close, protecting her as well as Myri could.

(Amaranth!) she called her love and farewell to her baby. The only baby she would ever bear.

Then she gave herself up to the tremendous heat and friction that channeled through her.

Better to live as a dragon and be able to watch and protect her loved ones than to die and break the chain of power that built an impenetrable border between Coronnan and her enemies.

*   *   *

Part of Powwell watched Thorny hunch and relax in rhythm with the breathing of every magician in the circle of power. He had one hand on the shoulder of the magician to his left. His right hand—where Thorny perched—rested flat against the black glass so he couldn't stroke his familiar's spines. Thorny wiggled and rubbed his nose against Powwell in mute understanding of the problem.

Only a small piece of Powwell's awareness remained in the spell. The magicians of Coronnan didn't need his mind, only his talent. If he could separate his thoughts enough to touch Thorny, then he could focus on Kalen.

The communal vision of the growing wall between Coronnan and SeLenicca stood back, looking at the entire problem. Nimbulan's genius as a Battlemage centered around his ability to view the entire field, thousands of men and multitudes of small skirmishes. Powwell needed a closer look at one particular section.

The magic of the spell offered him the thoughts of every man sitting at the glass table. These men didn't interest him. He needed to hone in on the thoughts of Moncriith and Yaassima. Only they could tell him what happened to Kalen.

Thorny slid off Powwell's hand onto the table. Only the tips of the hedgehog's spines brushed his thumb. Was it enough of a separation? Powwell tapped Thorny's sense of smell. *Find the Bloodmage,* he ordered himself and the hedgehog.

Suddenly his awareness jerked away from the court-yard, beyond Coronnan City. He skimmed along the communal vision of the border. At a narrow pass far South of the primary action, Powwell's augmented senses skidded to a halt, backed up and flew into the canyon.

The smell of old blood, of hot rocks, and desert dry-ness lingered there.

Powwell added sight to smell. Moncriith came into view, his red robe standing out among the dark uniforms of his troops.

"Run forward. Everyone run forward!" Moncriith screamed as the magic barricade threatened to blockade the narrow pass. His men scrambled in all directions to avoid the pulsating energy most of them couldn't see. Discipline dissolved, and the soldiers ignored their leaders. Sergeants and lieutenants abandoned their posts as well as their men.

Steeds screamed and reared. They fought the traces that bound them to sledges and prevented flight.

Yaassima slowed her steps in deliberate defiance of her captor's orders. Strong rope, fortified with magic, encircled her neck in a tight noose and bound her hands before her body. If she moved so that her hands were low enough to secure her balance, she choked. If she raised her hands to ease the pressure on her throat, she stumbled with every step.

The soldier assigned to her tugged sharply on the ex-tension of rope, pulling her forward. She had to take several rapid, short steps to remain upright.

Then she gave in to the Kardia and plunged forward, sideways across the path, careful to land on the un-marred side of her ruined face. The soldier had to stop or choke her to death. Moncriith had ordered her alive until he needed a sacrifice for a battle spell.

Men tripped over her and sprawled across the path beneath the descending wall of magic.

Powwell felt the Kardia tremble, both in the protected courtyard in the city and through the pass where Yaas-sima and Moncriith kept their thoughts shielded from

him. He tried harder to penetrate Yaassima's mind. She
had no magic and shouldn't be able to block him.

Suddenly his vision split again. He watched a small
shower of rock and dirt slide down the hillside into the
pass through eyes that could only be Yaassima's. But
her thoughts and memories remained cloudy and indis-
tinct. A blast of heat nearly shattered his partial rapport
with her. The morning air of deep Winter heated to the
noon temperatures of high Summer.

Powwell thought she was remembering her fall into
the pit, and he nearly shouted in triumph. At last, he'd
see precisely what happened to Kalen.

Then he realized the heat came from the Kardia itself.
Heat akin to the molten lava in the pit. Yaassima was
laying across a thin ley line that suddenly reversed its
flow of energy and with great speed returned . . . returned where? Where did ley lines begin?

No matter. The channel of the retreating magic
scorched and collapsed, taking the crust of the Kardia
with it. All around them, a spiderweb of cracks opened
and spread. The slow spread of the ruptures in the land
contrasted sharply with the frantic movements of the
men. Movements that accomplished little in getting them
out of the path of chaos and death.

Powwell heard a few of their shouts and screams over
the crashing of the Kardia.

The soldiers jumped and scrambled away from the
fissures that followed them in all directions. Some
jumped forward, over the rising magic wall, many backward and up the sides of the hills. The hillsides crumbled
beneath the trampling feet, showering more debris down
into the pass. If they weren't careful, they'd bury the
pass and Moncriith with it.

Yaassima laughed. Her burned and shattered body
trembled with pain. Still she laughed. "You're dead,
Moncriith. You are dead already and don't realize it!"

"Come!" Moncriith hauled her up, none too gently,
by the armpits. "Follow me, all of you." The Bloodmage
made a panicky dash for Coronnan, dragging Yaassima
with him.

A few soldiers followed them. Most opted for retreat
into SeLenicca.

Yaassima continued to laugh at the crumbling of Moncriith's grand invasion.

Powwell tried to retreat. Yaassima wasn't thinking of her fall into the pit. She thought only of watching Moncriith die.

"Stop laughing," Moncriith ordered as he paused for breath and looked back at the wall that separated him from the majority of his troops. He grasped Yaassima's shoulders with clammy hands and shook her. Back and forth. Back and forth until her neck ceased to support her head. Back and forth until her senses whirled and the constant pain of her burns and aching joints intensified beyond endurance.

And still Yaassima laughed. That evil laugh that took delight in watching others in pain. She raised her hands and encircled Moncriith's neck with her preternaturally long fingers. She laughed as she pressed her thumbs into the Bloodmage's vulnerable wind pipe.

Her laughter choked and gurgled when Moncriith moved his scarred and sweaty palms to capture her own throat.

The magic wall spurted upward, engulfing Yaassima and Moncriith. They froze, trapped with the magic.

Powwell yanked his mind out of Yaassima's failing body.

Then the wall collapsed again with uneven energy, crushing the Bloodmage and the Kaalipha into a bloody heap.

The wall suddenly grew higher, threatening to capture Powwell's mind. He willed himself back into his own body, back in the safety of Coronnan City.

I failed, Thorny, he moaned. *I didn't learn anything about Kalen. I've failed her again.*

CHAPTER 40

Myri's vision returned to the body anchored to the Kardia. She didn't need to see the magic, only fuel it. Wings broke free of the tight human skin on her back. Her neck elongated. The vestigial spinal bumps sharpened and shot outward as full horns. Purple-tipped crystal fur erupted from her too smooth skin. Fire rose. Fire glowed. Fire streamed forth as she absorbed more heat, and yet more heat from the Kardia.

Shayla showed her a swelling in the wall at the border. Up and up it rose, separating the army. The power fueling the spell fluctuated up and down. The wall grew and collapsed. She channeled more power into the spell. The wall grew again, up and out. It flowed in a continuous line of energy.

Only a few troops remained East of the wall inside Coronnan. Other men moved to go around the wall and found their passage blocked.

Panicked by the separation, the soldiers in front turned and beat on the barrier, screaming for an opening to return them to the safety of their comrades.

Up and out the barrier grew. It linked and looped across the tops of hills, blocking other passages.

Myri drew more power from the draining well. The boiling lava of Hanassa's living volcano fed the ley lines, draining out of the mountain, collapsing the caves of the pit and the dragongate. The ley lines that snaked across the land ceased flowing outward, reversed and drained back into the well. Scorched channel became burned-out husks in the wake of the reversed flow. And still she pulled power into the spell.

At the border, soldiers hopped and danced to avoid the scorching Kardia beneath their feet.

And still the wall grew.

Myri grew with it.

The wall was nearly complete.

She was nearly transformed into her true dragon-self.

A moment more and she would fly free of the bounds of gravity. Free and empty of love.

* * *

Nimbulan watched with horror as his beautiful Myri stretched and expanded, draconic features becoming more and more pronounced. He had to stop her.

How?

This was the person she was born to be.

He loved the woman she had chosen to be.

They couldn't separate now.

The spell demanded his attention. He had to break away from the magic long enough to force Myrilandel back into her own form. The wall was nearly complete. They didn't need so much power now. She could let go. If she would.

"You can't leave the circle," Scarface hissed in his ear. "If any one of us breaks contact, the entire thing will collapse. We'll be right back where we started from and too exhausted to start again."

"I know." His talent was necessary to the completion of the defense of Coronnan.

His talent.

Once before, he had separated from his talent, left it in an inanimate object. He wasn't sure if the glass table was totally inanimate, not the way the magic swirled through the eddies and waves of minerals.

The hand upon his own clutched him with talons that grew by the minute. Myri's bulk increased, threatening to crush his hand.

If you break contact with the table, you'll lose your talent forever.

"I have to take that chance." Quickly, he located the burning blue beacon behind his heart and pushed it into the table. Blue light joined the glittering black and gray. It melded with the combined talents of all the men sitting in the circle.

Nimbulan slid his chair back a little, allowing Scarface to slide his hand from his shoulder onto Lyman's. The circle remained complete, his talent remained in the combined mass of magic. Scarface's mind took over the completion of the wall.

Keeping his right hand on the table, Nimbulan grasped Myri's still human face with his left. "Beloved. I need you. Our daughter needs you. Return to us, please.

She wrenched herself away from him, tears flowing freely. "I must be a dragon to survive the power I give to this spell and Coronnan."

"The spell is nearly complete. Give back the power you drain from the Kardia."

She shook her head and stepped away from him. Only her talons remained in contact with the table and his talent embedded in it. The power continued to flow through her into the spell.

Then she looked up to the skies where Shayla and the other dragons flew. A heavy film dropped over her eyes, protecting her from the brightness of the sun in the upper atmosphere.

"You forsook dragonkind twenty years ago. Come back to the body and the life you chose. Please. I love you, Myrilandel. My life is incomplete without you." Moisture gathered at the corners of his eyes. His heart threatened to wrench out of his body as she took another step backward.

"I can never give you the sense of completeness and belonging you find in this Commune of magic. You belong here. I belong to the skies."

"No." The words wrenched out of him. His throat nearly closed with unshed tears. "Myrilandel, I love you more than I love my magic." Deliberately he lifted his hand from the table, leaving his talent forever embedded in the rare and perfect black glass.

*   *   *

Myri's concentration shattered with the touch of Nimbulan's hand. Kardia, Air, Fire, and Water fractured and separated within her body and her mind. She shrank in size and awareness. Heat drained out of her, back into the ley lines. Dimly she knew the web of magical power stopped abruptly at the new border wall, unable to restore the empty channels to the West.

The spell, the dragons, her own safety ceased to have importance as Nimbulan collapsed in her arms.

The very touch of the air against her skin sent waves of burning pain throughout her body. She was back in her own body with only vestigial traces of her dragon heritage. Nimbulan's clothing seemed to rub her raw. His weight on her aching muscles and stressed bones sent her to her knees. She couldn't let go. She had to hold him, keep him close. The silver cord connecting them faded to invisibility.

His aura looked different, dimmer, smaller, less dominated by the blue of his magical signature. The blue pulsed within the glass table, adding a different luster to the black minerals and the combined magic of the Commune.

She didn't know how his magic had detached from him and merged with the table, accessible to all in the Commune except him. Desperately she grabbed for the blue. But the glass was impervious to even dragon talons. Her now human fingernails couldn't scratch the glass.

"Nimbulan, beloved, what have you done to yourself?" She held him under the arms, sobbing her fears into him. "Don't you dare die on me. I've just found you again. I can't let you leave me again!"

She fought to keep him from sliding to the ground. If she could hold him long enough, the silver cord would come to life again. It had to. Neither one of them was fully alive without that bond.

Other hands reached out to relieve her of the burden. Familiar hands. Powwell, Scarface, and her brother Quinnault. She stared at the table, blinking away tears as the men settled her husband on the ground. The spell must be complete, for the magicians stood and stretched, talking quietly. They rapidly shifted their gaze from Nimbulan to the table and back again. Amazement touched their expressions.

"How did he separate himself from his talent?" one man asked.

"I've never heard of such a thing," replied another. He shuddered at the concept of life without his magic.

How would Nimbulan survive without the talent that had defined his life for so long?

"Such a waste." Lyman shook his head sadly. "He didn't have to sacrifice everything. You would have returned to your human body once the spell was complete."

"Are you sure, old man?" Myri knelt at Nimbulan's side, checking his pulse and breathing, loosening his tunic and shirt around his throat and chest.

"Shayla has mated again. The chances are good that she carries purple-tipped twins again. You could not have stayed a dragon once they are born, for there can only be one purple-tipped dragon at a time."

"How do we know that I would be able to come back? You had to find a new body when you left the nimbus. My human body would have been destroyed by the power I channeled and the transformation."

Nimbulan's chest shuddered, and his breath came in ragged gasps.

"You tried to leave me," he whispered through cracked and weary lips. "You tried to join the dragons. I feared you might ever since I learned of your heritage. I dreaded the day you would leave me." He turned his eyes up to hers briefly, before they sagged wearily shut again. The fire had gone out of the green orbs.

"But you never came for me in the clearing. You didn't communicate by magic or by message," she sobbed.

"I can never make up for that lapse. The bad habits of a bachelor interfered with my judgment. I need you, Myrilandel. I need you more than you can ever know." He sagged against her again.

Lacking the silver cord to tell her the state of his heart and pulse, Myri resorted to conventional checks. Nothing blocked his air passages. His heart fluttered and beat irregularly, but not so far off rhythm to endanger him. His skin looked gray but not waxy. Lumbird bumps rose up on his skin and he trembled as if very cold beneath his heavy formal robe and everyday tunic, shirt, and trews.

"I think he needs sleep more than anything," she said, sinking back on her heels. "He'll be in shock for a time."

"As are you, sister." Quinnault rested a heavy hand on her shoulder. She couldn't lean into his warmth, or accept the contact.

"You have called me 'sister?' Are you ready to accept me as family, or must I be exiled again for being a female with magic? Exiled and denied the right to nurse my lawful husband through this terrible trauma?"

*   *   *

"No, we will not deny you the right to nurse your husband, Myrilandel," Katie announced. Her little chin came up in a proud gesture her husband was coming to dread.

"She has to be exiled," Konnaught shouted across the courtyard. A guard stood behind him, carrying a small satchel. "If you are throwing me out of Coronnan, then you must do the same to her!"

Quinnault had forgotten that the boy would sail into exile as soon as the tide changed.

A nasty smile split Konnaught's pudgy face. "She's a witch, and we don't allow witches in Coronnan. The Council will depose you and that foreign hussy you married, if you let your sister stay. Then they'll bring me back as their king."

"Be careful how you address your queen, boy. You no longer have a title or lands. Within the hour you will be a penniless peasant on your way to the Monastic School in Sollthrie. I signed the order last night," Quinnault said slowly and evenly so there could be no mistake in his threat.

Konnaught didn't slink off. He stood straight and defiant, Lord Hanic and two other lords directly behind him. Quinnault met their eyes, girding himself to show no emotion.

Quinnault sighed. Too many of the lords preferred Konnaught's philosophy that titles and land granted privileges and the right of exploitation. Responsibility for the land and people who lived upon the land was a sometime thing with them rather than a way of life. If Quinnault was going to hold sway over those lords, he had to obey his own laws. His entire reign, the benign government he'd fought so hard for, all depended upon law.

He turned back to his wife and sister, hoping to find a compromise. "Katie, Myrilandel, the people of Coronnan have made a law against solitary magicians. For the good of all we have to control magic. Only the Commune can do that. Myri can't gather dragon magic and join the Commune.

"What good is a law without compassion!" Katie stamped her foot and shouted at him. "There is no justice in exiling her after she saved the kingdom from invasion." Her eyes blazed and bright color tinged her cheeks. Her absurdly short curls bounced about her ears. She had never looked more beautiful.

Quinnault was tempted to kiss her. That would solve nothing but his own need to hold her close and ease his instant passion. He still had a Council of Lords who could override any decision he made with a two-thirds majority vote. That was a law he had requested. The kings of Coronnan couldn't be dictators.

"Compassion and justice are concepts that have been missing from Coronnan for three generations. The people will have a hard time understanding why their king breaks the law for such vague ideas," he said, sighing.

"Then isn't it about time they were exposed to such 'vague' ideas?" A smile tugged at the corners of Katie's mouth. The humor that was never very far from the surface threatened to break through. "All of you recognize the 'vague' idea of diplomatic immunity."

The lords and magicians nodded.

"If SeLenicca sent a magician as ambassador, his diplomatic immunity would exempt him from the law. You'd have to let him stay or risk war."

"Granted, Katie. But Myrilandel isn't the ambassador from one of our neighbors," Quinnault replied. He tried to keep his voice firm. He nearly lost that battle facing the humor that glowed from Katie's face.

"She is the ambassador from the dragons! She is the one they selected to develop the Covenant. Without her, you have no Covenant, no dragons, no communal magic. She is the cornerstone of that *treaty*. That makes her an ambassador and exempt from your laws." She smiled triumphantly.

Quinnault nearly danced her around the courtyard in glee. "Ambassador Myrilandel of Shayla's Nimbus, prepare to present your credentials."

"What credentials?" She cocked her head puzzled.

"Oh, we'll think of something later." He bent down and hugged her tight. "Welcome, sister. Welcome home."

"Someone take this poor man to a comfortable bed and get the healers to look at him," Katie ordered, pointing to Nimbulan who shuddered and trembled on the ground. "And find a good hot meal for both of them. I can't believe no one thought of this before," she finished, shaking her head.

"Thank you, Your Grace." Myri dipped a slight curtsy toward Katie. She reached for her baby. Katie relinquished the precious burden reluctantly, gazing fondly at Amaranth's innocently sleeping face.

"She is beautiful. I wish you joy of her," Katie whispered. She ran a gentle finger along the baby's cheek. "I look forward to watching her grow."

"Messages are coming in from the border, Your Grace," Lyman said, standing at Quinnault's elbow.

"Did we succeed?" he asked the magician. He studied the man closely, looking for signs of the dragon within him.

"We succeeded admirably. Three of King Lorriin's seven generals and their troops are trapped on this side of the border. They have offered their swords in your service rather than return to SeLenicca as failures. King Lorriin isn't known for his forgiveness."

A happy grin burst from Quinnault. The wars were over. He'd made a peace that could last. He and Nimbulan. And Katie and Myri and dozens of others.

"There is more news from the few magicians on the other side of the border," Lyman continued. "Moncriith and Yaassima killed each other."

"You are free of them, sister. They'll not stalk you again." Quinnault touched Myrilandel's arm reassuringly.

"I must go back to Hanassa," Yaala said. "I have to see what damage Moncriith did before he left. He said the dragongate had collapsed."

"There is no word from Hanassa, child. There never is. It is a city state that remains outside the life of the Three Kingdoms," Lyman said kindly.

"Hanassa is a boil on the backside of the Three Kingdoms," Nimbulan said weakly from the ground at their feet. He didn't rouse enough to sit up or even support himself on an elbow. "Hanassa causes trouble and is a constant pain. The Kaalipha wanted us to think they are separate and aloof, but her assassins and raiders dart in and out, striking where they will. Even without the dragongate they will plague the rest of the world. None of us will be safe until that boil is cauterized."

Quinnault didn't like the magician's color as he closed his eyes once more, too exhausted to say more. Myri knelt beside him, quickly checking his pulse. She placed her long-fingered hand on his brow, brushing her husband's graying hair away from his eyes.

"Take him inside, quickly. He needs more healing than I can give him." She beckoned several young men to fetch a litter. Powwell came forward with a wineskin. He moistened his master's lips with a few drops.

A sense of loss washed over Quinnault. Through this whole adventure of establishing the Commune and the School for Magicians, finding a solution to the civil wars and building a permanent government, Nimbulan had been at his side. Nimbulan, adviser, helper, friend. He had no other friends. Kings didn't have friends, they had courtiers.

"I'll go to Hanassa, Master Nimbulan," Powwell whispered. "I'll go back and make sure the dragongate is closed forever. I'll find Rollett and Kalen, too, and bring them back to you safely."

"That will be your quest, boy. But not until you have more training," Scarface said. "Don't you lords and nobles have a government to run or something? Leave the healing to magicians. We'll keep you informed of any new messages." He dismissed the assembly with a stern look. His ugly scar creased more deeply with his scowl. The implied violence of his wounds sent mundanes scampering for other chores in other places.

Then Scarface turned to the magicians, assuming a leadership role naturally. "We have a conspirator with Rover blood to find. We'll start with the woman under guard and then devise a test for the latent potential. There are communications to monitor. Lambing season and Spring planting will be upon us very soon, we need to know which fields will produce the most food and which need to go fallow. Come on, we have work to do." The masters gathered in a knot and spoke in arcane phrases with many wild gestures.

Six young men ran up with a hospital litter. With Myri's guidance they rolled Nimbulan onto it and carried him back inside the school. Myri walked beside her husband, keeping one hand on him at all times.

Nimbulan lifted his own hand and placed it atop hers. "I love you," he whispered.

Quinnault's heart wrenched for the couple, and for his own loss of a trusted adviser and friend.

"I hope I can be your friend as well as your wife, Scarecrow," Katie whispered to him.

"You read my mind again."

"I read your grief. Our grief. He is a great man. We will miss him greatly."

"He left a great legacy for us all. Never again will magicians waste their talents as Battlemages. He ended magic as a weapon of death and destruction and made it an instrument of peace and prosperity." Quinnault returned to the business of continuing the legacy of the last Battlemage.

EPILOGUE

"Come to Papa, Amaranth," Nimbulan coaxed his giggling daughter.

The little girl, barely a year old, stood on unsteady legs, clutching her mother's skirt. She eyed the distance between her parents skeptically. Then, boldly she let go of the cloth that kept her upright. She swayed, lifted one foot off the ground and sat abruptly on her diapered bottom.

Her lower lip stuck out, and a tear threatened to overflow her wide eyes. Hints of fire-green highlighted the iris—closer to the color of her father's eyes than her mother's. But her light blonde hair and pale skin came from Myrilandel's heritage.

"Up!" Amaranth demanded, holding her pudgy arms out to her father. She had learned early that Nimbulan was always willing to hold her in his arms. Her mother wasn't as easy to persuade.

"That's all right, Amaranth. You'll walk when you are ready." Nimbulan plucked his daughter off the ground and hoisted her high in the air.

"Maybe if she walked, she'd slow down for a day or two," Myri chuckled. "She's into everything as it is." She bent to stir the stew that simmered over the central hearth of the hut in the clearing.

Nimbulan and his family retreated to the peace and solitude of this little hut often. As often as their duties in the city allowed. One of Myri's dragon brothers could usually be persuaded to fly them here at short notice.

Directing the School for Magicians—University now— no longer dominated Nimbulan's life. Others could do it better, others who still had magic at their fingertips.

He still sat in Council with the king. But Quinnault

had his new wife and a myriad of other advisers to guide him and Coronnan into a new era.

Nimbulan enjoyed the slower pace of life in the clearing more every time they retreated here. Myri certainly flourished in the rural setting. The demands of life at court and her duties as ambassador for the dragons stressed her empathic talent to near exhaustion. She needed the sanctuary of the clearing more than Nimbulan did.

"It's starting to snow," Yaala said, entering the hut with a fresh armload of wood. "Something smells good." She bent her head to draw in the aroma before she dropped the bundle of sticks and logs.

"Then you won't be going back to the capital for several weeks yet," Myri said. "Neither will we." She grinned widely.

"Why do you think I stalled so long." Yaala grinned. Her teeth gleamed in the firelight. "I don't like relying on your brother's hospitality, Myri. Having servants wait on me hand and foot gets boring after about ten minutes. This 'Princess in Exile' nonsense has gone on too long. I need to be doing something, even if it's just chopping firewood."

"There's lots of that to do," Myri replied.

Nimbulan shifted Amaranth to the crook of his right arm, giving her a favorite toy to chew on—a wooden rattle he'd carved himself. He had the scars on his fingers from his first attempts to guide the knife without magic.

Joy simmered in Nimbulan, like Myri's stew. It warmed his heart and grew more savory with time. All of his little regrets about unfinished work and lost magic faded. Only the question of Rollett's and Kalen's fate continued to nag him.

Myri cocked her head as if listening. "Someone is climbing the path from the village. Someone with determination."

"What does Shayla say?" Instinctively he looked toward the South-facing doorway. Shayla had retreated to her lair in the mountains, awaiting the birth of her next litter.

Shayla's voice was something else Nimbulan missed. The dragon hadn't talked to him much, but now that he had no magic, he couldn't hear her even when she directed her mental voice to him.

He wrapped his free arm around Myri's shoulder, almost hoping physical contact with her would open his mind to Shayla's words. "Anyone we know?" he asked.

Nimbulan set Amaranth on the floor where she promptly crawled to the pile of firewood and began investigating the new logs with all of her senses.

"Take that out of your mouth, Ammi," Yaala plucked a piece of bark out of the baby's hands.

Nimbulan reached for his winter cloak. No one would be able to enter the clearing without Myri's permission. He shouldn't worry. But he'd spent too many years as a Battlemage not to worry about unannounced visitors.

"It's Powwell!" Myri cried, reaching for her cloak at the same time.

Together they dashed out the door to meet the boy at the boundary of the clearing.

Nimbulan didn't see the magical boundary swirling bright pastel colors as it parted to admit his former apprentice. One second he saw only trees. The next, Powwell stood in the arching shadow made by two leaning trunks of the Tambootie.

"You've grown! You have a beard. You're taller than I." Myri fussed over the young man.

Fifteen now, Powwell stood broader of shoulder and longer of leg than Nimbulan remembered.

"Are you hungry? Of course you are. Supper is nearly ready." Myri hugged her foster son.

"I'm fine, Myrilandel. Just a little weary." Powwell hugged her back.

Nimbulan watched the boy's hands clench. An air of heavy sadness bent his posture.

"What has happened, son?" he asked joining Myri's embrace of him.

"I figured out how to get into Hanassa, but I need help. I can fetch Rollett back for you, Nimbulan. But you'll have to go with me."

Excitement leaped in Nimbulan's heart. A chance to rescue the journeyman he'd had to leave in Hanassa so many moons ago.

Myri stiffened within Powwell's embrace. She said

nothing. Nimbulan didn't need magic to know she waited warily for her husband's response.

"I'm sorry. I can't, Powwell. My place is here." He held Myri tighter. "I promised I'd never leave you again, Myri, and I won't." Disappointment threatened to choke him. "I wouldn't be much use to you anyway, Powwell, not without my magic."

"I'll go," Yaala said from the doorway of the hut.

"The trip will be dangerous, Yaala," Powwell warned.

"That doesn't matter. Hanassa should be mine! The time has come to reclaim my throne."

"We have to leave immediately. The gateway at the city will only be open for short periods this Winter." Powwell stood straighter, adjusting his pack.

"It will wait until the snow has stopped and you have packed some provisions," Nimbulan said, ushering them all toward the warmth of the hut.

"Have you also thought of a way to find Kalen in the void?" Myri asked so quietly Nimbulan almost didn't hear her.

"Of course." A big grin creased Powwell's tired face. "That's why I waited so long. I had to find a way to free both my—sister and my fellow journeyman. Finding the right opening into the void is going to be chancy. That's the gateway that will only be open twice this Winter and for very short times."

"Then you have accepted Kalen is your sister?" Nimbulan had to ask.

"The dragons say she is. I have to believe them."

"Go with our blessing, Powwell. You, too, Yaala." Nimbulan almost choked. His instincts screamed to keep these vulnerable people close. He'd lost so many good friends and students he couldn't take a chance on letting Powwell and Yaala go into danger alone.

(A journeyman must quest to become a master. A quest by nature must be taken without a mentor,) Shayla reminded him.

"Shayla, I can hear you! Has my magic returned?"

"No, love," Myri said quietly. "The dragon spoke through my voice. You are still mundane. Are you terribly disappointed?"

"Not really. Your love and the life of my daughter is magic enough." Together they ducked into the hut.

Amaranth squealed in delight at sight of them. She let go of the woodpile that supported her and toddled toward him. She giggled as she wavered and nearly sat down again, but she kept walking until she clutched her father's cloak for balance.

"Up," she demanded.

Nimbulan lifted her high over his head, laughing and rejoicing in his life and his loves.